SCREAM ALL NIGHT

ScREAM ALL NIGHT

DEREK MILMAN

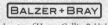

BALZER + BRAY

An Imprint of HarperCollins*Publishers*

Balzer + Bray is an imprint of HarperCollins Publishers.

Scream All Night
Copyright © 2018 by Derek Milman
All rights reserved. Printed in the United States of America.
No part of this book may be used or reproduced in any manner whatsoever without written permission except in the case of brief quotations embodied in critical
articles and reviews. For information address HarperCollins Children's Books, a
division of HarperCollins Publishers, 195 Broadway, New York, NY 10007.
www.epicreads.com

ISBN 978-0-06-266565-2

Typography by Jessie Gang
18 19 20 21 22 PC/LSCH 10 9 8 7 6 5 4 3 2 1
❖
First Edition

FOR BRIAN, WHO ALWAYS PULLS ME TOWARD THE LIGHT.

FOR RACHEL, WHO WOULD HAVE LOVED THE STUFF ABOUT MONSTERS.

FOR MY FAMILY: MOM, DAD, JORDAN, LORIN, ISLA. AND HENRY, WHO HAVE READ
EVERYTHING I'VE WRITTEN (OR WILL ONE DAY WHEN THE TIME IS RIGHT.)

PART I

CHAPTER ONE

RETURN TO MOLDAVIA

SLIGHTLY BEFORE DINNER, KEENAN HOUSE, THE GROUP HOME WHERE I live, gets a call that my homosexual exorcism is scheduled to take place next Thursday at four.

"But I'm not homosexual. And I'm not possessed," I say to Len, my counselor.

"You sure?" asks Len. He cracks open a PBR and takes a long, gurgling sip.

"Bet you're both," says my roommate, Jude, pulling on his boxing gloves.

"Actually," says Len, belching, softly punching his gut, "I think it's your brother calling."

Oren. Of course.

Late-afternoon sunlight smears across the cinder-block walls through broken, yellowed blinds. I throw down my graphic novel, which I was actually half enjoying, and roll out of my sagging lower bunk with a groan. I walk down the hall and grab the phone.

"Why are you calling me?"

"'Cause I know you have lots of homo demons inside you," says Oren, stifling one of his loud, chirpy laughs. "And I thought maybe it was time for a devil cleanse."

"Uh-huh." I hear projected voices in the background—like announcements on a PA or something. "Where are you?"

"Hospital."

"What?"

"We're burying Dad next week. Funeral is Thursday."

"Dad died?"

"No, no."

My dad has been slowly dying for forty years. Emphysema, hairy cell leukemia, diabetes, arthritis; it's like he just went shopping one day for chronic diseases and never made any returns. More recently, he's been sliding into dementia.

Thing is, this might really be it. The doctors are pretty sure. "He has two weeks *max*," says Oren.

"Shit." I bite my thumbnail—an old nervous habit instantaneously reborn. I'm suddenly terrified that my family, who I was legally emancipated from three years ago, might be planning something deeply, morbidly insane. But it's not as bad as all that.

Just a live funeral.

"A what?" The phone slips out of my hands. I juggle it back to my ear.

"Dad's final wish was to be buried alive," says Oren.

"His what was *what*?"

Oren's voice takes on that swoony, nostalgic glaze that always makes me want to stab him in the face with a corn holder. "Just like Veronica Bellwether in *The Curse of the Mummy's Tongue*, his first film."

I hear my eyes blinking. "Is this even legal?"

"I highly doubt it. I've made arrangements for you to be picked up at the orphanage at noon." He lowers his voice. "Are they assaulting you over there, Dario? I mean, *sexually*."

I know what he meant. I roll my eyes. "Only on Tuesdays."

"Do they pilfer your valuables? Beat you with pillowcases filled with bar soap? Glue your eyes shut while you're asleep? Ejaculate into your socks?"

I refuse to tell Oren that maybe one or two of those things has happened maybe once or twice.

"Have the other wanton orphans there ever tricked you into one of those atomic sit-ups?" He cackles. "Those are cruel."

"I'm not going. And don't call me again." I hang up.

I stand there, staring at the phone. There's a goopy brown stain on the wall above. Chocolate? Roach repellent? Something worse? I start to itch. Just hearing Oren's voice gave me hives, dammit.

"I need the phone," says Hal, an eighth-grade albino with ADD, standing behind me.

I clench and unclench my hands. "I need a moment. And I need Benadryl."

5

I head back to my room, pop two caplets out of the foil, and swallow them down with the remains of some warm Gatorade. People say you can slap hives away, but that's a load of crap, and trying just makes you look like an asshole.

Antihistamines always give me terrifying dreams. That night, with Jude snoring loud as ever above me, I dream I'm locked in a closet. Someone with a nail gun is shooting at me through the slatted door; I see the shadow of a hulking man outside, morphing into unnatural, demonic shapes. When I can't dodge or duck the nails anymore, they start piercing my flesh, and I slowly transform into that dude from *Hellraiser.*

I wake up exhausted. I hate that.

That day, after school, I get another call. Expecting Oren again, I bark into the phone to *stop calling me*, but actually it's Hayley.

"Oh," I say, startled and a little embarrassed. "I'm so sorry. I . . ."

"It's okay," she says.

There's just crackling on the line because neither of us knows what to say. The sound of her voice literally flattened me against the wall. I look cartoonish, like someone being chased by a ghost.

My body starts catching up to the barrage of emotions ballooning inside me, their colors merging into a muddy black, so all the physiological shit starts. I scratch like crazy under my chin. My eyes burn.

"I think I'm allergic to these random phone calls from home," I tell her.

"Home," she says with a little laugh. "Is that what you still call it?"

"That word just fell out of my mouth."

"I haven't talked to you in so long."

I nod, to no one. "Almost six years, I guess."

"How are you, Dario?"

"I'm fine. I'm not going to this thing. Oren shouldn't have told you to call me."

"He didn't."

"Oh." Hayley calling me out of the blue makes everything seem more real and serious. I never made a purposeful, conscious choice to cut off contact with her. It was just part of the new reality I chopped open for myself when I left home. It became an unspoken rule that it was easier for both of us if we didn't keep in touch. Hearing her voice, which hasn't changed one bit, is like remembering a dream.

"I think you might regret it later if you weren't there," she adds.

I scratch at my neck. "Why?"

I have a vision of her then: a girl in a flowered dress stained by splotches of buttercups and dandelions, strawberry-blonde hair curled at the ends, blowing behind her in the breeze, running through a meadow on a sun-streaked day.

It's part memory, part . . . Claritin commercial.

"I think you should say good-bye to your dad."

I close my eyes and lean my head against the wall. "Did he even ask about me?"

After a moment: "No."

There's a wash of silence. For some reason I think of a battlefield, quiet and still, dying flares raining down on bloodstained grass, stamped flat.

"It's also me being selfish," she says. "I don't want to be there without you. It wouldn't feel right."

I take the phone away from my ear and press it against my forehead for a second. She says something else, but I can't hear her, like she's drifting away. I put the phone back to my mouth. "Sorry. What?"

"I said: I don't know what else to say. That's all I've got."

"This whole thing sounds insane, Hayley."

"Are you surprised?"

My family doing something utterly insane doesn't much surprise me, no.

"Let me know if you change your mind," she says.

"I will." I breathe in, filling my lungs. "Thanks for calling, Hay."

"I feel like I had to."

"It's . . . good to hear your voice."

"It's good to hear your voice too, Dario."

There's a second of dead air, as if she's waiting, or we're both waiting for something more, before she hangs up, with a messy rattle.

I'm so startled by Hayley's call, at first I can't fathom what she's really asking me to do: Go back home. Say good-bye to my dad. Forever. I never thought I'd go back there. But I was stupid to think this moment wouldn't come. What if Hayley is right? What if I'd regret it for the rest of my life if I didn't see him again before his death?

Later, I run the idea by Jude. He's sweating profusely, attacking a standing punching bag in a basement storeroom stacked with moldering files documenting every adoption that went awry. "So now, what? *What?* You want to go back there?" He whirls around to face me, spraying sweat into my eyes.

"Don't you think I should? It's my dad's funeral."

"The trick is staying away from all that shit that brings back the bad feelings."

"Yeah. I did. For years."

"Remember what you were like when they brought you in here? You were an uncontrollable mess."

He's right. I was not in a good state. I had anger issues that needed to be dealt with. Those first few months I'd cry myself to sleep every night.

"Like a rabid wolf abandoned by its pack," he's saying.

"I've put time and distance between me and that stuff."

"You think you've moved on from your crappy childhood?"

"I think I'm better now, yeah. I think we might disagree on this."

Gradually, I had moved away from the dark thoughts, the negative emotions, and embraced life here at Keenan. I don't think it's totally dangerous to revisit the remnants of my childhood. In fact, I think as Hayley said, I could regret not going. And that could haunt me. Getting closure might not be such a bad thing—now that I have this one last chance.

I try to explain all this to Jude.

"Fine. Go! But just for the day! That's the rule. You come back right after."

"Okay."

"That's the rule," he repeats, all muffled, through his mouthpiece.

"Why are you wearing that mouthpiece? The punching bag won't hit you back."

He squints. "Don't get sucked in, Dar. Don't spend the night there."

"There might be, like, hors d'oeuvres or something after the—"

"Huh? *What?* Just come back right after!"

Jude, oiled with foamy sweat, adopts a mock predatory crouch. He looks like a panther, disturbed in its rainforest ravine, that isn't going to take any more shit. He can be a little controlling, but I know he means well. "When did your dad die?" he says. "You didn't mention—"

"Uhhh . . ." I back toward the door, wanting this conversation to be over because I kind of made up my mind already. "Uh, he's not dead yet."

Jude's eyes become bewildered slits. "What?"

I tell him about the live funeral like it's something people just do on occasion.

Jude smacks his gloves together. "This is real? Like, *this is fucking real?*"

"Apparently." I start scratching my neck, my arms.

"Christ, look at you."

I regard my angry, red, mottled skin. "I know."

"You think you're past it all, but look at yourself."

He may have a point. But this is just stupid: getting a rash just because someone called from home. This is childish crap that I need to get over. I have to confront them. I have to confront my past. Then there won't be any more hives.

"This is just residual weakness," I say, regarding my skin. "I can get stronger. I need to get stronger."

"You are strong. You were strong when you left."

"Even stronger."

Jude gives me a hard look, shakes his head at me and socks the bag. "Just make sure someone there has an EpiPen."

Oren sends a black hearse, because you know, *why the hell not?*

Sunglasses on, I slide down the cool leather seats, wanting to be swallowed up by the car, which smells like Windex and pine trees. After about thirty minutes of queasy twists and turns over hills and quaint covered bridges, I see the sign approaching.

Moldavia Studios.

As the ivy-covered gates swing open, I get this flashbang of anxiety, and my confidence weakens. I sit forward and open my mouth, about to tell the driver, *Please, for the love of God, just turn the hell around.* But we're already through the gates, crawling up the long, winding driveway. I catch my breath again, which keeps fluttering away like a kite, as the castle looms over me, guilting me for being gone too long. The hearse lurches to a stop. I just sit there for a second. Then I open the door and step outside into the chilly, late-April air.

My father is ninety-one years old, meaning he was seventy-four when I was born. My older brother, Oren, is twenty years older than me. He probably should have become a surrogate father to me, given our weird family dynamics. But Oren has always been . . . *Oren.* Too consumed with the studio, and its innumerable daily needs, to deal with anything else. And slowly, as my dad began descending further into dementia, Oren became Moldavia's de facto studio chief as well as its principal producer.

And my mother was committed to a psychiatric hospital when I was seven. So no one was really looking after me by the time I left this place. When I was twelve, I rode my bike over a small cliff. I broke my collarbone and two ribs. I was in the hospital for five days before anyone from home realized I was gone. A week later I had a lawyer. Two weeks after that, I began the process of moving into Keenan House.

Now, I make my way onto the sloping meadow of the east lawn. The grass is always a healthy, gleaming green, impeccably maintained, and seemingly never ending, as it stretches for miles. They filmed *Undead Nocturne* out here— four weeks of twilight shoots, chasing that thin window of cerulean light, actors twirling through the grass in gossamer rags, their herky-jerky zombie ballet restless, tragic, and hilarious all at once.

It became one of our biggest cult classics, bootleg DVDs circulating for years on eBay in the cinema geek underground. We went massively over budget on that one. Someone had to remind my dad we make B-movies here, and he's not Bertolucci. He might disagree.

In the early days, Moldavia had distribution deals with various Hollywood studios, but as interest waned, Moldavia began distributing its own films. Film scholars and pop culture writers frequently compare the studio, and its weirdly inclusive family, to Andy Warhol's Factory and John Waters's Dreamlanders.

"And here's Dario," says Oren in his deep, booming voice, arms extended, "the prodigal son." He's holding court by a long table draped in white linen, near the entrance to the lawn, where a bartender is handing out glasses of wine and champagne.

Oren rips himself away from the small, intense crowd. I'm not sure who they are. They look like a combination of random mourners and obsessed horror fans (Oren calls them "squeezers"). But that makes no sense, since outsiders aren't allowed through the gates. Oren is holding a white-tipped cane even though he can walk just fine.

He's wearing a dark-purple tuxedo, white shoes, and a top hat.

He takes my arms and extends them out like he's

measuring me for a suit. "Ack!" he says, doing that thing where he makes random noises. He frowns at me—my faded Fangoria T-shirt, my ripped jeans—like I'm the one who showed up dressed all wrong.

He clucks his tongue. "You didn't have a suit, Dario?"

"You look like Mr. Peanut's closeted uncle, so let's not judge."

"Come, come," he says, pulling at me, wanting me to meet the gaggle of mourners/squeezers, all of them decked out like they're attending a Mardi Gras party in the underworld. But my eyes are locked on Hayley. She's coming toward me with the sweetest smile, champagne flute in her hand, auburn hair flowing in nervy, seismic curls over her shoulder. A quiver runs through my body.

"Just a sec," I say to Oren, wriggling out of his grasp and away from the hungry crowd. I steer Hayley into a more secluded spot.

"I'm glad you came," she says, hugging me.

"Yeah, well, I had no other plans, so."

"I'm surprised, actually."

I'm not sure what to say. I'm kind of surprised myself.

She lowers her head. "I wasn't sure. About calling you. But I felt it was the right thing to do. I'm so sorry, Dario."

"About calling?"

She takes a sip of champagne, giving me a slanted look with the glass to her lips. I never forgot her eyes are the color of bruised pears. "About your dad."

I nod. "So this is . . . actually a real funeral, then?"

She considers this. "More a . . . send-off."

"A send-off?"

"Yes. Gosh," she says, reaching down to readjust her perfectly white high heel, "you really grew up."

Yeah, you too, I want to say, but don't. She fixes her smile on me, sipping champagne. Her pearl-colored blouse neatly tucked into that black skirt makes me think of bad porn about offices after hours and misbehaving secretaries. It feels wrong to be having these thoughts. This is Hayley, Hugo and Aida's daughter. I want to punch myself in the head.

"You should see this." She leads me down the lawn. Past a row of sycamores there's a roped-off area, a hole in the ground with a mound of neon-green Astroturf, and a man with a shovel.

I rub the back of my neck. "He's really being buried on the grounds?"

She nods. "It's what he wanted. Isn't it . . . sort of beautiful?"

"It's creepy as fuck, Hayley."

I'm not processing any of this the way I should. I feel removed, like this is happening to someone else, and I'm just a witness. But no matter what happens today, I'm going to see my dad, that's for sure. I can't even remember when I saw him last.

My dad was great at keeping me at a distance—and he'd make a point of it. That's when I hated him the most. But I hated myself when I'd realize how desperate I was for any kind of connection with him. It was tough accepting that I simply didn't matter to him. That I was nothing more than a footnote to his famous, busy, bloated life, his persona always larger, more immediate than me. As a kid, I found that trying to get something more from him was always a losing game that I'd keep playing.

"Are you okay?" Hayley asks me.

"Yeah." My skin feels kind of hot, though.

She points to an old oak, which once had a tire swing attached to it. "We used to play in the pachysandra under that tree. Remember?"

Hayley and I would throw a jar of swirled marbles into the air and then hunt in the pachysandra, like truffle-sniffing pigs, for every single one. I was six; Hayley was eight.

The castle and grounds have been passed down through generations of my mother's family—a family of business magnates and industrialists. Mental illness ran in their DNA as fervently as fair skin and blue eyes runs in others.

My great-grandfather was an insane gardener. Literally. Both those things. I'll never forget coming outside one day when I was little, just as spring had sprung, to find exotic flowers blooming everywhere—the grounds exploding with crazy combinations of color, like I had just entered an acid-coated Oz.

Of course a week later it rained jumping spiders, their webbing coating the tops of trees and shrubs like shredded silken parachutes. The crew ran around tearing off their shirts, flitting them out of their hair. A production assistant was reduced to tears.

Hugo told me that some of the blossoming trees, imported from exotic locales, also held exotic spider eggs. Soon after the flowers bloomed, the eggs hatched too. That's when I first learned that with beauty comes a little bit of terror. That pretty much sums up my childhood here: something cool would happen immediately followed by something traumatic. I could never deal with that.

I give Hayley a half grin, half grimace.

"What?" she says.

"I just don't get how you've been able to deal with this place for so long."

She shrugs. "I grew up here."

"Me too," I say, feeling weirdly defensive all of a sudden, because we both know it was only to a point. I left. She stayed.

"I have my own apartment, in the Hitchcock Wing, overlooking the Shakespeare garden," she says. "I'm head of accounts now."

"Really? Oren made you head of accounts?"

"Well, your dad did."

"Wow. Congrats!"

I'm happy for her, but I also suddenly feel a little jealous. A question I used to ask myself a lot bubbles up to the surface: *What if I hadn't left?* Part of me never stopped wondering what my life would have been like had I stayed here.

"Thank you," says Hayley. "The studio's failing, though."

"But hasn't it always been? Wasn't that, like, always the point?"

"Well. It wasn't explicitly the *point*. Criterion reissued *Black Blood Picnic* and *The Vomit of Sergei Ramona*."

I press my sneaker into the grass. "I heard."

"That was huge for your dad. He felt validated, he was so proud."

I nod. "Good for him."

"Hey, we still make four features a year, and we have solid VOD sales. People still buy DVDs, if you can believe it. Parts of Central Europe love us—we're huge in Slovakia, for some reason, and our films still get a theatrical release there. But it isn't enough. The landscape is changing."

"You mean people don't want to watch grainy creature features anymore? Because it's not, like, 1952?"

Hayley, noting my sarcasm, folds her arms. Any talk of the studio or my dad instantly creates this rush of bitterness in me. I offset that by making fun of this place—since it's super easy. But it's my family legacy, so it's interesting to see Hayley be the one all defensive and proud about Moldavia.

Keeping her eyes on me, she takes another sip and taps her fingers on the rim of her flute. "Well," she says, "your dad was considering an offer from Rusty Blade Films to buy the studio."

"Really?" This surprises me. Rusty Blade makes soulless torture porn—everything my dad hates, and everything Moldavia stands apart from. They made like a billion dollars from this insanely gory series called *Backpacker* about spoiled rich kids in Europe who get kidnapped and put in snuff films.

In the last one, the bratty daughter of a Silicon Valley titan dies by getting wormed. That's right: *wormed*. Little green inchworms are dropped down her throat, one at a time (it's a long scene), while she slowly chokes to death, to the delight of pervy mobsters with unplaceable accents wearing Karl Lagerfeld sunglasses who bid millions for the only existing tape.

If my dad was going to align himself in any way with Rusty Blade, he might have actually been considering his estate and our inheritance, given his condition. But that really doesn't sound like him, so maybe it was the dementia.

The grave digger walks by, dirt-coated shovel slung over his shoulder. "Alas, poor Yorick!" I shout after him, but he doesn't turn around. I'm about to ask Hayley what time this whole thing is going to start, when Oren breaks free of the gaggle of clucking squeezers and starts making this hooting noise, hands cupped over his mouth.

I frown at him. "What the hell is he doing?"

"I think we're starting," says Hayley.

The crowd, more of them than I thought—who the hell are all these people?—start to converge on the center of the lawn, by the open grave. They creep from all corners of the vast estate in tight clusters, like a half-finished watercolor painting that got tipped upside down.

Suddenly, I see all these familiar faces popping out of the crowd—faces I haven't seen for years, faces I had forgotten about, some with a little more age on them now—carpenters and grips and electricians, the dudes in the props department, the people in the kitchen, the makeup crew. Hunter Yates, the studio's marketing director; the kids from the scenic design and special effects teams, teenagers when I knew them—now in their mid-twenties. A few of them hold babies.

There's Elena Scaler, otherwise known as Mistress Moonshadow, a principal Moldavia actress, who films her famous web series, *Live from Moldavia*, somewhere deep in the bowels of the castle. I see Lorenzo Mayberry, the aging Italian lead actor of several Moldavia classics, standing in a clump with his costars, a small repertory company of Moldavia regulars known as the Spine Tinglers. Many of them have acted in Moldavia films for decades. Lorenzo, an icon in the horror underground, suffers from vertigo and narcolepsy. As my dad once famously snapped on the set of *The Grinning Gargoyle*: "Why the hell couldn't he just be a drunk like everybody else?"

"My God, Dario, is that you?" Franklin Fletcher, the chief legal officer of Moldavia, and one of my dad's closest confidants, cuts a clean path toward me, moving one or two squeezers aside with a gentle push of shoulders. He's dressed in a well-tailored dark suit, which matches his personality: organized, humorless, and efficient. I shake Franklin's hand. He has a firm grip. "You're all grown up," he says, removing his tinted glasses. "I'm so sorry about your father. He lived a long life, and no one can say there's a single minute of it he regrets."

There has probably never been a truer statement made.

I doubt my dad regrets a single thing he ever did, said, or made.

"How is the orphanage treating you?"

"We call it a group home," I reply. "And I'm pretty happy there."

Franklin flicks out his wrist to check the time on his gleaming Rolex—the same color as his slicked-back hair. "I'm glad to hear that. How old are you now?"

"He's seventeen," says Hayley, who's moved in close by my side, her fingers lightly grazing my arm.

"My goodness," says Franklin. "Soon you'll be off to college."

"We'll see." Pretty much nothing else could heighten my stress right now than hearing the word *college*. It's just another decision to make, more uncertainty. And I'm already lost in the disorienting maze of whatever today is going to be.

"Plenty of time to decide, I'm sure," says Franklin.

"Not really."

Franklin doesn't hear me. He's scanning the crowd and then turns toward the castle, where a long white carpet is being laid out, leading all the way from the glass doors of the rear atrium to the gravesite.

As it gets more crowded, other people start coming over to me, hands grasping, in a Dickensian sort of way, like only I can anchor them in this storm of madness. Barbara Pandova, who helped design the iconic mummy monster in *The Entombment of Freddie Fell*, gives me a kiss on each cheek.

Samantha Childress, the icy but brilliant head costume

designer, wearing this lavender scarf-and-gown ensemble, gives me a hug. Joaquin Joseph, a carpenter when I knew him, and now an internationally recognized production designer, starts sobbing into my shoulder. With each new person, there's another punch of emotion flooding through me, threatening me with a total loss of control.

People are paying their respects. This is an actual funeral. Even though—*Jesus Christ, does anyone realize this?*—my dad isn't even dead yet! He's really going to be buried alive. This is literally his last hour on earth. I wonder what that must feel like: to know everything is about to end. Every dream, thought, or fear he's ever had—thrust into oblivion. Everyone he's ever known he'll never see again after today.

Surprisingly, I've never thought that much about death; it was always an abstract concept, rendered even more unreal growing up around fake ghosts and monsters. But all of a sudden, I feel this prickling coldness. And now, the appropriate emotions, as if governed by a system of ingrained etiquette, seem to decide what's going to take the lead. As the floodgates open, I get a terrific lump in my throat and my chest starts to feel leaden. "Shit," I say, softly, to myself, digging my nails into my palm.

I feel grief. I was not expecting that at all.

The crowd of mourners seems to be multiplying. I'm losing the familiar faces in the throng of squeezers, some of them decked out in garish costumes and clownish makeup, many of them dressed, I now realize, as characters from classic Moldavia films.

Some of them hold calla lilies, my dad's favorite flower, which makes an appearance, however briefly, in almost every one of his films. Ginger Borenville in *Wolf Wife* dies with one in her teeth after getting shot by a silver bullet from her philandering hairdresser husband (played by Lorenzo, of course).

Hayley explains to me that the funeral is semi-public—open to fans who purchased "tickets" through the painfully outdated Moldavia website.

I turn to her. "Are you serious?"

She nods, slowly.

I guess that explains all this insanity. Why am I even surprised? Of course this is what my dad would want; he always maintained an obsessive relationship with his hard-core fan base—drawing them in while simultaneously keeping them at arm's length.

I'm older now, my hair is long, tied up into a droopy man-bun, and I haven't shaved, but (and I was afraid this was going to happen) I get recognized anyway.

Once word begins to spread that I'm here, at least a dozen squeezers come up to me asking for an autograph. Thing is, like it or not, I am firmly enmeshed in Moldavia lore since *Zombie Children of the Harvest Sun*. When I was twelve years old, my dad made me the star of one of his films. I played the main zombie kid, Alastair, who unites an undead army of hungry children against their *very much still living* parents and teachers. Hayley was in the movie too, and so was her mom, Aida. They were both great, in smaller roles.

Like me, they never appeared in another Moldavia movie again.

Zombie Children was critically panned. It has such a low score on Rotten Tomatoes they had to come up with a new level of bad, like I think it's literally certified *shit*. But for squeezers the movie remains a late Moldavia favorite and has become this big cult thing. I'm probably the only kid in a group home to ever receive fan mail.

Just seeing the grounds again, and remembering growing up here, is giving me a reaction. Hives creep up on the inside of my wrist. My throat constricts.

My dad does his own thing, so there were no union rules, no child labor laws being enforced. *Zombie Children* was filmed entirely on the grounds, behind closed gates, as all Moldavia films are, with cast and crew living in the castle for the duration of the shoot. Although I had various tutors homeschooling me, or whatever, that stuff was always an afterthought.

Hugo usually did the normal dad stuff with me: playing catch, taking me on walks during my bits of downtime. My dad worked me hard, day and night, pretty much bullying me into giving what's considered one of the great modern-day horror child performances, despite the overall movie being considered crap.

My dad was notorious for overworking his actors. He'd film screams until voices were completely shot. He felt there was a real terror that would creep into a scream after a certain point. He was always after that moment, that elusive truth. The scene in *Hiss for a Kiss* when disgraced fortune-teller Charlotte Lockwood sees a cobra slithering across her dining-room table is supposedly the longest scream ever put on film—at two whole minutes. "Scream all night!" my dad would say, gleefully. It became a catchphrase. He started saying it whenever he was about to film a new scene.

He was even harsher with me. He knew he could push me further—and be brutal in an unchecked way—than he could with any other actor he ever directed.

More squeezers run over to me, like I just escaped my booth at a horror convention. They're getting more aggressive— wanting selfies and hugs, oblivious to the fact that I'm at my own dad's funeral. I make a beeline away from them, my pulse racing.

Everywhere I look, I see a scene from a Moldavia movie. I spot the shrub where the half-devoured remains of Lionel Gimpin were found in *Shapeshifter*. I see the yellow rose-bush where Parma Quiota was summarily dispatched by a gang of serial-killer ghosts in *The Stranglers of Strangelove Cove*. I see the tree where Puritans hanged teenage witch Betsy Norris in *Dial W for Witchcraft*. Over by the lattice gazebo demonologist Uriel Orloff was struck by lightning in *Coal Black Soul*. And by the big old fountain, where stone angels perpetually piss water, the vengeful countess Antonia Rigg started feeding her possessed pet Rottweiler junk food in *Devil Dog*.

I'm also very much aware of who I don't see: namely, Hugo and Aida.

"You doing okay?" Hayley's managed to find me in the scrum. As I turn to her, I start a little, because I didn't notice the gold locket around her throat before. Now the light is hitting it just right, so it gleams. That's my mom's locket. I recognize the engraved profile of the little boy with the sapphire eye. His face snaps open; my mom had a little photo of me at two years old trimmed and glued inside.

I don't get a chance to ask Hayley about it. The glass doors of the atrium suddenly open, and four men in kilts, playing bagpipes, come marching down the long, white carpet.

I'm a little confused, since there's not a drop of Scottish blood in my family.

Seven pallbearers, all in white tuxedos, appear behind the bagpipes, carrying out my dad, who also wears a white tux. He's sitting up, leaning against the back of the velvet-lined dark-wood casket as if he's taking a dip in a Jacuzzi. The pallbearers follow the procession of the bagpipes, all of them solemnly marching down the carpet from the castle to the gravesite. "Who the hell are we burying, Braveheart?"

"Bagpipes feature prominently in *The Psychic Sisters of Edinburgh*," says Hayley. "He must be paying tribute. It's one of your dad's late favorites."

"I didn't know." I haven't seen any of the recent Moldavia films.

Hayley looks at me. "You stopped watching them, didn't you?"

"Yes." I watch the procession. "Hayley, what is all this? This is *madness*."

My dad, clearly out of his mind, is blowing kisses and throwing calla lilies at everyone while holding a lit cigar in his other hand. People throw lilies back at him, so it all looks like one bizarre calla lily fight. Another pallbearer drags my dad's oxygen tank behind the casket, head down, looking pretty grim, like he never got the memo that this is actually a giant yard party.

"This is what your dad wanted," she says. "You know he gets what he wants."

"How could he want this? Everyone's acting like he's already dead. We're actually going to bury him alive?" I can't fully comprehend what I'm seeing.

"This is how he felt he could take on death. He wanted to go on his own terms. Make his death a celebration of his life, leave with dignity."

"*Dignity?* Hayley, he's not in his right mind!"

"Thank you for coming!" my dad is saying. "Thank you!" He looks frail and shrunken, more so than I remember, which makes a weird match to his bright, maniacal energy. He got so old. He spots me, and his face changes: the lower half sort of falls, goes slack. He looks as if he's desperately trying to see something through a wall of cotton.

"Dario?" he says, recognizing me, but seemingly baffled by my presence. Then a fan runs over, stealing away his attention, and I wonder if that's all I'll get. I didn't know what this was going to be—Jesus, who would?—so there was no way to prepare.

It's funny how Hayley told me I might regret it if I wasn't

here. There's this pinch of regret I always fend off whenever my dad comes into my thoughts—that I left him here, a lonely old man, and maybe there was a chance things could have changed; a chance for mutual forgiveness. That pinch just got sharper, because now I'll never know.

As he gets closer to his grave, I start to panic. I grab Hayley. "I should . . . um . . ."

"All right," she says, nodding at me, understanding. Hayley motions to Oren and then waves at Franklin. She hustles me quickly through the crowd of leering faces and vulgar costumes. Franklin stops the procession and pushes everyone out of the way so Oren and I can approach the casket. "Step aside, please," says Franklin.

"Why'd we stop?" says Oren, running over, hands out, in the manner of an annoyed wedding planner.

"He wanted to say something," says Hayley. She frowns at Oren. *"Don't you?"*

"It's okay," says my dad, taking my hands in his—they're cold, limp, trembling.

"Dad," I say. Up close he seems practically dead already. His eyes are milky, sunken, clouded over with cataracts. He's so skinny and wasted away he's almost skeletal. He's lost the remainder of his thin yellow-white hair. "Dad . . . ," I say again. I can't seem to say anything else.

"It makes me happy to see your face again," he says.

I remember us sitting at the kitchen table, eating yogurt together when I was four. He's about to be buried alive, and I'm thinking about yogurt. My dad puts his cigar in his mouth, and grabs Oren's hand too, so now he's holding on to both of us.

"Okay?" Oren says to our dad, smiling gently.

"Okay," he says back, grasping our hands.

"WE LOVE YOU SO MUCH! YOU'RE A GENIUS!" a fan shouts.

My dad sticks his chin up, amused, always happy to be called a genius.

"Dad," I say again. I'm choking here. Why can't I speak?

My dad drops our hands. He takes us in like he's trying hard not to forget our faces. Then he looks away, his face tight and determined. "It's time," he says.

"Onward!" Oren yells.

I have the sensation of something fading forever as the procession continues, and I fall back into the teeming crowd. I can almost see all the questions that will never be answered blowing away like dandelion seeds—scattered, tiny dark shapes against the flush of the sky, and then just gone.

When they reach the grave, the pallbearers begin their routine of quickly running straps through the handles of the coffin, preparing to lower it. The crowd quiets as my dad sits all the way up in the casket and clears his throat.

"Quiet!" someone shouts.

"As many of you already know, I'm terminal," he says, chucking out the remainder of the lilies from the coffin in a single fistful. "But I am blessed to have spent my life devoted to my sole passion—making films of horror and fear, envy and spite, love and loneliness, ghastly apparitions, and vulnerable, freakish creatures of the night; stirring emotions through the most powerful medium that ever was. I've always done exactly what I wanted—taking control of my life, and stilling it, in a chaotic world. Thank you to the Moldavia family, and to all of you who watched my films with the same passion we put into making them."

"Thank you!" some lunatic shouts.

He coughs. "I have been sick a long time. But I have resolved not to let this disease win. Instead, my death shall be my final work of art, a tribute to the first heroine I ever put on celluloid, Veronica Bellwether, who was buried alive in a musty sarcophagus somewhere in the hills outside Kutná Hora."

People cheer at the mention of Veronica Bellwether. I can't tell if my dad has scripted this farewell speech or if he's just making this up as he goes along.

"It has always been my lifelong desire to be buried alive," he continues, "emulating Veronica's tragic demise, so she and I could commune eternally in the misty zone of the imagination, where everything began for me. This has always been my first choice to exit this life. I leave you happy, content, and at peace with the world."

My dad waves, signaling he's done. People get quiet.

As they start slowly lowering the coffin, a Britney Spears song pierces the grief-stricken silence. It slowly dawns on the mourners that this is a ringtone, and everyone looks accusingly at everyone else. My dad is still waving, meekly, almost bored, as they lower the open coffin, but then he plugs his cigar in his mouth, reaches into his jacket pocket, takes out his phone, and holds it to his ear.

"Joe? Hey. Yeah. How are ya?"

My mouth opens. "Is he . . . *taking a call*?" I ask Hayley, leaning into her ear.

"Um. I think so," she says.

"How 'bout that? Was it Ed?" He lies back, chatting, as they continue to lower him down into his own grave. We all move closer and peer down into the dark hole after him. The pallbearer trying to maneuver the oxygen tank into the open coffin is clearly struggling. This was obviously never rehearsed, or given much thought at all, and when he loses his grip on the tank, he careens into the other pallbearers, who all lose their grip on the straps lowering the coffin.

Everything tumbles.

The casket tips backward, the oxygen tank smashes against the side, the neck of the tank breaks with this horrible clang, and the lid of the tank pops open. I hear the rush of oxygen just as my dad's cigar flies out of his hand. "Gosh!" he exclaims, halfway down, gripping the sides of the casket, trying not to fall out. He says it again: *"GOSH!"*

Then the straps come free and everything falls at once, hard and far, down into the hole, followed by a loud, tremendous fireball, which shoots out of the open grave like hell upending itself. Chunks of mud and splinters of coffin belch out of the flaming grave, sending the mourners flying back, screaming.

"Holy shit!" I scream, my hands flying to my face, just like that famous painting, all madness and furious swirls. "My dad just fucking *exploded.*"

Franklin, always the coolest cat in the kingdom, brushes off his suit and removes his mud-coated glasses. "Well," he says, "that was his second choice."

CHAPTER TWO

HORROR IS HELL ON LITTLE BOYS

EVERYONE'S CLOTHES ARE SPATTERED WITH DIRT. SOME PEOPLE HAVE superficial cuts and burns, singed hair and eyebrows. But by some miracle, no one is seriously injured. Everyone assumes my dad was killed instantly from the explosion. Oren takes charge and determines this by cupping his hands over his mouth, and yelling down into the grave: "Hellloooooo down there? Dad? *Dad?*"

When there's no response, Oren motions for everyone to quickly finish up the proceedings. And we all obey, in a slightly rushed manner, family members and close friends each taking a turn shoveling a heap of dirt into the hole, which makes this awful dull thudding sound as it hits what's left of the casket, way down below.

Two gravediggers take over, shoveling and shoveling, while most of the random squeezers head out, clutching purses and props, looking dazed and bedraggled, even stupider now in their Moldavia "costumes." Oren tells the real mourners to head into the music room, where the services will continue.

"I will be giving the eulogy," he tells me, clamping a hand on my shoulder as we linger outside by the door. "But tell me now if there's something you'd like to say."

I shake his hand off me. "You're talking about giving a *eulogy*?"

"What do you mean?"

Oren is still pretending this is a real funeral that went off without a hitch. It's like he has to prove at every step how inept he is. "Dad didn't die in some cushy hospital bed. Do you not get what just happened out there?"

"This was his first choice. You heard him."

I slam my hands over my eyes and slide them roughly down my face. "Technically, we all killed him, you idiot!"

"He's not suffering anymore. He was ninety-one years old. There are worse ways to go."

"Like what, Oren? Getting eaten by a shark? Having your parachute fail?"

Oren folds his arms. "Well, he didn't mention those options—"

"What is it going to say on his death certificate? *What did he die from?*"

"Everything," says Oren, with a long sigh.

"That's not an official cause of death."

"I'll take care of it all," says Franklin, heading inside, giving us each a look.

Goddammit. *This family.* Why does literally everything have to be three thousand times more traumatic than necessary? Every single thing that would happen normally in other families, guided by tradition, planning, and decorum, has to become an all-out horror movie with us. We can't just make them. We have to *live* them.

Something twists open inside my stomach.

"You look pale," says Oren.

"I—just—can't—I . . ." I run over to a bunch of daffodils and bend over them, my palms grinding into my knees. *God, please, no,* I beg the flowers. But they're not having it. I haven't eaten today, so I just dry heave dribbles of bile all over them.

Oren runs over. "I'm sorry. Are you okay?"

"This is my fault," I say, heaving. "I would have stopped this."

"But you—"

I raise my arm in the air to stop him. "Don't say I wasn't here!"

"But you weren't."

I gurgle onto the flowers.

"You could have had more of a say if you were," says Oren.

I spit and spit, trying to get rid of the taste of bile.

"I didn't know you cared enough. I thought you hated him," says Oren.

"That's what you thought!" I shout into the flowers.

"Well, didn't you?"

"I don't know." I straighten up, wiping my chin. "He hated *me*."

"Gosh, Dario, is that what you think? Dad didn't hate you."

"Stop, man, just stop." I can't listen to Oren contradict the cruel logic that's guided my choices up to now. I can't have that reality upended at the moment. It's too much to handle. "Why did you really want me here?" I ask, resting a sweaty palm against my throat, trying to steady myself.

"To say good-bye to him, Dario—one last time. I'm sorry this was painful."

"Someone's always sorry around here!" I spit some more, over my shoulder. "And what are you even sorry for? For turning this into a circus? Of course you knew this was going to be painful for me!"

"It was painful for all of us."

I can't help it. I just start to laugh, darkly, this throttled noise boiling up from my guts like something ugly and mean I swallowed finally being regurgitated along with everything else. I cough and I laugh and then I spit some more.

It feels like the consequences of every tough decision I made in my life (and questioned relentlessly) have been laid out before me—a pulsating grid of connected dots leading to today, when my senile dad gets blown to bits while being buried alive.

I tend to my own wounds so much that I can forget about

everyone else's feelings. It's a problem. I've recognized that in group therapy sessions. Leaving Moldavia felt like I was making the decision to survive my own whacked-out life. But it came with this heaping of guilt, which never felt fair to me. I worked hard to neutralize all of it—but not hard enough, clearly, because now I feel responsible for this mess.

Oren takes a conciliatory step toward me. "Listen, Dario—"

"No, Oren—"

"Dario, I tried to honor—"

"Honor *what*? Dad's mind wasn't clear! This was chaos! But what do you care? It's always easier to turn your back on things and be sorry about everything years later, right?"

I'm filled with disgust when I think about Oren's lifelong habit of looking the other way, particularly when it came to me when I was a kid, but even here, even now.

I leave Oren standing there and rush inside the castle.

The music room is one of the rooms no one ever really used and I never went into, even though it's one of the nicest in the whole castle—large mullioned windows face the east lawn, the super-high ceiling is all baroque, and the walls are hung with centuries-old Italian tapestries. A huge mirror hangs over the mantel. There's a harp in one corner, a grand piano in another; the room looks like it hosted all these dances and concerts, with people in lace and corsets giggling and nibbling finger sandwiches, but none of that ever happened in here.

The mourners sit on cushioned chairs that have been set

up facing a podium, which sits on a small raised platform. There's nowhere to spit, so I just clear my throat loudly, trying to get rid of the taste of bile, and take a seat.

Everyone looks typically mournful, but with this extra topping of distress and grit, like we're sequestering inside from a hurricane that just made landfall. A hundred heads swivel around as Oren closes the two large doors with a bang. It sounds like the first thing you hear in a climactic scene in an English boarding-school drama.

Oren swiftly takes the stage, placing some rumpled papers on the podium. Then he does this totally unnecessary bow and places his hands in a prayer position. I wonder if he's going to direct everyone to jump up, roll out our mats, and get into downward-facing dog. He brings his thumb and index finger together, looks out at all of us, and says: "What is love?"

That's when I know this will probably be the first eulogy in the history of funerals to require two fifteen-minute intermissions.

I inhale, deeply, and gaze out the window.

"Dario! You are not giving me what I need!"

The crew is getting restless. Hulky shapes are shrouded by heavy coats behind equipment—booms and cameras and barn door lights with orange glowing gels, cords and cables snaking everywhere. I can feel the electricity fizzing in the air. It's late. It's freezing. No one has eaten. My tongue is numb from sucking ice cubes all night. Undead boys can't have their breath show.

I shake my head. "Let's just do it again."

Roll sound. Roll camera. ACTION!

I try to stave off this feeling of failure, of disappointing my dad. I lower my chin, flatten my gaze, and try to muster up the same throaty grunting and sloshing of saliva that I did for the previous eighteen takes, leading my army of undead brethren to the burning schoolhouse. I smell the pyrotechnics. I hear the breathing of the twenty extras behind me—none of them kids like me, just adults on their knees, blurred and insignificant in the middle-distance background (most of them members of the kitchen staff).

CUT.

"Goddammit! Something's missing! Where is Alastair?"

I punch my palm. "I did what you said, just like last time."

"Don't you dare give me that look. Alastair is hungry. Ravenous! He has to kill. He's angry he's been reduced to an animal. He's filled with rage. There's only superficial fear on your face. Alastair isn't a mouse! He's not a goddamn pussy. He's the enraged leader of a zombie army!"

Every take has felt the same to me. I don't know what he wants. He's pushing me somewhere only he can see.

"Do not kill the lights, and we are not breaking!" he screams to the first A.D., who just ran over, whispering into his ear. "He's gonna get it. Go."

ACTION!

We do another three takes, but my dad doesn't like them, his frustration steadily building. I'm trying so hard not to cry, but I'm losing my grip on that. And now my dad is just starting to seethe instead of communicate.

Take twenty-three:

I lift my chin up for only two seconds, the biting cold freezing the tears to my face, before he screams CUT. There's a swollen silence that rolls in like a breakneck tidal wave through the heavy night and then he's charging me, back-handing me hard across the face.

I go flying into the frozen grass.

"Get the hell back up!" he's saying. My ears are ringing. "Are you angry now, Dario? GOOD! That's what real anger is. FEEL THAT?"

I don't feel anything. Not anymore.

"Now pretend every survivor in that schoolhouse is me," he says.

We do three more takes in a row—me with a swollen lip, a bruised cheek—and then he says, "Check the goddamn gate," and walks off the set, muttering into a walkie-talkie.

Later, I'm sitting on the frigid metal steps of the hair and makeup trailer, parked a mile away from set, on the base camp of the northern lawn. Semi-frozen tears skate down my cheeks. My shivering is so intense I'm almost mesmerized by it—watching my knees involuntarily knock into each other like I'm removed from my own body. I want everything to be numb.

Hugo carries some equipment while two other burly construction guys, members of his crew, follow behind him. He sees me sitting there, hands off the equipment to his men, and heaves his tattered down jacket over my trembling shoulders. He's wearing worn cords, a flannel shirt over thermal wear, which slopes over his bulging gut, a thick skullcap the color of his dark beard. "What you still doing out here, kiddo?"

I just shake my head and stare at my hands.

Hugo nods. "Horror is hell on little boys. You're doing a good job. People will remember Alastair." He frowns at my swollen mouth. "You gotta put ice on that. You want me to punch your dad in the face for you?"

I shake my head slowly. "Don't want you to get in trouble."

"There's not another head carpenter who could do this crap, work these hours, for at least five hundred miles. Your dad needs me more than I need him. Say the word."

He's right. No one, not even my dad, ever messes with Hugo. "It's okay."

"Dario, I ain't gonna say how he treats you is right, and I ain't gonna lie to you and tell you he loves you more than his schlocky films, 'cause we both know that's bullshit, but one day you'll realize you can either be defined by him or defined by everything you are that he could never be. So that's what I gotta say on that. Wanna eat?"

I don't say anything. Hugo looks toward the castle, clearly starving and freezing, like me, but I can't move yet. So Hugo rests a heavy hand on my shoulder and just stands there, as if guarding me, and when I fail to move, he remains; he doesn't ever take his hand off my shoulder until what feels like hours later, when I finally unstick my butt from the icy metal step and walk silently toward the castle. Hugo follows

me at a respectable distance without a word of complaint or
so much as an impatient sigh.

"What is . . . *effervescence?*" says Oren, wincing at his defenseless audience, having lost his train of thought for the eighth time. The room has gotten so hot and stuffy. I rub my eyes. Christ, Oren. It's the shit they put in soda.

Oren blathers on about our dad's love of filmmaking, going on tangent after tangent, one tangent splintering off into subtangents, touching on everything from our dad's childhood in a small Romanian village to Italian horror to seventies-era slasher films, to the world going digital to— for some reason I'll never know—C86, a little-known British genre of jangly indie music from the mid-eighties.

It's like Oren barely knew our dad. He's not memorializing him like a son, he's celebrating him like a biographer, or worse . . . *a fan.* Oren is so removed from who our dad was as a human being, his mind so muddled and incapable of sustaining a single line of focused thought, that his eulogy just becomes this flood of mental puking, which is painful to watch. He might as well be reciting our dad's Wikipedia page.

Finally, mentioning a few of our father's proudest moments on celluloid (after briefly digressing into Harriet Tubman's early life, and rising real estate prices in the Bay Area), he gathers his papers, nods to everyone grimly, and leaves the podium.

Since Oren requested he be the only one to speak, the

exhausted mourners all stand up as one and hurriedly make their way out of the music room like Oren might at any moment change his mind and realize he never got around to debating the environmental impacts of fracking, or exploring the various conspiracies surrounding the Kennedy assassination.

CHAPTER THREE

THE TWO-A.M. SUCCUBUS

EVERYONE'S ADJOURNED TO THE GREAT DINING ROOM IN THE LUGOSI Wing of the castle, where pastries and other hors d'oeuvres have been set up on a black tablecloth draped over the long oak table. Silver candelabras drip wax. A fire rages in the marble fireplace, flickering moodily off the plum damask walls. There's a commissary on the basement floor where everyone usually eats, but the main dining room is used for special occasions, like premieres or the occasional birthday party.

And now, of course, the reception for my dad's *live funeral.*

I try to avoid everyone awkwardly picking at the food and murmuring condolences to me, and I find the bar toward the back of the room. I grab a bottle of Bombay Sapphire and pour a healthy amount over some ice. I drink it down fast and relish the burning in my gut. Franklin wanders by to tell me that tomorrow morning will be the official reading of the will, and everyone is hoping I'll spend the night in the castle.

Of course, with everything else going on, I didn't think about a will, and that there'd be an actual reading of it. But that's what people do before they die, I guess—leave wills. I obviously won't be mentioned in it, and everyone hoping I'll spend the night here—when that was not my original plan, as Jude could tell anyone—seems like Moldavia already trying to exert its influence over me.

And there it is again. As a kid, I always ascribed anthropomorphic qualities to Moldavia itself and all of its inhabitants, as if they were one collective force, tugging at me. The fact that I'm doing this again, and so soon, makes me uncomfortable.

"Look, I should really get back tonight," I tell Franklin.

"Arrangements have already been made with the orphanage," he says. "And with your school."

I crunch down hard on an ice cube and grind it. I like Franklin a whole lot, but what's up with no one consulting me on spending the night here and missing school?

"I apologize," says Franklin. "It's one night. We'll have you back before noon."

I'm too drained to make this into a thing. I ask him where exactly I'll be sleeping, and of course he tells me in my old room, and that it's already been prepared for me. "Are you all right, Dario?"

I chug the rest of my drink down. "I mean . . . I've had better days?"

"Of course."

I look for a place to put my empty glass down. Every available surface would automatically absorb me into a group conversation I do not want to have right now, and I'm getting more and more irritated that now I'm being forced to spend the night. I think part of me is afraid I won't be able to escape. "I just wasn't expecting to spend the night," I say. "I didn't bring anything."

"We'll take care of that," he says. Then a caterer grabs his elbow and asks him something stupid about shrimp, and he's off somewhere else. I take the opportunity to make a beeline out of there. I can't deal with Oren right now, or anyone else from the Moldavia inner circle. I just want to be very alone.

I put my glass down on an end table and veer down the dark wood–paneled halls, trying to dodge the onslaught of memories, which come faster, in sneakier ways now. It's like being slapped in the face repeatedly by an unseen force. I stop at the bottom of the red-carpeted grand staircase, in the great hall of the Corman Wing, which leads up to the master bedroom suites that once housed our immediate family and other highly ranked Moldavia staff like Franklin, Mistress Moonshadow, and Hugo and his family.

Hayley stands at the top of the staircase, ten years old, wearing a black dress. She rolls a green marble down the stairs. I watch as it slowly bounces down, like a glass planet ripped from its solar system. When it reaches the bottom, I pick it up and clasp it in my fist. She clambers down and stands in front of me. "My dad loved you," she says.

"I loved him back," I tell her. I want to say so much more, say just how sorry I am, but I'm feeling too much, and I can't express it all. I don't know how.

Aida, Hayley's mom, sees us from the top of the staircase and hurries down. She's so pretty, with her thick mane of strawberry-blonde hair, eyes the color of a spring garden, this sprinkle of freckles around her nose. Her slight, lilting Dublin accent always calms me. She kisses me on the forehead. "Come on, sweetie—we have to go," she tells her daughter, taking her hand. "Dario's dad needs him. We'll see him later."

Both of them look back at me over their shoulders as they walk off.

My room is barren because I never really had much—no books or toys or video games. And not to be too Oliver Twisty about it, but not much was ever really mine. I never had *stuff.* I didn't have model airplanes dangling from the ceiling or rock band posters on the walls—the crap kids always have in movies. What I did have I took to Keenan House. The rest went into storage somewhere deep in the bowels of the castle.

I always liked my room, though. It's big, yet cozy, and unchanged: same thick scarlet rug, same antique four-poster bed, and spindly lamps, props from old Moldavia movies set in haunted mansions. My worn leather armchair is still here too, in a far corner. The cathedral ceiling is a refreshing change of pace from my claustrophobic dorm room, and so is the walk-in closet, with its wide shelves and lemony light.

An armoire with little doors and drawers is the only other piece of furniture in here. Tall windows overlook the grounds; outside I can see the candles surrounding my dad's gravesite flickering in the night. For a moment I think maybe my dad didn't die, or isn't dead yet, and the wind will carry his screams from below ground, begging to be dug up. I shudder that thought away fast.

A cordless phone sitting on the floor actually works. I call Keenan and get Jude on the phone. He's out of breath. He was probably boxing. I explain the situation, that I'll be spending the night. There's a long silence. But then he says softly: "And how are you doing, are you okay?"

I sit on the edge of the bed and run a hand through my hair. A tough question, considering all the shades of bedlam I experienced today. "I'm surviving."

And that's all I say. I don't want to get into everything. He'll get all worked up, protective and shit, which I can't deal with right now. Plus, I think I am holding up pretty well, all things considered. There are lots of memories here—good ones, bad ones, whatever; it doesn't matter. Soon I'll be putting this place behind me again.

"Make sure you get home tomorrow," says Jude. "Call me if there's a problem."

"I will." There's a knock at my door. "Okay. I should go."

I hang up the phone and open the door. A sweaty, nervous little kid is standing in the hall wearing a jacket and tie. "I have your kit, sir."

I blink at him. "You have my what? Who are you?"

"I'm Gavin, I'm an intern, and Franklin wanted me to get you settled."

"We have interns?"

"Yes, sir."

"*Sir*? My name is Dario."

"I know, sir. May I?"

Gavin enters, and I follow him into my bathroom. The white-tiled walls are spotless, as is the bottle-green floor. Wow, my very own bathroom that doesn't smell like days-old urine; honestly, this is probably what I miss most about this place.

Gavin, who can't be more than ten or eleven years old, has opened this leather shaving kit and is placing each item on a fluffy towel beside the sink: a razor and shaving cream, a bar of soap, a tube of bath gel, a striped wooden tooth-brush, a box of toothpaste, a tub of turquoise pomade, a jar of strawberry breath mints—on and on it goes. As I watch this kid arranging everything so fastidiously, I suddenly wonder if I'm supposed to tip him. "Uh. That should do it."

He looks up at me. "Sorry about your father, sir."

"Thank you. You don't need to call me—"

Gavin suddenly puts two hands over his eyes and stifles a sob—literally, *a goddamn sob.* I take a step back, nearly trip-ping over the edge of the bathtub. I have no idea what's going on. Why is this kid crying? I haven't even cried once today.

"Uh. Are you okay?"

Hands still clapped over his face, Gavin gulps and then

starts making these awful heaving sounds: *huh, heh, huh, heh, heh, heh, huggghh* . . .

I stand there, helpless. I'm five seconds away from walking out and just leaving him in here, when he immediately stops and composes himself. He takes his hands off his face, revealing red eyes filled with overflowing tears.

"If there's anything else you need, sir, just let me know."

"How would I—"

But he's already rushed out of the bathroom. I look at all the luxe grooming products neatly laid out for me by the sink.

What the hell was that?

My bed is soft and so much higher off the ground than I'm used to. It's strange being in it again. As my eyes get heavy, I have the oddest thought: Why does it feel like I'm somewhere far away and totally unfamiliar, instead of back home? Did this place ever feel like home to me?

Home, Hayley said on the phone. *Is that what you still call it?*

When I wake up, it feels like minutes later. There's something in my room.

It takes me a moment to remember where I am and everything that's happened: There was a funeral. My dad exploded. I'm back in my old bed.

There's a sifting sound. I roll out of bed, but it's too dark to see anything. It sounds like a colony of bats is clustering on the ceiling. I really, *really* hate bats.

I crawl toward the nearest lamp and switch it on; a single

one of these things casts only a sliver of the palest light—but just enough to illuminate the outline of the actual succubus suspended from my ceiling. I've never screamed so loud in my life.

Every defense mechanism kicks into gear but in the most awkward way possible. I lie flat, stiff as a board, arms clamped to my sides as if trying to camouflage myself into the carpet and disguise all movement. My panicking brain has no idea what predator it's trying to defend against. But now it's too late.

She descends from a low-hanging cloud of rippling black smoke, covered in rainstorm-colored strips of decayed skin, her face bone white, her eyes a glaring, sulfurous yellow. Her long black hair streams behind her. When she parts her gangrenous lips, she bares demonic fangs. She hisses, and I feel her acid breath burning my face off. As I prepare to be dragged, faceless and deformed, to the underworld, I spot wires and a harness behind her and finally recognize the pretty sophisticated makeup.

It's Elena: *Mistress Moonshadow.*

She lowers down until she's only an inch away from my face.

"Oh. My. God."

"Dario," she purrs as I lie there, petrified. "It's good to see you home again."

It takes me five whole minutes of slithering around on my belly to turn on each separate lamp so I can finally see.

Then I stand, shakily. "Come out from there." I wave her out from behind the door, where's she's hiding, hissing, still in character, as if even these low-watt bulbs will melt her into oblivion. She peeks her head out.

"You set up a . . . *fly system* in here while I was asleep?" I ask.

She glides into the center of my room, right over to me, her gaze hungry and intense enough to keep my blood pumping. "It's a basic pendulum system. I'm playing Silvana the Succubus in *No Chance in Hell*, which we're finishing production on. I wanted to see how effective her getup was."

"Uh, pretty effective. And don't worry, I didn't really want those ten extra years of my life."

She flashes me a fangy grin, but it lacks its usual bite. Her outfit looks like someone's weird destroyed shower curtain. Shine a bright light on anything around here and it'll crumble before your eyes; I always have to remind myself of that. "I'm sorry about your father, Dario," she says, a tremor creeping into her voice. She takes my chin in her hand, appraising. "You're a handsome young man," she says. "You turned out well. You look just like Lucien."

She sits on my leather armchair, removing her wig. The sexy dark gleam is gone, turned off. Just like that. Now she just kind of looks like a sad, middle-aged Goth who's wearing too much makeup, which she removes, mirror-free, in circular swipes with a pink cloth. It's like she's getting older and erasing herself at the same time. "I don't know what to do," she says, with a sigh. She rests the cloth against her knee. "Honestly, Dario, I'm a little afraid."

"That doesn't sound like you." Her vulnerability seems so unnatural.

"Actors are superstitious creatures. I've only been Mistress Moonshadow through your father's lens, through his eyes."

"Yeah, but you created what you are."

I remember a review of a movie Elena was in called *Death Every Morning*, where she played a bloodsucking femme fatale. The reviewer said she was the only actress in modern cinema "with the true and absolute ability to creep like a cat— making us rejoice in feeling equally delicious and in mortal danger at the same time."

"Everything at Moldavia was a collaboration with Lucien," she explains. "We're used to being directed, told where to stand, how we'll be lit, how we'll live, how we'll die—until we're all resurrected, and do it again for the next film. Do you think we know how to function without him here, guiding us?"

That hadn't occurred to me. With my dad gone, people might not even know how to exist here. The actors, at least, have spent their whole lives as these wacky characters. Do they even know who they are as real people anymore?

I walk around the room, turning off a few lights, because it suddenly seems too bright in here, which seems an affront to Mistress Moonshadow. Then I plop down on the floor, in the middle of the room, rubbing my lower back. "Who is going to be directing the films now that my dad is gone?"

"You should talk to your brother about that," she replies.

I nod, picking at the carpet. "Okay. But you still managed to scare the crap out of me. I literally almost had a heart attack and died right there on the floor."

She stands, examining her shiny long black fingernails. "That means a lot." She sighs. "I think I'll head to bed. Would you be a gentleman and escort me to my room?"

"It would be my pleasure." I jump to my feet, link her arm, and lead her to the door. When I open it, I scream even louder than before.

Gavin is standing there, right outside my door, all still and intense.

I'm literally clutching my chest like an old lady. "What are you *doing* out here?"

"To see if you needed anything, sir."

"Have you been standing outside my room all night?"

He looks down at his feet.

"You don't need to stand out here," I say. "Don't you have your own room?"

"Down the hall, sir," he says meekly.

"Stop calling me *sir*. And go to bed. I'm fine."

"But Franklin said I should see if you needed anything."

"He didn't mean for you to just stand there all night! That's creepy, dude."

The kid looks sheepish; he really wants to please.

I frown. "Didn't you hear me screaming?"

"Yes. But I didn't want to bother you."

I raise my eyebrow. "Right. Well, just go to bed," I tell him. "Really. I'll find you if I need you." He still doesn't move. "Shoo. Shoo!" I wave him away, and keep waving, until he finally retreats down the hall.

I walk Mistress Moonshadow to her suite. The front room is bathed in a peachy glow from vintage tripod movie lights standing in the corners. Everything is draped in shimmering, gunmetal-gray fabric, hanging from the ceiling like sails, and wrapped around several white mannequins scattered around the room. Pieces of black, purple, and gold costuming hang from brass hooks on the walls. I laugh a little, 'cause *c'mon.*

"Good night, Dario." She blows me a kiss, followed by a mournful, deflated smile, sashaying toward the tunneling abyss of her bedroom—*her lair.*

As I head back to my room, I see a strip of light under Oren's door. Not wanting to go back to bed just yet, and feeling a gnawing loneliness, I get this unexpected urge to talk to my brother. I don't know. I feel a little bad about how I acted earlier; I'm also curious about what Mistress Moonshadow just told me. My dad wrote and directed every single one of Moldavia's 150 or so features. I can't imagine anyone replacing him.

What are Oren's plans, exactly?

I knock softly. When there's no answer, I peek inside. Oren is lying on a futon. He's dressed in red long johns, watching *Suspiria* on mute while he listens to the soundtrack on vinyl through Skullcandy headphones, which are attached to a record player on the floor, next to the album's spooky jacket. I remember Oren does this. He likes to storyboard movies in reverse. It's his way of studying how all the shots are composed. *Suspiria* was directed by my namesake, Italian horror master Dario Argento.

Oren's room is slightly bigger than mine, but it's way more cluttered: VHS tapes and DVDs are scattered everywhere, as well as magazines and books and all these loose papers and torn-open envelopes. It's basically the room of a shut-in who watches lots of Moldavia movies. On the walls are framed black-and-white photos of severe-looking old people in nineteenth-century immigrant garb. I'm not going to ask about the empty mayonnaise jar perched on the windowsill with a spoon sticking out of it. Oren sees me standing there and slips off his headphones.

"Dario. It's such an odd sight to see you at my door."

I lean against the doorframe and nod. I never really know what to say to Oren, and I always seem to realize that too late.

"Was there something you needed?" he asks.

"Um. Just wanted to say . . . nice speech about Dad."

Oren picks at a loose thread on his shirt. "No it wasn't."

"It was good."

"Thank you for saying so. But I'm no Henry the Fifth."

"Right. Well, are you okay?"

"I'm deeply sorrowful," says Oren, accompanying this statement with a loud moan as if to prove it. "But at least we knew this day was coming. I was emotionally prepared. Yes, there were a few hiccups, but for the most part Dad got what he wanted in the end. I'm comforted by that fact."

It kind of says everything that Oren is *comforted* by how today went.

"And how are you doing, Dario?"

He does seem genuinely concerned, which makes me relax a little. I puff out my cheeks and slowly exhale a stream of air. "I . . . don't know. Not sure."

"Grief is a complicated process," he says, as if reading the first sentence of a really bad self-help book.

But I don't feel grief. I just feel numb. And that's starting to concern me. So I guess I feel concerned? And maybe a little lost. But overall, I don't think I'm feeling what I'm supposed to be feeling. So now I'm wondering what the hell is wrong with me.

"What's going to happen now?" I ask, trying to stabilize my thoughts.

"What do you mean?"

"Well, now that Dad is gone, who's going to be directing—"

"I am taking over all directing duties!" Oren says proudly, and loudly, like he's announcing a presidential appointment.

I can't stop my lower jaw from falling open a little. Oren. Directing. Holy shit. Who in God's name would have approved that? But then of course I know: the same man who wished to be buried alive in his own backyard—our dear old departed dad.

It's suddenly painfully apparent that no one bothered to think through the aftermath of the most planned "natural death" of all time.

I try to reassure myself that I have a tenuous connection to Moldavia now. None of this is really my problem. But still

I imagine tentacles unfurling, and coming for me through the castle walls. If things reach a certain level of untenable chaos, *this could somehow become my problem*. And that scares me—the idea of getting pulled into Moldavia's insanity like quicksand.

But I should have known Oren would step up to the plate. He hasn't been watching and studying classic horror films his whole life for no reason.

"Did you ever direct anything before?" I ask.

"Not yet!" he says, his eyes lighting up like someone just plugged in his face. "But I've shadowed Dad my whole life. I'm taking over *No Chance in Hell.* Three scenes still left to shoot on that. Then we're going into production on *The Killer Cauliflowers.*"

"The *what*?"

"It's my own script."

I furiously scratch an eyebrow. "You're spelling *Killer* with a *k*, right?"

"I am."

I know he isn't. "What is it about?"

"An evil shaman puts a spell on a rival farmer, and his vegetable patch gives birth to these mutant vegetable monsters that attack all the villagers. We're trying to hit that sweet spot of the Eastern European horror vegan market."

"Oh. That sweet spot."

"Dad loved the idea."

"He did?"

"Yes. There was just a lot on the docket, and he kept

pushing it back so he could focus on projects that were already in planning stages."

I wait for more—for Oren to tell me he's kidding, but he doesn't.

"Are cauliflowers scary, though?" I try to phrase this in a calm, constructive, test-screening sort of tone, but my voice warbles and sounds too high. I can't imagine our dad loving this idea at all.

Oren sits up. "You've seen the *Pumpkinhead* films?"

I gnash my teeth a little. "I know of them."

"It's like that."

"I don't think that monster was literally a pumpkin, though." That movie is about a dad whose son gets killed by teenagers on dirt bikes. Then the dad finds a witch, and they create a horrible monster to get revenge on the teen-agers. So . . .

"This is going to be an instant classic," Oren informs me.

I nod, imagining cauliflowers, which I guess are pretty weird looking if you think about it long enough. And appar-ently Oren did.

Maybe this could work? Maybe Oren could pull this together? Maybe he's really an undiscovered auteur, a latent genius? Oh man, I really want to believe all that.

"Um . . . maybe just rethink the title?" I suggest, like that's the only issue here.

"Any ideas?"

"*Haunted House Salad?*"

"Oh."

"*The Creeping Crudité*?"

He cocks an eyebrow. "You're mocking me."

"Just a little." I'm joking because I don't know what else to do.

Oren reaches for his headphones. "Well. It's nice to have you back here, however briefly. How much school do you have left?" He frowns. "How does all that even work?"

"How does what work? I go to school like anybody else. Then I go home."

"Home. To that bacteria-ridden orphanage?"

"There's bacteria here too, Oren. Just different strains." I rap my knuckles against the door. "Anyway. Look. I'm sorry I freaked out earlier."

"I understand. It's a lot. I'm sure it's hard to be back."

"Yeah. It is." I hesitate; it's not exactly uncharted territory trying to talk to Oren about the bad shit that went down here when I was a kid. But he's never directly acknowledged it, and I've always wondered if he *could* without being dismissive. "You know I had a rough time growing up here. Right?"

Oren makes a strangled *hmmph* sound, like *here we go again.* He sticks his hand out. "I *assumed.* You did get *emancipated.* You did move to an *orphanage.*" He rubs his chin, glances at the TV screen, then back at me, his eyes searching, offering a hint of vulnerability, of something more. But then I see him swallow everything; his demeanor resets into his default mode with me. "You have some bad memories? Is that it? We all do." His voice is flat, listless.

I look down, and nod. "Bad memories" doesn't really

sum it all up, but it's clearly easier for Oren to digest, so let's just go with that.

"Is it about Mom?" He's fiddling with his headphones. He's treating this conversation like I've paid him for therapy, and I'm his most needy patient.

Oren doesn't like to talk about the stuff that went haywire with our family. I wish there was an easier way to connect with him. All that pain keeps us apart, but it's also the main thing we have in common.

"For sure about Mom," I answer. "But also making *Zombie Children*."

"I was supposed to be first A.D. on that one," says Oren. "But I got pneumonia. I was bedridden for weeks. So I wasn't able to protect you during—"

"There were other times."

"Other times?"

I hate when he repeats shit back to me as a question, in that light, innocent tone of his. I level my gaze at him. "When you could have protected me."

"From Mom? Oh, I doubt—"

"After. *After she left.*"

He fucking knows what I'm talking about.

I step into his room. There's a heavy pause. I run my hand down the back of my neck, trying to unknot all the muscles that are suddenly tightening up.

Oren turns his attention back to the movie and writes something down, staring at the screen, licking his lips in concentration, lightly shaking his head. "It's just that . . .

sometimes you have a tendency to whine."

And here we go with this.

Oren loves to bait me. He has a couple of things in his repertoire, this routine he's created just for me. One of them is mocking Keenan House, and everyone there, as decrepit thieving vagrants fighting over morsels of food in a leaking, reeking hellhole.

That dovetails into the other thing he loves to do: paint me as this selfish ingrate who left Moldavia as part of some extended tantrum. That's convenient for him, I'm sure, because it absolves him, offsets whatever guilt he feels at being a shitty older brother, and masks the real reasons I had to get the hell out of here.

But the thing is, *it works.* He can really piss me off. I've been determined not to let him get to me since I've been back. "Look, man," I say, keeping my voice steady, "I can't keep going down this path with you where I constantly have to justify why I left, or apologize for leaving—"

"I haven't asked you to do either—"

"When really, you should be the one apologizing to me—"

"Ohhh, is that right—"

"Yeah, it *is* right." I take a breath. I unball my fists. I'm not going to take the bait. "I just don't like this . . . *defensiveness* I've been feeling since I've been back."

"Yes, well, you can't blame others for the way *you feel*, Dario—"

"Partly because you think I'm this self-involved brat who just abandoned—"

He holds out his hands. "Your words."

I let out a low whistle. I put my hands over my eyes, trying to quell the anger rising up. I hate that he still plays these games. I keep trying with him, just like I did with our dad—and it's impossible to get anywhere.

I turn my gaze to Oren's TV and let the movie give me a dose of escapism. It's about a witches' coven disguised as a ballet school. It's filmed in bright, off-putting candy colors. I smile at that. It's a bold choice. I like bold choices.

"Look," says Oren, "I'm sorry you felt like you needed to escape your home. That I wasn't there for you, that I ignored your plight. Okay? Happy now? This family has had its tragedies. I suppose we both had our own concerns and put ourselves first. That's the Heyward way, though, isn't it?"

I look at him. "Is that really supposed to be a fucking apology?"

"That's what you really want from me? An *apology*?"

"Jesus." I walk over to the window and squint outside. It's so black and quiet and vast out there that the night swims in my eyes. Oren's right. What would saying sorry even accomplish? It's just bullshit people say so they can move on, like pressing a button or something. Forgiveness is pointless, in any case. Usually the damage is already done.

I barely know Oren, and that's sure as hell not my fault. People with much older siblings generally don't know them well, usually because the older sibling leaves home. Not the other way around. Everything around here is too backward to get a proper handle on. I feel like an asteroid flying through space. I can't catch up. Moldavia and the fragments of what once was my "family" are so unknowable to me at this point, it's like *why even try.*

"This was always your true home, even if you renounced it," says Oren. "We're still your family, even if you renounced us. You left part of yourself here. Maybe you're just now realizing that."

It's statements like that that make the hives and all the itching come back.

Oren puts his headphones back on and redirects his attention to *Suspiria*, where a blind man is getting his throat torn out by his possessed guide dog in a German plaza.

I step away from the window and shake my head at him.

"Good night, Dario," he says, not looking at me.

He gives me a little wave as I close the door. As I'm walking back to my room, I run into Hayley, carrying a cup of steaming tea on a saucer. She starts a little, like she forgot I was back.

"Does anyone sleep around here?"

"Apparently not you," she says, taking a sip of tea. "Sometimes I walk the halls at night. Insomnia."

We just stare at each other, something we keep doing. I guess we're still not used to seeing each other all grown up.

"Wanna see something cool?" she says.

I follow her down drafty stone hallways until we reach the grand ballroom in the Carpenter Wing. The room has been cleared out and turned into a huge makeshift graveyard, with real mounds of dirt. Papier-mâché ghouls, reinforced with wires, are crawling out of ripped-open graves.

The matte paintings stacked against the walls, created by Joaquin Joseph's production design team on the upper floors of the castle, depict toothlike gravestones protruding through miles of foggy, moonlit night. This was always the thing about living here: you never knew what room was going to be turned into what.

I used to spend time in the library of the Lugosi Wing, where old books were stacked from floor to ceiling. It was the only place I could read and be alone for a while. But one morning I walked in there and found all the bookshelves gone and the room transformed into an evil chemistry lab for Dr. Vernon Landover in *The Cyberian Experiments*. Glass vials were bubbling, beakers were smoking, and there were mashed-faced fetuses in jars filled with brightly colored liquids.

They needed the library because it got great afternoon light.

Hayley and I sit across from each other on the ground, in the middle of the huge dirt-filled set. The room looks so real, and the castle is so drafty anyway, it feels like we're sitting in the middle of an actual graveyard.

I stare into my lap. "Hayley . . . I wanted to say . . . I'm so sorry."

She blows into the cup. "About what?"

"That I didn't go to the funeral."

She frowns.

"Your mom. I loved Aida so much."

Hayley's eyes instantly get shiny. "She loved you a lot too."

I was trying all day to bring this up and I didn't know how. "I should have reached out."

She nods. "It was pancreatic. We knew for a while. It wasn't a shock." She takes another sip of tea. "How did you hear?"

"A horror zine, I think? Online." I hug myself as the wind whistles outside the castle walls. "I could have called, or sent flowers or something. I totally suck."

The edges of Hayley's curls glint in the weak bronze light. She looks contemplative. I can tell she's holding a lot back. "You left. This place wasn't a part of you anymore."

Except I'm realizing, more and more, each minute I'm back, how untrue that is. It's just been one long fight with myself pretending Moldavia didn't matter anymore. Oren's right: I left part of myself here. I spent two days sobbing when I heard about Aida. I missed school and everything. I should have called Hayley. But I had to continue my pathetic illusion, proving nothing. As a result, I wasn't there for her, and I never got a chance to pay my respects to her mom.

It hurts to think how Hayley's continued on here, without me or her own family. There must be a constant onslaught of memories, just like there are for me—except she still lives here. They're not temporary for her.

Hayley takes a sip and gives me a little nudge. "How did things go with Oren? I saw you coming out of his room."

I lean back on both hands. "He says he's taking over as principal director."

Hayley nearly chokes on her tea. "Let's not make any assumptions. We haven't even heard the will yet."

"Do you know something I don't?"

She rests the empty teacup beside her on the saucer. "Not at all. But Oren doesn't get to just appoint himself anything."

"You might want to tell that to Oren."

"He'll figure it out."

The politics of this place confuse me. There are so many mysterious rules. I've barely been back, and I already feel lost in its fumes. I don't get how Moldavia's engine is supposed to run, with all its moving, intricate parts. But Hayley seems to know a lot more, which makes sense, I guess, since she's been here all this time. She also seemed very in tune with what my dad was thinking about his funeral, and how he wanted "to take on death." I can't imagine him talking about that with just anyone. He pretty much expressed everything he thought or felt through his films.

I wonder how afraid and alone he actually felt at the end there.

Hayley catches me eyeing the locket around her throat. She reaches behind her neck to undo the clasp. "You should have this. It really belongs to you."

"No, no, no, don't." I put my hand on her arm. "Just . . . what's the story?"

"Your mom didn't want to keep it at the hospital. There

had been some thefts. She gave it to me as a gift on my six-teenth birthday."

"Then it's yours," I say. "Can I . . ." I motion to the locket, and Hayley nods. I snap the face open. It's empty: there's no photo of me inside anymore. It's like I got erased.

It was an ordinary cloudy afternoon when my mom told me she was leaving Moldavia. We were standing under a cherry blossom tree on the west lawn. There was a light breeze. Blossoms fell on our heads in the creamy porcelain light as they came for her with a wheelchair.

Good-bye, my peach.

We used to visit her every week, then every month, then it winnowed down to three times a year, then only on Moth-er's Day. She seemed worse—less and less herself each time. I haven't seen her in seven years, two years before I left Mol-davia.

My mom is acutely psychotic, and to some degree mental illness is genetic. Oren may be old enough that he doesn't have to worry as much about getting sick. But the risk is always there. I'm at the age when my brain could break too. I wake up every morning wondering if today's the day I'll start hearing voices.

"Your mom kept the photo with her," says Hayley.

"You know about the photo?"

Hayley nods.

When I left this place, I left a hole here. I knew I would. But I never realized Hayley would take my place so easily. She belonged in my family more than I did.

Hayley could see my mother and not have the same terror of becoming her. And my dad could let himself care about Hayley without worrying he might lose her too.

I briefly make eye contact with the glassy stare of a knobby wraith peeking at us from behind a painted Styrofoam birch tree. I look at Hayley and laugh a little.

Hayley smiles at me. I rub the tops of her hands with my thumbs.

We both lean forward. Our lips brush.

I kiss her softly. She kisses me back. And then we really start kissing, deep and intense. We fall asleep holding each other, our mouths still touching, but only a little.

"Because you're wasting our time!"

He's given me another bloody lip—this is his thing now: he'll beat this performance into me if it's the last thing he'll ever do. Alastair is decaying. Bruises and blood only make it more real.

He has a certain image of what Alastair should look like. He even has ideas about how Alastair breathes. Being emaciated is a part of that. He wants my rib cage protruding. Sometimes he'll wake me with two fingers shoved down my throat (he always seems to know when I sneak food at night). When I start vomiting, he drags me to the toilet, holds my head over the bowl by my hair until it's all out of me.

He senses I'm his chance to some greater respect. Maybe this is the film that won't be forgotten, regulated to the midnight circuit, to cult status. Maybe this will be his true masterpiece, mainstream even, dare we say it, admired by his fans and peers alike.

He wants me to hate him. He's trying to get me to hate him in that perfect way only he can pick out from the other shades of rage that trickle out of me, which he deems boring, weak, uncinematic, unauthentic, not a true facet of Alastair's core torment.

Does he think the hate boiling inside me can be flipped off like a switch once we're done filming? The answer is: he doesn't really care.

This is the last Alastair scene to be filmed, but not the last one in the movie.

I have to climb a wooden ladder to the roof of the custom-built firehouse where my latest victims cower inside: the dwindling survivors of a zombie apocalypse. After I get to the roof, I'll shimmy down the chimney like a skinny, undead, prepubescent Santa Claus, something the audience won't see; it will only be inferred by the sound of screams, ripping flesh, the breaking of bones.

We've been at it for hours. He's saying I'm not moving fast enough, my gait is wrong, my posture is off, I don't have enough intention—we've done so many takes now the ladder leading four stories up is slowly coming apart. But my dad says it'll hold for another take, or at least till I reach the top of the roof.

"But it might not, you stupid sonofabitch, and your son could break his neck!" Hugo roars at him, and my dad roars right back that the ladder will hold.

"If he climbs it one more time, you are gambling with his life."

Truthfully, I'd rather climb the goddamn ladder than deal with the aftermath of saying no to my dad. How messed up is that?

My dad asks if we have another ladder. Hugo says that this already is the second ladder and we even have a third, but he has to fetch it from the props department, all the way back at the castle, because there's only so much he and his crew can carry.

"Dar's wasted enough of our time," my father spits. "We're losing the light! This is my magic hour. I'm going for it. Let's go, let's go!"

"You are going to kill your son!"

"The ladder will hold him! He weighs thirty goddamn pounds! The ladder would even hold your fat useless ass!"

"WHERE DOES THIS END, LUCIEN?"

"Picture's up."

"Quiet on set!"

"Take twenty-three."

I don't know why he does it except maybe just to save me, to literally save my dumbass life, but Hugo throws off his jacket and begins to climb the ladder.

"Christ, what's he doing?" my dad screams. "You see, Hugo? It holds!"

Except it doesn't.

The ladder could have just collapsed after Hugo hit the third rung, but the goddamn thing is as stubborn as my dad,

71

so it waits till he's all the way at the top before it splinters and comes apart into a million bits and pieces. Everyone screams and then goes quiet, in one big shocked intake of breath, as Hugo falls backward, his flailing body a shadow puppet against the copper twilight. It seems like he falls forever. . . .

And then Hugo is the one who breaks his neck.

The next day, while my dad is hugging a sobbing, inconsolable Aida, I watch from the crack of a doorway in the small storage room where I've been hiding and silently crying all day. His hand drops a little further, lightly squeezing her ass. She couldn't be more diplomatic, gently removing my dad's hand and clasping it in both of hers, a gesture that marks boundaries, yet offers forgiveness, while she mourns.

It's such a clean move that it's impossible to forget just how many times I've seen him do this shit. When my mom was still here, when I was in sight, when Hugo was in sight, when Hayley was in sight. My dad didn't care. He was asserting his authority over his films, the studio, the castle, and all of its inhabitants.

This is my vision, *he was telling us.* You're all just pawns on my chessboard.

That's the moment when I lose it. I'm strong and lithe enough to knock him to the ground. I pound at his face until I feel his nose crunch. And when his hands defensively go to his face, I pound his stomach, his chest, his ribs, wanting only to feel more crunching and more breaking. It takes three crew members to pry me off him.

I feel disgust. Not because of what I did, or even what I was reduced to, but because there's a part of him inside me, and I know this at twelve; I realize it so completely that all I want to do is exterminate it. So I get on my bike. And I pedal away, out the gates, as far away from the estate as I can go, and when I see the edge of that cliff coming I don't even bother to slow down.

In the end it didn't even matter that I was hospitalized. My dad already had what he needed. He just wanted to see if he could push me further, into something so desperate and bestial no one would ever forget my performance—or his film. Not this one. He had already gotten me there. He just didn't know it yet.

Only the camera did.

My dad visited me in the hospital. He fell to his knees, begging my forgiveness, telling me about his hardscrabble life growing up poor in Romania, which pushed him to an almost sociopathic perfectionism in his work, a frantic will to succeed, and stave off failure, which he confessed filled him with shame. He regretted he risked so much, put me in the center of his own internal storm of madness. It was cruel and unfair of him.

Ignosce mihi, he murmured, soothing me with Latin, kissing my hands.

Actually, none of that happened. I just like to pretend it did.

Franklin, the lawyer, my dad's trusted confidant, was the only one who visited me in the hospital. And that was because I had been there for so long without anyone claiming me, the authorities got involved, and I was assigned a social worker.

I told Franklin then and there I wanted to leave my family, leave Moldavia.

I knew I couldn't take another day there.

Franklin was silent for a long time. Then he said: "All right, Dario. We can prove neglect. We can prove abuse."

Franklin stood and moved to the door, hands behind his back. This was the only time I ever saw him truly weighed down by something. I saw it in the rounded slope of his shoulders, heard it in the heavy, churning silence. "Your father and I have known each other a long time. We're well aware of each other's flaws. We respect that about one another." He looked at me. "Are you sure this is what you want?"

I told him it was.

So I left Moldavia at twelve, although I had to wait until I was fourteen to get legally emancipated. That had to go before a judge, but then, with Franklin's help, it was done, and I finally wasn't a Heyward anymore. Not that Heyward was even my dad's real name. He legally changed it from whatever vampirish Romanian last name he was born with and never spoke of it again to anyone. Another lost tale, another apparition.

I wake up, blinking back tears. Hayley is still lying beside me. The locket glimmers around her neck. I sit up, hugging my knees. Then I feel Hayley's hand, cool and firm, on my back. "I'm sorry," I say, sniffling, wiping my eyes.

"Your dad died. It's okay to be sad."

"I was thinking about Hugo."

Hayley rests her chin on my shoulder.

"I couldn't get the scene right," I say. "Your dad was just trying to protect me. . . ."

She wraps her arms around my chest and speaks softly into my ear: "Is that what you think? Is that what you've *always* thought? That it was your fault?"

I wipe my nose with the sleeve of my shirt. I have actually always thought that.

"It was an accident," she says. "My dad was being reckless. In no way was his death ever your fault."

This is bullshit: that she feels like she needs to console me. She was the one who lost him. I turn to her. She has a hard, determined look on her face, like this is the story she's come to accept—*Hugo was reckless*--and there can't be another version of it. But there are tears in the corners of her eyes, like paratroopers waiting for their turn to jump.

I lay the back of my hand against her face, and she presses her cheek into it.

We stay like that for a while, until she says we should probably clear out of the fake graveyard. We kiss once more. It feels so natural, like we've been kissing each other for years. Then we both make our escape through the predawn hush of the castle.

I shower the dirt off when I get back. There's a caged light over my showerhead that changes colors—Argento hues, like he personally lit my bathroom with his infamous colors—an emergency red rising to a sunrise orange, and then down again to a cold underwater blue. I close my eyes and let the water pour over my head.

Even in the hot shower, I'm still trembling when I think about how it felt to kiss Hayley. Maybe she's the real reason I came back here—to see what would happen between us after all this time. She softens everything, takes me out of my head. She gives me hope that the world can stay sweet and pure. She's always done that for me.

Coming back here, seeing Hayley now, is like being lost in time. I think about time itself, and how Moldavia can muddle it. I think about being unable to sail freely into the future because of the past chasing us, chaining us. I think of tentacles again. Coming through the walls. Wrapping around my ankles.

CHAPTER FOUR

THE LAST WILL AND TESTAMENT OF LUCIEN JOSEPH HEYWARD

THE NEXT MORNING, WE'RE GATHERED IN THE BILLIARD ROOM OF THE Romero Wing.

There's a purple pool table under a ceiling light shaped like a ginormous, upside-down funnel, and a shuffleboard table in a far corner, beneath a row of small windows. Vintage pinball machines line the walls. Because of its size and smoky light, this room was used as the study for Horace Rivers in *Grave Robbers and the Whores Who Love Them*. In the infamous scene when Horace opens the cursed gold cigarette case containing the severed mummified fingers of beheaded gypsy Leonora Quell, this was where his eyes liquefy and pour out of his sockets like milk.

This room also boasts the largest collection of crystal

skulls in North America, although I'm skeptical of this claim and not exactly sure who's tallying it, because most of them are props, not artifacts. They line the bookshelves. Crystal skulls, like calla lilies, feature in many Moldavia films.

We sit at a black, oblong table. Only Oren, Franklin, Hayley, and I are here. Oren is unironically wearing a black Victorian waistcoat, a white shirt with ruffled collar and laced eyelets in the front, and ripped black leather pants. He looks like a pirate who got lost somewhere in the Renaissance and wound up at an S&M club in 1973.

Hayley's hair is tied back in a ponytail. She wears a perfectly pressed white blouse and charcoal-gray skirt. I'm definitely super into her steely corporate day look. Oren gestures at me, lazily, with the back of his hand. "Why is he here?" he asks Franklin. "He's not a member of our family anymore."

I lay my hands flat on the table. "Didn't you say last night this is still my real family, my real home, all that crap?"

Oren cackles. "Yeah, but not *legally*."

"Oren, please," says Hayley with an impatient sigh. "I'm even here."

"Dario got emancipated," he announces, like maybe no one knew. "He moved to an orphanage for unwanted children and deformed burn victims."

I hold out my hand. "What burn victims? No one there is burned."

"I'm pretty sure all the kids there are *burned*," says Oren.

"Not one person there is burned. What are you even talking about?"

Franklin clears his throat. "All of you need to be here; all of you are mentioned in the will. Lucien—the testator—appointed me executor of the estate. I will be handling the probate process, dealing with creditors, distributing assets, and—"

At that moment, Gavin enters the room holding a silver tray with a pitcher of orange juice, glasses, a neat stack of doughnuts, and multicolored packets of tea.

"Oh goody!" says Oren, reaching.

Franklin shuffles his papers while Gavin serves everyone breakfast. "Since you're all here," says Franklin, "I thought we might have a formal reading of your father's last will and testament, even though the document is part of the court record—"

"Do we have any more of these strawberry glazed doughnuts?" Oren asks from the side of his overstuffed mouth. "Sorry. But. They're so yummy. Please continue."

"So," says Franklin.

"It's the jam in particular." Oren brushes off his leather pants, sees us all staring at him, and straightens his posture. "Sorry. Go ahead. Please."

My father, who declared himself *of sound mind*, ensured that my mother would get proper care for the rest of her life at the institution where she resides, Kingside Park Hospital—in their residential treatment program. They never divorced.

There's stuff about paying off a shitload of debt to a

shitload of creditors, and then the remaining assets are to be divided between Oren, Hayley, and me; special trusts were set up for each of us. I'll get this money, if there's any left, when I turn twenty-one.

And the grand finale:

"'I hereby appoint my son Dario Lancet Heyward chief executive officer of Moldavia Studios . . .'"

Oren stops chewing. Hayley's eyes open wide. I get a massive head rush.

Franklin pauses, twirls a pen.

"Go on," says Oren, stormily, staring into his clasped hands.

"'. . . with the stipulation that he is to return to Moldavia and live here full-time. In which case he has six months from the time of my death to achieve financial stability for Moldavia. If he manages to achieve solvency before those six months are up, or if there is sufficient evidence to reasonably conclude that Moldavia will be solvent within that period, Dario is free to leave the estate. If Dario should refuse this, or if solvency, or the likelihood of solvency, is not achieved in six months, the Moldavia name and library are to be sold to Rusty Blade Films, with the profits of the sale to be shared equally between my two sons as well as Hayley Fionnoula Marsh.'"

Oren loudly digs his nails into the table.

Franklin continues: "'If Moldavia is not solvent, or not likely to be solvent, within the stated time above *and* if Rusty Blade no longer wants to buy Moldavia for market price, based on an impartial appraisal of the estate, I direct the estate to be liquefied. Any leftover profits, after all debts are paid, as well as the rights to the Moldavia library, are to be shared equally between my two sons as well as Hayley Fionnoula Marsh.'"

The fates of the crew and the actors who live here (including Franklin), who gave their lives to Moldavia, are not mentioned in the will at all.

"He clearly wasn't of sound mind," says Oren, aggressively licking pink frosting crusted on his upper lip.

"Then you murdered him yesterday," I tell him.

Franklin tells us that Cassidy Blackwell, the founder and CEO of Rusty Blade, is coming to Moldavia in about three months to tour the estate and the studio facilities.

"Why three months?" says Hayley.

"His schedule," Franklin replies. "Cassidy's filming all around the world." He explains that Cassidy's visit will just be preliminary—an invite extended by my dad before his death.

"Cassidy Blackwell will just want to liquefy everything and use the cash to fund one of those dreadful slasher flicks he shits out every year," says Oren.

"Those do very well," says Hayley. "Especially in foreign markets."

"I cannot believe this!" says Oren, slapping the table. "My father wants some moody, restless teenager to take over our studio?"

"Some moody, restless teenager?" I've sunk way down in

my chair, hands pressed against my knees, as if to hide from what's happening.

"Well, you know," says Oren, waving me away.

"I'm still your brother, you dick."

Franklin explains that a will is one of the most ironclad legal documents, and contesting it is a lengthy and complicated process.

"I know that!" Oren yells, standing. He walks over to the pool table and leans over it like he might puke onto the eight ball. "Typical," he barks into the table.

"All right, take it easy," says Hayley.

"What are your plans?" says Oren, pushing himself off the table, barreling toward me. "Do you intend to depose me as principal director and producer? Or are you going to refuse his request and let the studio, *our family legacy*, crumble to nothing?"

For a second I can't even speak. I just hem and haw. "I . . . have no plans," I finally manage to croak. "I just found this out like you did! Clearly!"

"We employ more than one hundred personnel," says Oren. "What will happen to them now?"

"It's not like we're paying them anymore," says Hayley.

I frown. "What? What does that mean?"

"Dad was running this place into the ground," says Oren. "We haven't had the money to keep any salaried positions here for over a year now. People work for room and board. And regular meals."

"How come?"

"Dad wasn't of sound mind," says Oren. "At least not toward the end. We still needed to respect his wishes regarding his burial, Dario."

I turn to Franklin. "Are you being paid?"

"Your father paid me a small stipend, which was generous of him," he says. "That will be ending now."

"Then why do people stay here?" I ask, incredulous.

"Don't you get it?" Oren snaps. "They have nowhere else to go. Once people come through these gates, very few come out again."

He's right. This is a house full of misfits, everyone unmoored from the world outside these gates. They don't belong out there. They live in a constantly moving dream world of imagined horrors, spurts of gore, skulking monsters—creatures more aberrant than themselves. After all, it takes true misfits to make believable monsters.

I scratch my arms. I'm breaking out in hives again. This goddamn place.

Providing for my mom and Hayley was the right thing to do. My dad must have been guided by some measure of regret or kindness I never knew he was capable of. Making no provisions at all for the rest of the Moldavia family, to safeguard their jobs or lives here, seems cruel at first, but maybe my dad wanted them to be free. And taking the studio away from Oren shows my dad was probably thinking very clearly when he wrote his will. Oren is too scatter-brained to change a light bulb, let alone lead a failing movie studio back to solvency. But giving the studio to *me*—not even

Hayley or Franklin—feels petulant and mean.

Oren and I look at each other across the table. I feel my dad's hand from beyond the grave—pitting us against each other.

"The time frame is *absurd*," Oren sputters, looking away from me with revulsion. "Dad never intended for this to work. This was a game to him. One last game. I gave my life to Moldavia."

"We all did," says Hayley.

"You're nineteen!" Oren bellows. "You did not. Give. Up. Your. Life."

And with that, he swings open the door, bends his body backward like a human slingshot, and flings himself out of the room, slamming the door behind him, rattling a few of the crystal skulls in his wake.

"Well," says Franklin, gathering his papers.

"What *are* your plans?" Hayley asks me, softly.

I shrug, sitting back in my seat, feeling like I just got punched in the gut. I didn't want to come back here. I didn't want this.

"It's your future," Franklin tells me. "It's up to you to decide what that is."

"What were you going to do after you graduate?" Hayley asks me.

"I thought about maybe getting a summer job or something." I wanted to help out at this little indie bookstore I like. I kept picturing myself restocking Cormac McCarthy books while the summer sun set outside, people spooning ice cream out of pink paper cups asking me to recommend good beach reads. It was a really nice, silly fantasy that actually made me feel pretty calm whenever I imagined it.

"And after the summer?" says Franklin.

Hayley frowns at me. "Dario. Did you have a plan for after the summer?"

I cough into my fist. "Well, I sort of got into Harvard."

The two of them just stare at me. Everything is suddenly so quiet.

I applied on a whim. I did no research. I only applied to Harvard . . . because it was *Harvard*. I never thought I'd actually get in. I never gave much thought to college at all.

"You *sort of* got in?" says Hayley. "What does that mean?"

"No, I did. I got in." I shake my knees a little. "Free tuition." I should have known I had a real shot. I have a perfect GPA. My test scores were through the roof. They loved my essay about growing up at Moldavia and then at Keenan.

"Well, I'm not surprised at all!" says Franklin. "You're a brilliant boy."

"That's amazing," says Hayley, looking totally startled. "Congratulations."

"Why didn't you say anything?" says Franklin.

I bury my head in my hands. "Because I'm not sure I'm going!"

"Lord, *why*?" says Franklin.

"I mean, I feel so lucky . . . about everything. But I don't know if college or academia is for me—classes and homework and tests and essays. I don't know."

And that's the thing. I've been living in some kind of institutional setting for most of my life. I want to be free for a while, be a real adult, travel and see the world. I accepted their offer because of the May deadline, but I'm still not sure it's the right choice for me. I can't go just because I got in. That can't be the only reason.

I didn't want to bring this up earlier because everyone will say exactly that: *I got in, so now I have to go.* Jude says that. I don't want that kind of pressure. And my fantasies about working in the bookstore have started to morph into something more long-term. "I've been thinking it might be nice to live a quiet life somewhere secluded and peaceful and work with my hands," I tell them. "I even thought about going to automotive school and maybe getting a job in a small town as a mechanic."

"You're going to Harvard," says Franklin, standing, giving me a firm squeeze on the shoulder as he leaves the room. "Or I'll break your arm."

"Yeah." I smile at Hayley. "I figured he'd say that. That's what everyone says."

"Harvard is a huge opportunity," she says. Her eyes are flicking around rapidly, like she's imagining the same opportunity for herself.

"I know."

"Work with your hands?" she says, with a half smile.

I shrug.

"Dar," she says, leaning across the table, "you wouldn't

have applied there—*Harvard*—if some part of you didn't want to go. And have that experience."

"I wanted to have something . . . just in case."

"So Harvard was the backup?"

I rub at a spot on my shirtsleeve.

Hayley taps her fingers lightly on the table. I know she's proud of me, but I also sense something closing off inside her, a half-open gate shuttering down again.

"I'm sorry I didn't tell you sooner," I say.

She looks at me. "Your dad would have wanted you to go."

"Seems like he wanted me to run the studio."

"Had he known," she replies.

My dad must have known I'd have *some* sort of plan after Keenan. I mean, I wasn't going to play the ukulele in a bus station. Forcing me back here, and having me be solely responsible for the fate of the studio, would be disrupting any plans I'd made for my own future. I want to think good, happy thoughts about this little decision. But it feels like revenge. "Did you know . . . what he was doing with his will?" I ask Hayley.

She shakes her head. "Honestly. This is all news to me."

"You should be studio chief."

Hayley dismisses that idea with her eyes. "I never told your dad any of this," she says, "but I started thinking about my own future when he got sick. When I knew the end was near."

"Away from Moldavia?"

She nods. "It might be cool to move to a big city, go to

87

school myself. . . ." She gazes out the window. "But it just never felt like a real option."

"Do you feel trapped here?"

She smiles to herself, and looks down at her hands. "I rose up the ranks. I helped make Moldavia what it is today. I'm part of its story now. But I lost a lot—and not just both my parents. Moldavia is like a child; it takes all your attention. It's always *moving.* It murders any other plans you might have entertained. Things can get pretty lonely here too, despite how it seems."

I got out before Moldavia—and all its tentacles—started strangling my life, cutting off circulation to any other kind of future I may have wanted for myself. Before I got in too deep. Listening to her—this is the first time, in a while, when I feel relief, not just guilt, about leaving. But I also feel bad for Hayley. That she didn't get that choice.

"You need to do what's right for you," says Hayley. "You can't start worrying about everyone else's futures, and Moldavia itself, before you consider your own future, and what you want to do with *your* life." Hayley sits back and folds her hands on her lap. "And maybe I need to as well," she adds, softly.

"Then what happens to everyone here? What happens to the studio?"

"You heard the will. We sell to Rusty Blade."

"But this is our legacy. Oren would be destroyed."

"He'd get over it."

"He'll say I'm being selfish."

"Sometimes you need to be selfish," says Hayley.

Before I head back to Keenan, Hayley and I go for a walk. We don't say much. My mind is in total turmoil. But it feels great having Hayley by my side.

It's still early morning. Dark clouds are moving in, casting their shade over the grounds. We walk across the south lawn as it gets darker and darker. We reach a certain spot where I remember one night the amber moon swung over a cluster of tents spread out on the black grass, all of them lit from inside.

I stop walking. "The Curdling," I say to Hayley, with a little laugh.

The Curdling is a Moldavia trademark. Every Moldavia movie has it: a shocking, gross-out "scream scene," usually near the end. It comes from *bloodcurdling*, and it always divides audiences. Some think the Curdling goes too far, while others, the true die-hard Moldavia fanatics, hoot with terrified appreciation. The Curdling in *Zombie Children of the Harvest Sun* was the penultimate scene in the movie, which we shot way ahead of schedule, on a night when we were supposed to film something else.

"When I left Moldavia," I tell her, "I wasn't prepared for the fact that people would know me already—from that movie, you know? It was weird."

"You were a little celebrity?"

I laugh. "A cult one. Do you ever think about making that movie?"

"Not so much anymore. I remember the ending, though."

"Holding a knife to my throat?"

She takes my hand in hers, which sends a charge through my body.

"Yeah," she says. "I always wondered what came next."

I stare out at the lawn as more ominous clouds roll in and blot out the sky.

My dad pulls me into one of the tents, where the cameras huddle close over Aida, who lies on a blanket, dressed like a country peasant. Her eyes are wild, and she's crying. I've never seen anyone cry like that before. Every time her anguish softens a bit, my dad whispers into her ear, her face goes scarlet again, and she clamps a hand over her mouth, tears pouring out of her eyes. My dad slyly directs the dolly grip and camera op to move in, framing her in a tight close-up. Then he whispers, "CUT."

I didn't even realize they were rolling. I have no idea what's going on.

"I thought Valerie was playing the part," I say, standing stock-still, staring down at Aida, feeling uneasy.

"I want Aida to do this," my dad says.

"Why?"

"Stop asking questions," he says. "Focus. This is the Curdling."

They paint my mouth and chin with sticky globs of fake blood. My dad tells me I have to pretend to chew on Aida's throat. She's playing Lara, a farmer's wife, who along with her daughter, Abigail (played by Hayley, waiting in an adjacent tent), are the only two survivors of the zombie apocalypse. Alastair's last living victims.

"You'll just be tickling her," says my dad, seeing the uncertainty on my face, before the cameras roll again. He calls, "ACTION." I go at her throat, kissing and licking her. I make it sound real and gross, lots of slurping and fake chewing sounds, while Aida continues to sob. But I can't imagine why she would be so upset by this, and now it's upsetting me. But then it gets even stranger.

"I want Alastair to find this giant hunk of candy!" my dad bellows, standing behind the camera, next to Jip, "and I want him to devour it like it's the last piece of candy on earth. He wants to make Lara jealous that he has this candy, and he's gonna eat it while she dies. You understand? It's the last piece of candy he'll ever have."

I nod. But what they hand me looks nothing like candy any kid, living or undead, would ever want to eat: this hunk of rubbery red gelatin; oval shaped, smeared with grape and strawberry jam to make it more palatable.

I crouch in a corner, in the shadows, where they set my mark. The camera glides in on the dolly track, real close, and they film me gnawing on this cold, hard log of Jell-O. I make smacking sounds with my lips while keeping my eyes on Aida, off-camera, who's crying hard every time my dad whispers in her ear. And all I can think is: what's she crying about? It's just some stupid Jell-O.

Of course, editing tied it all together. I was too young to know what the scene was really about at the time. In the actual movie, we see Alastair tear out Lara's throat, but she doesn't die right away.

And she's pregnant.

And he's still hungry. . . .

So in the movie, there's a cut to someone else's long, yellowed, curling, gross-ass fingernails tearing open a prosthetic silicone womb filled with fake blood and guts (some of it made out of pasta) and a Jell-O fetus, made by the creature effects department.

The movie cuts back to me devouring Lara's unborn baby, while she screams in a wrenching close-up: the last thing she sees before she dies. That's what I was really eating. I never knew it. Kind of horrible, yeah, but it was silly. The whole movie was.

In the final scene, I discover Abigail hiding under a table in another room of the farmhouse. The scene was filmed in super-tight closeups; that's why they set up all the tents. They already struck down most of the sets, having filmed the wider shots weeks earlier. I drag her out of her hiding spot and lie on top of her, pinning her down.

I'm about to go for her throat, but I stop. Her beauty stops me, and in that moment we see the last shred of humanity left in Alastair, which is what makes him so tragic, that there's still part of a human soul inside him—enough of one to be stopped cold by a young girl's beauty. This is the scene in the movie that gained its cult following. This is the scene in the movie that made it hard for fans to forget about Alastair.

Abigail reveals a large kitchen knife that she was holding behind her back. She holds it to my throat with trembling hands. But she can't kill me. I see beauty in her and she sees innocence in me. So even though I'm probably going to kill her in a moment, she can't bring herself to kill me first. We just stare at each other, Hayley and I.

And that's how the movie ends.

CHAPTER FIVE

NO FAVORITES

THE HEARSE DROPS ME BACK AT KEENAN HOUSE LATER THAT MORNING. After a pretty dull school day, I'm back in the basement rec room full of sticky tables, hard plastic chairs, wonky shelving holding worn-out board games, and thin slits of window from above, helping Oscar, a fifth grader, with his math homework when Jude charges in. "Yo, Dar!"

I look up. "Hey. Let me finish up with Oscar."

Jude sticks out his tongue. "Oscar, bah! *i Déjanos solos, tenemos que hablar!*"

"*¡Necesito ayuda con esto!*" the boy shouts.

Jude growls. "Later, eh? *¡Haz tu propio trabajo!*"

"*¡Esta mierda es difícil!*" Oscar rolls his eyes, sulkily picks up his homework, and leaves the room, but not before flipping off Jude. Jude stamps, pretends to lunge at him, and the kid flees with a little yelp.

"He has a test Monday."

"The Common Core can suck me," says Jude. "What happened at Moldavia?"

I only tell him about the reading of the will. He immediately goes into his *Godfather* thing. "They're not pulling you back in."

"I didn't say I was going back."

"Harvard." He points at me. "You have a responsibility to all of us."

I throw up my hands. "All of you? What about what I want, man?"

Jude starts boxing the air. "Not everyone gets to go to Harvard. I'll be lucky if I don't spend my life in jail."

"Don't talk like that. Don't be a moron."

An Irish-Italian amateur pugilist with Mommy issues, Jude's dream is to be the welterweight champion of the world. He walks around Keenan House wearing only silver gym shorts, black high-top Everlast boxing shoes, and cherry-red boxing gloves. His nose has been broken nine times. It literally looks like someone stuck a potato in the center of his face, but that hasn't stopped him from sleeping with every female our age or older who's come through these doors, including a few key staff members—or so he claims.

That's actually Jude's sign-off to me every night. Instead of "good night" or "sleep well" he'll say: "Dar, just remember I fucked every woman here."

Once he said: "Nancy. I did her too."

"Nancy? *The resident nurse?* She's like seventy years old."

"You'd never know it," he replied.

He may be a pathological liar. Or he may not be. But he definitely knows how to work it. I've seen his charm in spell-binding action, and it's something to behold.

I don't know how Jude wound up here. We never really talk about it. I'm sure he has a dark past. Keenan House is a nonprofit residential foster care home for kids who have been really kicked around—most of them way worse than me. But the facilities are nice, the campus is relatively serene, it isn't all Christian and shit, and that's why Franklin pulled the right strings to get me in. I take a bus to a public high school nearby (same one as Jude, though he has his own circle of friends) and come home to a bunch of overworked, half-drunk counselors pursuing various PhDs who look after us, and mean well. I was already too old to be adopted when I got here, as was Jude.

It always made me sad, though, to see that yearning in the younger kids, like Oscar, who got so goddamn close with three separate couples before these assholes changed their minds at the last minute. Yet Oscar soldiers on, hoping for more chances, wanting to be wanted so badly, needing a family to make him feel whole. Fuck, man.

None of the younger kids seem to understand why I ran away from my own family; it's incomprehensible to them. But I needed the opposite of family. No more families for me, with all the depraved circuitry that runs through them. I craved the stark, institutional structure of Keenan. There are definitely a lot of troubled kids who come and go here: bruised and abused (B&A, Jude says), with drug problems, on suicide watch, and all that shit. I knew I'd be here for six years, I carved out my place, and I've been happier on my own.

I've only ever roomed with Jude, and despite his lawn-mower snoring, we get along great, have a mutual respect. An older-brotherish protective thing comes out in him with me. Even though we're the same age. He's pretty much my best friend.

I mean, hey, I was totally open-minded about being friends with kids at my school, but the whole Alastair thing got in the way. I was naive. I had a group of friends, but then one of them took an unflattering photo of me chomping on a meatball sub in the school cafeteria and posted it on Instagram: *Alastair still craves human flesh! #Alastair #WhereTheyAreNow #Gross #HungryDeadBoys #ZombieChildrenOfTheHarvestSun.*

The post went viral, and I felt totally betrayed. I retreated into myself and never came out of my shell again. People apologized, but I ignored any attempts of various kids to get to know me after that. I didn't trust their intentions. I've never been all that good at the whole friendship thing anyway (or accepting people's apologies). Whatever.

I love Jude's mysterious, sometimes pervy, secrets; his unknowable quirks are way more interesting to me than anyone else's boring old bullshit. Sometimes, when he can't sleep, he'll dress up as a Mexican wrestler (a *luchador*), mask and all, and pace the halls, freaking out the younger kids. He also has a hidden stash of Japanese tentacle porn stuffed in a sock drawer, and in a scuffed-up metal cabinet that Jude once forgot to lock, I found a skateboard made of solid gold. The thing glinted off my guilty, prying face like that briefcase from *Pulp Fiction.* Who knows where the hell he got it.

Deep down, Jude is a dirty romantic; he plans to explore the Seychelles Islands just so he can behold, and cup in his large battered hands, the coco de mer: a plant shaped like a penis and testicles. And then he plans on falling in love with "a sexy treasure hunter who doesn't take any shit." That kind of sums up anything anyone ever needs to know about Jude.

In a beat-up Adidas shoe box that I keep under a loose floorboard, I have my own little secret: an iPhone. Oren gave it to me as a gift for my sixteenth birthday, sending it along with an iTunes gift card. We aren't allowed to have personal cell phone plans here (we have to use the communal cordless off the kitchen), but I use the iPhone to make curated playlists of John Coltrane, Miles Davis, Art Blakey—I'm a bit of a jazz head.

The iPhone is the nicest thing I've ever owned. I cried my eyes out when I first got it, and I had to immediately smash the screen with the heel of Jude's boxing shoe—not out of spite, just so it wouldn't get stolen. In a house full of broken people, the things you keep close to your heart better be broken too.

†††

I know the terms of my dad's will dictate I have to return to Moldavia. The tentacles I was imagining coming for me have become a little too real. But I've been in total denial about going back, and having real responsibilities there. Still, Moldavia looms. Like it always did, in a way. I was just able to ignore it better before the will.

A week after I get back from Moldavia, I'm in bed listening to *Miles Davis at Newport*, picturing smoke-filled jazz clubs in the 1950s, and ladies in sequins clutching champagne flutes, when I hear screams. Jude bursts into our room wearing his *luchador* getup: blue-and-silver mask, red cape. He's completely naked otherwise. He stands still for a moment, pallid moonlight striping his bulky body. He looks at me and starts wildly swinging his dick back and forth, trying to guess the rhythm of the jazz track I'm listening to.

I roll my eyes, put the pillow over my head. "Come to bed, you schmuck."

"Yes, dear."

Jude cannonballs into the upper bunk, nearly toppling the whole bed over. He sticks his head down, still masked, wiggling his fat tongue at me. "Remember. I fucked every woman here."

There's a soft knock on the door. And then Len's voice: "You guys?"

As soon as Len, our sad-sack but good-hearted counselor, opens the door and tentatively steps inside, our bed begins to shake like mad: Jude pretending to jerk off.

"Oh shit, sorry!" says Len, backing away, awkwardly

juggling his can of PBR and a half-eaten slice of pepperoni pizza.

"Jesus!" says Jude. "Why can't you knock?"

"I did!"

"He's just messing with you," I tell Len.

"Sorry," says Jude. We actually all adore poor, miserable Len.

"Dario, it's after hours, but you have a phone call," says Len. "It's your brother and he says it's important, so I agreed you could take the call."

I sit up, removing my headphones. "Oh."

As Len leads me out, he says: "You should go to Harvard." And then he scratches his ass. "Pam told me today that I've put on some weight." He pulls at his flannel shirt. "What do you think?"

"You look the same to me." Pam is the library science grad student Len has been in a tormented relationship with for as long as I've known him. Len is a reminder that all sorts of unhappiness await us in our adult lives, beyond these walls. "Just be you, Len." I don't know what else to say. People usually say that.

He frowns. "Sometimes I wonder if me is enough for Pam."

I tap my chin with my finger. "Pam knows where the door is."

"So you're saying I should tell her this is who I am and deal with it? Or try to maybe become a better, healthier person based on what she's always telling me about my personality, career goals, and general appearance? I know she means well. . . ."

This role-reversal thing I've always had going on with Len, where I'm the one counseling him, has ceased to be weird for me. "Look. Are you happy with you?"

Len rests the can of beer against his cheek. "I like me," he says, somewhat assuredly.

"Are you happy with her?" I never know where I get any of this advice. It's kind of instinctual—stuff I'd ask myself if I was in the same position. I try to care about the people who try to care about me.

Len inhales long and hard. He takes a slug of beer, considering this, and nods vaguely, like I just solved everything wrong in his life. Then he smacks me on the back and hands me the phone as he shuffles off, gnawing at his slice of pizza.

I put the phone to my ear. "Oren."

"Dario. I didn't know about Harvard. Congratulations."

"Thanks. Did you just find out or something?"

"No, no. I've been meaning to call. Just got caught up. You have to go, of course."

I nervously pick at a spot of peeling paint on the wall. "We'll see."

"It's what Dad would have wanted."

Here we go with this again. "How do you know that?"

There's a sound like Oren just dropped the phone; I hear him curse, the sound of stuff, like papers shuffling. Then he quickly comes back on the line. "I know you can defer after you've been admitted to college. Kids take these gap years now. I read about it. I read . . . these blogs."

"Yeah." Harvard actually encourages gap years.

"You know we have to make a decision regarding Dad's will?"

"I know."

"So what were you thinking?"

I wasn't. I was putting Moldavia off for as long as possible. I'm finishing high school. I have other decisions to make about college and summer jobs, and part of me was hoping Oren and everyone else would just decide to sell the studio to Rusty Blade and I'd find out about it later.

"Listen," says Oren, "what if we say: come back for the summer and see how things go. Just for the summer, Dario. A trial period."

"The will stipulates I have to live at Moldavia full-time for six months—"

"I have an idea."

I wonder if there's anything scarier than Oren uttering those four words.

"Something that would bring the studio a lot of attention," he says, "something that could really put us back on the map . . ."

He pauses for dramatic effect. I'm instantly overcome with a quaking anxiety.

". . . is the return of one of Moldavia's most iconic actors back to the family fold!"

"I am not going to star in your broccoli movie."

102

"It's killer cauliflowers, Dario." He sounds hurt. "Let me finish!"

"I'll save us both some time. *No.*"

But he's launched into this P. T. Barnum thing now. "The return of Dario Heyward! Not seen on-screen since his legendary performance in *Zombie Children of the Harvest Sun!*"

I hold the phone an inch from my face and intensely give it the finger.

The last thing I want to do is stoke my cult following—resurrecting this awful thing from my past that I always prayed would finally burn itself out in the loneliest recesses of the internet, where it thrived like *E. coli*. But I can hear Oren's voice excitedly blaring out of the earpiece. "Alastair has become such a *thing* in the years since. You know that, right? *People are obsessed.* There'd be a ton of excitement in the horror world. Fanboy freak-outs all over societal mediums."

I swallow, take a breath, and put the receiver back to my ear. "Social media."

"Right, yes, that."

"I'm going to say no."

"We'll give it the summer. Just the summer! If you're miserable, off you go to Harvard in the fall. If we're able to save the studio, you can do some well-deserved traveling after we wrap, typical gap year stuff, and return to Harvard a year later! Knowing you finally did something selfless for your family."

"I don't know how to run a movie studio," I say through my teeth.

"Leave that part to me."

"I just don't think this is a good idea. Going back. Also, there's a process. I'd have to defer enrollment, write a letter to admissions, probably very soon, outlining what I'll be doing, get it approved, maybe even reapply for financial aid—"

"Dar!" He's growing impatient. "Just think about everyone else for a moment instead of yourself! What if we have a real chance to save the studio? What about Hayley and everyone whose lives are here? If we go under, Dario—if we're forced to sell—what would happen to them? They'd all be displaced," he says, lowering his voice like he's narrating a Holocaust documentary. "We have to . . . Dario . . . Hello? *Hello?*"

I'm miming smashing the phone receiver into the wall.

This is obviously all part of my dad's master plan—forcing me home to get back at me for leaving. And on top of that, Oren is playing the *Dario's being selfish* card, with the added bonus points of throwing everyone else's fate into the mix, twisting and twisting and twisting my arm.

Hayley told me to focus on my own future. But it's not that simple. I do have guilt about leaving Moldavia, and Oren knows that. I'm not sure I want to go to college, and even if I decide I want to, I can take a year off. It's worse in a way, because what Oren's asking isn't totally ludicrous. It's just family shit, and that happens in life.

So, for the hell of it, I ask him what role I'd be playing in his vegetable movie.

"There's a hell-bent leader of the mutant cauliflowers," he says.

"Why does there always have to be a leader?"

"Even dry vegetables need leadership, Dario. His name is Stanhope."

I squeeze the skin where my nose meets my forehead. "Stanhope?"

"Yes."

"You wrote a mutant cauliflower character named . . . Stanhope?"

"I'll direct. You star. If it turns out we have a hit on our hands—because of your name—maybe we can actually save the studio after all! And then off to Harvard you go—with a clear conscience."

Clear conscience. Fuck you, Oren.

"Isn't it worth a try?" he says. "So we know we at least did *something* to save the studio, and preserve our family legacy? I don't have Harvard waiting for me. This is all I've got. This is the only life I know."

I can't take any more of his pleading and his selling. "I'll think it over." I hang up the phone before he can say anything else.

I punch the air. *Fuck! This! Shit!*

Jude was right. They're pulling me back. How could I tell Oren no? I'd be consumed by even more guilt for the rest of my life. It feels like Moldavia has erased my free will, my ability to make my own decisions about my life. It's enraging and unnerving, it really is.

But then I think about Hayley. And instantly, all that anger evaporates.

Jude is snoring when I return to my room. If someone put a leaf blower in the upper bunk, in place of him, it would actually be quieter in here. I put the jazz back on, but I'm too upset to listen, so I take the headphones off, fumbling with the phone. Whenever I'm frazzled, I always accidentally hit something on my phone that says *No Favorites*. I put my iPhone away and just lie there.

I actually do have a favorite Moldavia movie, even though I never told anyone. It's called *The Lovers of Dust and Shadow*. It's often overlooked. My dad made it right after my mother was committed. I think it's the one movie that proves my dad really had a soul, however corrupted it might have been.

In the movie, a handsome Hollywood stunt man falls in love with this rich lonely countess in the countryside of some unnamed locale. But she has this horrible disease: the more she loves someone, the more of her body rots and turns into dust. And the disease is contagious. But the two lovers, despite repeated attempts to go their separate ways, can't live without each other. Love turns out to be the real disease, in a way. And they figure, *screw it*, and get married, knowing they won't have a lot of time. But they'd rather have some time rather than none. They need each other *that much*.

So they both slowly decay, as their love grows deeper and deeper. She's sicker than he is, and in the last scene of the movie he's holding her on a deserted beach as what's left of her crumbles away in his hands, scattered to the wind. Then he carries her empty gown, all that's left of her, *her scent*, holding the gown delicately to his nose, so he can keep the fading essence of her with him for as long as possible, as he slowly walks into the sea, drowning himself.

My dad could be cruel and tyrannical. But yet, somehow, he was able to make this delicate love story. People's dichotomies fascinate me. And freak me out.

I was too young at the time to know what was going on, but my dad watched his true love—*my mother*—basically disintegrate before his eyes. And then he had to send her away because of me—someone he had no interest in knowing at all.

My mom never really believed I was her son. That was at the core of her delusions. Although she loved me (at least for a time, I guess), and wore the locket to prove it (probably to herself), she began to suspect I was something *other*. Namely, that she had been impregnated by a race of aliens, who she called the Red Ferrets.

Moldavia is a hectic place, and she wasn't getting the proper care there. No one was looking after her. And one night, when no one was looking after me either, the Red Ferrets told her to bring me to them. "Let's buy you some new toys," she said, even though it was pretty late at night. I rarely saw my mom by that point, so any chance to be with her was precious to me. I was happy for the first time in a while.

She duct-taped my mouth shut and shoved me into the

back seat of our silver Volvo. The night was neon and taut like it was lit with the fuel of her hallucinations. She sped down the highway going ninety, skidding and sliding down muddy side roads until she reached a bus stop. She left me on a bench, with my mouth still taped, and drove away.

I was there, by myself, for over an hour before someone called the cops.

"There are worse things than dying," the dude in *The Lovers of Dust and Shadow* says, faced with the prospect of losing his love. That line always stuck with me because of what he was saying: suffering can be worse. Pain can be worse.

It really is a beautiful film.

Of course, after I left Moldavia, my dad's first feature was *The Possession of Prodigal Peter*, about the boorish, bratty thirteen-year-old scion of a wealthy real estate family who gets possessed by a horrible demon. But the kid is so foul and empty inside, grinding the family fortune into the ground with his unrelenting needs and wants and demented behavior, the demon can't last inside of him and makes a break for it.

You actually wind up feeling sorry for the demon.

So, yeah, I stopped watching Moldavia films after that one.

I fall asleep thinking about Franklin and Hayley and Mistress Moonshadow and Oren, and all the rest of them, feeling strangled by the night, and I have this dream about a drowned world—a deluge that plunges everything underwater: Keenan House, Moldavia, my school, the whole world. But for some reason I can breathe underwater. I'm the only one who can. So I try to find Jude and Hayley and Oren, but they've already drowned, sinking into the cold depths, arms outstretched, hair waving like anemones. I cry out for them, but only a useless string of bubbles shoots out of my mouth.

And then everything gets darker and heavier as I start to sink too.

In the morning, before school, I wipe away the drying sweat on the back of my neck, call Oren back, and tell him what I want to do.

PART II

From the opening chapter of *Guts, Cuts, & Gory: The Underground History of Moldavia Studios* by Sheckleton Burke, Doubleday, 1996 (out of print):

Legend has it that socialite and heiress to the Moldavia fortune Isabella Moldavia, just nineteen years old at the time, met her future husband while accompanying her father, Rudolph Moldavia, on a business trip to Braşov in the summer of 1977. Lucien Heyward's real name has never officially been known (though various sources, unconfirmed, report his birth name as either Drahoslav Pîrvulescu or Iorghu Groza).

Isabella, a tall, young woman with flowing dark hair and bright green eyes, was never entirely comfortable with her beauty or her family's wealth, and was known to be mercurial and something of a rebel. She was charmed by Lucien's overtures at a Transylvanian tochitură picnic, under the looming shadow of the landmark Liars Bridge. Lucien promised to write her, and after she returned to the United States, the two of them fell into a heated correspondence that continued for the remainder of that summer and into the following fall.

Ten months later, Isabella's mother, Rosemary, died of influenza, and only a few weeks after that, Rudolph was dead of a stroke. Isabella inherited the family fortune as well as the estate, already on the National Register of Historic Places. (Her twin sister, Serafina, was killed in a tragic carousel accident at a beachside playground when the girls were seven.)

Isabella, lonely and restless, invited Lucien to visit the castle, and against the advice of her closest friends and relatives (of which she had few), a mere three months later they were married. The age difference sparked gossip in the society pages. Isabella was twenty years old. Lucien was fifty-three. A year later, Isabella gave birth to a son, Oren Jacob Heyward, who as a teenager would work his way up from kitchen lackey to grip to second A.D. on most of his father's films made during the "golden years" of the studio's output.

Lucien Heyward was already an infamous lothario and raconteur in Braşov before he met Isabella. His family owned a struggling movie theater chain, Cosmescu Cinemas (allegedly, a fruitless trip to Cairo to spearhead efforts to expand the chain to the Middle East inspired Moldavia's first feature, *The Curse of the Mummy's Tongue*), and Heyward had been making low-budget exploitation films since the age of thirty. Using an old Cine-Kodak camera, a gift from his father, and a cast of rough-and-tumble Romanian nonprofessional actors, many of them his own cousins, Heyward filmed in the basements, balconies, and lobbies of his family's empty cinema houses. These early films linked gratuitous sex and alien invasion in uneasy ways. This led to local notoriety that grew beyond the borders of Brașov once Heyward's opportunistic father sniffed the upside of controversy and allowed his son's peculiar, ribald films to play as featurettes before every movie shown at a Cosmescu Cinema house.

In a bizarre turn of events, Heyward was hired by Romanian pharmaceutical company Terapia Ranbaxy to direct educational training films for the company's employees, though Heyward always maintained grander ambitions. Many assumed he would take advantage of his sudden marriage to Isabella and his newfound U.S. citizenship to penetrate the gates of Hollywood at a time when exploitative horror films, many of which would go on to become classics of the genre, were on an upswing. Instead, Heyward did the opposite, shutting himself behind the gates of the Moldavia estate and building his own studio on its grounds. Heyward's first feature under the Moldavia banner, *Mummy's Tongue*, with its winking callback to an earlier era of Saturday-matinee serial films, put the studio on the map after Jamie Montana of Billington Pictures purchased the distribution rights. The film was a sleeper hit and gained Heyward a lucrative distribution deal with Columbia Pictures and a roaring reputation as an eccentric hermit auteur.

Made on a shoestring budget with a cast and crew of visiting Romanian relatives (and one Hungarian fugitive wanted for bank robbery), and shot entirely within the walls of the castle, the film remains among the most beloved of Moldavia's output. After the film's success, Heyward was able to write his own ticket, and ads placed in the trades led to an influx of top production staff longing for a change of pace from the grind of Los Angeles (and a chance to work with a self-exiled Hollywood outsider and enfant terrible whose phony name was on everyone's lips). Many of the actors and below-the-line talent that came through the Moldavia gates during this period formed the core family of Moldavia Studios, and it is a testament to either Heyward's raffish charm or cultish ability to inspire fascist loyalty that many never left.

Heyward quickly squandered the remainder of his wife's fortune on the studio's next dozen (and far less successful) features, including the disastrous, unwatchable, and overbudgeted *Brain Breakfast*, even though the camp value of some of these failures earned *Rocky Horror*–level cult followings. As Heyward began to embrace the underground, knowing he'd never achieve conventional mainstream success, his distribution deals with several Hollywood studios collapsed. But the director amassed a die-hard fan base and a loyal collective of mysterious Eastern European investors who would fund Moldavia's features over the next several years. Heyward remained free to make what he wanted as he wanted at his own frenetic, ritualistic pace—for as long as he wanted to.

The deteriorating mental state of Isabella was

something few were privy to. Five years after her marriage to Lucien, she had not been seen in public in some time. Mental illness had been a frequent scourge upon her family. Her father had been hospitalized for a supposed nervous breakdown three years before his death, and her mother spent an extended period of time in a psychiatric institution after she disappeared and was found days later wandering the woods around the estate, filthy and raving, her pockets full of acorns.

Despite the studio's airtight privacy and policy of isolation, rumors still ran rampant through high society that Isabella was not well. In response, Heyward retreated even further behind Moldavia's gates. He refused to grant interviews or speak with his own investors, and no outsiders were allowed on the grounds of the estate. The only connection Moldavia had with the outside world, in fact, was through its films (at an increased pace from two to four features a year) and the weekly food and supply trucks that would wind their way through the hills to the castle. They were required to stop and unload just inside the gates, while the rest of the estate was hidden behind an imposing blockade of fir trees.

Increasingly, Hunter Yates, the studio's marketing wunderkind, a former Hollywood publicist who had weathered a scandal or two of his own, and Franklin Fletcher, a high-priced Manhattan corporate lawyer who escaped the world of mergers and acquisitions for the ghosts and ghouls of Moldavia, handled all communications and business dealings for the studio. Lucien Heyward continued to pump out overly stylized B-movies, some of which took on a sadder tone, further alienating the studio's core audience, yet gaining new fans who were attracted to Moldavia's shift into a melancholic brand of what noted film critic K. J. Stimpell called "haunted horror films."

Heyward certainly seemed more and more like a haunted man. His breakneck pace, particularly when he churned out surprisingly sensitive and at times truly doleful horrors like *Mama Has No Intestines Anymore* and *The Loneliness of a Long Distance Poltergeist*, seemed infused more with loss and loneliness than the fun, pulpy monster mayhem the studio had built its reputation on. Heyward escaped his difficult life in Romania only to feel the need to escape his own breaking heart. . . .

CHAPTER SIX

THE SURFACE OF THINGS

MY MOM WAS FORTY-ONE YEARS OLD WHEN SHE HAD ME, AND SHE was already clearly mentally ill. I probably shouldn't have happened. Was I an accident?

I've pondered how consensual my conception might have been. But I can't question it for long. It's too loaded and mysterious, and it quickly gets relegated to shelf space in the back of my mind.

Ever since I can remember, my mom was always a wavering presence around the castle. There were moments of soft-focus hugs and laughter: singing with her as she played the piano, listening to the stories she read to me, feeling her love, or at least aware of it. But those moments were few and far between.

I'll never forget that emptiness invading her eyes like something drinking her pupils away through a straw, replaced by a remote sharpening of her gaze that seemed to say: *I figured it all out. I see more than any of you ever will.*

Whenever I saw that look, I knew she'd be disappearing again. I was a little kid; I thought I'd done something wrong. All I wanted to do was get her back again.

Over time, I started seeing less and less of her, until any appearance at all became almost mythical. And when I did see her, it was awful: She hissed at me. Called me horrible names. I'd wake up and she'd be standing over my bed, scowling at me.

After she abandoned me at that bus stop, they took her away for good.

Then I was gone from this place too.

And now I'm coming back.

Oren sent me a wood-and-brass steamer trunk to pack my stuff up in. It looks like something left over from World War I. Jude and I stared at it for a full minute before we burst out laughing. A few days later, Jude received his own trunk.

I told Oren I would only return to Moldavia if Jude could come with me. That way, we could watch over each other. Oren readily agreed, saying they could use him on the crew, since they've been short a guy after "the electrocution incident of last November." I didn't mention that to Jude, though Oren assured me that "the guy is fine, just resting back home in Peoria."

Two weeks ago, Jude and I graduated from high school.

Both of us are about to turn eighteen, which means we'll be booted from Keenan House. Jude, like some Neverland reject, seemed to assume he would never grow up, and made no real plans. I was legit worried about this. His only post-Keenan plans involved him "helping out" at his friend's motorcycle shop, and couch surfing.

The problem with "Ben's Bike Shop" is that no one actually repairs or sells any bikes. The place is so clearly a front for a drug-running operation I have no idea how it hasn't been raided by the DEA. Jude tends to fall into the wrong crowd too easily—with people he meets in the world of underground amateur boxing, or whatever. It's a major flaw of his. Now I know he'll have a place to crash too—at least for a while.

Jude agreed to accompany me to Moldavia, but he made me promise I'd eventually go to Harvard. That was his condition. Although, honestly, with all his talk about me getting *pulled back in*, I've never seen him so excited about anything.

Knowing I'll have Jude with me is a huge comfort—he's such a major part of my life; there's no one I'm closer to. But I'm still filled with this nagging dread about returning to Moldavia and filling my dad's shoes as studio chief. I have absolutely no idea what to expect.

Leaving Keenan got super-emotional. Stupidly, I never realized there would be a literal last day. There were lots of tearful good-byes with the other kids (especially since I know many of them are doomed to live difficult lives). Walking out of our room one last time was wrenching. I gave Len a hug, and wished him luck with Pam and his doctorate. He urged me again to go to Harvard.

Jude and I move to Moldavia at the end of May, right before what's left of spring melts into the early swell of summer.

Oren apparently wants to make an impression, so he sends the hunter-green Rolls-Royce to pick us up. The car was used as Balzac Best's chauffeured ride in *The Goblins That Only Ate Cake*, Moldavia's rough attempt at crossing gross-out gore with a tender look at class distinction, released in 1982. While it was meant as social satire, the movie failed on every level. Once again Rotten Tomatoes had to, like, rewire their algorithms in order to include it in their database, since the film scored so low their website wasn't sure how to even process it.

Whenever a fancy-ass car is needed in a Moldavia movie, the Rolls-Royce is used every single time. They don't even bother to paint it a different color. But Jude doesn't know that. He's grinning, running his hands all over the leather interior. We roll through the gates, and Jude's eyes go wide when he sees the immense castle and the sprawling grounds. The property stretches over hundreds of acres, licking the edge of Peabody Lake a mile and a half away, where beach scenes are filmed.

Oren has the entire Moldavia staff standing outside in a ring, flanking the circular driveway like we're in a *Downton Abbey* episode and we've just returned from war.

I roll my eyes. "Jesus."

"Whoa," says Jude, clamping a fist over his mouth.

Oren steps forward to open the door. "Welcome, welcome!

I'm Oren Heyward," he says, making intense eye contact with Jude, shaking his hand firmly. "We're so happy to have you. I've heard so many wonderful things."

"Thanks!" says Jude, a little starstruck. Oren is wearing a three-piece yellow-and-brown houndstooth suit. The brown porkpie hat would seem like overkill only if you'd never met Oren before, which Jude hasn't, so he's staring at him gleefully.

"Ack! C'mere!" says Oren, opening his arms wide and giving me a tight, overly dramatic embrace that's all for show, since we don't really hug. "My baby brother. Home at last."

"All right, calm down." I look around for Hayley but don't see her anywhere. Hayley and I haven't talked at all since I was here last, a month ago.

Oren flicks his vest. "Do you like the suit?"

"You look like . . . if Sherlock Holmes had a pimp," I say.

"It's an old costume piece. But it fits me like a glove, right? They're here, everyone!" Oren screams (which he always does when he's excited).

"Where's Hayley?" I ask Oren as some guys lug our trunks inside.

"Oh, she'll be down. Come!" he screams. "Let's get you boys settled."

That night there's a thunderstorm. Through my windows I watch the grounds get pelted with windswept rain. Lightning bolts corkscrew out of the sky, leaving wisps of smoke in their wake. The thunder echoes and quakes, muffled by the stone castle.

"Perfect," says Jude, staring out, mesmerized.

Jude insisted he room with me, so an additional bed and bureau were carried in by some of the larger crewmen. Jude is the toughest guy I know, but he has his own kryptonite just like everyone else—he doesn't like to sleep alone. We both unpack as the storm rages outside, running to the window like little kids at every crack of thunder.

Having taken note of Jude's boxing gloves, two electricians come over to surprise Jude with a seventy-pound Everlast punching bag, which they attach to our ceiling with a customizable chain.

Jude nearly falls over himself. "This is so awesome, man!"

We eat an early dinner at a long, communal table in the basement commissary, while the wind howls through the walls, and the medieval wooden chandelier, gently swinging, flickers a bit. Everyone except Hayley makes a brief appearance to greet us, but then they all quickly retreat to their respective departments, spread throughout the castle, prepping scenes for tomorrow's filming.

It's definitely busy around here, as always. You'd never know we were nearly bankrupt. And no storm, however big, would ever slow things down. Moldavia is weatherproof—weeks of consecutive shooting could take place exclusively indoors. All the large rooms function as sound stages.

After dinner, I give Jude a little tour. Gliding through the castle, I hear the usual Moldavia sounds: hammering, power drilling, sawing, the crew shouting.

The various departments are all hunkered down in their own warmly lit circles of concentration. The production design team has the loft-like upper floors of the Romero Wing to themselves. Lightning strobes through the dormer windows as everyone works on matte backdrops of hellish, eclipsed, moon-raked skies. Paints and brushes and cans of pungent chemicals are scattered everywhere over heavy tarps.

The makeup crew, one floor below, in a lab-like room of vanity mirrors and barber chairs, is testing out various deformities, dripping paraffin wax over dummy heads, using photos of actual acid victims as inspiration. The lighting department, next door, is shuffling through an autumnal spectrum of colored gels.

Costumes and props are at the end of the Hitchcock Wing. The wardrobe department is comprised of narrow corridors filled with moth-protected garments dangling from hangers, each with their own ID numbers. In smaller rooms, people sew and drape costumes, presided over by their mad queen, Samantha Childress. Sketches are hung on the walls. The costume crew inhabits a world of fabrics and threads, classic rock, old tailor's dummies, and slinky measuring tapes.

The props department resembles the historical society of some lost city. Its ticking, gleaming collection of clocks and silverware, dolls, candlesticks, daggers, magnifying glasses, and tons of other random stuff, all exactingly filed and organized on rustproof Metro shelving, stretches into the rumbling darkness.

Jude keeps cupping both hands over his mouth and doing a little hop-dance at every new thing he sees, trying to contain his excitement. I keep wondering where Hayley is. "Who you looking for?" says Jude.

I shrug and shake my head.

Lastly, we peek into the photography department. Camera equipment lines the windowless walls. Jip, still Moldavia's resident cinematographer, with tufts of white hair poking out of a baseball cap and his Dutch accent gloppy as ever, is too consumed by a discussion of lenses with a goggle-eyed camera operator to even notice us at the door.

As the storm gradually passes over, and the tumult outside settles into scattered faraway grumbling over the hills, the castle resumes its creaky, snooty dignity. Jude and I lie in our beds as the reality of Moldavia, and the fact that we're actually here, that our time at Keenan is over forever, slowly washes over us.

We're not kids anymore—just like that.

"Why'd you leave here?" says Jude. "I can't believe this place even exists. I can't imagine how cool it would be to grow up here. It seems like . . ."

I know what he's going to say. "It seems like it would be awesome." The fact that it was the opposite seems almost like a nasty prank.

"They make real movies here!" Jude sounds like a little

kid. I'm jealous—Moldavia is blank slate for Jude. He doesn't have my memories.

"I know. But I had to get the hell out."

"Yeah, you did, didn't you?" says Jude, dropping his voice. "I guess we never told each other everything."

It was probably easier that way. But easier isn't always better. There's a brief pause; we listen to the dripping aftermath of a storm contending with an old drainage system.

"I'll tell you something real," says Jude. "I wear that wrestling mask because I don't feel as ugly with it. My nose and shit, you know."

"You're not ugly, man. You slept with every chick at Keenan!"

"Almost. One or two got away."

We both crack up.

"What really happened here?" Jude asks. His tone is a little cautious.

So I tell him—a little about my mom's illness, and what it was like making *Zombie Children*. After, Jude just grunts, as if he's clearing something stuck in his throat. "Here's another thing: I never show anyone the tops of my feet," he replies. "Because of all the cigarette burns."

I squeeze my eyes shut. *That's* why we never went into all this. Who the hell wants to picture their best friend being hurt?

"This place does seem pretty awesome," I say. "But people see the surface of things. The outside. You don't know what goes on inside."

"You came back here for every reason other than your-self," says Jude. "For the studio, for your family . . . *for me.*"

It's funny how some people can see you as selfless and others just the opposite.

I hear Jude sitting up quickly in the dark. "Wait. You dawg. There's more to this."

"What?"

"You have a girl here, don't you?"

"How the hell would you know that?"

"I have a sixth sense about this kind of thing. Also, I saw you looking for someone all day in this puppy-dog kind of way. Had to be a girl."

"I looked like a puppy dog?"

"Just a little."

I shake my head. "She's not *my girl* . . . just someone I knew growing up."

I tell Jude about Hayley, and what happened with her when I returned.

"Let's go find her." He's on the edge of his bed, putting on his sneaks.

"Not now. It's too late!"

But he's already moving toward the door. "I want to meet this chick."

Jude swings open the door, screams, and flies back.

I hurtle myself out of bed, run over, and see Gavin stand-ing in front of the door wearing an oversize black suit. Jude is out of breath, speechless, pointing at him. "That kid . . . was just standing there. . . ."

"Gavin," I say, catching my breath, "this is Jude."

Gavin nods at him. "Nice to meet you, sir."

Jude looks baffled. He keeps pointing at Gavin like he isn't sure he's real.

"Gavin. We've talked about maybe not standing in front of the door like that?"

"I'm sorry, sir. I just wanted to make sure you two were settled."

"We're good. But seriously, it's terrifying." Not to mention the fact that Gavin resembles a confused child ghost from another era.

"Just let me know if you need anything, sir."

"Stop calling me that. Please. And how would we even find you if . . ."

Gavin runs off, disappearing into the shadows.

"Where'd he go?" asks Jude, actually looking behind him. "Who *is* he?"

I rub my eyes. "An intern."

We walk into the long, drafty hallway. "So what's Hayley look like?" says Jude. As I begin to describe her, he interrupts: "So basically like that?" He's pointing down the hall. I shove him back inside; we peer out through the crack in the door as Hayley hurries down the hall holding a teacup, just like the last time I ran into her. She's even wearing the same nightgown. But this time she looks pissed.

CHAPTER SEVEN

AWAY

"WRONG!" OREN SHOUTS AFTER HER, HIS HEAD STICKING OUT OF HIS doorway. But Hayley doesn't turn around, and then she's gone. Oren sees me standing right there. "Oh, hello." He pats down his bright-yellow long johns, seemingly not at all concerned that he looks like a crazed banana.

"I'm going to bed," says Jude, gesturing inside our room with his thumb. "I'll let you guys chat." I nod at him, and Jude slips into our room, closing the door behind him.

"What's going on?" I ask Oren.

"We were running lines."

"Running lines? For what?"

"Ummm . . . we begin principal photography tomorrow?"

"Are you acting in the movie as well?" I didn't even consider that.

"I wear many hats," he replies, brushing back his frizzed, static-electrical hair. "Literally, sometimes. And yes. I'm acting in *The Killer Cauliflowers*." He looks around the hall-way, and then he beckons me. "Come in, come in."

Oren has *Mother of Tears*, another Argento film, play-ing on his dusty, twenty-year-old TV, which is perched on a banged-up dresser with underwear poking out of every drawer. The volume is turned down, but I can sense the malevolence of the world from the pace of the images, the gothic soundtrack thrumming faintly in the background.

Oren starts rummaging, throwing papers around. "I've been tweaking the script," he says. With a grunt, Oren removes a pile of what I think might be dirty laundry from a desk chair. A vintage olive-green Smith Corona typewriter is revealed on his small wooden desk. "Ah!" He rips a piece of paper from the machine and then crawls under the desk, collecting more loose pages.

"You write on an old typewriter? Who are you, Orson Welles?"

Oren hops up at the name, as if he and Orson Welles are frequently confused. "Well, I—" A gust of wind blows through the open window, scattering the pages out of his hands, while simultaneously blowing his hair into a spiral of mad-scientist madness. *"Merde!"* he exclaims, slamming the window shut before chasing after the escaped pages.

Despite my brother's frenzy and general slobbery, the mustard-colored walls of his room and its nestling lived-in-ness, are weirdly soothing. He also has a small fire crackling in his fireplace. I sit on the edge of his futon, moving a plate with a half-eaten ham sandwich that's slowly turning green out of the way. "Why were you yelling at Hayley? She looked kind of mad."

Oren is frozen in space, hands slightly grasping, trying to remember something. Then he just slowly gathers a few last pages off the floor. "She gives me criticism on my writing. We don't always agree, but sometimes her feedback can be . . . helpful, I suppose."

"Oh, yeah? What were some of her suggestions?"

"Oh, people and their suggestions, you know." He thrusts a bunch of pages at me. "I have a lot of faith in this script! I'd be interested to know what you think." I start reading the first page, but Oren interrupts me, intoning: "We begin in the moonlit vegetable patch of a lonely widowed farmer named Juston Bieberman, played by me."

"What?"

Oren scowls, annoyed by the interruption. "What."

"Justin *Bieberman*?"

"That's my character's name. The lonely widowed farmer."

"Seriously? Justin *Bieber* is . . . like a huge pop star."

"Ah," says Oren. "I knew I heard that name somewhere. That happens during the creative process." He flutters his hands around. "You get lost in the words. The rush of ideas, images. We should rename? How about—"

"Just let me read this, man."

"Mort Sephiroth?"

I stare at him.

"No?"

"This guy is *a rural farmer*, right? You can't name that kind of character after someone who sounds like the Jewish grandfather of a *Final Fantasy* villain."

"So what you're saying is . . . we should mull this further?"

I move to the door. "I'm going to bed."

"Wait." He piles a huge stack of pages in my arms. "That's the whole first act."

The title page reads: *The Ciller Cauliflowers* by Oren Jacob Heyward.

I knew he was going to spell killer with a *c*.

I give him a wary look.

"I was thinking," says Oren, "your friend might make a great antagonist in the film! How would Jude feel about being an actor rather than working behind the scenes?"

"He'd be thrilled, I'm sure." I smack the pages against my leg. "Should I read all this tonight?"

"Yes. I'll get the next hundred and fifty pages of the second act to you by morning. I'll have Gavin or Franklin or Peter or Linda wake you and let you know where we'll begin our day." Oren continues picking up pages from the floor as he blathers on. "Sharon should get some breakfast over to you boys, or it might be Peter, or Gavin. . . ."

I leave the room with him crawling around in an unraveling fog of his scattered thoughts. It'll probably be a few minutes before he even realizes I've left.

Jude is snoring when I return to our room. Careful not to wake him, I go inside the closet, turn on the light, and drop

Act One of Oren's screenplay onto the floor. He's given me nearly seventy pages. I sit on the floor and lean against one of the empty steamer trunks. When I was a kid, I used to hide in this closet.

I'm scribbling in a leather journal. Sometimes I write about playing Alastair. And about my life: wanting to be someone else, wanting to be somewhere else. Sometimes I write stories. A lot of them are escape stories. I don't have any books. No one reads me stories anymore, so I write my own. I give some to my dad for inspiration, written out on separate pieces of paper, but he always says: "Don't distract me, Dario," and crumples them up right then and there.

Aida gave me the journal, along with a ballpoint pen with my initials engraved on it, for my tenth birthday. When things get bad there's a buzzing that rises in my ears, like a hornets' nest broken open. Writing makes the buzzing ease off a bit. Sometimes I just don't know what else to do.

The door of the closet opens and Hayley stands there with an ice pack in her hand. I turn away and the journal falls into my lap. I don't want her to see my face.

"I always know where to find you," she says, kneeling in front of me. "Look up." She lays the ice pack right below my eye, where it's swollen and throbbing. We're both quiet. I only hear our tight, clutched breathing in the enclosed space, and suddenly I'm aware of what it's like to really show my bruises to someone—inside and out.

I pull away. "It's getting cold."

"It's supposed to be fifteen minutes on, fifteen off."

"My face is freezing."

Hayley blows her hot breath onto my cheek.

There's more silence. I don't know what to do with silence, so I take her chin in my hands and kiss her on the lips. It's the first time I've ever kissed a girl, and I don't expect the feeling—like I'm giving a piece of myself to her that I'll never get back. It makes me afraid. And she doesn't react like I thought she would. A tear comes to the edge of her eye and just trembles there, caught in an eyelash.

"What's wrong?" I say, reaching forward and lifting the tear delicately off her eyelash like it's a tiny piece of precious glass.

She shakes her head.

"What?"

She looks up at me. "I want to tell you to do something."

"So tell me."

"But I don't really want you to do it," she says.

I take her hand. I wish we could never leave this closet.

"It would hurt," she adds.

"Then I wouldn't do it!" I say, laughing, confused.

"I mean, hurt me."

"Then I really wouldn't do it."

Her lips tremble. "Yeah, but . . ."

I hand her the journal and the pen. "Sometimes writing stuff down is easier."

She flips to the next page, hesitating, biting the tip of the pen.

"No, no," I say, flipping to the end of the journal. "Write it on the very last page."

"Why?"

"Because if it'll hurt you, I don't want to read it. I just want you to write it."

"Then what's the point?" she says.

"Tell me part of it. Right now. Tell me only the last word. And write the rest."

She leans in. Her lips tickle my ear. "Away," she whispers. She flips through blank pages; she stops on a page, scribbles something, considering it carefully, tapping the pen against her teeth.

I want to kiss her again but I don't.

She closes the journal, clips the pen onto it, and hands it back to me. "I didn't write it on the very last page. It's toward the back. You'll have to search to find it."

"So it'll always be there if I need it."

I feel safer with Hayley around. She knows this and has been on set, as much as possible, during the filming of my scenes. My dad behaves differently when she's there—he doesn't push me around as much. He knows he's tamer when she's there, so he's been getting sneaky about the shooting schedule.

Hayley presses the ice pack against my face, determinedly, until the cold melts away. It's like she's trying to freeze something broiling in us both. Then she looks down at the dead ice pack. "I think we have another one."

We walk down the hallway into her parents' suite. It's

dark in there. In the bathroom, I hear Hugo and Aida argu-
ing. I always had this dumb impression everyone besides me
was happy-go-lucky around here. This is my first glimpse of
something else. "Wait here," says Hayley.

I hear Aida sobbing.

I hear Hugo: "Can't let him touch you again. I'll murder
him . . . have to just go, Ai. Before . . . something . . . maybe
it's time."

". . . doing to that poor boy. It'll be worse for him if we go."

". . . take him with us."

"That's kidnapping."

I just stand there, unable to move.

Aida and Hugo burst out of the bathroom, releasing a
plume of steam and a triangle of light like they just tum-
bled out of a magical dimension. Hugo has a towel around
his shoulders. Hayley appears from another room, shaking a
fresh ice pack.

"Oh!" says Aida, grabbing the ice pack from Hayley and
making a beeline for me. She embraces me; when I wince and
pull away, she raises up my shirt, revealing a web of bruising
on my side. My dad shoved me again, and I fell on something
hard.

Aida turns to face Hugo, fingers still gripping my shirt,
breathing hard through her nose. Hugo is leaning against the
bathroom door, sipping from a metal flask. When he sees me,
he looks down. Aida presses the ice pack gently to my face
and says to Hayley: "Take your dad downstairs, collect our
laundry, and bring me up a seltzer with lemon, please."

Hayley and Hugo leave the room.

Aida takes me over to the bed, and like I'm six or seven years younger than I am, sits me right on her lap, and starts rocking me. She has strong arms, but everything else about her is so delicate. "There will come a time when you'll need to be strong and leave this place for good. You'll know when the time is right. And then you need to go. But when you go . . . let the wounds heal. Don't let them sink under the surface and fester inside you. Promise?"

"Promise."

"And once you go, you can't ever come back. Promise me that."

"Promise."

"One day you'll look back on your time here, and all of us, and you won't feel the pain you do now. When that moment comes, you'll know you've made it through all the darkness God drew for you, and come out into the light."

CHAPTER EIGHT

THE CILLER CAULIFLOWERS

I SEARCH THE CLOSET FOR THE LEATHER JOURNAL AND PEN, BUT I can't find them. I never took them to Keenan with me, so I hope they didn't get lost. I never peeked at what Hayley wrote. When she said what she wrote would hurt her, it ascribed supernatural powers to it in my mind, like it was a curse or something.

I plop down on the floor. With nothing else to distract me, I take a deep breath and start to read Oren's script.

EXT. VEGETABLE PATCH -- NIGHT

A moonlit vegetable patch on a farm in Nova Scotia. In the distance there is an iceberg melting. JUSTON BIEBERMAN, a lonely farmer of twenty-one years old, steps onto his porch smoking a pipe and staring at the sky. He curses the sky with anger, holding up his fists, which block out the moon. Then he removes his fists from the sky and stares at his fists.

> JUSTON BIEBERMAN
> (staring at his fists)

My fists . . .

His fists are hard and callused like the fists of a farmer or someone who has punched a cabinet. He regards his fists.

> JUSTON BIEBERMAN

I had the fists of a young man, but now they are not that. They are the fists of someone who has experienced grief and hunger and whose cauliflowers did not turn out good. I am hungry and want some crops, but the winter froze them and I am upset my wife, SELENA GOMEZ BIEBERMAN, got run over by a tractor because a moth flew in her mouth. I did not want to feel these things and I know I am feeling them because of that EVIL SHAMAN FARMER who lives down the road from me and put a curse on my farm because he wants to grow nicer vegetables than me. I have to kill that foul shaman!

My thumbs are pressed against my tightly closed eyes. "It's not really funny."

"It's pretty funny."

I woke up Jude because I *had to*. He's crouched beside me on the floor of our bedroom, wearing his tighty whities (and

Mexican wrestler cape, which he apparently now sleeps in), lit by one of the dim lamps. I'm afraid if I turn on more light, the script will somehow get *worse*, if that's possible. Jude is slapping himself and giggling as he flips through each page. Ordinarily I would find this hilarious, too, except Oren is seriously about to start filming this shit tomorrow, and it's supposed to be the movie that saves Moldavia from extinction. (I did laugh a little after Jude read the first page and asked if the movie should be renamed *Fisting*.)

"I don't understand any of this," says Jude, turning over another page.

I pace the room. "How does Oren not understand that anyone might have a few minor snags growing crops if *an iceberg* is floating down the street?"

"I'm not sure. . . ."

I look down at the script, and then back at Jude, as if hoping Jude can magically make this script better. Or vanish. "God," I say. "I don't know what to do."

Moldavia movies were proudly and stalwartly of the B variety. They had an inherent look and tone about them, and despite their silliness, for the most part they were well made. People gather to actually watch them, not make fun of them. There's a fine line—fun bad vs. truly *bad* bad—that my dad was careful not to cross, even if he didn't always succeed. The Moldavia name was sacred to him.

Although I stopped watching Moldavia movies when I got to Keenan, Jude had seen a few. He was careful not to bring it up around me, but he had definitely seen *Zombie*

Children of the Harvest Sun. One Friday night we both got wasted at some horrible dance thing with another, rougher, group home; the girls, heavily tattooed, many of them wearing distressed white leather, looked like they'd sooner cut you than dance with you. But one of them thought Jude was hot and she had a bottle of Jack in her purse.

We stumbled home, drunkenly cackling at nothing, a little sick, and found the DVD of Moldavia's *Conjoined Connie* in Keenan's DVD bin in the rec room. Jude swore that DVD was in the collection, and I didn't believe him until we found it. So we watched it together in that last chunk of night when the sky starts to turn cobalt.

Conjoined Connie is fucking ridiculous, but there was a certain art to it, especially the acting of Yolanda Deir Nasterfeld as both Connies. I hadn't seen it since I was a kid, and I couldn't deny a new appreciation for it; mostly because of Yolanda, who funneled genuine torment into her performances. She was my first introduction to some of the truly messed-up people who came through the Moldavia gates, the ones who gave my father that certain gleam in his eye, the ones his camera loved most.

My dad was naturally attracted to people plagued by demons. I was just a sad kid with a sick mom. So he played upon that pain—getting inside my head, exacerbating my fears, inflaming my loneliness. I was only halfway to the edge. It was my dad who tried to push me over it. And he almost succeeded.

When I first got to Keenan, I was prone to violent

outbursts. Two snarky dudes who provoked me both got their noses broken. It was like I was still punching my dad in the face—over and over again. At first, there was the hornets' nest—the furious buzzing in my ears. Then everything would drop away, leaving me in the middle of a pulsing red tidal wave. It was like I slid out of myself. My mom, at her worst, also had no control over herself. That link terrified me.

The last time I pummeled someone, it took three counselors to hold me down. If it happened again I was out. So I let them help me. I didn't write in journals anymore—that reminded me of the past. Group therapy helped unravel some of my anger issues, and Jude gave me boxing lessons, which gave me a healthy outlet for my aggression.

I didn't want to become someone like Yolanda Deir Nasterfeld.

Yolanda, a Hollywood actress, sometime porn star, and alleged retired Mafia hit woman, came from a place in Italy called *Toscana nascosta*. She was known for her husky voice, her slinky black dresses, and her heavy smoking. Apparently, she would refuse to ever put out a lit cigarette, creating untold continuity issues. She made a few notable films with Moldavia, but then one day declared she was done. She was found a month later, dead of a heroin overdose, in a seedy Culver City motel.

"If only she hadn't left," everyone at Moldavia mumbled, as if this place really did shield you from all the evil temptations outside. But some of these people just had haunted lives. It didn't matter where they were.

Oren, however, is haunted in an entirely different way: by self-delusion.

He not only fails to understand narrative and write believable dialogue, but he also doesn't seem to know how human beings behave. It's like he's an alien disguising himself as a human who decided to write and direct a movie about humans.

This is what's written, fifteen pages later, when Juston Bieberman—the Farmer Obsessed with His Fists—walks down the dry, bramble-ridden dirt road (in Nova Scotia!) and confronts this "evil shaman farmer" whose side anyone watching this movie would instantly take:

INT. HUT OF EVIL SHAMAN FARMER -- NIGHT

JUSTON BIEBERMAN walks into the hut. There are pots and pans in there. It is cramped and dirty. The SHAMAN FARMER is standing by the fire, stoking it, and also eating marshmallows. He wears a tan robe.

SHAMAN

Hello. Would you like some marshmallows?

JUSTON BIEBERMAN

Don't tempt me with your candy, Satan's spawn!

SHAMAN

(throws down marshmallow)

What intense rudeness. I have invited you to dinner
here at my hut and you insult me! Juston, was it you
who stole those cauliflower seeds from my shed?

JUSTON BIEBERMAN

Is that why you cursed my crops? And my wife, Selena
Gomez?

SHAMAN

The night is cold. I can cook us a ham.

The SHAMAN moves around the hut preparing the ham and getting
salt.

JUSTON BIEBERMAN

(staring at his fists)

When a man can no longer sleep because of the grief,
he knows he has been cursed, and it was you, Macaulay.
We used to be friends in the old days. I never stole
seeds from you then or now. What an insult.

SHAMAN

You stole my seeds, but I never cursed you for it.

JUSTON BIEBERMAN

I never stole your seeds.

SHAMAN

You took my seeds and my trust. But I offer ham.

JUSTON BIEBERMAN

How could I eat a man's ham whose seeds I did not take?

SHAMAN

You cannot even eat a man's ham.

JUSTON BIEBERMAN

I love man's ham. But not his seeds.

SHAMAN

I am insulted by this accusation. Get out of my hut!

JUSTON BIEBERMAN
(shaking his fists)
I miss Selena Gomez! She was my flame of desire. I wish
only death and conjunctivitis on you, Evil Shaman.

SHAMAN

I am not evil, just a nice, hardworking shaman.
Ohhhh. A man's cauliflower crop is a reflection of his
soul -- for you, cold and flavorless.

JUSTON BIEBERMAN

I am nothing without my cauliflowers. I will kill
you.

SHAMAN

(pointing a glowing stick at Juston)

I did not curse you then, but now you are cursed.

JUSTON BIEBERMAN

Do not!

Evil yellow laser rays shoot out of the SHAMAN's stick.

SHAMAN

Bastard farmer! You are cursed to behold the living
embodiment of your greed and selfishness. Your dead
cauliflowers will be reanimated as vegetable demons
from the foulest pits of hell!

THE SHAMAN screams and breaks open, and light shoots out of his
open chest. The hut collapses all around them as THE SHAMAN
laughs and flies into outer space.

THE SHAMAN lands on the moon, walks around on it, laughing,
and pulls out the American flag and dances around with it. Then
he flies to Mars and hops around the red sand. Then he flies
around Saturn's rings, still laughing, and swings around vines
in the jungles of the Amazon, rolls around the sand dunes of the
Sahara desert, and strolls around the streets of London drinking tea. He points two evil fingers at Big Ben and changes the
time, just for fun.

Then he returns to his destroyed hut in Nova Scotia and confronts JUSTON BIEBERMAN, who is not cowering, but standing very strong.

SHAMAN

You should have had my ham.

What's most amazing about this is . . . *well, everything.*

But also within the span of a tiny paragraph, Oren managed to raise the budget of *The Ciller Cauliflowers* by about $300 million. The rest of the pages Oren gave me are mostly, incredibly, Juston and the shaman *continuing their argument* in the shaman's hut about whether or not Juston Bieberman stole this fucker's seeds.

I start nervously pulling at loose strands of my hair. "I'm playing Stanhope."

"Who's that?" says Jude.

"We haven't met him yet. He's like the leader of the . . . the, uh, killer cauliflowers. Oh, and Oren wants you to be in this too."

Jude's face lights up. "In the movie? *Really?* Are you serious?"

"Oh, c'mon, man, you don't really want to be in this crap, do you?"

"I don't know? Maybe?"

There's a knock at the door. Expecting Gavin, I open it a crack, but Hayley is outside, hugging herself in a gray shawl. "Did you read it yet?" she asks.

"Uh, hi. Yeah. Most of it."

"Can I come in?" she says.

"*Yeah* you can," says Jude.

She steps inside, extending her hand to Jude with an amused smile. "Hayley."

"I've heard a lot about you," says Jude, grinning, shaking her hand while elbowing me in the ribs.

Hayley laughs, clearly charmed by Jude, like everyone always is. "It's nice to meet you. I love the cape." She looks at me. "I know it's late. I saw light under the door." She points at the script on the floor. "Oren told me he gave you the first part. How far did you get?"

"Far enough. You read it too?"

"He read most of it aloud to me while he was working on it."

That sounds like a form of slow torture.

"This movie can't happen," she says. "We can't waste the time or the resources. If Oren attempts to make this, we're cooked."

"I'm sure we can persuade him to cut the part where the shaman flies to the moon and then visits London."

Jude laughs a little, looks at me, sees my face, and stops laughing.

"It's more than that," she says. "This studio needs a hit. *Desperately.* It needs something people will actually watch. We can't afford to make another *Brain Breakfast.* Not now." She points at the script again. "If we make *this*, it'll be a disaster."

"Yeah, this makes *Brain Breakfast* look like *Citizen Kane*. What the hell has Oren been smoking?"

"It's not what he smokes. It's the tea he drinks."

I stare at her, slowly blinking.

"Oren grows mushrooms out in the fields," she explains.

I'm so confused. "*Magic* mushrooms? How long has he been doing that?"

Hayley looks at me like I just started speaking in tongues. "For years, Dario. That's nothing new."

Okay, well, I didn't know about *that*. Things clearly took a turn after I left. Or I was just too young to know what Oren was getting up to when I was here. I cannot imagine hallucinating at Moldavia.

"I think Oren only wrote the part where the shaman goes to the moon under the influence of psilocybin," she says. "What's really scary is, the rest of it he wrote *stone-cold sober*."

Yep. That's terrifying. "Well, good luck telling him the truth about his script."

Hayley holds out both her hands like I'm about to ram her. "Oh, no. I can't be the one to break his heart."

"Well, I can't do it! I'm his estranged brother."

Hayley's eyes shoot to the ceiling. "You guys are not estranged! And you're not just his brother. You're the de facto studio chief now. Welcome to your new job."

"Well, I don't know what to do. So I guess I suck at my new job."

"You're gonna be great," Jude whispers to me with a wink.

Hayley paces the room. "I've *tried* telling Oren about his script. He's hypersensitive and doesn't listen—he does this thing where he turns your criticism into a huge compliment. I've never seen anyone do that before. It's bizarre."

"Bizarre? Look who we're talking about!" I say.

Over the years, Oren and Hayley seem to have developed a tension-filled sibling-like relationship where they just disappoint each other in different ways.

"Tomorrow's the first day of shooting," she says. "I don't even know what scene he's doing. No one does. He was supposed to finish *No Chance in Hell*. There are three scenes left. But Oren halted production on that so he could dive right into this cauliflower thing." She sighs deeply. "Which is not how we do things around here."

"Well, have you told him that?"

"I've tried! And he knows that! But he had the crew transform the parlor in the Karloff Wing into a giant vegetable patch with the facade of a farmhouse."

"That is *so cool*," says Jude.

I want to take charge. I want to show Hayley that I can run this place, fix everything, mitigate shit, but I just wind up wringing my hands and giving her this helpless look.

Hayley lowers her voice: "I wish I could tell you we have time to play around, but we don't. We could get lucky, though. In the past, I've seen the crew turn against something that's really sucking. If that happens organically, maybe Oren will see reason, and you won't need to fire him off his own—"

"Whoa, whoa, whoa," I say, jumping back, "that sounds extreme."

"Sorry, but you need to be prepared to pull the plug on this."

I draw my knuckles across my forehead. I'm sweating.

"Also," she says, "we already have the sets, costumes, props . . . something else will have to be made using the materials we've already spent our entire budget on."

"Okay. I'm not Cecil B. DeMille. I just got here."

"We'll let him get through his first day of shooting," she says. "That way it won't look like you're usurping him *completely*. We have to let him fail a little first."

"That's our plan? Let Oren publicly fail?"

"Only for one day."

I sit, shakily, on the armrest of the leather armchair, totally overwhelmed.

I didn't envision killing Oren's dream as my first major decision at Moldavia. I was already so wary of coming back here, but I was also hoping I'd finally manage to feel like I belonged. Creating an adversarial relationship with Oren right off the bat won't foster any sense of belonging; it's just going to make me regret not trusting my instincts about coming back to Moldavia in the first place.

I came back because of my dad's will, because my time at Keenan is over, and because I have no other home, but also because of what Oren thinks of me: that I'm a self-centered brat. I need to prove to myself that I'm better than that. Better than my dad, better than Oren, even. So here I am, hoping for closure to my horrific childhood. And also, there's Hayley.

"In the morning Madge wants to do some makeup tests on you," says Hayley. "Freakify you."

"Okay."

She sighs. "Anyway, I should get to bed." As she moves toward the door, she looks over at the open closet with the light spilling out. She stops for a second and glances at me, and her face softens. Then she turns to Jude. "Welcome to Moldavia. I'll be seeing you around."

"Yeah, you will!"

I follow her out into the hallway, closing the door behind us.

Hayley flicks her eyes to Oren's door, down the hall. "Keep your voice down."

"Look, are you upset with me?"

She looks startled. "Why would I be upset?"

"I didn't see you all day. I thought you were ignoring me."

"I was working." She narrows her eyes at me. "I'm always working, Dar."

"Yeah, okay." I feel unsure all of a sudden. "I know you thought I should consider my own future. Be more selfish about that. But deferring college is a small sacrifice to make if I can preserve our family legacy, and everyone's jobs—"

"That's what Oren told you, right?"

I stare at her, chewing my lip. I am basically repeating his pitch.

"Do I have the facts wrong?"

"So did you call Harvard and tell them you're deferring?" she says.

I take a breath. "Um. No. Not yet. . . ."

Hayley puts her hands on her hips. "If you were confident coming back was the right thing to do, it seems to me that small administrative detail would be the first thing you'd want to get out of the way."

"I'm confident," I say. "I'm here."

"Then you should let Harvard know. Because the longer you dither, the less likely another student can take your place in the entering class."

"Fine, I will. I didn't realize you were moonlighting as dean of admissions."

I don't understand why Hayley is giving me shit about this. She seems so angsty. I guess there are a lot of changes happening, and uncertainty, but she almost seems a little disappointed in me that I came back and didn't take her advice.

Hayley lets out a sharp wisp of breath. "I just want you to understand what all this entails. This isn't going to be a summer vacation. I hope Oren didn't sell you on that."

I cover my face. "I got super-stressed so fast," I say into my hands. "I thought coming back was the right thing to do. But I didn't know about the script." I rub my hands together. "No one warned me about that."

She taps her foot. "I've been trying to talk him out of this idea for months. The script has been a slow, steady descent into the mess it is now. But"—she throws her hands in the air—"I don't know what to do anymore. Maybe he'll listen to you."

I smack my lips. I bet that'll go smoothly. Can't wait for *that* conversation.

"I'm glad you're back," she says. "I'm sure it was a tough decision. I didn't know if I would see you again."

I didn't know if I would see her again either. And I didn't like that. The sweetness of just being with her right now cuts into my rising panic about what I got myself into.

"It's just . . ." Hayley's eyes get all scrutinizing. "I don't want to be the reason you came back."

I shake my head, vaguely, because she was definitely part of the equation.

"Well," she says, glancing behind her, "we should probably get some sleep?"

"Okay." I nod, and we quickly hug before Hayley hurries off to bed.

When I go back inside my room, Jude is grinning at me, rocking back and forth on his heels. "Now I get it," he says. "Noooowwww I get it!"

I shake my head, closing the door. "I'm in over my head, man."

Jude is practically dancing around the room. "Nah, this is going to be *awesome.*"

"Ugh!" I pound the door. "My fists!"

CHAPTER NINE

STANHOPE, ALIVE!

I DECIDE TO LET MOLDAVIA GUIDE ME A LITTLE, AND SEE FOR MYSELF just how off the rails Oren's little cauliflower project is. I have to properly assess the situation before I can nix the flick.

It's been four and a half hours, and Madge doesn't think I'm hideous enough.

"Oh, what we're doing to that beautiful face!" she frets, opening drawers, rifling through plastic containers in cabinets as I sit back in the chair and stare at my transformation in the mirror. Earbuds dangle down in my lap, playing faraway jazz.

They're using rubber and foam latex as prosthetics, as well as globs of putty and mortician's wax, to turn me into the scariest vegetable monster that's ever been put on celluloid, since we have loads of competition there.

What they're going for is some sort of Cronenberg-style

melding of teenager and cauliflower. But the nature of my mutation, and of who I am at all, is a mystery because *not even Oren* comprehends this script—or his own characters. All we know is that Stanhope is the humanoid result of a shaman's curse.

Oren gave the makeup crew loosely scribbled notes on a Post-it that no one could decipher, and then ordered several crates of cauliflowers so everyone could just, like, *stare at them*, hoping for inspiration, which made for one thrilling afternoon, I'm sure.

There are photos of cauliflowers all over the walls. There are also these creepy sketches Madge made of Stanhope as this hulking hybrid vegetable-boy. The only awful part of the makeup so far was the contact lenses, the color of dirty snow, which make me look like the victim of a shipwreck in the Arctic. I just hate putting anything in my eyes. Every few minutes Deb, Madge's assistant, asks me to turn to her. She snaps a bunch of photos, and texts them to Oren, who's somewhere else in the castle.

He texts back every time: More. Much more!

"More of what?" says Deb.

"We need sealer," says Madge, and Deb runs off somewhere.

"What do you think?" Madge spins me around in front of the mirror.

"I'm just glad I'm not an asparagus." A few hours ago I looked like someone smeared with doughnut glaze, but as they continued layering on the prosthetics, I got freakier.

Now I'm starting to look like a giant wasabi pea.

Madge gets back to work. I lose track of time and nod off. When I wake up, I almost scream at my reflection. My neck is sprouting these cabbagy leaves, and my face is the actual head of the cauliflower—my dead gray eyes peering out of all these waxy white stems and florets. I look like a vegetarian-friendly version of the Elephant Man.

"Congratulations, you're one of the healthiest foods in the world," says Madge.

Oren's been texting that he's ready to see me.

I have so much cranial makeup on, I have a hard time making it down the staircase. I stagger, reaching out. Then I see something moving out of the corner of my eye. I yelp and almost fall down the stairs, but it's Oren. He's straddling the bannister, slowly sliding down it, with this insane expression on his face: bug eyes, delirious grin. He's wearing a flowered yellow shirt with a super-wide collar, purple ascot, and fleece riding pants with leather patches on the knees.

"Please don't sneak up on me," I say, teetering, but it comes out all muffled.

Oren squints. "What did you say?"

"Please don't sneak up on me!"

"Your keys are in the beak of a commie?" he says.

I try to grab onto him and almost fall down the stairs again.

"I'm sorry," says Oren, "I just can't understand you." He hops off the bannister, looking at me. "Amazing! Look at you." He spreads his arms. "Stanhope is alive!"

But I don't feel particularly alive. I feel like I'm the living embodiment of Oren's cluttered mind and his cracked logic—a horror movie in itself, but not one I want to watch or be in. Oren puts his fist under his chin, takes a step back, and studies me. "You know, I think I'd prefer you to be one of those *purple* cauliflowers."

I adjust one of the prosthetics on my face so I can speak better. "No."

Oren runs a finger across his lower lip. "You don't see him as purple?"

"Who?"

"Stanhope."

"I don't know who Stanhope is supposed to be."

Oren looks aghast, like there have been volumes written about Stanhope and his origin story, and I just haven't been doing my homework. "He's the leader of the killer cauliflowers, of course!" he bellows. "Who else would he be? *The pool man?*"

I take a breath. "No one seems to know who he is, though. Like . . . as a character."

"Well, I don't know why that would be. You definitely look like the Stanhope I imagined. Less purple, perhaps, but let's not dwell."

"Let's not."

He takes a sharp inhale. "So. What did you think of the script?"

God, I've been dreading this moment. My mind instantly goes into overdrive, wondering how honest I can be without hurting his feelings. "I think it needs work," I say, treading carefully.

"Well, of course. This is my first go! What's your recommendation?"

Burn it. Never write another word again. Never speak of it again.

"Maybe, like, sharpen the dialogue a bit? Figure out what the story's about?"

"What do you mean?"

"Figure out what you're trying to say."

Oren places a hand over his heart, as if someone just told him he won a Pulitzer. He affectionately adjusts one of the cauliflower stems sprouting on my forehead. "You mean the story is so compelling, I should just swim around in it some more to further perfect what's already so close to perfect it's astounding."

I don't think I said that. I look around for a witness, but I can barely see out of my foggy lenses, and I'm feeling very unsteady on my feet.

Oren pokes my chest with his index finger. "Keep going."

I'm feeling more and more uneasy. "Uh. Develop the characters. Figure out what the movie is really about. Like, what's the subgenre, the theme, the general tone, or the point? Because like . . . nothing's clear to me. I have no idea what you're going for at all."

Oren hugs himself. "I'm so glad you loved it."

"I'm saying—"

"I know," says Oren, suddenly wistful, "it's strange . . .

we've been out of touch for so long but still I was all nervous what you were going to think. Isn't it great how the script mashes genres in a totally unique way while asking: What does life mean? What is death? Why do bad things happen to good people?"

"Is it . . . really asking those questions?"

"It asks *so many* questions," he says, his voice swoony.

It's clear Oren hasn't heard a word I've said, and now I'm getting scared. He's so lost inside his head, and his fantasy of all this, I'm not seeing a way in. There probably won't be a happy resolution to this.

"Anyway!" says Oren, clapping his hands. "Shall we?" There's a red golf cart with an angry monster mouth painted on the front parked at the bottom of the staircase. Oren motions me in and takes the wheel.

"When did we get one of these?" I say.

Oren steps on the gas, and my huge cauliflower head slams back hard against the seat as we go flying through the castle. "A month ago. It's saved me tons of time! And it's so fun, right?"

A few crew members leap out of the way, trampling over electrical wires, as we race through the halls, making these wild twists and turns at top speed; the wheels squeak across the slick marble floors. After a few minutes of this, it dawns on me that something is wrong. "Where are we going?"

"The Karloff Wing?" His voice goes up at the end a little.

"Oren. *Are you lost?*"

His face is all scrunched up, intensely focused ahead.

But suddenly we're back at the same staircase. "Good," he says, pointing at it, putting the cart in reverse.

"We just went in a big circle."

"I . . . lost my keys here."

"You don't have keys! You live in a castle with a bunch of rooms that never lock!"

How often does Oren actually leave his room?

He hops out of the cart.

"Oren!" I shout. "Please don't make a thing of pretending to look for your keys."

But he's doing it. He's pretending to hunt for his keys around the edge of the staircase. "I had them earlier," he's muttering, making a big show of patting his pants down. My head is starting to feel really heavy with all the wax and shit piled on it.

"Ah!" Oren yells, pointing down, like he found them.

Fifteen minutes later, after we circle around some more, Oren finally breaks down and *asks directions* from a passing member of the kitchen staff, and we arrive on set.

The exhausted-looking crew is standing in what once was the parlor of the Karloff Wing but is now a leafy pumpkin patch filled with fake pumpkins that look totally real; the facade of a dilapidated farmhouse towers over us. The set is amazing.

"My brother is here! Stanhope is here!" Oren screams as he careens in, nearly running over our gaffer as he skids to a stop.

I get out after him, wobbling, top-heavy, trying not to fall over. Everyone just stares at me silently.

"So what do you want to do here?" a young goateed guy asks Oren. He wears an earpiece and holds a clipboard. I soon learn his name is Eric, and he's Oren's first A.D.

It's obvious everyone has been here all day, in a state of inactivity and confusion, and no one's eaten yet. Jip is standing behind the camera, hands on his hips, a viewfinder hanging from his neck, muttering to his camera op.

"So what's going to happen," says Oren, making large gestures, "is that Stanhope is going to rise from beneath the soil and fly over the pumpkin patch. At that point, lasers will shoot from his eyes. Stanhope will declare himself leader of the Killer Cauliflower Revolution, and then he'll give that speech about the state of humanity."

"What speech about humanity?" I say, but it comes out all muffled.

There's silence, then the sound of feet shuffling. "We're set up for that other shot you wanted to do," says Eric.

"Which shot?" says Oren.

"The one where the farmer guy—"

"Juston Bieberman?" Oren interrupts.

Everyone cringes at the name.

"Right," says Eric, flashing me a pleading look. "Where he comes home from seeing the shaman and makes tea."

"Oh!" says Oren. "Well, I'm not in costume for that."

There's a tense pause.

"We thought that's where you've been all this time," says Eric. "Getting dressed."

"I don't know all my lines yet. Time got away from me. I . . . misplaced my keys. . . ."

"We lost a lot of time," says Eric, quietly. "Most of the day."

"Ah," says Oren, clearly trying to hide his panic. "Time."

The script supervisor, this nervous-looking woman in a dark hoodie and glasses, flips through the call sheet; pages of the shooting script, today's scenes, are attached. "There's no dialogue here," she says. "The shot is just you coming home from seeing the shaman." She squints at the script. "And then you put on a pot of tea."

"Well, let's do Stanhope's speech. He's already in makeup."

"I thought today was just a makeup test for him," says Eric, frowning. "He's not even in costume."

"What speech?" I say.

"Last looks!" Oren screams.

"We're not remotely ready!" someone screams back.

"It will take hours to change the setup," says Eric. "Hours."

"What if we just move a little more quickly?" says Oren.

"It doesn't work like that," I tell Oren. "They have to relight everything. That takes a lot of time."

Eric glances at me, and then Oren. "Um. So . . ."

Oren picks up a megaphone. "Can we set up his flying rig?" Oren asks into the megaphone, making everyone jump a foot into the air. "Where is the Laser Man?"

"What is a Laser Man?" I ask, holding my ears.

Oren looks at me, dumbfounded. "The man . . . who makes all the lasers."

Every single time I wonder: Is Oren kidding? The answer is always: *Nope.*

"I want them to look like they're really shooting out of your eyes!" says Oren.

Eric stares at Oren. "There's . . . no such man."

Oren's eyes go wide. "No Laser Man?" It's like someone told him the Easter Bunny just died. "I don't understand. Is he on vacation?" Oren tries to say something authoritative into the megaphone, but it just rings with deafening feedback.

"Where did you get that thing?" I ask.

Oren holds it out, displaying it for me, all excited and proud. "It was ordered for me last week. On Amazon dot com."

"There's only, like, thirty people here," I say.

"Please," says Oren, "we won't get anywhere if you just argue."

I try to level my gaze, but my head is so oversize I almost tip over.

"What do you want to do here?" says Eric. Maybe only I realize this is the second time he's asked that in under ten minutes.

Oren discards the megaphone. "Listen up! I know this is my first time at this end of the lens! It's a historic day! I came of age on the set of *The Minotaur's Masseuse* as my father's second A.D. I remember handing him cups of coffee as he composed his shots. It was almost like I could see through his eyes, but they weren't my eyes, they were his eyes. We have to go on—*through my own eyes, not his eyes.*"

Everyone starts to get restless, so Oren just amps it up.

"We're not going to get bought out by a studio that placates the masses, keeps making the same soulless crap over and over! We're still a family at Moldavia! We owe our fans! And our future fans! And ourselves!" Oren traverses the set, fists clenched at his sides. "We have to fight!"

Hayley appears on set, watching Oren, her tongue pressed into her cheek.

"Fight!" Oren shouts, tripping over a cable.

Eric quietly suggests they wrap for the day, and Oren immediately agrees.

The crew breathes a collective sigh of relief. They're famished and beleaguered, but they all manage a smile for Hayley as soon as they see her. They fan around her, like she's the sun of their solar system. She talks with a few of the production designers, tapping at design sketches with a pencil, waving at people, while deftly shutting up a few crew members who seem to be mocking Oren, by giving them a single sharp stare.

She comes over to me with no reaction to my appearance whatsoever, like she runs into vegetable hybrid monsters every day around here. "So," she says, "what's your plan here, studio chief?"

Things are so chaotic, there wasn't even a chance for the crew to mutiny. But I saw their desperate faces. I felt the tension. How does Oren *not* feel that? I wonder if he's really that oblivious. "Obviously, we have to pull the plug," I say.

Hayley nods. "Yeah, we need time to figure out what can replace this."

Oren runs over to us, carrying a bunch of pages under his arm, dropping a few behind him. "Hi, guys. So that was a little rough, *admittedly*, but it was my first day. I bet Robert Altman's first day was rough too, right?"

"I'm sure he knew how to get to the set, though," I say. "I'm also sure he knew what scene he was shooting."

"Who knows, though, right?" Oren starts shuffling through the pages.

I clear my throat, loudly. "Listen, Oren—"

"Dario." He looks up at me, his eyes glossy. "Truthfully, I . . . I froze. I felt like I didn't know if I could do it. I kept picturing Dad shaking his head at me. I really saw him at one point, looking down at me, a free-floating specter, *a specter*, telling me I could never do this, I could never be him, that I was a talentless fool."

I look him in the eye. "But you aren't him."

"I know! But how can a creative man work when confronted by his father's mocking specter? Could James Cameron work under those conditions? Could Werner Herzog?"

"I don't know," I say. "Let's call them up and ask *that very question*."

"I panicked. Instead of getting in costume, I started worrying the script wasn't good enough. That I could go deeper, really explore the psychological vicissitudes of these characters—all their foibles and peccadilloes—"

"Are you talking about the cauliflowers?" I ask.

"I want this to be truly great!" says Oren. "Different from anything we've ever done. So I ran upstairs and crouched. I crouched under a table in a sewing room and I started rewriting the whole script. *Why? Why did I do this?*"

I feel like my wax face is starting to melt. "Oren. You're hysterical."

"I did this," he says, taking great heaves of breath, "I crouched there because I wanted this script to be perfect, and it's not perfect yet."

Hayley and I look at each other.

"I ate a salad," says Oren, spreading out his hands, really setting the scene for us.

"What?" says Hayley, frowning.

"Yes, for lunch, about a year ago," says Oren. "I looked in the salad, and there were some tomatoes and sprouts, lettuce of course, and this single lone cauliflower, this little fellow. And then it just hit me. There's a film in this."

The world will never know what might have been if Oren had eaten a meatball sub or some cottage cheese that day. He's totally adrift from reality, and sinking under his own whacked-out ambitions.

The second A.D. approaches Oren and makes him sign off on tomorrow's call sheet, forcing him to confront a schedule someone else had to make for him. "So tomorrow," says Oren, "we're going to make up for today. Promise. We're going to shoot two major scenes in quick succession. Juston

Bieberman's return to his farm and then Stanhope rising out of the earth and giving his speech about civilization."

"What speech about civilization?" I say.

Oren looks baffled. "I didn't give it to you?"

I shake my head; a cauliflower floret hits me in the eye.

Oren starts madly flipping through pages. Then he hands me a stack of rumpled, tea-stained paper. "You only need to learn the first twenty pages for tomorrow."

I snatch the pages. "Oh, is that all?"

"I guess we'll have to wait on the lasers. I really thought we had a Laser Man."

I clap my hands together. "Oren, look, I'm sorry, but—"

"Dario. I wasn't sure at first how this could work. It's hard . . . being a visionary—lonely, in a sense. But it is nice to have you back, supporting me. We all grieve in different ways. I didn't expect, after all that prep and fanfare, how shocked I'd be by Dad's death. How much it *crushed me.* Working on this script, preparing my *directorial debut* is the only thing that's kept me sane over these last weeks." He lays a hand on my arm. "Maybe, *finally*, we'll truly become the brothers we were always meant to become."

Oren exhales, dramatically, and runs over to talk to Jip. They point at the farmhouse, having a heated debate. Oren continues the conversation while looking through the wrong end of a viewfinder.

"I can't believe he pronounced *debut* with a full-on French accent," says Hayley.

"I don't know how to take this away from him."

"Look, Dario."

"What?"

"No, *look*."

She points at everyone on set—they're all breaking for the day. I hear the sound of children. A few crewmen are reunited with their wives (who must work in different departments). Two of them have newborn babies. I watch these dudes put down their equipment and rock their wailing babies. A little boy, maybe five or six years old, finds his dad, one of the carpenters; the guy picks him up and lifts him in the air.

"I get it," I tell her, feeling the pressure. "There are kids and families here."

I guess I always knew, growing up here, that kids live here. But seeing it now, from the other side, is a totally different story. Whole families depend on this place. Every decision I make matters.

Hayley crouches down and ruffles the hair of a little red-headed boy. She looks up at me. "He knows how to press your buttons. He knows how to manipulate you, and he does it well. He's more devious than you think."

"He's just a little kid."

Hayley rolls her eyes. "Oren, you twit. *Oren*."

"Oh." I duck to the side as two crewmen walk past, carrying a skeletal wooden doorframe, a piece of the set, I guess. "Yeah, I know."

"Just don't fall for all that impish guile," says Hayley.

I suck in my lips. "Is it an act?"

"Not totally," she says, "but he knows what he wants and how to get it. He knows you came back here because you've been yearning your whole life for a real family."

I take a step back, sawing my arms through the air. "Whoa. I've been purposefully avoiding all that crap for the last six years. Is that what you really think?"

Hayley smiles at the little boy and then turns the same smile on me like a follow spot. "Am I totally wrong?"

I don't get the chance to respond. More kids run over, circling her. Of course she knows every single one. While I wait for her to pull out a magical umbrella and float away, Franklin comes over dressed in a natty pinstriped suit. He leans over and whispers something into Hayley's ear. She stands and flips her hair over her shoulder, and they converse in low voices. Hayley gestures at me. "Okay. Tell *him* how it works."

"Well," says Franklin, removing his glasses, "in order to keep the studio running, every day is scheduled down to the hour. The studio has to work on a fairly regimented schedule so we can churn out a certain number of features a year."

"We can't lose days like this," Hayley adds. "Your dad would give the production staff an estimated budget and they'd make a production schedule of the entire shoot in advance—since sets needed to be built, costumes made. We would never divert from that schedule unless something went very wrong."

Franklin explains about stripboards, and cards color

coded by location. I get a headache encompassing every part of my head.

"Oren was a good A.D.," says Hayley. "He's a capable producer too. He isn't so bad at the behind-the-scenes stuff—if you tell him exactly what you need and when."

"He's basically an Irish setter," says Franklin.

"But he has zero experience as a director, actor, or writer," says Hayley. "And we can't afford to play around right now while he figures out what movie he wants to make."

We watch Oren zoom off in his cart, waving, while everyone dives out of his way.

"He's just so excited," I say.

"All I can do is tell you how your dad ran this place," says Hayley.

The way Hayley acts with the little kids, with the crew, diplomatic and balletic, makes my heart swell; she's smart and capable, and there's a boundless kindness wrapped around it all. I don't want to let her down. But I don't want to break Oren's heart either—he's just starting to see me as a real brother. I never knew how much that even mattered to me till now. Christ. Is Hayley right about all that?

I'm in an impossible position.

"Cassidy Blackwell from Rusty Blade Films will be visiting in about two months," says Franklin. "He may come prepared with an offer. He had some sort of loose understanding with your father that we're not privy to. It's preliminary, as I said. *However*, if our goal is to preserve the Moldavia legacy, we want to be in as strong a position as possible . . .

just so we can look at all our options objectively."

"Jesus," I sputter, wiggling my fingers around like mad, "that's in no time. . . . How am I supposed to . . . ? This is *so* stressful. . . . How can I possibly get the studio back on track by then? How? *How?* I've inherited a sinking ship!"

"We're here to help," says Franklin.

"Then help!" I take deep inhales until I catch my breath. "Sorry. I have to think," I tell them, pulling at my face. "And I can't think in this . . . *fucking* . . . cauliflower thing. Where's Jude?"

"In your room," says Hayley. "He was lying in bed reading comic books last time I checked. Oren never told anyone when or where he was needed."

Everything was a disaster today—day care, meals, the filming itself—because there was no shooting schedule. No one knew what was happening. This is also my first official day as studio chief—a fact not lost on me or on anyone else, probably.

And I feel bad for Jude. He needs somewhere to be. He doesn't like to be alone. I managed to let him down too. Franklin tells me everyone is heading down to supper now.

"I'm really hungry too," I say, looking around. "And I can't eat wearing all this makeup. I can barely move my mouth."

At that moment, someone from the makeup crew sidles up to inform me, having overheard this conversation, that we should probably get started now, because it might take up to three hours to remove all the makeup and prosthetics.

CHAPTER TEN

SMITHEREENS

WHEN I GET BACK TO OUR ROOM JUDE IS TOTALLY NAKED EXCEPT FOR his cape and gloves, glistening with sweat as he attacks the Everlast bag. He's got his mouthpiece in, pivoting, feinting, parrying, in a fantasy match of his own creation. To him, that bag is hitting back as he pants and grunts and jabs. It's only now I realize that in Jude's mind he's fighting someone specific; someone he never got to fight before. He's not just fighting—he's fighting *back.* I never looked closely enough, or watched Jude fight—he usually does it alone. But it's a rage I recognize right away.

I lean against the doorway. "Who is it?"

Jude sees me and looks up, a liquid fury spiraling in his eyes. He takes out his mouthpiece and steps away from the bag. "Who is what?"

I point at the bag. "Who are you fighting?"

"My stepdad."

"Who's winning?"

"He is. He always won."

There's a reason why we chose each other as best friends. It was something unspoken and primal that meshed; something familiar we saw in one another that we couldn't necessarily put into words. I step inside the room. "When are you gonna win?"

"Oh, I will one day," he says. "Don't worry. I know where he lives now."

I rub my mouth with my fist. "What did he do to you?"

"It's not what he did to me," Jude whispers, vaguely, his eyes flickering around the room, everywhere except me, meaning he doesn't want to talk about this.

I see a few empty dishes on the floor, and an empty glass. "You ate?"

"A while ago. Did you?"

"No." I sit in the armchair and throw Oren's stack of pages onto the floor; I stare at them and then gaze out the window. It's already dark out. "I'm really sorry. I'll make sure you're more involved tomorrow. Today was a total shit show."

"Hayley told me. She brought me up the food. It was good." Jude unfastens the Velcro straps on his gloves. He lopes around the room, locating his clothes, piling them into his arms without actually putting any of them on. "You don't need to worry about me. I'm just happy to be here. I'll know you'll find me if you need me."

"Do you want to . . . box some more? Or . . ."

"Nah." Jude waves away the punching bag like he's

dismissing some drunken asshole mouthing off in a dive bar. He takes his gloves off and throws them on his bed. "You should eat something."

As soon as he says that, we both look up to see Gavin standing there. He's holding a silver tray with a lid on top like we summoned him from a magical world. Gavin walked all the way inside the room without either of us noticing him standing there. Jude yelps and covers himself, running into a far corner, shrieking.

"Sorry," says Gavin, removing the lid to reveal a steaming, mouthwatering fried chicken dinner with biscuits and coleslaw and apple pie and a glass of pink lemonade. "I didn't mean to startle you. I have your dinner, sir."

I stare at him. "You are human, right?"

Gavin sets my tray on the floor, stacks Jude's empty dishes on his tray, and then carries everything out, smiling good-naturedly, without another word. Jude is cowering in the corner. "Is he gone? *Is that kid gone?*" Gavin scares the shit out of Jude.

"He's gone."

"Jesus." Jude starts putting on his clothes, shaking a little.

I sit on the floor, the plate of food between my legs, Oren's script beside me.

"So what are you going to do?" asks Jude, pulling up his sweatpants. "You're the studio chief now. If Oren doesn't know what he's doing—"

"He's been waiting for this moment his entire life."

"Yeah, well. You're not doing him or anybody else here any favors by pretending he knows what he's doing."

"He will feel like I'm out for revenge if I tell him he can't make this movie. He will make this personal." I can already see where this is going.

Although Oren doesn't want to sell to Rusty Blade either, so it's really him getting in his own way (and everyone else's way too). This is madness.

"Revenge for what?" asks Jude.

I rip a hunk off a chicken leg and chew silently for a moment. "Oren wasn't always the most *protective* older brother in the world," I say, swallowing hard.

"How so?"

"He didn't always step in when my dad would get out of control."

Jude nods, understanding.

"I don't know what everyone expects me to do," I say. "There's no one else who could write and direct a movie around here! Oren's our only option. He shadowed our dad for years. He was the one closest to his process."

"Guess he didn't retain much," says Jude. "Or he doesn't know how to translate what's in his head. Not everyone can do that." He pauses, looking at me. "You were pretty close to your dad's process too."

I shake my head. Not as close as Oren was.

I acted in one movie, and I'm still trying to mentally and emotionally recover from the experience. Oren has been grooming himself to take over for years. But no matter how hard he *wants* this and how long he's been waiting in the wings, it's painfully clear Oren cannot succeed our dad. I eye Oren's new pages warily. I put my hand on the first page, splattering grease all over it in dark, angry spots.

"Go ahead," says Jude, watching me. "Read what's next."

"I really don't want to, man."

"No. I think we need to see what comes next."

EXT. VEGETABLE PATCH -- NIGHT

JUSTON BIEBERMAN walks home in the dark thick night under the mocking incandescent moon. When he gets to his FARMHOUSE, the patch outside is bursting open like a pregnant beast. STAN-HOPE GOLDSTEIN, a mutant humanoid teenage cauliflower, rises fifty feet in the air. LASERS shoot out of his eyes, destroying a nearby tractor and frightening cows.

                    STANHOPE
                    (flying)
          Are you the farmer Bieberman?

                    JUSTON BIEBERMAN
          I am him. Who is asking?

                    STANHOPE
          I am Stanhope Goldstein, leader of the Ciller
          Cauliflower Revolution. We are here to ruin you,
          your farm, and it all.

JUSTON BIEBERMAN gasps as the black moonlit earth begins to shake and another Ciller Cauliflower emerges from the torn-open ground: Stanhope's assistant, PETER VON LUFTIG. Peter laughs along with Stanhope, flying in midair.

                          PETER
                  (laughing maniacally)
          I am Peter! I will help Stanhope destroy you!

                          STANHOPE
          We were summoned by the shaman. It is time to deal the
          deathly blow to you, Juston.

                          JUSTON
          NO, PLEASE.

                          PETER
                  (laughing maniacally)
          Ha! Yes! HA.

                          STANHOPE
              (laughing maniacally, shooting lasers)
          We are all flawed creatures growing in corrupted
          dirt. Life is meaningless and cursed. I am revenge for
          your antics, for the sin of envy and stealing seeds.
          Humanity is base and selfish. But I wouldn't know
          because I am a cauliflower mutant, which is why I am

asking you -- why do you go to war against your own
and eat beans and watch digital media?

PETER
(laughing maniacally)
Yes! This is true! Yes, Stan! Why? Oh ho!

STANHOPE
(laughing maniacally)
I can only destroy what I'm destined to: you!

JUSTON
(laughing maniacally)
No. NO! This is so wrong, you are stressing me out.

PETER
(laughing maniacally)
I am going to help Stanhope DESTROY YOU!

STANHOPE
(laughing maniacally)
I only know my wicked nature. I am a teenaged
cauliflower, so I like to eat and have sex a lot and
play Candy Crush on my phone, but I know that I am
here to cause pain even if I don't know why. Do any of
us know what we do? My parents cast me out because
I was a mutant vegetable. I only know evil. My heart

is full of silty scum like the pond behind your barn.
Civilization won't have me. Humanity is bleak and out
of control. I am another man's creation, and just do
his bidding. I am lonely and sad but whatever. BAH!

More Ciller Cauliflowers begin to emerge from the ground, cackling and flying around like vegetable devils.

That's pretty much as far as we get. I flip ahead and skim
the rest of the pages with one hand. There are nineteen more
pages of Stanhope and Peter flying around this stupid patch,
questioning their existence while continuing to berate and
threaten Juston.

I look at Jude. "Did Oren actually write . . . *an existential
cauliflower*?"

"I have lines?" says Jude, trying to temper his excitement
that he's in a movie with the dawning realization that it
would be the worst movie ever made.

The weird thing is, if you really examine it—and, I mean,
who the fuck would—but if you look closely at what Oren
wrote, there's a genuine sadness—about being misunder-
stood, feeling lost, and not really knowing the world at all, or
who you are. But whatever it all means, whatever he's trying
to do here, we're in big trouble. We cannot make this film.
Nonetheless, Jude and I still run around the room, playing
our parts.

We can't help it.

"'Hello,'" I say into my phone, "'is this my assistant, Peter von Luftig?'"

"'It is!'" says Jude. "'I just arrived at the Killer Cauliflower Headquarters.'"

"'Oh good! How many farmhouses do we have scheduled to destroy this week?'"

"'It's a busy week! Five! But your weekend looks good!'"

"'Wonderful! Set up a game of golf with Trevor the Turnip!'"

This goes on for longer than it should, till we collapse on the floor, laughing until we're crying, and crying until it becomes something else: darker, more strained. Because it feels like we're playing one last carefree game on the deck of the *Titanic*.

Before I head to bed, I tiptoe into the hall holding Oren's pages, shaking them against my leg, anxiously. I want Oren to tell me where he's going with this cauliflower script, because it feels like one big joke, an all-out meltdown, or something worse.

It's late, but several crewmen are carrying furniture out of Oren's room. I ask one of them what's going on. He says Oren wanted to paint his room. I peek inside. There's a splattered tarp on the floor, cans of paint, paint rollers. For some reason he decided to paint his room black. He's only half done—one side is still yellow. Bumblebee colors. The windows are wide open. A breeze rustles the curtains, scattering loose papers everywhere.

The only furniture still in the room is his desk and chair. Oren is hunched over his typewriter, wearing a kimono with fat orange lobsters swimming against a crystal-blue background. He's typing furiously, ripping pages out of the machine as he goes. I cough, loudly.

He turns around, his mouth still moving. "Dario?"

I hold out the script. "Look, I'm sorry. This is . . . a total disaster."

Oren looks quizzical. "In a bad way?"

"There is no good way for something to be a disaster, Oren."

Oren turns to the typewriter, as if it could offer a different opinion, his fingers still making typing movements in the air. Then he looks back at me, baffled.

"Dad was very supportive of what he read," he says.

"Dad was in late-stage dementia."

"I'm still working on it, it's still forming, it's getting better every —"

"*Oren.* I'm confused. Explain this to me. You've watched Dad work for virtually your whole life. You know how movies get made here. There's a schedule, a known process to the way—"

"Hmmm." Oren pulls the kimono around him tighter, pointing his finger at me. "Someone's getting very power hungry around here."

I walk into the room. "C'mon, that's not what this is about."

Oren leaps up. He grabs scattered pages of the script and waves them around, like he's drying off a layer of invisible ink and underneath will be something better, his real intentions all along.

"You said it today," Oren intones. "*I'm not Dad.* Well, I have to work at my own pace, conform to my own style and aesthetic. Moldavia will have to get used to the way *I* want to make films."

"Moldavia is too financially endangered right now to take that big a risk—"

"Well, everyone is going to have to give me a chance—"

"Everyone wants me to shut this cauliflower shit down."

His mouth curls inward. His eyes widen and then unwiden.

"No one understands the script," I say.

"You mean the script is so astonishingly innovative—"

"God, *enough of that!* Sometimes criticism just means something sucks."

Oren strides across the room, his blue kimono flying out and flowing around him, as if it's trying to chase him and drown him. "It doesn't matter what people understand," says Oren. "*I'm owed—*"

"You're owed nothing! Dad appointed me studio chief. I have to make these decisions. It's not about you and how you had an epiphany from a bowl of arugula—"

Oren's eyes go cold. "It was *radicchio—*"

"Moldavia is a movie studio, not just a castle filled with moaning mummies and zombie brides. People's lives depend on us keeping Moldavia afloat. Don't you get that?"

"How dare you!" he cries. "You really think I don't know

that? You just waltz in here like—"

"*Waltz?* You asked me! You asked me to come back here!"

He glares at me, fuming. "Because I didn't think you'd have the nerve or the knowledge about the way this studio runs to try and—"

"Aha!" I shout, pointing. "There it is! You thought I'd just lie down and you could do whatever the hell you wanted, right?"

Why am I only now realizing this? Hayley is totally right.

Oren would never have wanted me to come back here if he didn't think I was someone he could push around. After everything I went through here as a kid, he has no problem using me for whatever value he thinks my name has, and then not taking me seriously as studio chief. Not to mention he has no idea what he's doing.

Oren grabs a fireplace poker and holds it up in the air for a second, menacingly. Then he turns and starts poking at the fire, scattering sparks and embers as logs overturn.

I cough, waving away smoke. "You're going to burn this place down."

Oren stands stock-still in front of the fireplace, his back to me. He stares at the flames, fire iron at his side. "Your time at that lice nest is over. So you figured, now that you're homeless, you'd try out your old family again, like an old sock. Give all us flawed, broken souls another chance. How *beneficent* of you."

I slam my fists into my legs. "Dad's will made me chief. It was come back here or sell this place to Rusty Blade."

"But now you're just out to crush me. Get back at me for—"

"For what? Tell me, Oren."

I want him to acknowledge the past. I want him to truly apologize for not being there for me, for being a shitty brother and a shitty human being, for always putting himself first. I want to hear those words come out of his stupid mouth.

"Tell me, Oren."

He raises his hand without turning around, shushing me.

I knew he would spin this so it would seem like my goal is revenge. "Tell me you're not losing your mind. 'Cause I'm getting scared."

"I have a few tricks up my sleeve," he says into the fire.

"What the hell does that mean?"

Oren sighs, replaces the poker, and turns around, smiling gaily, suddenly tranquil. "It means I know it was a rough start. But it's all part of the grand plan."

I untie my hair so it falls, messily, over my shoulders. I shake it out and lean against his door. "There's no grand stupid plan."

"No, *there is*," he says. "Of course there is. My mind is clear."

"Oren, listen to me. You better get your deluded ego in check if your goal is to preserve our family legacy. Because you're the one—*right now*—who is handing this place to Cassidy Blackwell on a giant platter."

"I need to work." Oren returns to his typewriter, sits down, and starts calmly typing, with ramrod posture, as if I just asked him to outline a sequel. He refuses to listen.

I slap the door. "We can't make your film," I say, not backing down, ignoring his passive-aggressive tantrum; it's pissing me off.

"Give me tomorrow," he says into the typewriter, "and I'll show you."

"What's going to change tomorrow?"

"Give me tomorrow. I have a grand plan. I promise you that."

I let my exhausted eyes settle on the crackling fire. Fire burning wood is the only thing that makes sense in this room right now. Oren types away. As I leave the room I hear the mocking *ding* of the margin bell.

"He doesn't have a grand plan," says Hayley.

"Yeah, I know that, but—look, can I come in?"

I surprised her, knocking on her door this late. She's wrapped in one of her shawls, propping the door open only a crack.

She hesitates. Then she swings the door open. Her room smells vaguely of roses. There are paintings on the eggplant-colored walls—these weird portraits—and framed photographs of her parents, propped on shelves. She has a lot of stuff, but it's organized in its own way, and everything is sort of feminine and pillowy, like we're inside a scented candle. I point at the stuffed animals piled up on the bed. "It's kind of girly in here."

"They all have names."

"I'll bet they do."

She walks over to her desk and snaps her laptop shut. But before she does, I see FaceTime open.

"Who were you chatting with?"

Hayley smirks. "Nosy a little?"

"Just curious."

"Nobody." She sighs. "You know Oren is playing you, right?"

I wink. "He can't play me if I'm playing him."

Hayley throws her head back. *"Christ."* She moves across the room toward her desk. She rummages through a small box. I hear the sound of a lighter clicking. She walks over to her window, cracks it open, and sits on the ledge, taking a long drag on a joint. She waves the smoke away, and holds the joint out. "Want some?"

I decline, even though I kind of do.

"Look," she says, "you two boys better grow up already and get past all this, because things are going to get tiresome around here real fast."

"I'm giving him one more day."

Hayley exhales a plume of smoke and tilts her head back at me.

"You said it yourself," I say. "He really needs to fail. He didn't get that chance yet. Tomorrow he will. He needs to see for himself. Then we can move on."

She points the lighter at me. "I said let him fail *only for a day.*"

At first I felt horrible that I was going to break Oren's heart. But Oren has been using my guilt against me this whole time, to wrest control, get what he wants, and make this stupid-ass vegetable movie. So I'll give him what he wants—*another day.* And then he can fail—epically.

Hayley arches her eyebrows. She knows what I'm up to.

"What Oren said about finally seeing me as a real brother," I say, shaking my head. "Bunch of crap. He claims to have something up his sleeve, so fine, let's see if he can pull this thing together." I hold my hands out. "I'm only being fair."

Hayley folds her body into the frame of the large windowsill. The broken moonlight sprinkles her hair.

I pick up one of the picture frames. Seeing Hayley with her parents, back when everything was still whole, gives me a twinge in my chest. I glance at the books lined up on her shelves—Oscar Wilde, Yeats, Beckett. There are books on Georgian, Palladian, and Neo-Gothic architecture that are kind of curious.

I turn to her. "It bothered me what you said."

She's watching me, her pupils dilated, like they've consumed their own galaxy.

"Yearning my whole life for a real family?" I replace the picture frame, a little harder than I intended. It rattles. "Shit, sorry," I say, straightening it. "Do you and Oren talk about me like that? Like I'm some lonely, unloved orphan boy yearning for a real home?"

Hayley laughs. "No."

"It hurt when I realized Oren didn't really mean what he said."

"Are you sure he didn't mean *any* of it?"

I'm not. But it still stung. I motion for her to pass the joint, and I take a drag.

"Is he losing his mind?" I ask, my voice doing that squeaky inhaling-pot noise.

She shakes her head. "Oren is just a narcissistic by-product of being sequestered in the crazy world of Moldavia for too long," she says.

The possibility of losing my mind hovers around the fringes of every decision I make. It haunts every thought. I've always used Oren as a sort of a barometer—to see if he would lose it too. But using Oren as a set point for normal comes with obvious complications.

I can't pretend I didn't come back here partly to see what was left of my family, and my relationship with Oren; partly to see how much time with Hayley I could have before it all might fade. There were so many loose threads. I'd regret not seeing everyone again while I was still lucid.

Hayley looks so incredibly beautiful right now. I give her a lopsided grin. "Wanna make out?"

She throws her head back and sort of laughs-shrugs. "Sure."

I hold her around the waist, bending her out the window like I'm dipping part of her into the night. Her hair blows in a breeze that rustles the trees outside. She closes her eyes as I work my way up her throat, to her lips. She blows pot smoke into my mouth, and then I'm kissing Hayley in the night wind. This turns out to be one of my favorite moments ever.

At some point I right her back on the windowsill and step away, but I don't remember doing that. Dazed, I gesture at the walls and ask about the paintings.

"Your mom," she replies, brushing a lock of hair behind her ear.

I give her a confused face, I think, but I'm not really sure what my face is doing.

"She paints."

The portraits are strange and pulsing, but I'm stoned now. I didn't know my mother painted. I feel like that's something I should have known, but how would I? I'm not a part of her world anymore. Patients in hospitals paint. Sure. That makes sense.

"She gave me some of them," Hayley explains, studying them. "She's gotten really good."

My eyelids feel sandy and leaden. "Yeah."

"Visits got to be a bit much for Oren. So I visit her now. As frequently as I can."

Something else I didn't know. I take a stuffed animal from her bed—a green plush alligator—and put it in her arms. She hugs it close. "This is Binky."

"Seriously?"

"Why does it bother you?" she says.

"I don't care what its name is."

"I mean, wanting a real family?"

I guess families, and never having had a healthy one, is my Achilles' heel. "Maybe I stayed away too long," I say, running a hand through my hair.

"No, you needed to stay away." Hayley always dismisses my self-doubts.

"I don't know. What do you want?" I ask her.

She chews on her thumb for a moment, studying the ceiling. Her eyes flick over to her closed laptop and then back to me. She shrugs. "Ask me tomorrow."

"I totally will." I really don't want to leave her room.

Sensing this, Hayley walks over, leans in, and kisses me lightly on the throat, right under my jawline. I rest my hand against the back of her neck. We press our foreheads together, rubbing noses. After a few minutes, standing there just like that, it becomes apparent that both of us should probably get to bed. So I extract myself, gently squeezing her wrist, and do just that.

I walk back to my room, thinking about how removed I am from where I came from. And how I've always had feelings for Hayley, but probably suppressed them.

Now that I'm back at Moldavia, I'm feeling stuff I didn't expect: this need for a real home, and to claim a family I never had, or felt I needed. I feel a weird surge of protectiveness in a legacy I didn't even know I gave a shit about.

I want a second stupid chance. I want to fix this place so I can reverse all the pain it caused me. So I'll always have somewhere I belong.

I get into bed and will myself to lose consciousness.

This has been such a long, confusing day.

"Who knows how long you have?"

My dad wakes me up, his hand around my throat.

I hear the sound of my own choking. He lets go and tells me to take a deep breath. I do, gasping, gulping in air. But then his fingers close around my windpipe, tighter this time. "Alastair is slowly dying. Every breath might be his last. I want you to feel that."

He lets go of me again. Gasping, I try to push him off me, but he shoves me back down and presses the heel of his hand into my chest, grinding it against my sternum.

"Every breath is weaker. He's fighting against death . . ."

He's already dead, *I want to scream.*

". . . fighting for his survival. . . ."

His hands go for my throat again, but I reach out and jab him in the eye. He pulls me out of bed by my wrists; I go flying and land heavily on the floor. He drags me by the hair into the bathroom. When he lets me go, moves to the sink, and turns the faucet on, he drops a handful of my torn-out hair, which floats down as gently as a snowflake.

I try and crawl out of the bathroom, but he grabs my ankle. I kick him hard in the stomach. He falls backward but regains his balance, and lifts me up by my shirt collar. Then his arm is curling around my waist, bending me over the sink. "Who knows how long you have?" he says into my ear. The sink is slowly filling up. He pushes me under as I make frantic bubbles in the water.

The door swings open. My dad yanks my head out of the sink. Oren stands there in a white T-shirt and boxer shorts, looking at us, slowly shaking his head. I reach for him. "Enough of this," he tells our dad. "You have to stop this."

I try to wriggle away, coughing up water, but my dad has an iron grip on the back of my neck. "Help me!"

Oren takes a step into the bathroom. "You're hurting him."

All it takes is one look from my dad, and Oren freezes.

Our eyes lock. There's this pitched moment that slowly deflates. Oren looks at me with an expression of frightened helplessness that slowly turns into disgust.

"I'm so sick of you both," he mutters. He backs out. The door clicks shut.

My dad, still clutching the back of my neck, makes this horrible guttural sound, and it takes me a minute to realize he's laughing. When his grip softens, I elbow him in the crotch. He grunts and stumbles back. I slip on the wet floor and fall hard on my tailbone. I expect my dad to lunge at me again, but he just sits there, propped against the tile wall under a window, resting a hand on his knee, laughing at me.

I sit against the door, rubbing my throat, trying to get my breath back. "I hate you," I rasp. My voice is wrecked.

"You're getting so good. You have no idea. The problem is you're soft like your mom. You have too much of her inside you. But Dario, she went mad. They tie her to her own bed in

that hospital. Who knows how long you have? It's genetic. You probably have a fifty-fifty chance of winding up just like her."

"Stop talking about her!"

He points at me. "That's Alastair!" he says, grinning, exposing his black and gold fillings, his rotten teeth. "That's him right there. That desperation. Tiny bursts of broken breath. A thin window of life left that's slowly . . . slowly . . . closing." He reaches out, framing me, making a rectangle with his thumbs and index fingers, composing a shot. "He's trying to hold on in a dying world. Show that to me." I stand up and grip the doorknob, but it's too slippery and I can't open the door. "Show that to the camera tomorrow."

I whirl around. "Is he supposed to be me?"

He grins at me again. "He was once whole and now his world is in smithereens."

He looks at me like he's seeing someone come apart before his eyes.

"I won't wind up like her!"

"Alastair is the monster rotting inside all of us," he says.

He peels off his face, revealing the meaty musculature beneath, glowing red eyes, and a hungry set of dripping, grisly fangs.

"Dario!"

Jude's hand is on my shoulder, and I recoil. I must have fallen out of bed. I'm curled up on the floor in the middle of the room, drenched in sweat. "You were dreaming, man," he says. I'm clutching my throat. "What the hell is happening?

I've never seen you like this."

"I want to go home, Jude. . . . I want to go back to Keenan."

"We can't," says Jude. "We left. Remember? *Jesus*, look at you." He turns on one of the lamps. I'm covered in hives. My throat is so tight I can barely breathe.

"Benadryl," I say, holding my hands. "I'll be fine. It's a panic attack."

"This was a mistake. Coming back here. I should never have let you do this."

"Find some Benadryl. Ask that kid! I'll be fine." Jude starts to run out, but I call him back. "Wait! Don't leave me. . . ."

Jude kneels beside me. I put my head in his lap. The bathroom door is open a crack. I see the sink, all quiet and still now, as the light spills in and glints off the porcelain, disrupting its stoic darkness, like something dead and buried slowly coming back to life.

CHAPTER ELEVEN

BLASTED

THE NEXT MORNING, JUDE AND I SIT SIDE BY SIDE, FACING OURSELVES in the mirror, as the makeup crew dutifully transforms us into Stanhope Goldstein and Peter von Luftig.

Madge and her assistants work fast, in a more focused way now, but the makeup still takes almost three hours, and I'm too wired from coffee, and too anxious in general, to snooze through any of it.

They're careful to differentiate Stanhope's particular cauliflower deformities from Peter's. It's obvious that Peter is a totally unnecessary character *anyway*, but there's so much already wrong with Oren's script, why dwell on that?

Plus I'm not going to rain on Jude's parade. He is *so* excited.

"Look at us!" he squeals, as Deb delicately adjusts the cauliflower florets growing out of his face so they're in a different arrangement from mine.

The makeup is only from the neck up, *thank Christ*, so it's up to the costume department to figure out the rest. They try out all different kinds of stuff on us—from black trench coats, which give us that cliché *cauliflower-gangster* look, to these skin-colored body stockings that make us look like a sexually ambiguous ice-skating duo in a super-fucked-up Olympics.

When we try on Mexican ponchos with sombreros, I realize Oren's begun texting the costume department with some last-minute ideas. It's a sad testament to how little anyone understands who or what we're supposed to be that we go through maybe twelve different looks before Samantha Childress—who refused to take any measurements, fitted us for nothing, and is pretending this whole thing isn't happening—gives us these cream-colored tunics, belts, and stretch pants. Now we look like Luke Skywalker twins at a Costa Rican yoga retreat. Oren texts back: Fabulous! Just as I pictured them!

Samantha rolls her eyes, carts off the remaining looks, and then we're off.

When we get to the set, escorted by a small entourage of makeup and costume assistants, it's total pandemonium. As soon as they see me, the crew all give me this *please save us* look. The second A.D. fills me in on the morning's events.

Oren is still in the process of filming the end of his first scene. Apparently Lorenzo Mayberry was awakened from his deep hibernation to play the evil shaman, wearing not a "tan robe," as the script indicated, but a shimmering, silver, three-piece suit that made him look like a futuristic game-show host. Having never been treated for his lifelong narcolepsy, he fell asleep twice in the middle of speaking his lines.

Then Oren decided Juston Bieberman should have a monologue on his walk back to his farmhouse, before the killer cauliflowers burst out of the ground, to show the character's "inner torment." Oren is dressed in white H&M overalls and an oversize straw hat (Samantha is purposefully making him look like a buffoon, and he has no idea).

He's trying to remember his new lines while simultaneously directing Jip to follow his new blocking, which is frustrating the hell out of the camera crew. The floor is a mess of colored tape, marking the different camera positions and Oren's own marks, which keep changing. Whenever Oren can't remember his lines, he takes it out on everybody else, like they're the ones messing up the shot.

"'But of course,'" he mumbles, stumbling out of frame, "'I would never steal the shaman's seeds. For what am I, except a good man who doesn't do that.'"

"Stay on your mark!" someone yells.

Oren waves him off, annoyed, and continues. "'I don't need stolen seeds. . . . I enjoy moonlight and long walks by a beachfront, and melons and nice books about pigeons and playing darts, that's me, a nice farmer fellow, I would sooner . . . sooner . . .'" He stops and looks down, holding the sides of his head, trying to remember what comes next. He kicks the ground, scowling at the crew. "Where are the songbirds? *Cut!*"

"What?" the camera op screams.

"I asked for a flock of songbirds to lift off at that moment!" He mimes birds swarming around him.

"What the hell are you talking about?" a production designer screams.

"I asked for songbirds!" Oren yells. "I need a flock of them to lift out of the trees and circle around my head . . . *singing.* Where's the bird wrangler?"

Someone tells him there is no animal wrangler at Moldavia.

"No birds?" Oren says, incredulously. "*No birds?* What is going on here? We had birds in *The House That Moaned Murder.* I distinctly remember that."

Someone explains those were just random birds flying above the outdoor shoot.

"Also," says Oren, his straw hat slipping over his eyes, "I need like a piece of straw or a stem to chew on. Don't farmers chew on stems or straws when they speak?"

Oh, dear God.

"Ah!" he says, seeing us, running over. "Look at you. I changed my mind about the whole purple cauliflower thing because this is just perfection."

"How is it going?" I ask, tentatively.

"Oh, you know," says Oren, taking off his hat, looking around, like he's not sure where he is or how he got here.

"I'm getting into my groove. I need a stem to chew on."

First A.D. Eric comes over, tapping his watch. He looks like someone who's just returned from a horrible war. "We're losing time."

"You know," says Oren, "I don't think we need this monologue after all. We have a usable take of me coming back to the farm *sans* monologue, right?"

Eric's face reddens. "Of you just walking home? Yeah. *From four hours ago.*"

"Great," says Oren. "Let's just use that and move on to the next setup."

"The crew will need lunch soon," says Eric.

Oren giggles. "Do I look like Chef Boyardee?"

"I didn't suggest you start grilling hot dogs." I'm starting to like Eric. "I'm just saying we need to get the crew down to the commissary soon. We've been here all morning. People need to eat."

"Sure," says Oren. "Let's just do this next scene and then we can all get fed!"

Eric emits a long sigh and says something into a walkie-talkie. There's a staticky reply, and then in a flash Jude and I are fitted with AMSPEC harnesses.

We get prepped to fly while they set up the rig. At least an hour goes by while they reconfigure the lights and change the camera positions. The floor is retaped. We barely rehearse, and then we're up in the air, dangling over the pumpkin patch. "Aren't we supposed to burst out of the ground?" I shout down.

"I'll get that shot later!" says Oren.

"Yes, but . . . we're flying over undisturbed dirt," I say, pointing down. No one's tending to continuity or any of the details at all, which concerns me.

"That won't be in the shot," says Oren.

"It is in the shot," says the camera op.

"Just frame them higher," he says.

"If we frame them higher, the light reflects off their wires," says the op.

"Can't we digitally delete that in post?" says Oren.

Yes, they *can* do that in post, the assistant camera op explains, but that takes time and resources. It's best to get everything as close to perfect during production—a good piece of advice that Oren doesn't seem to pay any attention to.

Oren, the camera op, and Jip have a heated conversation—or more like an *argument*, half of it in Dutch—about how they want to handle this, which results in them having to move the camera and change the lights while we just hang there.

"No, we can't do a three-hundred-and-sixty-degree pan!" someone shouts. "We'd have to move walls. It would take all day to relight!"

"I don't see why that's not an option, but fine, yeah, yeah," says Oren, waving away Jip. *"Wat je ook wilt!"* He comes over to us, looks up, and explains that for this first shot, the camera will be tight on our faces and he'll shout his lines off camera.

Oren throws a pair of headphones around his neck. He runs over and sits in a director's chair with his name chalked on it, intensely studying the shot on a monitor.

Someone tells Oren they're ready.

"Quiet on set!"

"Roll sound."

"Roll camera."

"ACTION!" Oren shouts.

"'Are you the farmer Bieberman?'" I yell down, trying not to crash into Jude.

There's a long pause.

"Darn it all," says Oren, clasping his head. "Sorry, I'm sorry. Can someone give me a shooting script?"

Someone literally hurls a script at Oren. "Great. Let's go again!" he shouts.

"We're still rolling!"

"ACTION!" Oren screams.

"'Are you the farmer Bieberman?'" I yell again.

Oren loudly pages through the script for way too long. Then: "'I am him. Who is asking?'" he shouts over at us.

"'I am Stanhope Goldstein, leader of the Killer Cauliflower Revolution.'"

At that moment a primal, earsplitting roar erupts from behind the farmhouse, and an enormous werewolf crashes through the front of the facade. Clipboards, pencils, papers, walkie-talkies, everything goes flying as people scatter, screaming. The towering werewolf, with glistening silver fur, yolky eyes, and fangs covered with bloody slime, lunges into the pumpkin patch. He drops into a predatory crouch and then rises up again, claws extended, howling a blood-curdling cry at an unseen moon.

"Holy shit!" someone screams.

Part of the set collapses on top of our fly system, sending Jude and me spinning out of control, in danger of coming loose and plummeting down right on our heads. "Help us!" I scream. Two brave crew members run over with ladders and quickly dismantle the equipment as the werewolf scampers around; we plop down safely on a pile of leaves only a few feet from the salivating monster. We rip off our harnesses and scramble away.

The creature begins to growl. *"I want human meat!"* he roars in a deep voice. The monster looks around at everyone cowering, trying to pick out his lunch.

Do werewolves talk? I'm not sure they do. This one sounds a lot like Lester Carver, Moldavia's super-tall, super-talented resident creature actor, who works with the creature effects department on the secretive third floor of the Whale Wing. They're led by eccentric genius Jasper Raines and his genius wife, Barbara Pandova, to create some of Moldavia's most memorable monsters.

The werewolf roars again, swiping at the air. The remainder of the set crumbles behind him, leaving the werewolf standing in a pile of wreckage, a cloud of dust partially obscuring him. Rust-colored light shines through the dust, backlighting the werewolf's silhouette and all his coarse body hairs, making them look like tiny needles.

Hayley appears at the other end of the room. Her mouth is open wide. Our eyes meet, and I get a sickening feeling. I acted like a child. I should have pulled the plug on this yesterday, but I let Oren get to me—*again.* And he was right: I wanted revenge. My judgment got clouded, and I almost got people killed. I had no idea it would get this bad.

"*Cut!*" Oren yells.

The werewolf gives a vague nod, turns around, and then stalks off the way he came, through the destroyed set, disappearing into the darkness beyond.

Blasted, my dad would say. He used to say that whenever a bulb randomly exploded, with a loud pop and a sprinkle of glass, but then it became synonymous with anything that went disastrously wrong.

There's momentary silence. Then everyone who took cover behind equipment, or ran to the far corners of the room in terror, starts to convene sheepishly in the center of the room to survey the damage. "The set is toast," says Joaquin, the production designer, shaking his head. "That's at least two weeks to rebuild." Work boots crunch over broken glass. Several walkie-talkies crackle. People cough, waving dust away.

I pick myself up off the floor, and help Jude up. "You okay?"

"Yeah," says Jude, a little dazed. "You?"

Oren runs over, looking thrilled. "I told you!" he says, clasping his hands in front of him. "I just needed today!"

"Oren, what the hell was that?" I say.

"I wasn't sure where to go with this whole cauliflower thing. It was getting a bit long at four hundred pages, and I thought: What if we subvert expectations? At the beginning, people would think this is just another movie about a farmer being attacked by mutant cauliflowers . . . but then, *boom* . . . it becomes a classic moonlit werewolf tale."

"That makes no sense!"

"People have a hard time understanding something truly unique. At first people never get it." He points at me. *"At first.* This would be different. Revolutionary!"

The crew has been listening in to this conversation, looking at one another in disbelief, and then looking at me like, *Do something.*

"We can rebuild the farmhouse," says Oren with a fleeting, nonplussed glance over at the destroyed set. "It was worth it to get that shot! In the meantime we can focus on more intimate scenes, particularly when the werewolf, Kevin Shane Modigliani, goes to battle with Stanhope and Peter for control over Dr. Frankenstein's summer villa—"

"This was your grand plan? To have a werewolf appear for no reason?" I have to end this now. This is only going to get worse the longer I prolong it.

"Dario. This horror film will reprogram audiences for generations!"

I think about Cassidy Blackwell coming, the possibility of having to sell Moldavia to Rusty Blade, and all those awful *Backpacker* movies they make. Still, this is so much harder than I thought it would be.

I take a deep breath. "Oren. I need you to leave the set now."

"Yes, we should probably break for lunch—"

"No." I have to rip the Band-Aid off. "I'm sorry. You're fired."

My words echo. There's an awful silence.

"I'm . . ." Oren opens his mouth but it just hangs there, open.

I turn around to face the crew slowly gathering around us. "Can everyone give us a minute, please?" They all make a show of murmuring to each other and pretending to go back to work, picking up loose nails here and there, but intently focused on what's happening between Oren and me.

"Dario," says Oren with an uncertain smile, "you can't really fire me."

I beg him with my eyes not to make this worse than it already is.

Oren, his straw hat falling over his eyes, starts backing away. "Can I please have another chance to get this right?"

"We don't have time . . . or the money. I'm sorry."

There's another endless pause while he stands there, his mouth still hanging open. Then he turns to everyone, and thumps his heart with his fist. The crew gives him a respectful, relieved, generous round of applause.

He takes in all this imaginary glory. Then he gets into his golf cart and zooms off. Everyone watches him go. The whirring of Oren's cart gets farther and farther away and then, closer and closer, as Oren suddenly reappears. I take a breath, steadying myself for a longer confrontation, but Oren looks equally as surprised to see us. He grips the wheel tightly, incensed, and then slowly steps out of the cart, pointing at the ground. "I . . . lost my keys. . . ."

"So what do you want to do?" Eric says to me, after Oren finally leaves for the second fucking time. The makeup crew sets up chairs, this whole triage station on the set so they can get Jude and me out of our sweltering makeup as quickly as possible.

"Oren suspended production on *No Chance in Hell*?"

"That's right."

"Is the set still intact?"

"Everything's ready to go," says Eric. "We just need three more days on it."

Suddenly, I'm making decisions. They're just pouring out of me, involuntarily, like I was always studio chief, and I always knew how to delegate and solve things. "Okay. Can you be my second unit? Finish production on that while we regroup and I figure out what we'll shoot next. I'm officially killing *The Ciller Cauliflowers*."

Eric agrees. He can rally the crew, and we won't lose too much time if we divert resources back to the other film temporarily, but I have to make decisions about what comes next fast. Then it hits me—I have *three days* to come up with another idea to replace this cauliflower fiasco.

I have some more back-and-forth with Eric about scheduling. Then he says something about them not resuming filming at all, *on anything*, for another two days.

"Wait, what?" I say. "Two days off? I'm confused."

Eric looks surprised. "It's Crepuscular Dusk."

I forgot the first Friday of every month begins a Moldavia tradition—two days off so everyone can rest and get their wits back from the seven-day-a-week, thirteen-hour-a-day grind. There's always a giant costume ball in the grand ballroom of the Carpenter Wing that begins at midnight of that first Friday. Resources like costumes and party food are recycled and redirected, so these soirees wind up costing the studio very little money.

Eric says this ball will take place in the slightly smaller ballroom of the Karloff Wing, since the graveyard set from *No Chance in Hell* is still spread out all over the other ballroom, and they're behind schedule.

Hayley and Franklin come over.

Hayley tries to tell me something, but I'm still in studio chief mode, so I quickly explain my plan to them, and they seem to think it's a solid next step, although no one has a clue what we should film next.

"I didn't handle this well," I tell Hayley. "I was just . . . so *pissed* at him." I wince whenever I think of Oren's face, that naïve devastation washing over him when he realized what was happening. "How is he? Have you seen him?"

"That's actually why I came over," says Hayley. "He's not great. He's standing on the roof."

"He's what?"

"He's on the roof," says Hayley. "Threatening to jump."

We run out to the west lawn, the remains of my vegetal face falling away like so much tempura. By now it's midafternoon, and the sky is becoming a bright, blank white that threatens anything. Firm gusts of wind stripe the lawn silver as the grass shudders. A bunch of the crew run out after us, and then the crowd slowly grows.

Oren is standing on the roof of the turret where his bedroom is. His window is wide open below him, and the curtains are blowing out. It looks like he climbed out his window and used a rope with a grappling hook attached to pull himself up onto the roof above. Oren is wearing a brown monk's robe with the hood up, hiding his face. He's holding a bell, which he rings once, grimly, as we all fan out in a loose Stonehenge formation around the open window.

Oren isn't that high up, and the turret, one of the smaller ones, is over a big flowerbed, so he would probably only sprain his ankle if he fell. So really, he's just standing there, looking like the cover art of a mediocre death-metal album, threatening all of us with the possibility of his own sprained ankle. Of course he could always fall the wrong way. As soon as I have that thought, I get scared. "Oren!" I yell up at him. "What are you doing?"

Head down, and shrouded, he responds only with another ring of the bell.

"Jump!" someone shouts. There's a nasty burst of laughter. I turn around and the laughter immediately stops. Some of the younger, scruffier dudes in the props department are looking down, stifling laughter. Assholes.

"Oren," says Hayley. "Come down from there. Let's talk."

Oren rings the bell once, takes a step closer to the edge. And then I just completely lose my shit. I fall to the ground and clamp my hands over my ears, desperately trying to shut out this whole experience. I press my forehead into the grass until it hurts. *"Oren, get off the goddamn roof!"* I scream into the ground.

I'm having flashbacks of Hugo. Oren is doing this on purpose. . . .

He's all that's left of my family. If I lost him because I was callous and vengeful, because of this stupid movie or this stupid studio, I don't know what I'd do. I'm furious at my dad for putting me in this position, and furious at Oren for fucking up his one chance and leaving me no choice. I pound the grass. "Oren!"

"Take it easy," says Jude, pulling me up. "This is a delicate situation."

"Do something!"

Jude walks toward the castle, looking up, shielding his eyes. "Oren, I totally get you," he says. "It's hard when you want to do something different, or *are* different, and no one understands you. Trust me, I know. I love the idea of the cauliflower movie suddenly becoming this old-fashioned werewolf thing. That's so cool. I totally saw it in my mind when you set up that amazing shot and freaked the fuck out of everyone. It was something Kubrick would have done."

Oren slowly turns his hooded head to face Jude. He's listening.

"Keep going," I whisper to Jude.

"And it was so generous of you to invite me here and put me in one of your awesome horror movies. I've already had the best day of my life. Please don't jump before I get to know you, and read more of your stuff. I think you're a genius, and one day everyone's going to know that. So don't hurt yourself, man! I've known too many people who have hurt themselves in my life, and I don't want to know another one, especially one I really admire."

We all wait and see, with bated breath, how Oren will react. He gives us an almost imperceptible nod and rings the bell again. He looks toward me.

"Please come down," I yell. "You're really scaring me now!"

"Your brother loves you," says Jude. "I know this 'cause all he did at Keenan was talk about what a cool guy you are. People are stressed right now, so decisions get made quickly and brutally. It's not worth dying over. Please, let's talk down here."

Oren starts slowly backing away from the edge. I feel such a powerful hit of relief, it's like I injected it. I turn to Jude. "Oh my God," I say. "How did you do that?"

"I've talked people off ledges before. I've helped people who were on the brink."

"Who? Who have you known who's hurt themselves?"

"People," says Jude with a shrug.

I hug him. "I love you, man. Thank you for talking my brother off the roof."

"Ooooh no," says Jude, pulling away, clapping his hands to his cheeks. "I actually didn't help at all—he's jumping."

"What?"

I turn back in horror just in time to see this brown blur drop over the roof and into the flower patch below, followed by the rustle and crunch of mashed flowers, a muffled *oof*, and a dull ring. It's the awful sound of a grown man who has lost sight of who he is, whose dreams just got dashed, jumping off a roof that isn't high enough, and landing on his own bell.

CHAPTER TWELVE

THE PSYCHEDELIC SOLDIER

OREN DEMANDS A WHEELCHAIR EVEN THOUGH HE DOESN'T REALLY need it. All those flowers broke his fall, and he's *totally fine*, but he's limping around and insists he twisted his ankle, so a wheelchair is retrieved from the props department—the very same one used by Becky Staples in *Tickle the Cripple*. Then Oren shuts himself in his room.

Jude and I have dinner in the commissary, where the general mood is tense and uncertain. People are gossiping in hushed groups about the day's events. Moldavia is already a pretty strange place, but I think today set a new precedent.

I can barely eat. I'm too upset. After dinner, I take a plate up to Oren. His door is open a crack, so I just shoulder it all the way open. "Hey, it's me." I walk inside.

Oren is lying on his bed, still in his monk's outfit, his right leg raised on a stack of pillows, a frosty-blue ice pack resting on top of his ankle. He's covered in Band-Aids from all the thorns he said "tore at his flesh like teeth from angry little devil babies." Someone finished painting his room black and he changed all the light bulbs to red, which cast rivulets of unnerving light everywhere. Hexagons and other occult symbols are painted on the black walls in glowing ultraviolet. His room is now *Satan chic.*

Oren is watching *Black Sunday*, another classic Italian horror directed by Mario Bava. He's always watching shit about witches. He eyes me as he sips a cup of tea.

"I brought you some grub," I say. "Thought you might be hungry."

He points at an empty plate on the floor: wadded-up napkins and chicken bones.

"Oh, okay. Can I sit down?"

He doesn't object, so I sit on the edge of his bed, and since he's not going to eat, and I'm really hungry all of a sudden, I start eating all the food I brought up for him.

I look around. "Why'd you paint your room black?"

"I wanted a change," he says icily. "I find darker tones soothing."

I finish eating and push the plate away. Oren ignores me, pretending to be engrossed in the movie. I can practically taste the bitterness in the air. But neither of us seems to want to be alone, or without each other. I feel sick about everything. But I'm also still kind of angry when I think about what just went down.

"After what happened to Hugo . . ."

Oren holds up his hand to stop me. "Don't even—"

"How could you do that? How could you jump off the goddamn roof like that?"

He looks at me. When I see the hurt in his eyes, I feel heartbroken.

"Everyone thinks I'm a fool," he says. "Today was the most humiliating experience of my life. I just wanted physical pain to replace the psychic pain. I wanted you to see that when you're around . . . people seem to fall from great heights."

I flinch. "That's a fucked-up thing to say."

"I have no future. You're still young. People have said yes to you. No one's ever said yes to me. You don't know what that's like." He closes his eyes, blinks back tears. "I thought you would stand up for me. You're my family. I thought finally . . . I had someone in my corner."

Oren really knows how to push every single one of my buttons.

"I have no purpose here," he continues, "or anywhere. You don't know. . . . To want to be able to do something so badly . . . but realize you . . ." He trails off, staring into the fire.

Oren wanted this so bad; but he wanted something he's not very good at. He can't even bring himself to admit it. That's what this is all about. My dad must have known. He's orchestrating this circus from beyond the grave, letting me clean up the mess he left behind. I have to be the one to tell everyone all the terrible truths.

I feel so rootless right now, connected to nothing and no one. I can't listen to Oren go on, feeling sorry for himself. I wish he would just grow up already, and see reality. But I don't know what it's been like for him here. He's lived here his whole life, dreaming one day that his vision would be Moldavia's vision.

"I know how much you wanted this," I tell him. "But Jesus, man, it's like you wanted to crash and burn out there. How can you not know what you can and can't have? There's no Laser Man. There's no animal wrangler. You can't switch genres on a whim, have a werewolf suddenly appear, and destroy the entire set the production design team spent weeks building! How could you not know that?"

His jaw clenches, and his chest heaves. He moves the ice pack and then reaches behind him to adjust the pillow under his head. The light from the TV flickers off his stoic face, protruding out of the haze of his room like a tragic Romantic bust.

He sniffles. "You enjoyed it. Firing me."

The truth is: I thought I would. But I didn't at all. No one enrages me like Oren, but no one else inspires this level of pathos and remorse in me either.

"I know I didn't protect you," he says, flatly.

I glare at him. "You mean when Dad beat the shit out of me? When he tried to drown me?"

"You think I didn't bear the brunt of most of his rages?" he says.

"He almost killed me. And you just stood there."

I clench my fists by my sides. Those bad feelings are starting to well up.

"You think I haven't been haunted about all that?" he says.

"I think you worshipped him. You were willing to let him get away with anything so you'd get what you wanted out of him." I grin cruelly at him. "Well, how did that work out for you?"

Oren's whole face crinkles, like my words are a nerve agent.

He turns his head toward the fire, the flames reflecting in his eyes. "The truth is, I relished seeing you almost drown in that sink," he says, quietly.

It's so horrible I almost laugh out loud—because I know it's true. He'd have to be carrying a hell of a lot of fury to look the other way for so long. And then take advantage of my damage so he could win what he thought he deserved.

"My loyalty?" he says, his voice rising. "My sacrifices? My obedience? My patience? *My love?* All of that meant nothing. You were always the favorite. Dad thought you were lit from within. With me, he only saw a clumsy shadow on the wall."

I put my head between my knees. "That's what this is? You were jealous of me?"

"Two decades being ignored in this family and then you came along and it was: light shining down from the heavens! *And you never even realized it.*"

I sigh into the floor. "You should have gotten out."

He sits up. "You think I haven't thought about it? I've had fantasies about traveling the world . . . maybe working as an au pair in Prussia."

I spring back up. "*Prussia?* Prussia hasn't existed since World War II."

"Okay, so somewhere else, then—"

"But how do you not know about the demise of Prussia?" I push my fists into my forehead. "How could you let yourself be isolated and ignorant for so long?"

"*Let myself?* I didn't get to escape like you did. I was too old. I didn't have that opportunity. I never went to school."

Like Hayley, Oren really did sacrifice everything to Moldavia. He never got any kind of education. How could my dad allow that? Especially since he clearly had no plans to provide some other future here for Oren.

All this happened before I was even born. I didn't know; I was too young. Oren was always just here. I accepted that like I accepted everything else about this place. It never occurred to me that Oren should be graduating from college, out in the world. It never occurred to me that everyone was living in unnatural seclusion here, where all the flowers are imported and have spiders inside. I just knew I wasn't safe here.

"I wanted to have something be my *own creation* for once," he says. "I wanted to show everyone I could make something of myself. That I'm not a joke." Oren pours himself another cup of tea from an orange kettle sitting on a hot plate by his bed. "Dad always intended for you to be next in line."

This seems like a leap. "How do you know that?"

"I always sensed it. Everyone did. Yet you were the one who left. Ironic, isn't it?"

I guess it is. I'm so exhausted all of a sudden.

"Can I offer you some tea?" he asks.

"No, thank you."

"Have some tea with your poor crippled brother." He grabs an empty mug and pours me some. I take a sip. The tea tastes like licorice and fermented raspberries. "It's my own little brew." He laughs. "I created that, at least."

We sip tea in silence.

"You're not a joke, Oren. You just have nowhere to grow here. You can't explore your potential trapped in this castle. And I don't really believe I was Dad's favorite—"

"Believe it," he says, sitting up, kicking a bunch of papers toward me. In the dark I can't make out what they are, there's so much mess on his floor. "Dad always wanted you to come back. That was his big plan all along."

I frown. "What are you talking about?"

"He was working on a sequel to *Zombie Children*."

I don't believe him. Moldavia doesn't make sequels.

Oren picks up the stack of papers. "He actually finished a rough draft," he says.

I don't believe that either. My dad never wrote a script. He would film from his treatments—individual scenes would be fleshed out later. Dialogue would get written during production, even in the middle of a scene. Sometimes that was painfully obvious.

"He worked on it for years," says Oren.

"He didn't work that way. He didn't write whole scripts. And he didn't take years either."

"This was a more personal project," says Oren. "His *most* personal project. Maybe you didn't know him as well as you thought."

"Bullshit."

He shows me the title page: *Alastair and Abigail.*

Parts of my body start to feel prickly and numb. "For real?"

Oren nods.

"Is it any good?"

"You know," says Oren, lifting himself off the bed, wincing, and packaging himself into the wheelchair, "I never could bring myself to read it."

My mouth feels swollen and dry. My dad wanted to reconcile, and I never gave him the chance.

"But you don't want to dwell on the past, right?" says Oren.

"I don't want to revisit all that painful shit, but I also have no idea what—"

"I figured you'd say that," says Oren, wheeling himself over to the fireplace. "Which is why you don't need this." He deposits the entire script into the fireplace. I watch the flames rise and consume all the pages.

I stand up, shakily. "Why did you do that?"

He cranes his neck around. "You have all these painful memories of making *Zombie Children*."

"I'd want to know what the sequel was about," I say. "We need ideas!"

"Revisiting Alastair would only dredge up more pain for you."

"But it was about me! *Alastair was always about me.*"

"Aww. And maybe Dad told you, somewhere in that script, how much he really loved you and regretted everything. Right?"

"Dammit!" I gesture uselessly into the fire.

"Don't worry," says Oren. "He wrote a treatment first. It's in his office." He puts a finger to his chin. "But I should probably burn that too."

"Don't. Touch. It."

That treatment is the last piece of my dad I'll ever have. It could offer an insight into everything I never knew about him. He may have even told me stuff through it that he never got a chance to say to my face. Suddenly, all I want is that goddamn treatment.

"Are you really sentimental?" Oren asks me, a frown slicing down his face. "Or do you just have no clue what to do now?"

I stumble into the center of the room, blocking his trajectory toward the door. "I just want to take a look at it."

"Well, I think it's a potential trigger for you, given everything you've said about being traumatized while playing Alastair."

I chop my hands through the air. "Oren—"

"So the question is: *Are you faster than me?*"

He positions his wheelchair in front of me like a Formula One racing car.

But it's like I'm looking at him through a kaleidoscope. I sway backward on my feet. "What's going on? Why am I seeing two of you?"

"Hmmm," he says, his face spraying into tiny cubes.

I look into my empty teacup. "Did you . . . *Are there mushrooms in this tea?*"

Oh, no he didn't.

"Shrooms . . . ayahuasca . . . a few other choice botanicals," he says in a low voice.

This can't be happening. But it is—everything is crawling.

"You seriously put hallucinogens in my tea!"

Oren pulls the hood over his face.

"Who are you, *the fucking Scarecrow*?"

"You only have a few days to figure out a whole new idea for a feature film, Dario! I thought I'd help provide some creative inspiration."

"I don't want to hallucinate!" I shout, groping for the door.

"Well, don't worry, then, it should only last about twelve to fifteen hours."

"Oh my God." I drop my cup on the floor and run out of the room.

I have to get to my dad's office. I have to find that treatment.

Except it feels like I'm moving through syrup. I slam my

shoulder against the wall, hard, as the hallway tilts to the side like a listing ship. "The walls are moving!" I yell. And they are. They're covered with beetles, their iridescent colors spotting the walls like tiny Christmas ornaments. "Oh God, there's going to be bugs," I say, grasping my head. "This is going to be bug themed."

I stumble into my room, hoping to stabilize, but I don't see Jude. The windows are open and the curtains are billowing out; lightning flashes rapidly, like someone fast-forwarding a thunderstorm. The room is full of bright-blue butterflies fluttering everywhere, clustered on the ceiling, flapping their wings. "Okay, that's not so bad, that's sort of pleasant," I say, but out the window, in a sudden flash of lightning, I see my dad's grave torn open—like he crawled right out of it. "Okay, I don't like that. I don't like that at all."

"What don't you like?"

I smell his cigar before I see him, sitting behind me in a tall, aristocratic armchair. He's wearing the white tuxedo he was buried in; gray spiders crawl up and down his face as he puffs on his cigar. All the butterflies have turned into spiders.

"No! Bring back the butterflies!" The room is teeming with spiders: white spotted, red striped, black, furry, all different kinds and sizes. They start dropping down on their invisible webs, shooting down my shirt, getting in my hair, into my ears.

I start dancing around the room, shaking them off. "Where did the butterflies go?"

As if in answer to my question, I get pummeled with

a wave of nausea. I bend over and throw up a torrent of peacock-colored vomit. There's weak, wounded flapping in the enormous puddle, and I realize I just puked hundreds of dead, mangled butterflies.

Oh God, this is so fucked up.

"Sit down, Dario," says my dad, indicating another armchair across from him. I topple into the chair. My dad waves the smoke away so I can see his face. He smiles at me warmly. He's wearing a gleaming golden crown. He comes around behind me and places the crown on my head. "You're king of the castle now," he says.

"Why did you do this to us?"

He sits back down in front of me. "Do what?" he asks, puffing on his cigar.

"Force me to come back here. Displace Oren, who wanted this so bad."

"Oren is useless. You've seen that for yourself! You're the only one who can lead the studio, Dario. After all, you created my favorite Moldavia character of all time."

My words get stuck in my throat. "Alastair was your favorite?"

"You gave him so much humanity! You understood my vision better than anyone else ever did. You had that dark light inside you. Only you can save Moldavia."

"I don't know how to save this stupid place."

"It's all about Alastair. You know that."

"You knew I could get sick like Mom. You're the one who first told me that! I wanted to make decisions about my own future. But you *forced me back here.*"

"You made the choice," he says, with a nonchalant shake of his head.

The bathroom sink is in front of me all of a sudden. He's slowly dragging me toward it as it fills up with water. I shove him off me. "Crawl back to your grave. Molder away like every other corpse, why don't you."

He laughs. "I'll never truly decay. Not in your mind. You hate me too much."

"You don't matter to me anymore!" I scream.

But I wonder how true that really is.

I stagger out into the hall, stretched taut like taffy. Oren is at the opposite end, sitting in his antique wheelchair with spinning brass wheels, hooded and cloaked. He comes at me, rolling as fast as a bowling ball. When he gets closer, he pulls down his hood, but there's nothing under there—just a swarm of bats.

"No bats!" I cry.

I pass by Hugo and Aida's door, which is wide open; sizzling, cryogenic blue light spills out. They're holding each other in a tormented *La Bohème*-ish way, frozen like a diorama in a museum. I hear Aida's voice echoing: *"Let the wounds heal. Don't let them sink under the surface and fester inside you. . . ."*

"I tried!"

"You broke your promise," she calls after me. "You came back!"

"I didn't really have a choice," I mutter as I run past their room, down the dark hallway, trying to get to my dad's office, but I'm dizzy and disoriented, and I wind up in the last place where I should be right now.

The Whale Wing.

The creature effects department resembles a top-secret government research facility, with dissected monster creations designed by Jasper and Barbara, lying on metal slabs. There is an array of life-size Frankenstein-type creatures leaning against the walls, their gray, rotting skin stitched loosely together, eye sockets empty, oversize hands reaching out, grasping. These are Jasper and Barbara's own versions of Frankenstein's monster. All the classic monsters used in Moldavia movies were rebooted and rethought so Moldavia wouldn't have copyright issues with Universal.

There are shelves lined with quarts of UltraSlime, tubes of food coloring, Karo syrup, adhesives, fake pus, and vials of stuff that makes you look frozen, dusty, or oily.

A gaggle of mummies stands in a corner; they've all been partially unbandaged, revealing desiccated corpses beneath, with crooked toothless grins. Winged, bat-like creatures with sharp incisors hang from the ceiling, the light shining through their spread, veiny, membranous wings.

I walk through the various rooms, noting every ashen-faced witch, every Gorgon head. I pass a wall of glass eyes in upsetting colors, another wall of mounted rotting limbs, severed from God knows what. I find a room devoted to what

I can only describe as experimental werewolves: giant lycanthropic creatures in midtransformation, in various stages of body hair growth, with various sets of supernatural, apex predator dental work.

Then the lights go out.

I sink to the floor and curl into a ball. I can hear, in the darkness, all these creatures freeing themselves from their fastenings. I hear their breathing, the stretching and creaking of malformed bodies and mutant spines. I hear their paws and claws clicking across the floors. The lights flicker on and off, serving only to show me, mockingly, that every creature has now been unleashed.

There's a low growl, a wet panting in the darkness, right next to my ear.

I scurry away into a hallway. At the other end, a coffin is being lowered down; my name is carved on the side. A shaft of light spills down, a sprinkling of soil from above, before the shoveling begins—that horrible thud of soil on wood.

"Get in," a voice says. It sounds like my mother.

I run down more hallways, up another staircase, until I finally stumble into my dad's old office, which is just as he left it: big oak desk, shelves of books, file cabinets, pictures on the walls—glossy black-and-white stills from classic Moldavia films. I run over to the file cabinets, but someone calls my name from the other end of the office suite. So I keep moving, deeper inside.

The labyrinthine office is connected to his editing suite (my dad cut his own 35 mm movies on an old Moviola, only switching to Avid fairly recently, when Franklin convinced him to go digital), which is connected to a small art studio with a drafting table (my dad designed the poster art for all his movies).

I hear water running in the bathroom, at the end of the office suite. I inch open the door. He's sitting on the edge of the bathtub, puffing on a cigar. He looks younger than he did before, like how he looked when I was a little kid. He's wearing a maroon silk smoking jacket. He holds out his arms.

"My boy!" he cries. "We're finally getting to know one another."

"You're a little late."

The cigar smoke, the color of milk spilled on asphalt, spirals around him. "So much judgment, Dario. Don't think for a second you don't have some of me inside you."

"I'll get an exorcism."

"You demonize me. I bought you that lovely train set for your eighth birthday! Why is it always the bad stuff people remember, and never the good stuff?"

"Because the bad stuff leaves the scars."

He considers that, taking another puff on his cigar.

"Plus you lit my train set on fire for the last scene of *Drink the Blood, My Darling*."

"Oh, yeah!" he says, pointing his cigar at me. "Great scene, though."

"I wanted to be in *Zombie Children* because it was the only way I could spend time with you. How could you treat me like that?"

"Look what we created together! I gave you a slice of immortality. No one will ever forget about Alastair. Hugo was right!"

"But I want them to forget. So *I* can forget."

He throws his head back and laughs at this.

"Was nothing sacred to you? Not me, not Oren, not Aida, not Hugo, none of the people who lived and worked here, who gave you everything they had?"

"Your mother was sacred to me. But she was taken from me, and then nothing was ever sacred to me again."

"But to hurt someone . . . just to make something you made better."

"Your pain was already there. You know that. I just had to strum it."

"I was just a kid!"

"It was never about you, Dario. You never understood that!"

I move toward him. "Who the hell was it about, then?"

"We serve our fans. You had the honor of moving them, of staying in their hearts and minds forever. Everything has a price."

"I'd rather have just been a normal kid. You never gave me that choice."

He cackles again, shaking his head like I'm too self-involved and small-minded to understand him. I can't stand the sound of his awful laughter anymore.

I shove him backward into the bathwater, but he instantly dissolves into a burst of foaming bubbles. I'm left staring at my own startled reflection in the water, lit by specks of moonlight from the octagonal skylight over my head.

I don't even get the chance to drown him back.

I run back into his office, open his file cabinets, and start pulling out papers. I find one of those accordion file folders, tied shut. On the front it says *Moldavia Treatments (Discarded)* written with a black Sharpie in my dad's handwriting. I grab it. Then I get hit with another wave of nausea.

Holding the folder to my chest, I lie flat on the floor. Everything's getting a little less fuzzy. The heartbeat of this experience is starting to flatline.

Still, a surgical team in green scrubs enters the office in a rush.

"Hi!" says one of the surgeons, all cheery. "Are you winning the war?"

"War?"

"You're a psychedelic soldier fighting a psychedelic war."

"I don't think I'm winning. . . ."

"Let us help," says a nurse.

They vivisect me with a scalpel while I lie there helpless, then remove tiny furry creatures from my body; they're squirming—the size and shape of gerbils. They have peel-off googly eyes, the kind that are stuck on cheap toys, and they squeak and chirp as they hop out of my bleeding, torn-open chest.

"The Goggins!" yells one of the surgeons. "Don't let the Goggins get away!"

"Are they all out?" I ask.

"Almost," says a nurse, looking down at me. But it's Oren. I can tell it's him behind the surgical mask. "It's okay to close your eyes," he says. "I wouldn't want to watch this, either."

"I don't. I don't want to watch this. . . ."

I close my eyes and enjoy the fireworks behind my eyelids; my short-circuiting synapses, ricocheting through my brain, as I start to fall asleep. My breathing shudders, and the whistling in my ears becomes a low moan.

There's no reason I can think of why I'd ever open my eyes again.

CHAPTER THIRTEEN

CREPUSCULAR DUSK

SOMEONE'S SHAKING ME.

"Huh." My face is pressed into the floor, my body twisted. My left hand is heavy and numb because I fell asleep with it bent backward under my waist. I roll over onto my back. My vision gyrates, and I see two masked faces staring down at me. One is a bloody ghoul with a meat cleaver splitting it down the middle, and the other is an evil-looking ghost doll with empty marble eyes and a stitched-up mouth.

I can't even scream. I just don't have the strength.

"It's us," one of them says.

Hayley and Jude remove their masks. "Boo!" says Jude.

"Are they all out of me?" I croak.

"Are what out?" says Hayley.

"Uh." I look around. "Never mind." I rub my eyes. "What time is it?"

"It's Friday morning," says Hayley. "Crepuscular Dusk."

"Yes!" says Jude, a little too loudly. "Everyone's running around trying on costumes and making special requests with the creature effects department for the costume ball tonight!"

I pick myself off the floor and put my throbbing head between my knees. Oren never got to the treatment. I'm still clutching the folder with sweaty hands.

"Are you okay?" says Hayley. "You ransacked your dad's office."

"Oren spiked my tea." I grab my head. "I've been tripping my ass off."

"Oh no," says Hayley. "How bad was it?"

I try to stand up but I'm still too dizzy. "Really bad. But I'm okay now."

"Let's get you out of here." Hayley nudges Jude, and they both gently lift me up under my arms and help me out of the office. When we get back to my room, I collapse into my bed. Hayley hands me a glass of water and asks me what I want to be.

"Like, when I grow up?"

"Tonight. We're all dressing up. I can ask the costume department for whatever. How about the devil? Seems like a good one for you." She frowns. "What are you doing with that folder?"

I grip it tighter but don't answer. I'm too woozy.

She looks at me, concerned. "You should eat. I'll bring something up." She turns and rushes out of the room.

I lie there for a few moments, on my back, just trying

to stabilize. Jude has his thumbs inside the waistband of his gym shorts. "Are you about to strip and start boxing? Because I don't think I can look at your dick right now."

"Nah," he says. But he was totally about to. "Are you okay?"

I slide out of bed and swing open the curtains. It's overcast out. My dad's grave is undisturbed; dried-up wreaths and dead flowers still surround it. So, yeah, that's what I wanted to see, and now I feel better. I look over at Jude. "Go punch some shit. I need some fresh air anyway."

"You sure?"

"Totally." I put on a windbreaker, head outside, and make my way across the west lawn. I'm not tired or hungry or anything. I just want to walk.

The cool air feels good on my face as my mind settles. I walk till I reach Peabody Lake, where they filmed *The Lovers of Dust and Shadow*. There's a rocky beach here, deserted, part of the Moldavia estate proper. I sit on a cold, slimy rock.

I open the folder.

There's no treatment inside for a sequel to *Zombie Children*. Oren must have burned it before I had a chance to save it.

Everything else inside the folder is in a kind of malicious order.

First, there's a stack of letters tied with baker's twine, dated about ten years ago—right after my mom was committed. In these letters, my mom talks plainly about her fears of aliens invading and harvesting Earth's resources.

Underneath this stack is a treatment my dad wrote for a 2008 Moldavia film called *Invasion of the Immortal Wasps*, where he seems to weave some of my mom's delusions into this dumbass plot involving insect larvae and malevolent aliens from a distant star. That movie did pretty well. A lot of squeezers love it. Not sure why it's in the *discarded treatments* folder.

It gets worse.

There's another stack of letters. About two years later, when she was most likely on antipsychotics, my mom wrote to my dad—in a fairly clearheaded way—begging to see me. My dad wrote her back, refusing, and reinforcing her delusions that I was a product of alien rape.

In response, she began writing back, fleshing out these delusions, inspiring a film called *The Red Ferrets* about a lonely suburban mom who gets impregnated by an alien tennis instructor. The treatment for it is in the folder as well, although this film never got made. My dad, clearly out of ideas, broken, and not knowing how to grieve for my mom, was feeding off her delusions as some twisted way of coping. I'll bet he felt this kept them connected—purposely addling her mind, exacerbating her mental turmoil.

There is a letter from Kingside Park Hospital—an administrator warning my dad to stop writing her, that he was interfering with her treatment. All his letters were returned by the hospital, which is why they're in the folder. The rest of his letters—and there are a good half dozen or so—are unopened, still in their envelopes, sent back by the hospital.

They had obviously stopped giving them to my mom.

In her final letter to my dad, dated less than a year ago, my mother writes, pretty lucidly, that she forgives my dad for "fathering a boy within the same walls as our two sons." Once again, she requests to see me. "My heart still breaks for young Dario and what I did to him. Please, Lucien!"

I was emancipated by then. My father could have forwarded the request to Keenan. My mom obviously didn't know where I was.

I don't know if my dad was punishing me or punishing my mom. Or both. My mom and I have something in common I never realized—we both incurred Lucien's wrath for the same reason. We left Moldavia. We abandoned him.

I sit on the rock clenching and unclenching my hands until I hear someone behind me. I turn around. It's Hayley, crunching through the sand and beach grass, wearing a black cashmere cardigan. She sits beside me.

Hayley was close to my dad—he meant a great deal to her. And so did my mom. Hayley knows there are plenty of dark shadows lurking behind Moldavia's walls, but I decide not to tell her what I found in the folder. Instead, I ask her something else:

"There was an old letter my mom wrote to my dad. She said she forgave him for fathering a boy within the same walls as her two sons."

Hayley looks out at the lake. "My mom lost a baby here."

I look at her. "What? When?"

"While we were shooting *Zombie Children*. So your mom

may have gotten confused about all that stuff."

"My mom was gone by then."

"She and your dad kept in touch, though."

I think about Aida sobbing, my dad whispering in her ear while we were filming that climactic scene. I never knew what that was all about.

I thought Valerie was playing the part.

I want Aida to do this.

Why?

Stop asking questions. Focus. This is the Curdling. . . .

Holy shit. My dad did the same thing to Aida that he did to me, and my mom, and probably everyone he ever worked with. He used people's pain in service to his movies, in his forever quest to spelunk out of the underground, into a wider spotlight. He was shameless.

"Why did . . . that upset . . . why would that have confused my mom?"

She shakes her head. "It was my dad's baby, if that's what you're asking me."

"It is."

"Lucien never went that far, Dario."

I snort. "I'll leave an extra rose on his grave."

"But it's possible your mother wasn't sure if he had."

Is it possible Hayley might want to protect me from the truth so much she'd lie to me? Or maybe I'm just being paranoid.

I watch a seagull dive down and glide along the water, skimming the surface in a focused, brutal way. Something's being hunted. There's always something being hunted.

"Did my dad visit my mom much at the hospital?" I ask.

"He used to. Not so much anymore. Lately, it's just been me. But your dad wasn't really well enough."

I open the file folder. I take out all the letters and papers and envelopes, and I tear everything into small pieces. Then I cast all the pieces into the lake. Hayley watches me but says nothing.

"Ancient shit between my mom and dad no one needs to read," I say quietly.

"She asks about you."

My heart skips a beat. "Oh?"

But I guess that's no surprise, given everything I just found out.

Hayley lays her head on my shoulder. "Every time I visit. She always asks me where you are."

I hug myself against a cool breeze. "I'm glad you told me."

"I'm glad I told you, too," she says, softly.

We sit for a few minutes, looking out at the lake. A couple pieces of the torn letters float back and get caught behind a rock.

When I wake from a nap I don't remember taking, I hear crickets outside. Moonlight leaks through my window.

I eat a bowl of potato-chervil soup, which was sitting on a covered silver tray by my bed. As it gets later, I hear people shouting and laughing, running down the halls. It's not midnight yet, but the costume ball has already started.

I put on this cheesy devil costume Hayley left for me—hooded, salsa-red pajamas with little horns and a tail. Jude decides he doesn't need a costume—he just puts on his Mexican wrestler outfit, mask and all, since he feels more comfortable in that.

I was never really allowed to stay up for the costume balls, so I remember only glimpses. One time I peeked inside and saw this purple-lit extravaganza: mirror balls and champagne glasses, and sequins and glitter and gilded masks sparkling in this fevered way. I tried to run inside, but someone picked me up and carried me off while the music echoed through the castle until it was only a distant thumping.

Crepuscular Dusk is really just everyone pretending Halloween comes once a month. Some people take it really seriously, spending all their downtime designing costumes, consulting with the special effects wizards upstairs; there's no formal competition, but people treat it like one, and there have been some legendary costumes.

Kat Trenton, one of Moldavia's costume designers, once wore a long coat made out of dozens of coiling, battery-powered snakes. Henry Ashe, our resident still photographer, once went as a three-headed rabid bat with three sets of glowing eyes and foaming mouths. And Samantha Childress once went as a fairy godmother in a gown made out of silverware, with a magic wand that shot real sparks.

The Karloff ballroom isn't as big as the grand ballroom in the Carpenter Wing, but it's cozier. Two sets of French doors are swung open, looking out over the east lawn. Someone turned on the spotlights buried in the grass, so the grounds are aglow with rainbow colors reflecting off the glass doors. The ballroom was designed to merge the interior of the castle with the landscaping outside. There are Tiffany lamps, red-leather booths with candy-green-apple-colored tables that match the marble floors, lots of giant ferns everywhere, and leafy vines crawling up the stone walls.

A makeshift DJ booth has been set up in the back of the ballroom. I can't tell who's at the decks, but so far I've heard at least three separate remixes of "Monster Mash," which, while maddening, matches the general theme of tonight's ball. People have gone all out as usual, but there's something inherently classical about people's costumes this time. Of course, this is the first ball since my dad died, so everyone seems to be paying tribute to his "creature of the night" B-movie legacy.

I love seeing the drooling werewolves, the mummies, the vampires, the zombies, the witches, and various different takes on Frankenstein monsters. The makeup and costuming are top-of-the-line. The mirror ball spins specks of toxic yellows and greens. People are tearing up the shimmering dance floor.

Jude and I sit at one of the leather booths; immediately a waiter appears, dressed as some sort of wraith. "What can I get you boys? Great costumes!"

"Thanks, man. Do I know you?"

"I'm Will. I'm a production designer. You're Dario!"

"I am."

"I volunteered to wait tables for the ball. Tonight's menu is all unhealthy, amazingly delicious comfort food. Buffalo wings, chicken fingers, pigs in blankets, deep-dish pizza bites, devils on horseback. Anything, really. What can I get you?"

"What are devils on horseback?" Jude asks.

Apparently those are bacon-wrapped dates filled with blue cheese, so yeah, we just order everything. Jude orders a beer. I order a dry martini, Bond style.

The music takes a soulful swerve into some Otis Redding, and I nod in appreciation. In the booth next to ours the ghosts of two mountain explorers frozen to death (complete with icicles glued onto fake beards!) canoodle over some frothy cocktails and a plate of cheese fries. Jude takes off his luchador mask and lounges back in the booth, crossing one leg over the other. He gives me a euphoric look, and instantly I know what he's going to say because he looks more chill than I've ever seen him: "I've never felt so comfortable just being me."

I laugh. "This place is the Island of Misfit Toys."

"If I hadn't met you all those years ago, I just don't know."

"What don't you know?"

"Where I'd be now. You took me here and it turned out to be the one place in the world that I belong."

Of course Jude fits in here. He wears all his freakishness on his freaky sleeves. That's why I've trusted him the most in my life—he can't get more weird or damaged, it's just not possible. There's still stuff I don't know about him, but I know how far down the slope he can slide. I know the contents of his heart.

"I got to know some of the electrician dudes," he says. "They're called juicers!"

"I know."

"They came upstairs and were boxing with me." His smile fades a little. He looks into his lap. "I'm sorry. I know you've had a rougher time. You seem kind of upset."

I wave away his concerns. "I'm okay. I'm glad you're making friends. I'm sorry I haven't been around as much." I keep getting caught up in Moldavia chaos, and I feel like I'm being a shit friend to him. "We should just have fun tonight."

The waiter returns with our drinks and steaming platters of food, and we just dig in. Jude holds up his beer. "Cheers." We clink glasses. "This place is a beautiful nightmare, man. You gonna get out there or what?" Jude looks toward the dance floor.

I look around at all the monsters and ghosts dancing around. What a weird optimism they represent: that a part of us—our souls, our decaying bodies, our vaporous imprints—could go on. It's hilarious, in a way. Is everything we do here just giving hope to people's fear of obliteration? Is that what horror really is?

Jude laughs, pointing at a booth of blood-spattered vampires eating nachos.

"Listen," I tell Jude, "Moldavia is a drug. Just know that. People can get trapped here. This place is kind of messed up."

He shrugs. "But so is life, right?"

"Yeah, but this isn't real life," I say. "Look around."

He does, and giggles at everything he sees.

"That girl loves you," he says, turning back to me.

My heart leaps into my throat. "Hayley?" I ask, stupidly.

He nods, chewing on a chicken wing.

It's weird hearing this from Jude. I've gotten pretty clear about my own feelings, but I never assumed anything on Hayley's end. It's not something you can just ask. I guess it takes someone looking in from the outside to see the truth of things.

"Stuff happens for a reason," says Jude. "Maybe there's a reason you had to come back here."

"Because of Hayley?"

He takes a swig of beer. "Yeah, but maybe you need to heal some of these wounds from your childhood . . . in order to move freely to the next level of adulthood."

I roll my eyes. "My life isn't a Freudian video game, Jude."

His expression is serious. "Not everyone gets that opportunity. I was too young, too weak, too little, and then it was too late."

I just stare at him.

"I couldn't stop him from hurting her," he says. "And he'd hurt her over and over and over again." He points at me. "I know you know what it's like to be helpless. But I wish I could go back in time. As a bigger, stronger me . . . be home on that day . . . when he hurt her so bad she was never going to be right again."

His eyes are empty and cold. I put my hand on his arm. "Jude?"

"It's okay," he whispers. "I know where he lives now."

"That's not the answer. You have to promise me . . ."

He looks at me, his lips trembling a little. "Promise you what, man? You're gonna tell me you don't understand revenge? Wanting to make shit right?"

I just press my hand down harder into his. *"You have to promise me."*

He pulls away and sits back, splaying his hands innocently.

"Do you want to tell me what happened?" I say.

He shakes his head. "Nah, man. But I see the way Hayley looks at you. I'll be lucky if someone ever looks at me like that."

"Yeah, but—"

He kicks me under the table. "Speaking of."

She materializes out of the flashing, feverish haze: a fairy princess with gold-spangled wings, her face all glittery, hair wild and teased. She has on blue-black eyeliner and blood-orange lipstick. "I'm a fallen fairy," she explains. "Literally." She hoists up her gown, licks her index finger, and tends to a bleeding knee. "I tripped in these heels."

"Are you benched for the night?" I ask her.

She looks at the dance floor. "Fuck no. I'm dancing."

We all hit the dance floor. Jude accuses Hayley of being nerd porn, and Hayley accuses Jude of being a luchador heartbreaker. I wrap my arms around Hayley's waist but

Hayley pushes me away and wraps her arms around Jude, sticking her tongue out at me. Fine, let her tease me. I kind of like that.

The dance floor parts in the middle. Oren, confined to his antique wheelchair, cuts a path through the revelers. He's dressed as Dr. Everett Von Scott from *Rocky Horror*, plaid quilt thrown over his legs, fake mustache, striped tie, spectacles and all.

"Hello, hello!" he says. "I don't want to disrupt!" he cries, doing just that. "I don't want to steal away attention!" he yells, doing just that. "I just wanted to make a brief appearance to say hello." He spots me and comes to a halt because I'm standing right there, glowering at him. "And how are you, dear brother? *How was your night?*"

I bite my lip. "Very restful. Thankfully that tea you gave me was so weak."

Oren studies my face. "Oh?"

"Just like you: Watered down. Flavorless. Ineffectual. A little bitter." I give him a tight smile. "So how was your night?"

"My knife?"

"Your *night*," I say, hitting that last consonant.

He rolls his neck around, luxuriously. "I had a wonderful night to myself. I listened to some French Freakbeat and read some illuminating poems by Anne Sexton. The pressure is off me, Dar. I've never felt so free."

"Good to hear. Hopefully you'll heal soon? The kitchen could use some help mincing vegetables."

Oren rolls over my foot *totally on purpose* as he makes his way across the floor.

"Ow!" I scream, holding up my hooved foot.

"Whoops, sorry!" He waves a hand over his shoulder as he barrels across the room, greeting various people, so everyone gets a turn to pour on the sympathy and shower him with attention while he brushes it all away, pretending he couldn't care less.

The lights come up halfway. The music is turned down.

Someone wheels in a TV on a rolling stand. Mistress Moonshadow appears on the screen, flashing a well-lipsticked leer. Everyone gathers around. She's filming her monthly web series live from the castle. These are always taped in tandem with the costume ball and streamed on Moldavia's official website, followed by an old Moldavia flick. The whole thing is done for all the fanboys, made to drum up interest in the studio and its back catalog. Moldavia fans wait with anxious anticipation for these vlogs, or any glimpse, however brief, inside the castle walls.

Mistress Moonshadow shows plenty of cleavage in her leather vamp outfit. Her cherry-red wig, streaked with silver, flows behind her as she reclines against a velvet couch, surrounded by flaming candelabras, old wooden coffins, and lots of spider webbing strung all over everything. There are old-fashioned spooky sound effects in the background: creaking doors, cackling, heavy chimes on an organ.

Jude looks like he's in a trance. "Who is that?" he says.

"Mistress Moonshadow."

"Take me to her," he says, without blinking.

"Good evening!" Mistress Moonshadow purrs. "Live from Moldavia, I am Mistress Moonshadow! The halls of Moldavia once again wail with a thousand restless spirits! It's another Crepuscular Dusk!" There's a thunderclap, and the camera zooms in and out. "A kiss for my fellow Spine Tinglers, currently dancing the night away in the ballroom of the Karloff Wing, paying their deepest respects to the creepy crawlies of the underworld and to our dear departed master visionary, Moldavia's founding father, Lucien Heyward. Scream all night, guys. Elsewhere in the castle, filming is nearly complete on our next feature, *No Chance in Hell*, which stars me. Look for it soon!"

"I think I'm in love," says Jude.

"We continue our series of underappreciated Moldavia mystery thrillers from the mid-eighties with tonight's selection, *Life Buoy!*, wherein the H.M.S. *Mayfair* returns to port with all its passengers murdered except one—Daisy Barrington, the mistress of billionaire playboy Lance Boom. Starring Spine Tingler favorites Hefford Scott, Marjorie Jaropie, myself as Muriel Marcato, and Lorenzo Mayberry as Lance, this is the film that critic Daniel Gable described as 'a smear on the very concept of logic itself as it courses through any form of reality that sanity could accept.'"

The movie plays silently as the lights go down again and the music continues.

I spot Gavin across the room wearing his signature over-size funeral suit, serving food to a table of caped sorcerers.

He does everything neatly and super-formally, as always, and when he's done, he swings the tray to his side, begins to glide off, but then spots me staring at him and stops. For a moment, we just stare at each other.

I forgive you for fathering a boy within the same walls as our two sons. . . .

And then Gavin does the strangest thing: he drops the tray on a nearby table, turns, and begins to run.

"Excuse me!" I say, shouldering my way through the crowd. "Excuse me, please!" I step on a foot or two as I push my way through the crowd, my stupid forked tail getting in everyone's way as I try to keep up with Gavin, who is *so fast.* They literally start playing "Keep On Running" by the Spencer Davis Group. "Excuse me, sorry!" I knock into a fellow demon and spill his beer. "Sorry!"

I run out of the ballroom. I see Gavin turning the corner at the end of the cavernous black-and-white, marble-floored hallway, lined with gleaming knights in armor, each of them standing in a recessed alcove, pinpointed lights from above.

People call this hallway, which connects all the main rooms of the Karloff Wing, Medieval Row. Some of these knights were used as actual costumes in one of Moldavia's biggest flops that went on to have a roaring second life on DVD and late-night cable, *Dr. Jekyll and the Knights Templar in Hawaii*, which was unreal. My favorite thing about that movie was a review by Jamie Renquist, writing for *Gore & Gristle*, in which he stated: "It is possible *Dr. Jekyll and the Knights Templar in Hawaii* was entirely written, produced, and directed by a possessed bottle of tequila."

I find Gavin in the hunting room. The room has dark wood-paneled walls, mounted deer heads (I don't think they're real; my dad loved animals), everything draped with tartan blankets. If I was a Scottish recluse who liked aged cheese, silk pajamas, and Agatha Christie, this is where I'd go to get drunk and die. I sit next to Gavin on the sofa. He's fingering an empty crystal tumbler, looking down at the floor.

"Why did you run away from me?" I ask, panting.

"I didn't want to get in trouble."

"What are you talking about?"

He shakes his leg. "I stole something. I thought you found out."

"What did you steal?"

Gavin reaches inside his jacket and removes something dark, square, and leathery. He hands it over without looking at me.

"Oh, my journal!"

"I swiped it from your closet. I figured you found out it was me. I'm sorry."

I look at the cover of my old, sad journal and laugh a little. The last thing I want to do is crack open this stupid thing. I am so done thinking about and reliving that period of my life. "Did you find the pen, by any chance?"

He shakes his head.

I hand the journal back to Gavin. "Here. Keep it safe for me."

"Are you sure?"

"Yes. But why did you take it? And why do you keep it on you? That's so weird."

"Because I wanted to know all about you."

"*Me?* Why?"

"Because you're the one everyone talks about around here. I didn't remember you from when I was little."

"You've been here that long?"

"Yes. You played Alastair, the best Moldavia character ever. I love that movie so much. You're my hero."

I'm too confused by this statement, and everything he's saying, to be disturbed that a kid loved a movie I starred in where I chowed down on a dying woman's fetus. *"I'm your hero?"*

"You're such a good actor, and you stood up to him and you left."

I never saw myself as a role model to anyone. My tormented face is what you see staring at you when there are no better horror options on whatever streaming service you're currently frustrated with.

"It sucks you weren't treated well," says Gavin. "Your dad was nice to me. He took care of me. It made me sad when I read what it was like for you growing up here."

Apparently, he read my journal like it was a novel—the kind where you start to really care about the main character. I sit back and sigh. "You know, it isn't nice to read people's journals . . . and invade people's privacy like that. It's a little stalker-y."

"I didn't know how else to get to know you. I'm just an

intern, and you're *Dario Heyward*. I'm lonely sometimes. I found this by accident. I wanted to read what it was like for you. You wrote some really good stories. And cool stuff about making *Zombie Children*."

"How old are you, Gavin?"

"I'm eleven."

I do the math in my head. He was born about a year before my mom was committed. A lot of people who came through Moldavia had major issues—financial problems, addiction problems, whatever. Maybe my dad took care of him because his mom was unable to. Of course, there's another reason my dad would feel responsible for him. . . .

"Who's your mom?"

"She worked here. But she left."

"Why did she leave?"

"She was sick," he replies. "But it's okay." He smiles, shakily, and it occurs to me I've never seen him smile before. "She's getting better; she's coming back for me."

"That's great! Who's your dad?"

He peers at his refracted reflection in the tumbler. "I didn't know him," he says in a somber tone. "He left before I was born."

I nod and wait for more. But he doesn't say anything else.

I'm not getting the whole story here, but I can't make this into an interrogation. He's just a sad, lonely kid. I pat him on the knee and stand up.

I'm glad my dad took care of Gavin. Hell, by the end of

the night some chambermaid I never saw before is probably going to crawl out of a piano bench to tell me how kind and loving my dad was to her as a child. My dad seems to have lavished affection on pretty much everyone except me. And I guess Oren. But at some point, I have to move on from feeling slighted.

I turn to Gavin. "You shouldn't feel alone here. That's never a good thing. If you ever feel that way, come find me. And we can talk it out. Yeah?"

He nods. "Yeah. Thanks."

I feel like that's a good, solid beat to stroll out of the room on, so that's what I do. I walk out of there feeling like a goddamn hero.

Maybe half the kids in this castle were actually fathered by my dad. Jesus, *maybe?* Or maybe Gavin is just a type A kleptomaniac stalker. Right now, I'd rather just not know. I'm learning sometimes that's the best choice you can make around here.

The costume ball is still in full swing. They're playing a lot of danceable, Goth-inflected post-punk. Joy Division, Siouxsie and the Banshees, Echo and the Bunnymen. It got really crowded, and the costumes more profane (hello, sexy zombie nurse). I don't see Jude or Hayley anywhere, so I settle in a corner booth by myself.

Something about talking to Gavin and seeing that old journal really opened the hornets' nest, because that buzzing begins to kick up a real fury in my ears. I sink back into the booth, drinking cocktails, as everyone comes over to say something nice to me.

That's right, I'm the *Big Kahuna* here now, and people want to kiss up, make a good impression. Some kid comes over to me to tell me how cool I am, how thrilled he is to be here. I recognize him as one of the scruffy dudes on the props crew who was laughing at Oren when he was on the roof. Maybe he was the one who told him to jump.

He's like: *It's so good to officially meet you, man. My name's Addison.*

I'm like: *Now that we've met, Addison, go pack your bags, you're out of here.*

I enjoy watching his face fall and his eyes go wide. It gives me a visceral thrill.

Addison asks if I'm serious. I say I am, I explain why, and then I tell him to get out of my face. He backs away, destroyed, vanishing into the manic crowd.

Oren is still my brother—even if he's a total disaster of a human being.

I get up, find a bloodstained hockey mask someone discarded, and put it on my face. I barrel into the center of the dance floor and start thrashing around, dancing wildly by myself, getting lost in the lights and the music and the smoke and my fellow freaks jumping all around me. I untie my hair and let it fall over my shoulders.

A lady dressed as a mermaid announces the sun is

coming up. Somehow, the entire night went by. I'm a drunken, sweaty mess. I follow the crowds staggering out of the ballroom onto the east lawn. The magenta sun is rising over the hills, breaking through the layer of morning mist hovering over the dewy grass. And all these intoxicated monsters come stumbling out of the castle, into the rising sun. It's like some circle of hell ejected us out of its sordid depths. I laugh. It's beautiful.

And so is Hayley. She's coming toward me. Her costume is still perfectly intact after this whole night. Of course it is. "Hi there," I say. "Where have you been?"

She shrugs mischievously. We watch the sunrise together for a moment.

"Where's Jude?" I say. Hayley points over to my right. Jude and Mistress Moonshadow are holding each other. Jude's head is on her shoulder, his eyes closed. They're dancing in the grass to music that isn't playing anymore, the sun fraying the outline of their bodies; they look radioactive. I wasn't expecting this. But it's Jude. I should have known it wouldn't take him long.

Hayley and I look at each other, smiling.

We sneak back to her room. We kiss, both of us leaning against her wall. Everything feels charged in a new way, because we're not totally ourselves, we're lost in our costumes. The sunrise cuts around the edges of Hayley's window shades. Dust motes float in the rosy beams, which illuminate all the framed photographs of Hugo and Aida, like they're waking from hibernation. Then it's like they're staring at me. I pull away from her. "What's up?" she says, adjusting her fairy wing.

"It's just . . ." The room is slanting and readjusting itself around me. I'm suddenly feeling how much I drank. "It's been a really long twenty-four hours."

Hayley follows my eyes to one of the photos on a bookshelf. She reaches around me and flips the frame facedown.

"How did your parents meet?" I ask her.

She smiles. "My dad went to Ireland on a documentary film crew when he was right out of college. My mom accidentally served him two pints of Guinness at a pub he went to in Limerick." She laughs to herself. "Literally, in County Limerick. It was a rough place at the time, actually. They called it Stab City."

"I thought your mom was from Dublin."

"Originally. But she was studying there. She was in art school. My dad drank both pints, and asked my mom on a date. I think that second one gave him the courage. The rest is history, I guess—although my mom finished school, I know that. I don't remember how they wound up here. They told me . . . it's funny . . ." She shakes her head. "The things you forget."

"I like that story." I take her hands. "I do think I came back here for you, Hay. There were several reasons. Obviously. But that was a big one."

She squeezes my hand and sighs. She looks a little stricken by my admission.

I brush her hands against my cheek. "You know I may not have . . . forever."

"Don't say that," she says. "You have a future to—"

"I don't know if I do."

"You do." She gives me a firm look.

I take a lock of her hair and curl it around my finger. "I think I should see my mom." Hayley opens her mouth a little, like she's about to say something, but doesn't. "I just think it's time."

"Yeah, of course," she says quietly.

"I know you loved my dad," I say, "but he wasn't . . ," I'm trying not to say too much, but I had a lot to drink tonight and my tongue is kind of loose.

"I know about the letters," she says.

I clap a hand over my eyes. I have no idea what to say to that.

"Oren found them when he was going through your dad's papers after he died," she says. "Both of us collected everything we found that we thought was relevant. I don't think either one of us knew how to bring this up to you, or if we even should."

"Oren led me to them."

Hayley rolls her eyes. "Of course he did."

We're both quiet for a moment.

"Your dad did bad things," says Hayley. "No question."

"Then why did you love him so much?"

"I hated him too at times. Don't think I didn't." Her eyes briefly flash a fire I've never seen in her before. "But I was able to look past a lot of that. I saw so much pain in him. You know this place, Dario . . . it works in perverse ways. Lucien became a father to me. I needed that."

"Or did he need that?"

"I needed that," she repeats.

I offer her a strained, wobbly smile.

"I think you should see your mom," she says, hesitating a bit. "If you're ready. Because I'll tell you something—she *really* doesn't have forever."

"What do you mean?"

She takes a breath. "Talk to your brother about all that, okay?"

I pinch my upper lip. "Okay."

She looks at one of the overturned picture frames. "After my mom died, I left Moldavia for a little bit."

This catches me by surprise. "You did?"

She folds her arms. "What? Did you think I was some sort of enchanted princess who could never leave the castle?"

"No, I—"

"I took a little trip to Ireland . . . to pay tribute to my parents. Dublin. And I toured the Irish countryside. I found the bar where my mom worked, where they met. It was cathartic for me. It was like I finally got to say good-bye to them."

I really can't picture Hayley anywhere else but here, which is ridiculous.

"It was amazing," she says. "I've always been interested in Irish literature, and medieval architecture . . . all the different kinds of architecture there."

"I'm glad you got to go."

"I met someone," she says, her eyes sharpening.

That knocks the wind out of me. "The person you were . . . FaceTiming with?"

"He's a grad student at Trinity. Law."

"He's older."

Hayley shrugs. "A little."

"And you guys have been keeping in touch and all that?"

"It's not . . ." Hayley runs her hands up and down her arms. "It's not anything. We're just friends. Obviously. He's there. I'm here."

"You care about him, though."

"I barely know him." But the conflicted dreaminess in her eyes suggests something more. And, hey, it's not like she doesn't have a right to be happy.

"So what are you going to do?" I say.

"About what? I came back here and everything was falling apart. The bookkeeping, the schedules . . . Franklin can't do it all on his own. This place needs me."

I rub my stomach. "I'm not feeling so great."

"You don't look great."

In her bathroom, I splash water on my face. I look at my strained, sallow reflection. I don't recognize the person looking back at me. It's like I've aged five years since I've been here. I think about Hayley going to Dublin, meeting some guy. Hayley wasn't going to be confined to this castle, waiting for me. I'm such a dumbass for even feeling jealous. Overcome with a sudden, maddening thirst, I drink out of the faucet, slurping, soaking my chest. I wipe my mouth with the sleeve of my costume.

When I stumble back into Hayley's room, she's still in her costume, asleep on the floor, leaning against the foot of the bed. Her wings are folded and collapsed around her, the edges ignited by the sunrise suffusing the room. She looks like a little girl again, spun back into the past.

I make my way to the door, but I'm unsteady on my feet and slam into the side of her desk, knocking over a stack of papers. Buried under countless loose script pages and old call sheets and a few more books on architecture (which make more sense now) is something I definitely wish I hadn't seen.

A GED diploma, and a bunch of college applications.

Most of the applications are dated over a year ago, and they're only half completed. Obviously, never mailed. I flip through Harvard, Yale, Stanford, Oberlin, Amherst, Princeton, NYU. The most recent one is for Trinity.

"Oh God," I whisper, cringing, as my stomach lurches.

I've been such an idiot. When I left Moldavia, I never realized I was whisking away someone else's dreams with me. Someone else's future had to be sacrificed to fill the gap I left. *And it was Hayley's.* Oren was never going anywhere. I stole that from her.

Hayley always considered a future outside these gates.

Maybe she didn't even want me to come back here, so the studio could be sold, and she could finally make her escape. I never thought about that. But she cares about this place.

It's everything to her. Otherwise, she would never have returned. She wouldn't work this hard. I have to save the studio—for her, for everyone here.

I spend a full minute just kneeling over the mess of her unsent college applications, imagining this life she never got to have, squeezing my fists into my eyes.

Then I stumble downstairs and outside.

More people are gathering on the east lawn, hesitant to bid farewell to another Crepuscular Dusk. Two sylphs in diaphanous gowns come up beside me, linking my arms. The dawn hangs over us, heavy and humid.

The sun is up now, revealing all of us for what we really are.

And it's fucking blinding.

PART III

From the review of *Zombie Children of the Harvest Sun* by Corbert A. Mince, *Ghastly Ghoul Magazine*, issue #343.

Moldavia Studios has never shied away from exploring the desecration of innocence. Witness Yolanda Deir Nasterfeld as the tortured twins of *Conjoined Connie*. In a rough-hewn, bleached-out world of human desperation, each Connie fights for control of their (shared?) soul, with one sister's morality tried, and then eventually corrupted, by the other's murderously nubile manipulations.

Then there's Griffin Carlson (Abe Laybey) in *Escape the Night*. A lonely night porter with a penchant for the harmonica, he becomes a mass murderer overnight after succumbing to the demands of his vampire crush, Vanessa Van Reese (Chelsea Jewel), and isn't above severing the head of his own stepmother with a hatchet to satisfy his lover's bloodlust. In *Hex on My Ex*, heartbroken bookworm Trish Williams (Juniper Doss) tries and fails to ward off the seductive coven of witches down the street who have a lot in store for her cheating fiancé—provided she joins their gang.

These are all weak and wounded individuals, too easily swayed by temptation, too easily pushed down that well into the dark side. And it can be argued the very notion of what innocence is, and its slow dissolution, is as much a Moldavia trademark as calla lilies and crystal skulls. But is there anything more innocent than a child? And is there anything more chilling to watch than the slow, utterly realistic erosion of a child's innocence unfolding on-screen?

Moldavia has done zombie movies aplenty: *Undead Nocturne*, *The Famishing*, *Flesh of the Loveless*, *Carol's Feast*, *Everyone Got Eaten on Christmas Eve*, *The Dead Don't Devour*, *Zombie Dawn*, *The Dead Rise on Sunday*, *Plague of the Damned*, *Day of Decay*, *Prey For Me*, *Where's Quentin?*, *Unburied*, *The Faces in the Trees* (it can be argued) and even sort of . . . if you think about it . . . *Druid Flu*.

All of these are better movies than *Zombie Children of the Harvest Sun*: the writing is stronger, the pacing is tighter, the cinematography more striking, the costumes better designed, the settings more interesting, the direction less lazy; they're more fun, less boring, and make more sense.

What all those films *don't have* is Dario Heyward.

It's no secret by now that Lucien Heyward cast his young son as the lead role in *Zombie Children*, for the first time directing one of his own children and for the first time directing a child at all. For now, let's ignore the rampant rumors of a troubled production (a crew member was killed in a fall during filmings, there have been allegations of abuse) that managed to waft outside those impenetrable castle walls. After all, who really knows what goes on in there?

Moldavia's last few efforts have been easily dismissed, and rightly; they're weak. Lucien Heyward's vision may be wavering of late, but it is extant. With *Zombie Children*, Heyward seems to have reined himself in from some of the heavy indulgences that plagued his last few films. Oddly, and maybe even subversively, the film he's given us here is as much a character study as it is a straight-up horror. The horror is coyly intertwined with the grim fate, powerful sadness, and reflective soul of a country farm boy infected by a virus that kills the brain but keeps the mouth munching.

You've seen it all before: Heyward has taken every trope out of the zombie playbook, simply shaken it all up in a blender, and poured it out again. There's a mysterious plague. People rise from the dead. People get eaten. More people die and get eaten. People run through fields. There's barely a plot at all here to hang on to. What you haven't seen before is the most genuinely harrowing performance ever put on-screen by a child, all the more so for its being completely and totally removed from the movie. It is its own entity, a separate generator, existing at once inside and out of the picture itself, daring you to forget about it.

Heyward plays Alastair, in a mostly wordless performance. As the son of grizzled, plow-pushing, unloving parents existing in a fuzzy future Dust Bowl, he's the first bitten—by a half-rotted skeletal creature with loose tenderized skin (as always, the creature work by Jasper Raines and Barbara Pandova is outstanding) hiding in a hayloft. As the Alpha Zombie infects all his classmates in a bright-red schoolhouse that could have been whisked out of an episode of *Little House on the Prairie* (the movie either wants us to think it exists out of time or never decided on a time period), it becomes kids vs. adults in a sort of zombie retelling of *Children of the Corn*. Alastair reluctantly leads his undead mates on a messy crusade to lunch on all their cold, strict, uncaring adult guardians.

In its one unique though superfluous touch, the child zombies silently worship the sun, and take some sort of solace, even supernatural power, in its warm autumn rays. While this is never satisfactorily explained, it does provide some arresting images of predatory zombie children standing in a cornfield, hypnotized and recharging, framed by the large red orb of the titular harvest sun.

While the movie itself is terrible, what will elevate it to cult status is the idea of a zombie child (not lumbering and staggering like the zombies of lore, but quick, brutal, and agile) who is all too aware of his diminishing humanity, and abhors the monster he's slowly becoming. Through the varying emotions that crisscross his face, we see a young character accepting that he will never mature; that he will never attain the wisdom of adulthood reached by even the weakest of his hapless victims. He is futureless, frozen forever in his undead adolescence. No other actor in the world could have portrayed this with such heartbreaking truth than Heyward, even as he's strangled with a mostly unintelligible narrative. As the story unravels to reveal a specious nonstarter, we begin to realize this isn't fiction: this is an accidental documentary about a father trying and failing to understand his own son.

This is certainly the most quizzical work done by Moldavia's longtime cinematographer Jip Bekker. His tight, mostly handheld close-ups through backlit dust and grit are an arty departure for the studio, and mark a sharp contrast from the Dutch-angled medium shots of Moldavia's past works. This technique is particularly effective in the Curdling—one of the goriest and most disquieting ever in a Moldavia film, but all the more frustrating because it feels common, and undeserved by the mostly lifeless eighty-six minutes that precede it.

Peeping Toms and internet fanboys may appreciate the unintentional airing of a mysteriously famous family's dirty laundry, but watching as Heyward Senior, through the lens of his frank, searching camera, attempts to bond with his son is a grisly affair. Alastair begins wasting away before our very eyes—as if we're actually witnessing Dario Heyward grow more and more disenchanted with his father after seeing him for what he really is. Is this art or entertainment? Horror or docudrama? Or is it meant to be both?

Besides the startling physical transformation of Alastair (the boy must have lost close to fifteen pounds during the course of the film, which wastes away his face and hollows out his eyes), the bruises and contusions that begin to appear on his face, arms, and neck seem all too real. If it's Moldavia's makeup crew that decided Ashcan Realism was the new game here, and moved boldly in that direction, perhaps they should remember their hammy B-movie roots. If Coreen Colchester (Ondine McPhaden) *really* looked like she was cannibalizing herself in *Meat and Greet*, would the movie have been as fun?

There's a moment when Alastair realizes he can no longer keep going; something other than sheer survival takes over his instincts: beholding the beauty of a young, still-human girl. He sees in her the innocence he's lost. By now, this young actor has plumbed the depths of his role so adroitly, even his breathing has become a staccato congested rattling of attempted inhales—the very sound and rhythm of life trying to stave off death. A single tear rolls out of his eye, down his nose, onto the face of this girl, splashing her unblemished skin in shocking slo-mo. Has he just infected her? Or is this the last drop of his humanity finally unleashing itself from his decaying core?

The moment is unforgettable, agonizing, blistering, and all too real.

But it isn't much fun to watch at all.

CHAPTER FOURTEEN

DUELERS

THE PARTY REVELERS, GATHERED ON THE EAST LAWN, BEGIN JUMPING into the stone fountain, instantly destroying all the lovingly made costumes, smearing makeup, and trying (at least for a short while longer) to fight off the coming hangovers that will grip us all in their queasy vise for the rest of the day. I lose my mask in the fray.

A variety of creatures, their transitory magic whittled away by the new morning, pile in too, displacing the water, soaking the grass. A former vampire is making a big show out of drinking the "piss" from one of the peeing angel statues while everyone laughs at him.

I get flung out by a surge after a green-faced Martian, polyester alien pants rolled up to the knees, jumps in. And then I'm on my ass in the mud and the wet, trampled grass, my devil tail torn and dragging, heavy with water. I crawl away from the morass, and when I look back I see these ravaged monsters, like pummeled dreams, splashing around in firewater: the blazing morning merging all prismatic with the gushing fountain.

I just lie there for a second, not really wanting to move.

Oren wheels himself over. He peers down at me, keeping away from the scrum. Still wearing his fake mustache, but at an off tilt, he's out of costume otherwise, wrapped in his favorite lobster kimono. "You're drunk," he says disgustedly.

"You're an imbecile. I'll be sober in a few hours."

"What a fine studio chief you'll make. Look at you: doing our father proud."

"Shut up, Oren."

He guffaws. "Still seeing things?"

"Like a vision of Dad telling me how useless you are?"

Oren's face twitches.

"That's right," I say, flipping over onto my belly, starting to cackle, "even your own hallucinogens found a way to mock you."

"I'm not the useless one," he hisses. "Dad didn't try and drown me like a litter of unwanted kittens. I practically had to convince him not to stuff you in a laundry bag and throw you into the lake."

"Funny, I remember you doing *nothing*. The only thing you do flawlessly."

I claw through the mud, trying to get to my feet so Oren's voice stops booming from *above* me.

Oren circles around me with his wheelchair, *Baby Jane* style. "Dad knew you were a waste. He'd tell me so all the—"

"And yet he left the studio to me. *Didn't he, Oren?*"

"Pity is a powerful thing."

I get myself to my knees. "As the resident sad clown, I'm sure you'd know."

Oren rolls right up to me. His face is really red now. Being called a clown gets under his skin like nothing else. "Hugo. Aida. Dad. So many people around here met their ends thinking you were nothing but a whiny, willful little succubus—"

"*Incubus*, you moron. Succubus is a female demon."

"*I know.*"

I'm starting to hear those hornets buzzing. "Bringing up Hugo *again*. Is that all you've got? You should have just killed yourself, man. But Oren . . . you even failed at that. The irony's a little much."

People are starting to gather around.

"You don't get it," he says. "You were the mistake. You were never meant to exist. Your whole life is just the result of a dirty little crime."

Now I get to my feet. "What does that mean?"

It's Oren's turn to cackle at me.

"What does that mean?"

Oren turns his wheelchair around, facing away from me. But I grab it. "How's your ankle? All better?"

"Get away from me, Dario! Go suck the life out of someone else." He looks over his shoulder at me and sneers. "Maybe it's Hayley's turn."

I race his wheelchair toward the fountain. People who

are still cavorting in there turn to see us, and they jump out in one quick, desperate jumble as I slam the wheelchair into the side of the fountain, tipping it forward. Oren goes flying out, splashing into the water. He quickly stands, soaked, tripping over himself.

"Oh, look!" I yell, pointing. "It's a miracle! He can walk!"

Everyone stares at us, jaws dropped. Oren spits and coughs. He climbs awkwardly out of the fountain, giving me a murderous look.

Then he charges me.

We slam into each other and fall to the ground. His hands close around my throat. I turn him over, my hands around his throat. He turns me back over, his hands gripping my throat again. We're literally *taking turns* strangling each other.

"You're a parasite!" he roars. "A *barn fire* has more compassion!"

"You're the King Midas of Shit! Everything you touch rots! I'm embarrassed we're related—that I have any connection to you at all!"

A couple of crewmen pull us apart.

Oren looks totally nuts with his hair all wet, spiked up.

"Go on," I say, "convince everyone here you're not a clown now."

He points at me, his sleeve dripping. "I challenge you to a duel," he says, chest puffed out, spitting on the ground.

"You challenge me to a duel?"

An embarrassed sort of exhaustion has fallen over these

proceedings, but I can't help laughing—even harder than before—a vicious laugh I cannot contain.

No one notices Oren run over and grab a musket that's buried in a blanket in his wheelchair. He points it at me. But this just makes me laugh harder. I have literally never seen a human being look more ridiculous.

Then he shoots me.

There's a popping report, a small cloud of smoke. I feel a sharp tug on my shoulder as I fly backward, landing hard on my back. At first I think: I can't believe a blank would have that much firepower. But there's a dark circle of blood spreading on my shirt. And then I realize my fuckhead brother just shot me.

Like a fallen soldier on a battle frigate, I'm carried upstairs into my chambers by ten of the ablest crewmen. I hear Oren whispering to the special effects supervisor who handles the firearms: *My God, it was a squib load!*

That's not good. That's when a piece of ammunition gets stuck in the barrel when a gun is only supposed to fire blanks. That's how Brandon Lee died making *The Crow.*

They strip my bed and lay me down, cutting away my costume with scissors, and inspect the wound. Oren kneels beside the bed, pale as death, as people fill the room.

"What were you doing with a musket?" I say weakly.

"It was a leftover prop—it was sitting in the wheel-chair. . . ."

"Don't you even know how a duel works? You plan it in

advance! You take a certain number of steps, turn, and fire. Both people have to be armed!"

"I was just so damn angry. *Is he going to be okay?*" Oren shouts at a production assistant tending to me—someone apparently with medical experience.

The wound isn't serious, despite all the blood. The musket is so old, it just lodged a piece of an iron ball into my upper shoulder. It didn't go in too deep, and it didn't take a piece of my costume into the wound. I got a recent tetanus shot, so they just have to dig out the remains of the ball with tweezers, disinfect the wound, and bandage me up. I'll survive. They just don't have anything to numb the pain with except Tylenol.

"Can we get him a dram of rum?" Oren yells.

"A dram of rum? We're not in the Napoleonic Wars!"

After my wound is dressed, Oren chases everyone out and sits on the floor, beside my bed, while I lie there aching and bandaged and tired and still bleeding. Oren seems destroyed. For a while, we don't speak.

Then: "We have to start forgiving one another," he says. "For everything."

I stare at the ceiling. "I know."

"I forgive you," says Oren.

I blink at him. "That's real big of you."

"I meant—"

"I forgive you too." I scratch at my bandages. "I can't believe you fired a weapon at me."

"I was sixty-two percent certain that gun wasn't loaded."

I look at him, my lips pursed. "Part of you must really want me dead."

He lays his head extremely awkwardly on my knee. "Dario. No. *No.*"

I think about him standing in the bathroom doorway. Poisoning me. Jumping off the roof. Shooting me. We don't bring out the best in each other, that's for sure.

"The studio will be toast if there's infighting like this," I say.

"You're right."

"I need you to be my brother, not my enemy. I need you to stop fighting me." I lay my hot palm over my eyes. "I can't believe the horrible things we say to each other."

I don't know who I am sometimes when it comes to Oren. It makes me sick.

"I know," he agrees. "You're the only one I'm ever this cruel to."

I look at him, warily. *Likewise.*

"And I can't believe how good it feels," he says.

"Because you're holding on to *so much resentment!*" I shout.

"It scared me how quickly you became callous. You have some of Dad in you."

That's something I never really considered before. Maybe he's right. And quite honestly, given what my dad was capable of, that scares the shit out of me.

"What did you mean about me being a dirty crime?"

"Nothing. I was just angry," he replies.

He moves away from the bed and begins to pace the room, his hands on his head. The shades are still drawn, and his movements cast warped, spidery shapes on the walls.

"You were just angry?" I say. "*Really?* 'Cause no one tells me shit."

"Let it go," he mutters, waving his hands around.

I sit up, wincing a little. "This is Moldavia, and you're still a Heyward. You will have a place here. That's my promise to you. You're not really a clown. Okay?"

Oren nods at me, gulping air, trying to gain control over the shock washing over him.

"You may have shot me with a musket," I say, "but you also led me to that folder with all those awful letters. That was worse in a way. And so was burning Dad's treatment. That was a terrible thing to do."

"I didn't burn any treatment," says Oren.

"What?"

"He never wrote a treatment for a sequel! You said it yourself: *We don't do sequels.* I pitched the idea myself to Dad, but he was never interested."

I really hate the pitiful expression on his face right now.

"The truth is," he says, "I always felt bad about what happened when you were a kid. You were right. I just stood there and did nothing."

I close my eyes. "Oh."

"I wanted to make it up to you. I wanted to reunite you and Dad. I wrote the script myself. Dad refused to look at it. That's what I burned."

My eyelids flutter. I exhale a stuttering stream of breath. This breaks what's left of my shattered heart. I hate to admit it, but it gave me a flicker of hope that my dad wanted me to come back, that he hadn't forgotten me, that he forgave me for leaving. But that was just another lie. I fell for it again.

Oren kneels in front of the bed and clasps his hands under his chin like he's about to launch into a Shakespearean soliloquy. "I'm sorry I led you to believe—"

I wave him off. "I don't want to hear it. Honestly. Just. Don't."

We're quiet, neither of us looking at each other. I pull at the sheets.

"I feel awful about what I said," Oren mumbles, "and shooting you—"

"And drugging me. . . ."

"How can I make it up to you?"

"I want to see Mom."

This seems to be the last thing Oren was expecting me to say. "Mom?"

"Today, if possible."

"Today?"

"Are we just going to repeat shit back at each other?"

"No," he says, jumping to his feet. "I'm just surprised. *Why?*"

I prop myself up on some pillows. "What did Hayley mean, that Mom probably doesn't have forever?"

"Who the hell has forever?" says Oren.

I roll my eyes. "What did she mean?"

"Mom has been on meds for years now. The side-effect profile is brutal." He examines his knuckles. "She's not in the best of health anymore."

I didn't know that. Because I wasn't here, because I never asked, because I was always afraid of her—because she represents everything I might become.

"Can you make this happen?" I ask him, grasping fistfuls of sheet.

"I'll see what I can do." He taps my leg. "For now, get some rest."

CHAPTER FIFTEEN

GOOD-BYE, MY PEACH

I FALL ASLEEP. A FEW HOURS LATER OREN WAKES ME, POKING A LONG umbrella in the space between my nose and my eye. I slap it away and open my eyes. Oren is wearing a mustard-yellow newsboy cap and a dark beige raincoat. He has an unlit pipe in the corner of his mouth. "It's nearly two o'clock in the afternoon," he says. "How are you feeling?"

I quickly assess this by patting the bandage; it's not throbbing as much. "I'm okay." It's dark in the room. I pull open the curtains. Rain is pattering against the window.

Gavin comes in carrying a silver tray with a croissant, soft butter, little jars of jam, and a glass of orange juice. I take the tray from him and set it on my lap; he smiles at me sympathetically and leaves the room. I bite into the croissant.

"Eat fast," says Oren, opening one side of his raincoat and checking—*for real*—a gold pocket watch on a chain. "I made this happen for you today. We need to get going."

"Mmm," I say, my mouth full of buttery croissant, as I step gingerly out of bed. I'm still wearing what's left of my rumpled, muddy, damp devil costume. Oren flips open a red embossed notebook, intently studying whatever's inside. "What are those, clues?"

"Directions to Kingside Park Hospital," he says.

"Why don't you just use Google Maps?"

Oren looks up at me with an uncomprehending expression on his face.

"Never mind."

Ten minutes later, Oren is driving us through the rain-soaked hills in his old pimento-colored Volkswagen Beetle, which I didn't know was still in existence. I'm momentarily disoriented by the fact that I have no idea how long it's been since I left the grounds of the castle. Time plays tricks on you at Moldavia. Days turn into weeks into months. I know it's still early June. Plenty of time to still call Harvard and tell them I'm postponing for the year. Or at least that's what I keep telling myself.

I'm not entirely sure why I haven't done that yet. Maybe part of me needs Harvard as some kind of insurance; so I don't get trapped at Moldavia if things continue to go sour.

I let myself be hypnotized by the squeaky sound of the windshield wipers as they whoosh the world into view for brief semicircular flashes before the dashing rain blocks it out again. Oren takes his pipe out of his mouth as he turns onto a long stretch of road, steering with one hand. The Beetle's jaundiced headlights barely pierce the low-lying fog. I watch the misty scenery passing outside. "So you stopped seeing Mom, huh?"

"Not entirely," he says, in a clipped, slightly defensive manner.

"Okay. . . ."

"As Dad got sicker, I was in more demand at the castle. Hayley was much better at these visits anyway. She has a soothing presence on Mom. I don't."

It seems as if Oren has been avoiding our mom just like I have.

"It gets frustrating," says Oren.

"Mom?"

"The anosognosia," Oren replies.

I look at him. "Sorry?"

"Mom is a paranoid schizophrenic, Dar. Mentally ill people don't always realize they're ill . . . so they stop taking their medication. Mom has a history of not complying with her medication regimen. She cheeks her pills."

I guess that would explain how she seemed to get worse so suddenly when I was a kid. "In those letters, Mom talks about a kid Dad fathered at Moldavia."

"Mom is delusional," he responds, in the impatient manner of having to repeat the same fact to someone who's tragically slow-witted.

"Well . . . what do you know about Gavin?" I keep thinking about this kid.

"The intern? He grew up at Moldavia. Remember Yolanda Deir Nasterfeld?"

"*Conjoined Connie*? Who OD'ed? You're not going to tell me she's his mom."

Oren clears his throat and nods.

"But Gavin thinks his mom is coming back for him!"

"There's no point in breaking a kid's heart," says Oren. "Franklin became Gavin's legal guardian. Gavin just doesn't know that."

I lay my hand on the window and sigh. Gavin, who's just a kid, will find out the truth eventually, after years of building up hope. No one at Moldavia has the time for inconvenient truths, it seems. Everything just gets shoved aside, hidden, relegated, shelved until later. Mean little decisions keep getting made.

"Even Hayley agreed not to tell Gavin about his mom?"

"Oh, Hayley doesn't know about all that," says Oren.

I fiddle with the glove compartment. "Who is Gavin's dad, then?"

Oren chews on his pipe. "How would I know?"

"Don't you think it's all a little suspicious?" I say.

"What's suspicious?"

"That Dad took so much interest—"

"What if Dad just wanted to do something decent and kind? You always see the worst in him—"

"And you always look the other way!"

"I do not! Dad wronged us both," says Oren, gripping the wheel. "He just hurt you faster and deeper. But the damage he did to me was slower, subtler, spread out over time. You weren't the only victim."

"I know," I say quietly. I get that I wasn't my dad's only victim. I definitely get that now. But that doesn't make any of the pain go away. It doesn't lessen anything.

Oren removes the pipe from his mouth. "We're here."

Oren pulls into a parking lot. There's a sign covered with wet leaves that says Kingside Park Hospital. I only vaguely remember coming here. It's been so long.

The sound of unsnapping seat belts and opening car doors becomes a rush inside my ears as my pulse quickens. Suddenly, I'm facing the entrance to the hospital, super-nervous and unsure. I have no idea what I'm going to say to my mother after all this time.

The rain has let up, leaving only this pesky drizzle in its aftermath. The main administration building we're facing is a converted yellow-brick mansion with a curved driveway in front. More modern-looking glass buildings are attached to this main one like careless cosmetic surgery. I can tell right away this is going to be one of those places with musty air, muted voices, every footstep audible, the sadness trapped inside the paint.

"Hold up a beat," says Oren.

I turn around. He's leaning against the car, lighting up his pipe. Tiny bursts of flame and then a question mark of smoke. Behind him, in the near distance: pine trees, wisps of fog circling around their tops. His cap shadows part of his face, making him look almost debonair. I stop walking up the cement stairs to the entrance and grip the metal railing tightly. The smell of the tobacco is making me feel sick.

"When did you start smoking a pipe?" I ask. Oren looks at the pipe like he didn't expect to see it in his hand. Then I get it. "That's not normal tobacco, is it?"

"Noooo," he says, with a little laugh. "This is my own blend."

"Do you always have to be *on something*?"

"This is my Visiting Mom blend. I have different blends for different occasions. I can't face certain situations . . . without seeing them through a slightly softer lens."

"Well, maybe you should man up a bit. See the world as it is, you know?"

"Sorry. Not for me. I can't face this world alone."

But I'm standing right here, I think.

"Would you like some?" He extends the pipe out to me.

My lips are tight. "I want to go in now."

He nods. "Dar. Mom is chronically ill. It's been a rough road. If she doesn't stop taking her medicine altogether, sometimes the meds stop working, and no one knows why. She gets better, but then she gets worse again. I just want you to be prepared."

Suddenly, I don't feel prepared at all.

"Also, because of her medication, she may not look like how you remember."

I frown. "Like how?"

Oren knocks the pipe against the heel of his burgundy-colored riding boot. He looks at the sky, adjusts his cap. "I'm glad it stopped raining. I enjoy the first thirty minutes after a long rainstorm."

"Why the first thirty?"

"The birds," he says, but there's no follow-up to that. We just walk inside.

Oren speaks quietly to a woman at a desk; we're led into a waiting area. We sit on a bench. Wood-framed windows with wired glass smudge the outside. The walls are a peeling institutional pistachio green—from a certain time. I hunch over, studying my phantom reflection in the buffed, industrial-tile floors hospitals always have.

My head is pounding even though this place is pretty quiet. I hear subdued, echoing conversations down hallways. After a few minutes, a lady dressed like a school librarian speaks quietly to Oren. We're led down a hallway, and then to an open door.

My mom is dressed in a blue sweater and loose beige slacks, her long, graying hair tied back with a black ribbon. She stands with her back to us as she touches up a portrait on an easel: a man with fiery eyes, emaciated, whiskery, wearing a hobo hat. Cans of brushes and tubes of paint are scattered around the room.

My mom is a lot heavier than the last time I saw her. But I know that's what can happen with certain meds.

"It's okay, honey, you can step inside," says Librarian Lady. It's only then I realize I was hovering in the doorway, frozen, my heart thumping.

"Hello, Mother," says Oren as we step inside. Librarian Lady closes the door softly behind us.

My mother turns around, laying the paintbrush on the

easel. Oren places a hand on her shoulder, leaning in to kiss her on the cheek. She turns her head to the side, accepting the kiss, smiling faintly. Then she sees me and claps her hands to her mouth.

"Oh my," she says, swaying on her feet. She walks over to me and kisses my cheek. She holds my face in her rough hands, but not for too long. She has paint-specked, chewed-up nails. Her deep, hazel eyes make me think about someone trapped in a cold, dark cave whose only flashlight is slowly dying.

Oren sits on a worn sofa that faces a twin bed. The blanket is rose colored. The walls are rose. The windows are open a crack, and the limp curtains, which feel like they should be blowing in a breeze that isn't here, are also a pale rose.

My eyes wander to the portraits lining the walls. They're so *specific*. A bald man with baggy eyes in a yellow sweater, holding a cup of coffee, sitting in a leather armchair; a little blonde girl sitting on a windowsill holding a toy sailboat; a wrinkled old lady with white hair, a garland of flowers around her head, standing against a door; a black man in a peacoat standing on a pier beside a stormy sea.

"You painted all of these?" I ask my mom.

"I did," she says, twisting the bottom of her sweater.

The people are motionless, static, but there's so much going on in their eyes.

"They're so vivid. Who are these people?"

My mom looks over at Oren, mouth slightly open. She folds her hands in front of her chest.

"People she knows," says Oren, vaguely.

My mom seems to find Oren's explanation acceptable. She nods and picks up a canvas from a stack of them leaning against the wall in front of the open windows. She gazes at it thoughtfully and then turns it around to face us.

It's a portrait of a boy—sixteen or seventeen, maybe. His long black hair tumbles over his shoulders. He has a goatee and coal-black eyes, fathomless, making him seem brooding Spanish Renaissance. The portrait is mostly from the neck up, but he's wearing what appears to be a white doublet. The background isn't as specified as the other portraits—it's just a solid indigo. "This one is of you," says my mother.

I peer closer. "Wearing a doublet?"

"I haven't seen you in so long."

So she took me hundreds of years into the past. I look like I'm about to board the *Santa Maria* to the New World. "It's beautiful," I tell her. But actually, it gives me the creeps. The boy looks unloved, hurt, kind of infuriated.

"What I meant was," she says, circling her hands around rapidly, "I projected my own rage onto this portrait. I missed you."

"I missed you too, Mom."

Standing in front of the windows blacks her out into a kind of silhouette. "I meant . . . I missed . . . your life, Dario. I never saw you grow up. They took you away."

I look over at Oren. He doesn't meet my gaze. He's fumbling with his stupid pocket watch, holding one side of his raincoat out, intently studying the fabric inside like he just found out there's a treasure map stitched into the lining.

I turn back to my mom. "Who took me away?"

She looks down at the floor, moving her lips, and then at the paintings, almost like she's afraid of them. "I did things. I said things. That weren't . . . who I am," she says. "Not as a mother. Not as *your* mother."

Her speech is slightly slurred. She's trying to communicate through the thin sunbeam of psychotropics that are cutting through the black clouds of her schizophrenia. But I know what she's trying to say: that she's separate from the delusions that coat her mind. That it isn't really her who threatened me, who rejected me, who abandoned me at a bus stop. That was her illness, and she's separate from it.

But I already knew that. "It's okay," I tell her. "I know."

She seems relieved by this, like she's been waiting forever to finally confess this truth to me. "How have you been, my peach?" she asks me.

It's the way she says *my peach* that kind of shreds me up inside. It's what she used to say to me—something from a totally innocent time, which I'll never get back, when I had a real mother, when I had all of her.

I hate this . . . all of a sudden . . . *I hate this so much*—that I'm here, reminded of what it was like to be loved by her, which was so pure and simple, without any judgment.

I don't recognize this woman, trapped in the undulating maze of her mixed-up mind that's forever short-circuiting, regulated by ferocious drugs. I'm only getting brief glimpses of what once was, and it sucks.

I sit next to Oren on the couch, clasping my hands tightly in my lap.

Oren looks at me and then at our mom. "Dario got into Harvard," he says.

My mom looks at me proudly, her face round and flushed. "Of course he did." She looks at Oren. "I knew this, right?" She looks back to me. "When do you leave?"

"I'm not sure yet if college is what I want," I say. "Moldavia needs me."

Both my mom and Oren seem surprised by my reply.

"Oh?" says Oren, frowning at me.

"Moldavia will hurt you again," my mom says, with a shake of her head. "It won't ever stop hurting you. Everyone who was supposed to protect you there failed."

The way she's looking at me now—she sees *me* as the tragic figure here.

She gives me a sad, wicked smile. "You were the greatest horror creation Moldavia ever claimed."

"Mother!" says Oren.

"People do terrible things when they're scared," she adds.

"What do they do?" I ask. But I know she's talking about my dad. And if he was ever scared of anything, it was losing my mom. He wanted to preserve their dying love.

"I think I was born out of fear," I whisper-laugh to Oren.

"What?" he says, leaning toward me. "I didn't hear you, sorry."

My mom moves to a midcentury desk, rummages through

it. "That sweet girl loves you," she says. Is everyone going to tell me this?

My mom opens a drawer, takes something out of it. "Close your eyes!" She folds her hands behind her back. "And stick out your hand."

I look over at Oren. He has this forced smile plastered on his face.

"Close your eyes, stick out your hand!" my mom repeats, girlishly.

I close my eyes and stick out my hand, expecting anything, and possibly something horrible, but something small and papery is placed gently in my palm. When my mom tells me to open my eyes again, I see it's the tiny cutout photo of me that used to be in her locket. "The photo of me."

"It used to be in my locket. I kept it." She places her hand against her bare throat. "I gave the locket to Hayley."

"Yes," I say, closing my fingers around the photo, but unsure what to do with it.

My mom points down at my hand. "Does Hayley still wear the locket?"

Oren and I both nod. Carefully, I pocket the photo.

"Some people are pulled into orbit with one another—a planet and its moon," she says. She moves over to her easel, tending to her art supplies, sticking brushes into coffee cans. "Sometimes love is dangerous," she says. "It can lead to unnatural things. Regret. Monstrous creations." She turns around to face to us, wiping her hands on her pants.

"Sometimes we see the worst of ourselves reflected back in our children; all our fears, our flaws, like through a backward mirror."

To her, I'm a filthy, mocking reflection of everything wrong with her. This is kind of how she always saw me—as something alien to her. That's always been part of her narrative. And I'm getting more and more of a sense why.

She walks over to us, but instead of sitting on the edge of the bed, which would have been a more natural choice, she squeezes between us on the sofa. Oren and I both move over to make room, our clothing getting caught under us. Our mother, sitting between us now, takes both our hands. We sit there like that for a minute. I wonder what we'd look like if someone took our photo. It would probably be amazing, one of those uncomfortable-looking things that get circulated online and become memes.

Kid Who Once Played a Zombie and His Weird Brother Visiting Their Mom at a Mental Hospital.

"But I had another baby," my mom says, looking off, "didn't I?"

"It's just us," says Oren, patting her on the knee. "Your two boys."

"No, there was a third," she says in a thin voice.

I lean toward her. "Did you and Dad have another kid? Did *Dad* have—"

Oren gives me a sharp, bug-eyed look, like: *Don't encourage this.*

"Those babies are bones," she says. "Corpses behind the castle walls. Poisoned wine. Masons. Bricks and mortar. Tombs and revenge."

"Mother," says Oren. "Stop that! There are no dead babies buried at Moldavia."

"Disposed of. Behind the stone walls. Dead babies in little jester costumes. No longer drunk. With bells that no longer ring."

"Let's have some tea," says Oren, clearing his throat loudly, standing up, disassembling our odd little triptych. "How does that sound?" he says, spinning around and bending forward to face our mother, hands on his hips.

"That sounds lovely," says my mom. "You can go out into the hallway, speak with one of the nurses, and they'll take care of it. I can have a little time with Dario."

"Wonderful!" says Oren, needing no further excuse to barrel out of the room.

My mom stands up and wanders over to the window. It's started raining again, and she listens to it, her head cocked to one side, her back to me. Then she turns around, rolling her eyes a little at the closed door. "He treats me like a child."

Suddenly I'm frozen, locked out of myself. It's like what happened when I was trying to say good-bye to my dad. I feel panic; terrified I'm going to miss some last chance. Then I manage to speak: "I wouldn't like that either."

She gives me a mischievous look. "So I play with him a little bit."

I laugh. "You mess with him?"

"Maybe a little." She smiles. "You should go to college, Dario. See the world. Learn new things. Meet new people."

I didn't expect her to have an opinion on my future. It's gotten a lot darker and duskier in the room, which makes all the portraits seem more alive.

"You weren't treated right by this family," my mother tells me.

I look at her and start to feel so awful I don't even know what to do.

"I'm sorry about that, my peach."

"You weren't either," I say, wanting her to stop calling me that.

She sits beside me on the couch again. As my throat lumps up, my chest heaves, and tears spill out of my eyes. My head falls onto her lap. I'm imagining her as she was, from the past. I have to. Because I wouldn't let this woman, the one here with me right now, ever touch me. She runs her fingers through my hair like she used to when I was little, her nails lightly scraping my scalp. "They had no right to take you from me."

I can never connect to her delusions. I want her like she was. If I accept another version of her, it feels like a lie because it's not my mom, it's an imposter.

"No one took me from you," I say, my voice tight and garbled, knowing she does not like her beliefs challenged. "Who do you think—"

"Oh, Christ, Dario, I was a breeder!" she says, raising her voice.

She takes my head off her lap—not roughly, but not gently either. "I was impregnated by them." She stands and paces the room. "I know what's going on," she says, "bringing you back here like this—trying to quell me into submission. I know what they're up to."

I sit up fast. "Mom . . . don't . . ."

"They keep me locked up. They medicate me to keep me docile. I'm being sequestered and silenced." She looks at one of the portraits with a tragic, knowing sigh. "I paint all the ones I know. They walk among us, disguising themselves as humans. When the siren call comes, the rest of them will rise from beneath the purple sea, transform water into blood, sand into bone, plant fiber into muscle. They'll build their bodies from earth's raw materials, form an elemental army, join with their fellow sleepers, and they'll wake the dark world up."

"Mom," I say haltingly, "those are delusions. None of that is true. Please . . . come back to me. . . . Mom, please don't go away. . . ."

She fixes me in her livid gaze like I'm part of the system oppressing her. I recognize that look in her eyes—vacant yet alert.

"There will be a war with them—thrust from a supernova with no heartbeats, no souls," she continues, "who we thought were our children, our friends, our neighbors—those cunning serpents from Cassiopeia. *Those motherfuckers.*"

"Mom," I say, calmly but firmly, wondering where Oren is

with that goddamn tea. "I'm your youngest son. You wanted to see me. So see me."

"I see you!" she cries, her arms outstretched. "But I don't know what you are."

"Yes you do, Mom."

She reaches for me, but then she retracts her hands like I'll bite them off. "Good-bye, my peach," she says, so softly I almost don't even hear her.

She looks me up and down, her face brittle, suspicious.

I press my fingers into the back of my neck. "I'm right here."

"They come every night," she says, gesturing out the window. "They nest in the trees—I see their russet eyes staring in at me. But I'm too old for them now. . . ."

"Mom, I'm sorry." All I wanted in the world was to have her back. I thought I could do it somehow—because it had been so long, and she's been on all these meds, and then she *was* back and the world seemed calm and still and soft. And then she was gone again. She appears and disappears to me, a hologram through a faulty transmission.

"I don't know you," she says, brows furrowed. And I believe her.

She grabs my portrait, and starts kicking it—harder and harder with her scuffed, dull-blue, old-lady shoes, until my Spanish Renaissance face is pulverized, the canvas shredded to bits, ruined.

I back away, reaching for the door. For some reason I see

Hayley in my mind, a little girl again, at the top of the staircase, dropping that marble down all the way—*thump thump thump*—until it reaches my open, cupped hands.

A planet and its moon . . .

Then what seems like fifty people rush into the room and grab at my mom, trying to restrain her. I become a pinball in a nightmare arcade. But there's a moment I come face-to-face with my mom, in the throes of her psychosis. She's thrashing like a fish out of water, fighting all the orderlies, who are just trying to get hold of her arms.

And I think: She's missed her own life, not just mine.

And this could be me one day—not being able to trust my own senses, not knowing who I am. Reality as I know it could reveal itself as an illness other people tell me I have. And they'll fight to flush truth through my misfiring brain, drowning in a hellish matrix of my own making. So I move forward, through all the mayhem, and kiss my mother softly on the lips. They're rough, cold, and brittle like a dead, crisping rose.

CHAPTER SIXTEEN

TWICKING HAM STATION

OREN AND I SIT IN THE CAR, IN THE HOSPITAL PARKING LOT.

"Well, that went well," says Oren, sucking on his pipe.

The engine is running; the turn signal is on for some reason, clicking away, but we haven't moved from our spot.

"I'm sorry," says Oren, turning to me. "I've never seen her like that before."

"I guess . . . I've always been a trigger. . . ,"

I may have waited too long. But, weirdly, I feel almost relieved that I went, that I saw her. There's only a small, well-lit corner of her mind that was yearning to see me. For a second she shared that part of herself with me, and we sort of forgave one another for falling out of each other's lives. I never realized how much I needed to do that until it happened. I'll never get my mom back. I always knew that, I think.

"There's always hope," says Oren. "They're making

breakthroughs . . . new medications, technological discoveries . . . optogenetics. It's just faulty wiring in the brain."

I run my hand along the seat belt. "Yeah, just."

Oren chews his lip. He seems like he wants to say something else.

"What?" I say.

"Mom was the one who asked to be hospitalized. No one ever took her away."

I look at Oren, all blurry, through tears pooling in my eyes.

"She didn't trust herself anymore," he says. "She was worried she would hurt you. She never wanted to return to Moldavia."

I frown. "Even after I left?"

Oren nods.

Jesus. All this time, my mom was protecting me—from herself. She sacrificed what was left of her freedom to do that, even when it didn't matter anymore.

"She was more comfortable here," says Oren. "She feels safer here."

I lick my lips. "You didn't want to tell me this?"

"Because," says Oren, adjusting his cap, "I figured you'd think she was running away from Dad . . . that she wanted protection from him. You'd go dark with it."

I'd go dark with it. "Would I be wrong?"

"I think she felt safer here because she was afraid of hurting someone she loved."

I look at the main hospital building—all the quaint windows, with their blinds drawn, everything picturesque and dry after the rainstorm. You'd never guess the tumult and anguish raging behind those walls.

"Just thought you should know," says Oren.

I tap the dash. "Let's get out of here."

Oren pulls out of the parking lot with a lurch and a loud screech.

I watch the trees flying against the gray sky. After a while, I frown out the window. "Where are we going? This isn't the way back."

"Well, I wanted to take you to lunch," says Oren.

"Isn't it a little late for lunch?"

"A bit. But haven't you worked up an appetite after watching Mom have a psychotic break?"

"I could eat."

"Good. I planned this ahead as a little surprise."

"Planned what?"

He turns off the highway and down a few rough unpaved roads, and then I realize where he's taking me.

Twicking Ham Station was the only place we'd ever leave the castle to go to, usually for a special occasion like my birthday. Beside a reedy marsh, in these protected wetlands, in the middle of nowhere, sits an old-fashioned train car. The honeyed light emanating from its windows is the only speck of warm color for miles.

I remember minty milkshakes with cumulus clouds of whipped cream and nuclear-red cherries on top; spears of fried pickle with red-pepper aioli; creamy shrimp salad sandwiches on toasted raisin bread; waiters in green-striped seersucker jackets twirling around trays with tall burgers, discs of onion and tomato toothpicked on top, fries piled in paper cones. White Formica tables with red chairs, each with a window of its own, facing the marsh outside. When I was a kid I always begged to go.

"And this is for you, Birthday Boy," says Aida, handing me something wrapped in light-blue paper designed with spring flowers and shooting stars. She gives me a big, wet kiss on the cheek. People are hooting. Empty fountain glasses are everywhere, the milkshakes they contained having long been sucked away, leaving a chalky residue.

There are so many purple balloons, they filter out the light and form a sort of giant berry over my head. Streamers and party hats and party whistles. It all sparkles and squeaks. I'm choking inside the revelry, hot and tired, at the point in my own party when what's been looked forward to for so long is more than halfway over, and there's only the end of it now, the slow quieting down, leaving an uncertain emptiness ahead.

I tear off the wrapping paper. The gift isn't what I expected, but I don't even know what I expected. It's a leather journal and a ballpoint pen clipped onto it with my initials engraved, royally, in gold. "So you can write down all your thoughts," says Aida. "And maybe one day you'll have your own stories to tell. The world will want to hear them. When you feel sad, just write. It will help, Dario."

"Thank you. I love it," I tell her, even though I'm unsure at

first; I wanted a video game for a console I don't even have, and probably never will. But I know Aida is giving me all she can, and I love her for that.

"Here," says Hayley, grabbing the pen. She's wearing a pointy gold party hat and a cute polka-dot dress. She writes on the cover of the journal, on the blank space where the owner's name is supposed to be handsomely inscribed, claiming all the brilliance to follow: Dario's Lame Emo Boy Journal.

"Oh, Hayley," says Aida, waving her off with both hands, but laughing a little as she goes, rejoining a cluster of drunken adults near the bar. I'm laughing too.

"Maybe you should write me something inside," I say. "Just for me."

She laughs. "Maybe I will."

"Something important . . . too important to say to my face."

There are way too many adults and way too few kids here for this to be a normal kid's birthday party. But I'm not a normal kid having a normal childhood. A magician they hired got a flat tire and never arrived, and someone ordered a birthday cake, but something went wrong and that never came either. But everyone tried, although I haven't seen my dad in hours and have no idea if he left. And he forgot to get me a present. But everyone else is here at Twicking Ham Station, fighting to bring a semblance of celebration to my tenth.

Hayley leans forward and kisses me on the cheek. "Happy birthday," she whispers in my ear. I touch a finger to my lips, *and then to my heart. I saw a guy do this in a movie and thought it was cool. Hayley puts her hands to her mouth, stifling a giggle.*

We sit there while I get a few more small gifts from kind and generous crew members as the party rages on around us, pretty much forgetting about me, and I wait till it fizzles to nothing and it's over so I can go home.

Oren swerves into the mostly deserted parking lot. When we go inside, we're shown to a booth in the back. The place is pretty much like I remembered, but it's quiet inside—the time of day when old people wearing baseball caps chow down on what could be their last Thai chicken noodle soup. Any place is different when it's quiet and too bright. Oren takes off his coat, folding it neatly beside him. Then he takes off his cap, setting it on top of his coat, and starts flipping through the forty-five-page menu, humming. He orders us some burgers and fries and milkshakes and then orders himself a slippery nipple.

"There's alcohol in that," I tell him.

"Yes, I know."

"Don't you have to drive us home?"

Ignoring the question, Oren produces a package wrapped in plain brown paper, tied with string, like a parcel from the Great Depression. He pushes it toward me. "Happy birthday. It's your birthday, isn't it?"

I gasp. *Oh my God.* It's June second. I turned eighteen today. *Today.*

"Jude!" I say, grabbing the sides of my head.

"Jude?"

"His birthday is two days before mine. I forgot. We all forgot!"

"Okay, relax, I'll get him something when we return."

"I can't believe I lost track of time like that. We were so busy moving in and—"

"Open your gift," says Oren, impatiently.

I tear off the brown paper and stare at a book, totally confused. Oren leans back against the booth looking pleased and smug. "It's the autobiography of the popular actor Colin Hanks," he says.

I blink a bunch of times. "This exists?"

"Obviously! I ordered it from Amazon dot com." He holds up two fingers. "There were only *two copies left*."

Colin Hanks is on the cover, wearing this black Henley, his head propped against his fist, a wry smile on his face. The book is titled *Wake Up, It's Me*.

Sometimes I wonder what it would be like to spend a day in Oren's world. Everything would seem possible. You could lift a finger and expect a butterfly to land on it. "What made you get this for me?"

"I just knew you'd like it," he replies. "He's an actor, you're an actor." Oren shrugs like the choice was so obvious it was painful. "You know he's the son of *Tom Hanks*? The award-winning comedic actor?"

"Yes. I know."

"Did I do well?"

I look up at him. "I can't wait to dive in. Thank you."

"Oh, good." Oren smiles broadly and then flings the car keys at me, which hit me in the face, right below my eye.

"Ow!"

"Also, you can have my car," he says nonchalantly.

"Your *car*?"

At that moment, the waiter places Oren's drink in front of him.

"My slippery nipple!" he says way, *way* too loudly.

The cocktail looks vile, layered with different shades of brown cream. I feel sick just looking at it. He lifts the glass. "There's sambuca in this!" he says excitedly. "Cheers! Do you have a driver's license, Dar?"

"Yeah." I made sure I got mine while I was still at Keenan.

"I don't use the Bug much. I thought maybe . . ."

"That's very generous of you, Oren." And it is. I'm a little in shock.

"Well, today wasn't the best eighteenth birthday a man can have, was it?"

Nope. No it wasn't. I got shot and watched my mom go psycho.

"Aaaaaand here we are!" says the waiter, setting down our frothy strawberry shakes. Oren remembered I prefer strawberry; that's something I don't tell everyone. "Your burgers will be out momentarily!" The waiter skitters off in a blur of striped green.

"Mmmmmm!" says Oren, switching from his gross girly drink to the milkshake and then back again in one of the most nauseating maneuvers I've ever seen. He dangles the maraschino cherry over his mouth, puckering his lips, making more *mmm* noises.

"Oren."

He bites the cherry off the stem and flings the stem over his shoulder, coolly, like he's in some milkshake–themed Western.

I fold my hands together on the table. "Oren, Mom said some disturbing things about—"

"Not again!" He throws his head back, exasperated. *"There are no dead babies buried inside the walls!"* he bellows. At least three old people turn around; a few spoons clatter against bowls.

"Keep your voice down. Jesus. I know that. I know that!"

"Mom is mentally ill. And she likes Poe."

"What?"

"You know, *Edgar Allan?*" he says. "I used to go there and read to her. I think she was absorbing 'The Cask of Amontillado' into her delusions. Next time I'll read Harry Potter and we'll have more fun with her. Maybe she'll think she's the sorting hat."

"God, Oren—"

He throws out his hands. "It's okay to jest sometimes! Things are so horrifying, what else is there to do but jest? So we jest, we can only *jest*—"

"Stop saying that word!"

He sips his brown drink. "Mom suffers from command hallucinations. That's what they call it, the voices she hears.

They're not in her head. It sounds like someone's literally right behind her . . . telling her things."

I think of the hornets buzzing when things get bad. My palms get sweaty.

Oren holds the napkin in front of his mouth and talks in a deep gravelly voice: "The aliens are everywhere, Dario."

"Stop that."

"You're an alien child. The government knows . . ."

"Seriously, stop."

Oren folds the napkin on his lap. "Stop what?"

"Oren."

"They know so little about the mind, it's almost absurd!" he says. "And the newer antipsychotics aren't much more effective than the old ones. And the side effects . . ." He throws up his hands, shaking his head.

"Aaaaaand here are your burgers and fries!" says the waiter.

"You look so upset!" says Oren.

"Of course I'm upset!"

"Would you like me to give you a scalp massage?" he says as our food is served in what feels like an hours-long process of plopping down plates and side plates and arranging it all so everything fits on the table. When the waiter finally leaves, Oren sticks a fry in his mouth, leans over the table, and starts vigorously rubbing the top of my head. "There we go. . . ."

"Oren . . . get the fuck off me."

"Your hair is so soft! It feels like olive oil! Is that pomade? So delicate and fine."

"Sit back down."

"Sorry!" says Oren, flopping back down. He glares at his side salad and then pointedly removes all the cauliflowers, setting them on a cocktail napkin, which he brusquely pushes away.

We eat in silence for a few minutes. The food isn't as good as it looks. The burger is dry. The milkshake is too syrupy. The fries are soggy. Something's lost its luster here, or it's just my mood, or I'm just remembering this place wrong. What we thought was so amazing when we were kids doesn't always hold the same appeal later, I guess.

"You must worry too, right? Or you did at some point?" I ask.

"Worry about what?" says Oren, chomping down on his burger.

"Becoming . . . like her."

"I've thought about it before," he says, nodding. "Mental illness is genetic, clustered in families. Our grandmother was crackers, but"—he shoots out his hands—"we can only live our lives. I'm still here . . . you're here. I was always too busy with the studio to really stop and wait for it to hit me. I was lucky that way."

I dunk a fry in some ketchup, in one of those paper cups that are never big enough. "It was disturbing how much of what Mom said sounded like it was straight from *Invasion of the Immortal Wasps*."

"Not my favorite film," says Oren. He holds up his empty glass and bangs his spoon against it, signaling to the waiter for another slippery nipple. "Mom saw every Moldavia movie multiple times. I'm sure she retained a lot of those wild stories, stored them away somewhere in her unraveling subconscious. Just like she did with Poe."

"No, Oren. Dad co-opted her illness."

Oren frowns. "What do you mean?"

"Dad was a master collage artist! He took other people's pain, tragedies, and illnesses, and used them for his films. You read those letters!"

"I thought Dad was just trying to communicate with Mom in her own language."

I shake my head. "When are you going to stop defending him?"

"How do you know that's not what he was doing?" says Oren.

"You collected that stuff, with the *Immortal Wasps* treatment, and put it all in the folder together!"

Or maybe some of that was Hayley. Maybe she was the one creating that sinister little narrative through the letters, and my dad's film treatments, so I'd know the truth one day. Oren will do anything to preserve this romantic image he has of our family and how things were.

"Why do you think Mom said I was Moldavia's greatest horror creation?"

"Mom is delusional," says Oren.

"Didn't it ever occur to you that she rejected me, saw me as something alien to her, because I was? Because she didn't remember making me in the first place?"

"We don't know that," says Oren. "We'll never know what happened."

I lean across the table. "You said it yourself. You said I was a *dirty little crime.*"

Oren looks aghast. "I didn't mean that literally! That's such a horrible idea. I was so angry, and I just . . ."

"You put Dad on this pedestal—"

"He's dead," Oren mutters, choking back emotion, needlessly rearranging everything on the table. "Let me have that, let me keep him there. . . ."

"But Mom is right," I tell him. "I am Moldavia's greatest horror creation."

"Please," he says quietly, into his plate.

"Dad knew what he was doing; he was fascinated by people he thought were broken in some way. Eventually, he knew Mom would be too incapacitated to look after me. And he knew mental illness was genetic. So he'd have me as a fresh well of inspiration. I'd either go crazy like her or be traumatized by losing her. Either way he'd win."

It would explain why he pushed me so hard as Alastair. Right to the brink . . .

"You're saying *you were bred to go mad?*" Oren exclaims. "That's nuts!"

See what he did there?

I don't totally know what I'm saying anymore. Part of it is shit I've always feared the most, and part of it is frustration at Oren's ignorance and denial about Moldavia, and the truth about our dad.

311

"Did you know about Aida?" I say. "That she lost a baby?"

"No," says Oren, startled, dropping a fry on his plate. "When?"

"Aaaaaand here we are!" says the waiter, serving Oren his second slippery nipple.

Oren takes a long, pensive sip; a deep ruddiness spreads across his face, blotching his cheeks. "Aida lost a baby?" he asks, quietly.

"Yeah."

A vein on his forehead becomes visible, a strand of cooked spaghetti rising to the top of a boiling pot. "That's horrible. I didn't know. Hayley told you that?"

"That's why Aida played that part in *Zombie Children*, and that's why Dad cast me as Alastair. Aida lost a baby. I had recently lost my mom. The movie is about a kid who's losing a grip on his own humanity, lost in a depraved wasteland. Think about it."

He does. I watch the realization spreading across his face. He'll never believe all of it—I can't even bring myself to fully believe all of it; these are just dark little theories, but I think some level of truth is finally breaking through to him. I feel like I can't ever truly be close to Oren until it does.

"Maybe I got overlooked because I wasn't broken enough for Dad." He laughs. "I wanted to please him too badly. I fell into line too easily. I know you think I just blindly worshipped him. It wasn't that simple."

Oren lost out too. But he did blindly worship our dad.

"I was waiting for my chance," he says. "But now I know

he never took me seriously. I should have taken charge of my life. He taught me nothing on purpose. And I let it happen. He didn't want anyone else to dilute his vision. He was too arrogant to consider a successor, which is why he made a joke out of his will. He'd rather have Moldavia dissolved. It was all about his legacy, Dario. I was always going to be his assistant, not his *apprentice*." He downs the rest of his drink.

He's right. If Oren remained ignorant, my dad could keep making movies until the bitter end. If no one could replicate his process, that meant cinema history would regard him as a true auteur, because you can't replicate genius.

I think about babies buried in walls and spiders hiding in flowers and the castle digesting us from within like a carnivorous plant.

Outside, as yet another storm descends on the marsh, it's like I'm looking at some blank lunar plane, bereft of life, filled with moon rocks and curling space mist. Then it becomes a clean sheet of ice, a rink glowing in the murk, and I see Hayley and me skating by, holding hands, keeping our bodies close against the cold. But there's something else, something bigger. It's not just about us. . . .

We see the worst of ourselves in our children. . . .

"They have a child," I say.

Oren looks around. "Who? Who does?"

"Alastair and Abigail. In the sequel."

He looks astonished. "You want to make the sequel?"

"I think a sequel was a really good idea. What if Alastair

and Abigail have a child? Let's say . . . he turned her into what he is."

But there's something familiar about this idea. I've heard it somewhere before.

"How would they reproduce?" Oren asks.

"There's no logic in Moldavia films. Why start now?"

"Huh." He thinks it over, wiping a milky mustache off his upper lip. I wonder how much of Oren's whole deal is an act, a shtick to mask all his insecurities. "You and Hayley . . . reprising your roles . . . ," he says, his eyes wide and smoky as he looks at the roiling, greenish-gray sky outside the window. "You two. It was always obvious."

"What was?"

"She's your One. That's why that scene worked so well in the movie."

"My One?"

"One True Love. I think we only get one. Dad had one."

And he lost her. My mom knows Hayley and I love each other. That's why she told me to leave Moldavia. That's what she meant when she said Moldavia would keep hurting me. That's what she thinks is so dangerous. True love caused our mom and dad so much pain in the end. And also, she probably wants the bloodline to stop.

I reach into my pocket and take out the tiny photo of me at two years old that my mom used to keep in her locket. The glue on the back is all hard and yellowed.

"Ah, look," says Oren, gesturing out the window. The

rainstorm has made the wetlands seethe in this shimmering, electric way. "How cinematic." He peers out the window, framing it with his fingers.

"What about your One Love?" I ask him.

He smiles in a way that makes me think he's more deeply alone than I ever knew. I never saw that in him before. Or didn't want to. He's an incredibly weird man. But I don't need to be friends with him. I just need to accept him as my brother. And it matters to me that he's happy, and feels like he belongs.

Oren orders another slippery nipple, then another, and then another after that, slamming them down. Clearly, I'll be driving us back to Moldavia. That was probably the plan all along. "Look, we can do this," I tell him, fighting against accepting him as a tragic figure; today was just too much tragedy.

His eyelids look all droopy. "Do what?"

"Save the studio. Make this film. Do it together."

Oren gives me a sloppy thumbs-up, quickly finishing his last slippery nipple. I've lost track of how many he's had, but enough where he sort of muscularly collapses against the booth, eyes rolled back in his head, like a jellyfish that's lost its way. "You look so much like Mom." It seems almost like he's talking in his sleep, his mouth barely moving. "I bet no one ever told you that before. . . ."

No. But they probably thought it.

I help Oren dig out his wallet and pay, and then I lead

us out into torrential rain (Oren left his umbrella in the car), supporting all his weight, his arm wrapped around my shoulder, as we stumble through the mud.

"Don't worry about the passshtt anymore," he slurs. "Just consshentrate on yerrr future. Leading the ssshtudio to sss-holvenssshy . . . going to collegesh . . . if that'sssh what chew desshhide ta do. . . ."

Oren lies sprawled across the back seat while I get the Bug started. I peel out of the lot, down a bunch of slick, empty roads, and onto the highway, trying to remember the way we came. Then I'm driving on a highway for only the second time in my life.

Cars, wet stains of angry light, whoosh by like white blood cells off to attack an infection. After a few minutes, my headlights reflect off a green road sign that says: Moldavia Studios, 14 miles.

We both laugh. Before he passes out, Oren says that sign is meant for delivery trucks because we're so secluded; but squeezers also use it to guide them so they can stand outside the gates and leave calla lilies and cards and memorabilia while wondering endlessly what goes on inside, craning their necks for a peek they'll never get.

Once, many years ago, there was an interloper, an obsessed squeezer who scaled the walls and walked the grounds in abject disbelief he got that far before being tackled by a carpenter. My dad actually stopped what he was doing, ran out there, and shook the guy's hand. He told the guy, "Thank you for watching our films," and autographed a poster or some bullshit the guy had on him. Then my dad had him arrested, built the wall even higher, and strung barbed wire across the top like a North Korean prison.

It's true what they say: never meet your heroes.

CHAPTER SEVENTEEN

OTHER PEOPLE'S DREAMS

THERE'S NO GPS IN THE CAR, AND I DON'T WANT TO LOOK AT MY PHONE while I'm driving, but I have a really good sense of direction—*thank God*—so I manage to get us home okay. The guard at the gatehouse opens the gates; some baffled production designer, measuring tape in hand, lets me inside after I ring the service bell, wet and shivering. I leave Oren curled up in the back seat of my new car, parked in the driveway in front of the castle. According to the grandfather clock in the hall of the Chaney Wing, it's only eight p.m.

Jude isn't in our room. I stand there in the dim light, about to rip off my sopping-wet clothes, when I hear something behind me and turn around. Gavin is standing there. I didn't hear him come in, of course, but I've become used to him just spawning from out of nowhere, like a slain video game character restarting from the last checkpoint. He holds a steaming cup of tea on a tray.

"Oh, hey. You can set that down on the bedside table."

He does. Then he just stands there, swimming in his too-large suit, hands clasped behind his back. "There are warm, freshly laundered clothes in your closet."

"Thanks, Gavin. Listen, I need to tell you something."

"Yes?"

"There are too many secrets in this place . . . don't you think?" He looks at me as if he wants to answer this question in the way that will please me the most but isn't sure what that answer is. "It's about your mom."

"I was actually thinking about her today," he says.

This catches me off guard. "What were you thinking?"

He smiles, which always looks unnatural on him, like some app drew it on his face. "I was thinking about her coming back. We look at each other and see how we've changed, tell each other everything that's happened, and we realize nothing's changed that much. We're like how we were before, in a way, and it's all going to be the same, it's all going to be okay. . . ." His smile fades a little at the edges. "I know it's stupid."

"It's not stupid, man."

"It's not just today. I have this thought a lot. Like, every day."

God. This kid still feels hope. I know all too well what it's like to feel hopeless, especially at that age. I can't take that away from him. "I just wanted to tell you . . . it's okay to miss people. It's okay to want them back, the way they once were," I say.

Even though that's not always possible. I finish the rest of the thought in my head.

"Thank you for saying that," he says after a small pause.

I suddenly get this idea, and as soon as I get it, I realize it's risky, because I'm being inspired by shit my mom rambled today, which is already putting me down a path well trodden by my dad. "I have this idea for a sequel to *Zombie Children*," I blurt out. "Alastair and Abigail have a son. Would you want to act in the movie?"

He hesitates. "To play their son?"

"Right."

At first, Gavin looks intrigued but then apprehensive. After another small pause, while he mulls it over, eyes on his shoes (he's clearly read my journal entries about making *Zombie Children* very closely), he appears touched that I asked him.

"That would be really awesome," he says. "Thanks for trusting me to do it." He smiles at me. "You remembered your own idea."

"What do you mean?"

Gavin takes my journal out of his jacket pocket.

I run a finger across my eyebrow. "Oh, you, uh, still keep it on you, okay. . . ."

He flips through it a little too quickly (like he's memorized it) and stops on a specific page. He licks his thumb, folds the corner of the page down, and hands it to me.

"Let me know if there's anything else you need," he says.

"Thanks. By the way, have you seen Jude?"

"I think . . . he's with Mistress Moonshadow." Gavin walks to the door and stops momentarily, like there's something else he wants to say to me, but then he walks out, head down, closing the door softly behind him.

I change into warm clothes, sip tea, and sit on the edge of my bed with the journal on my lap. I read the section of the journal Gavin marked for me. I laugh a little at my twelve-year-old handwriting.

Zombies are dumb. Why are they even hungry? The body it's trying to feed is already dead! Has anyone ever realized that? I hate this I hate making this movie I hate my dad. It's not fun AT ALL. He's hitting me all the time and not letting me sleep or eat.

I think Alastair is lonely. He just wants to find someone to love him before he decays or whatever. No one ever loved him.

I told my dad it would be cool if someone like a girl sees something good in him so Alastair doesn't eat her, but transforms her into a zombie too and they fall in love that way. I wrote this out as a story but my dad just crumpled it up and said I should concentrate on playing Alastair. I really like my idea, though!

Maybe Alastair and this girl can have a kid themselves except this kid is born NORMAL! A normal kid with zombie parents who try to take care of this kid but have to resist their zombie impulses and not eat him. They have to abandon him so he will survive and start a new race.

I close the journal. So that's where I heard this idea before.

I commend my younger self for writing down some pretty cool ideas. Apparently, I wasn't the only one who thought they were pretty cool. My dad stole part of this idea for the ending to *Zombie Children*. And I never even realized it. I forgot I wrote any of this.

Missing Jude, I walk down the hall. Mistress Moonshadow's door is ajar. I walk inside, past all the mannequins, the billowing fabric, toward her bedroom. Deep inside there's a baroque bed engraved with skulls and vines, violet sheets, and a mahogany headboard in the shape of a giant spider. The headboard matches a bronze, spider-shaped chandelier hanging over her bed.

Jude and Mistress Moonshadow are in bed together, purple blanket thrown aside, sheets all rumpled. For a moment it looks like Jude is actually *suckling* from her, but then I realize he's asleep, his head against her breast. Mistress Moonshadow calmly pulls up the sheet, covering herself. "He's sleeping," she says quietly, stroking Jude's hair.

"Am not," says Jude, muffled, into her chest.

"I'm sorry." I don't know exactly why I did this, needed to see them like this. But then I sort of get it. I'm jealous. I'm scared of losing Jude.

Jude lifts up his head, his hair all crazy. They've probably been in bed all day long. He kicks the sheet aside. "Get in," he says, sticking his tongue out.

For a second, I almost do. But then I laugh. "I'm sorry we forgot your birthday," I say. "Happy eighteenth, man."

"Happy eighteenth to you too," he says, giving me the gift of his beautifully cockeyed grin. You know that moment when you get reminded of how much you truly care about a person? It happened with Hayley. It happened, in its own way today, with my mom, and then even with Oren. Now Jude. Maybe that's an unexpected gift of Moldavia. The flowers blooming brightly before the spiders crawl out.

I turn and quickly walk out of the room, embarrassed.

Jude represents everything I know, but I'm not ready to accept him as someone from my past just yet, although I can practically see the castle consuming him. I know people move away from each other over time, but he's not someone I want to outgrow.

My mind is whirring with ideas for a *Zombie Children* sequel. I'm pretty much dead set on making this work, I need more to go on, though—more inspiration, more material.

So I make my way to my father's office suite. I want to see if there are any other notes my dad may have cribbed from me about Alastair and Abigail, anything left over from his treatment for *Zombie Children.* I don't find anything like that. But in a drawer I find something else.

All the stories I wrote out and gave to my dad.

They've been uncrumpled and flattened as if ironed, in a neat pile, tied with the same baker's twine he used for my mom's letters. He saved every single one.

I either missed this last time because I was tripping so

hard, or someone purposefully left this here for me to find. It could have been anyone: Oren, Hayley, Franklin, even Gavin. Underneath the pile of pages is a reel of film.

I corral one of the camera ops to set up the film for me on a 35 mm projector. There's a screening room—forty upholstered seats, medium-size screen, old-fashioned concession stand, popcorn maker—in the Carpenter Wing.

Alone in the theater, I watch a bunch of outtakes from *The Possession of Prodigal Peter* on damaged film stock. This was the movie they made right after I left, ostensibly my dad's reaction to me leaving.

He's working with this very young actor (probably the poor kid of a long-departed crew member), directing him (and the actress playing his mom) during the big demonic possession scene, set in the kid's bedroom.

My dad is outwardly impatient with the kid, doing that thing where he *pushes and pushes* until he finally gets that exhausted despair that always seems to please him to no end—but he's not brutal with this kid like he was with me. Someone calls *cut*, the actors move out of frame, and then, only for a minute, my dad walks into frame while camera and sound are still running, fastidiously adjusting the blanket on the kid's bed.

Someone off camera says something to him that I can't hear.

Lucien Heyward turns toward the camera. "No. He's no Dario. *No one is.*"

Of course I don't need any more materials to create a

sequel and make it work. Everything I need is already a part of me, a part of my life and my experience being a kid at Moldavia.

I watch my dad sit on the edge of the bed. And then he just implodes.

He starts shaking, holding his head in his hands to cover his face. I watch him become, before my eyes, vulnerable: a grief-stricken man, racked by guilt.

The film crackles and burps, the colors bubble into a rusty sludge, and then I'm just staring at a blank white screen while the projector clicks, whirs, and flaps.

When I get back to our room, Jude is waiting for me, wearing black gym shorts and a red hoodie. He's sitting on the floor next to a big white birthday cake with candles that have been burning for a while.

I sit across from him. We look like those two kids at the end of *Sixteen Candles*. Without speaking, we blow out all the candles. Jude produces two plastic forks from his pocket. We each take a couple bites of cake. It's real good—not too sweet.

I don't ask where he got the cake.

All of Jude's stuff is gone from the room—packed up in his trunk. At first, I think he's leaving Moldavia, but then I know.

"I'm going to move in with Elena," he says.

In all the years that I've known him, Jude has never spent the night elsewhere. No matter whom he was sleeping with, or what he was doing, or how late he was out doing it, I'd always hear him snoring above me again before the sun came up.

"Also, I'm joining the electrical crew," he says. "It seems like I fit in with those guys."

I nod. "I'm glad you're finding your place here."

I also feel ambivalent about it. I'm responsible for Jude's future. I brought him here. But I warned him: people get trapped. Maybe he wants to be trapped. Maybe one day he'll leave. We're grown-ups now. We have to make our own decisions about this stuff. "What about the Seychelles?" I ask him. "Finding the coco de mer?"

He snickers. "There'll be time for that."

"Your stepfather?"

He gives me a razor-sharp stare. "I'm here now, so . . ."

I nod, accepting that. "Your mother?"

"Dude, she's long dead. I got no one else out there." Jude studies the cake. "Dario, you're the only family I ever had. I'll never have a brother. *You're my brother.* And you gave me an even bigger family here. And 'cause of you, I found someone."

"'Cause of me?"

"'*Cause of you.* So I want your blessing about Elena."

I laugh. "You don't need that. You're the heartbreaker, man! I don't want to see anyone get hurt. It's been less than twenty-four hours. You do realize that, right?"

Jude smiles and lays his strong, heavy palm on my shoulder. He knows.

I smear some frosting on his nose. He doesn't wipe it away.

I'm Jude! I'm a not-so-mean, not-very-lean fighting machine! he told me, smacking his gloves together, when we first met. I remember thinking: the world can't be that terrible if a total stranger is able to give me a smile that generous and wide.

"Do you want me to sit with you for a while?" he says, rubbing his stomach. "I can't eat any more of this cake."

"No, it's okay. I have work to do."

He taps his fingertip against one of the dead candles. "It's cool. Go do it."

But we sit and stare at the half-eaten cake for a few more minutes.

I go into Oren's empty room. The demonic occult symbols are still glowing in ultraviolet on his black walls. I sit down at his typewriter. I have vague ideas and half-formed images swimming in my head about Alastair and Abigail that take place years after *Zombie Children* left off. I have to take these loose abstract strands of thought and coalesce all of them into something filmable.

Zombie Children of the Harvest Sun failed because it wasn't really about anything. I mean, I guess it *was*, but it was mostly about my dad being indulgent, lost in his head, and trying to deal with me. And what audience would want to sit through that shit? There was no plot. But if Alastair and Abigail are really in love and have to find some way to survive, *especially if, somehow, they have a kid to take care of*, well, that's a pretty compelling story.

I wind up writing an entire treatment in one sitting. I type until my fingers ache. Then I gather all the pages and take them back to my room.

I enjoy a long, hot shower. The saturated colors from the caged shower light make me want to close my eyes and dream. As the light bathes the room in sci-fi acid green, I see a distorted shadow slowly approaching the glass door of the shower. I quickly slide open the door, flooding the bathroom.

Hayley stands there, wearing a pink nightgown. She looks surprised and frazzled, like she expected to see some-one else in the shower. She's holding my typewritten pages in her hand. I grab a towel and wrap it around my waist.

"Oh my God," she says, averting her eyes, clearly embarrassed. "I have no idea why I just walked in here like that! Why did I think that would be okay?"

I hold up my hand. "You're good."

"I heard you got shot! I was still asleep when it happened, and then you weren't here, and then you were, but I couldn't find you."

"It's okay, I'm okay."

"Where were you?" she asks me, her eyes narrowed into slits.

"Nowhere."

"Well, I came in to see if you were up, and saw these

pages on your bed." She opens her mouth to say something else, swipes some steam away, but then quickly leaves the bathroom, pressing a hand to the side of her head as she goes.

I go after her, almost slipping on the wet floor. "Wait!"

She turns around. "You have some good ideas here."

"Really? That's, uh, good." I am, in fact, pretty relieved to hear that. "I didn't expect anyone to sneak into my room in the middle of the night and read them, so . . ."

"Well, Dar, I didn't expect anyone to snoop around my desk and rifle through my unsent college applications, so . . ."

Oh snap. Fair enough.

She's looking at the bandage on my chest. I move toward her. Very lightly, she puts her finger on the wound. "Does it hurt?"

I shake my head. "All this time I thought you took my place here. But that's not what happened, is it? I took your place out there."

"That's not what happened," she says. "That's just what's in your head."

"Then why didn't you go to college?"

"Because those plans weren't practical. Yes, sure, sometimes I imagine leaving, living another life. But those moments always come when I'm at my weakest."

"You did more than imagine it, though—"

"Franklin and I are the glue that holds this place together. This is my home, and I chose it. I chose to be here."

"Or did it choose you?"

"Of course. That too." Hayley plops into the leather armchair, crossing her legs, paging through my outline. "But it's not all about me. Just like you coming back here wasn't all about you. I have to think about everyone else. I have my own legacy here now."

"I didn't mean to diminish your accomplishments." Knowing Hayley and Moldavia, I'm sure they're profound. Oren needs a lot of guidance, and my dad was on a steep decline for a while. Yet Hayley still managed to be there for my dad as he got worse, and to be there for my mom, who never got better.

She leans her cheek against her fist, her eyes flitting around the room. "Dario, we live in *a castle*, for God's sake. We make ridiculous movies about *monsters*. We're already living lives most people could only dream of."

"What about your interests in architecture? In Irish literature?"

"I'm interested in both! I might pursue them one day. Just not today."

"What about this guy you like? Seamus or Domhnall or Paddy Cloverleaf O'Malley—"

"Joe. His name is *Joe*."

"Well, what about *Joe*?"

She stands up, straightens the pages with one neat gesture, and places them on the armrest. "Joe is a great guy," she says. She brushes her hair back, and looks at me. "But I don't love him."

We just look at each other from across the room.

"I think everyone here reaches a point where they wonder if they're going to be a part of Moldavia forever, or if they belong in the outside world," she says. "But I have roots here. And they're deep. I could never just walk away. My parents sacrificed so much. Part of why I stayed was for them. Part of it was for your dad. Part of it was for your mom. Part of it was for me. And maybe you."

"Me?"

She looks toward the closet. "Our families sort of merged, didn't they? It's almost like we got married, but in reverse."

I laugh at that. It's kind of true.

"I knew you were being hurt," she says.

I hold up my hands. She doesn't need to go there.

"I was older than you . . . still too young to really protect you," she says, smoothing down her gown. "But I knew enough to tell you to get out."

I go over to her. "Hayley . . ."

She shakes her head. *"And I didn't.* I was too scared. I should have told you to run." She puts her hands over her face. "I was too scared of being alone. Of being here without you."

My stomach drops; it's the feeling you get when you plunge down a roller coaster. I want to find the right words, to dampen any pain she has, because it's unfair that she'd be hurting over this. I take her hands and squeeze. "I was scared too. We were both just kids. Please tell me you don't feel guilty about that."

Hayley kisses my hands. "That's not why I stayed. I wasn't punishing myself."

Or did she want me to live as much of my life as I could before I might lose my mind? How much of that has been in her head as well?

She loved my father as much as she could in my place. She loved my mother as much as she could for me. Did she love them because they were extensions of me, the closest she could get to me all this time? It's crazy, the complex web of shit that pushes people down their paths in life.

"Your dad even offered to pay for my college," says Hayley.

Of course he did. And he would never have done that for me, or Oren. My dad had this hidden side to him, revealed to only a select few—the side of him that actually cared about people. The side of him filled with regret for all the awful things he did. The grief-stricken side of him he was terrified to show the world—the side of him that could only be found in some of his films, like *The Lovers of Dust and Shadow.*

The sound of chirping birds has replaced the crickets. We're communing again nocturnally, on the delicate thread that runs through the silence of the world, other people's dreams, when everything is sleeping. It's our thing.

When we were kids, we were bound by our helplessness, which became more and more excruciating over time. That's gone now; but there are still traces of it—all that fear and defeat and sorrow between us, like the surging hush after a hurricane.

I want to find a different path with her.

I don't totally mean for it to happen, but the towel comes

undone and falls to my feet. Hayley looks at me, her eyes round and starry. I'm ephemeral to her, something astral. She, more than anyone, knows the transience of love, especially in this place. It's always been whisked away from her.

She takes off her nightgown. We stand there for a moment, taking each other in.

Then, as if we're dancers in a silent ballet, we move to the bed.

We only get hazy stripes of sleep, here and there, cutting into everything else we do: breathless, tender, and intertwined. When the final layer of night slips away, and morning light sweeps the room, I kiss every freckle on her back—like the reverse of the night sky. We talk about my ideas for the sequel. We hash shit out. We discuss the film, cocooned together in my blanket, until we hear footsteps, voices, sets and equipment being moved around downstairs: the castle waking up again.

CHAPTER EIGHTEEN

THE BALLAD OF ALASTAIR AND ABIGAIL

LATER IN THE DAY, HAYLEY AND I SHOW MY TREATMENT TO FRANKLIN. He's pretty enthusiastic. We have some preliminary talks, and a plan emerges: to dive into a speeded-up pre-production for *Alastair & Abigail* while principal photography winds down on *No Chance in Hell.* That's the best use of time and resources. So that's what happens.

Over the next week, Moldavia rises like Lazarus resurrected, all the various studio departments feeding off my vision for this film, which is still forming. I have lots and lots of meetings. I'm the director, so everything has to be approved by me. Hayley, Oren, and Franklin provide guidance, basically taking on the role of the film's producers.

During this first week, the production team draws up a schedule and a budget, and they immediately start building all the necessary sets. I'm in awe of how the dark wonder-land of Moldavia pieces itself together like some mysterious, well-oiled machine.

Oren wanted to be a screenwriter, so I make him one. My dad never wrote scripts for any of his films, but I want to work in a different way.

During the second week of pre-production, Hayley, Oren, and I squeeze in script meetings whenever we can. They also function as writing lessons for Oren. I task him with fleshing out individual scenes, dialogue and all, while I run off to have consultations with the costume department and makeup about how to zombify Hayley and me so it looks like our flesh is rotting.

Oren hands me individual scenes, and the production team begins to storyboard each one, guided by Jip. As the script gets developed, we all notice that grounded within my story, *cauliflower-free*, Oren's writing gets better and better. He just needed direction, to rein himself in. I think that whole cauliflower debacle was mostly Oren self-destructing anyway, mourning our dad.

I tell Oren I'm more than happy to share screenwriting credit, since the sequel was originally his idea. Seeing him smile at that, realizing he isn't purposeless here, is almost worth everything we went through. *Almost.*

Gavin brings me my meals at night, since I'm too busy to even make it down to the commissary. My bed looks like an overwhelmed aide-de-camp's tent during a troubled expedition to the Amazon. There are design sketches and script pages, schedules, and articles I printed out (and am consuming as quickly as I can) about filmmaking and the movie business, scattered everywhere. I don't have time to sleep.

I take a cup of tea off a saucer Gavin hands me and, without even looking at him, officially cast him as Ferdinand, Alastair and Abigail's son.

"Um." Gavin is hesitating again.

I explain to him, while studying Jip's storyboard, that I'll get the newer guys on other crews to take over his butlery duties while he films his scenes.

"But I've never acted before," he says nervously.

I look up at him. "I hadn't either when I made *Zombie Children*. Dude, you're the only one who can play this role. You're the right age, and you have the right temperament." I give him a reassuring smile. "It'll be okay. I promise."

He nods quickly, his lips mashed together, and leaves the room.

I don't tell him I see his continued hopefulness about his mom as kind of tragic, and that he has a naturally crestfallen quality that will be perfect for the role.

The next day, I cast the remaining roles (there aren't many) with some of the available Spine Tinglers. I cast various other crew members (as my dad used to do) who are the right size and shape for certain roles to fill out the more epic scenes. They always grumble about this, but hey, that's how the studio works.

Pre-production continues, and before I know it, it's the third week in June already.

Principal photography officially begins tomorrow—about a month and a half before Cassidy is scheduled to visit the estate.

The night before I direct my first scene ever, I find Hayley in the Shakespeare garden. We both had the same idea—get a little air, look at some flowers. We've hardly seen each other lately. We both had makeup tests, and we still have our zombie makeup on. The newly fallen dusk casts everything in a spectral blue that makes the roses look black, and our artificially pallid faces especially ghoulish.

"Nervous?" she asks me.

I nod. "A little. But kind of excited too. This is crazy." I bet no other incoming college freshman is spending his summer quite like this.

We kiss, but only lightly, because of all the makeup.

"I think it'll be different this time," I say, "getting inside Alastair's head. I feel different."

"Because you're the one in charge now," she says. "And you're all grown up."

What she really means is my dad isn't here anymore, and I'm not a helpless kid.

"How are you?"

"Abigail is a larger role this time," she says, tapping her teeth with her finger. "So I'm just hoping I nail it. But I think I understand her." She smiles at me. "She has to take charge; make decisions quick, some really tough ones too. She's very strong."

"And good with her teeth," I say, taking her hand.

It's hilarious that I'm going back all those years to the end of the first movie . . . giving Alastair and Abigail a future . . . almost like I'm hoping for one for us.

Hayley and I spend the night together, running lines. It's been a little while since she's slept beside me. Although I've been crazy busy, I was secretly really missing her.

Once we start filming, I'm pretty nervous at first. The first two days are shaky. But I hit my stride quickly. I just need to make fast and firm choices about the story I want to tell. Once I figure that out, it turns out directing movies is a blast.

The first scene is totally badass: Alastair and Abigail, twenty years after the conclusion of *Zombie Children*, attacking the camera in an extreme close-up (filmed with a 24 mm wide-angle lens) of our rotted tongues and moldy teeth.

So much is implied from that one shot. First, we obviously didn't kill each other. Second, Alastair turned Abigail into a zombie. Third, we're really hungry. And last, although twenty years have passed since we last saw these two, we've obviously only aged half that amount.

Since this film will be Moldavia's first-ever sequel and first-ever production not directed by my dad, I know my key to success boils down to two things: taking the studio forward (attracting the new and younger fans) while retaining the soul of Moldavia and checking off the requisite trademarks (appealing to the squeezers). So there has to be this perfect melding of the expected and the unexpected.

I take the whole idea of sentient zombies that my dad came up with for *Zombie Children* (an original, underrated concept muddled by poor execution) and decide to push it even further. As the camera pulls back (in an awesome tracking shot, our best camera op riding the dolly) we see Alastair and Abigail feasting on the remains of a cow, its gristly rib cage stabbing into the sunset. (Barbara didn't even need to build a fake cow rib cage; we already had one lying around in storage from Moldavia's 1981 adaptation of *The Importance of Being Earnest*. Rick Whorley, writing for *Evil Robot* magazine, said of it: "I am so confused by this film, I no longer even know how to take a piss.")

If Alastair and Abigail are eating farm animals, does that mean there are no human beings left on the planet? It turns out not. Their farm is soon attacked by a vicious band of bearded woodsmen, hunters dressed in cured zombie pelts, the ashen skins of slain zombies, toothy grins and all, stretched out into dystopian outerware (hints of black humor are a Moldavia trademark).

I have the production team transfer the remains of the farmhouse façade from *The Ciller Cauliflowers* outside and rebuild what's left of it (this doesn't take much time). Knowing the set was already in shambles, I wrote the script with that in mind, so there would be a minimum of rebuilding. This is to be Alastair and Abigail's dilapidated home. Gradually, as we continue filming, an inverted replica is reconstructed in the Karloff Wing for all the interior shots, which we get later.

The hunters assume Alastair and Abigail are roaming brainlessly through the farm, not that they're domesticated. Alastair and Abigail aren't ordinary zombies. They've had malevolent visitors before, and their farm is booby-trapped. As the hunters each get caught in bear traps, tumble into covered pits, and get felled by various other nasty snares, Abigail beheads them all with a machete, in an instant and total reversal of what anyone's come to expect from a typical zombie movie.

Chopping up the bodies, freezing all the human meat in fancy refrigeration units, Alastair and Abigail then return to their meal (after vacuuming the living-room rug, which got bloodstained), munching on opposite ends of a cow intestine while gazing into each other's eyes, in a zombie homage to *Lady and the Tramp.*

But the cow carcass has been poisoned. This leads to two full minutes of intense zombie vomiting (over-the-top, gross-out gore, another Moldavia trademark). The foaming greenish-black zombie vomit involves oatmeal, cornflakes, food coloring, Alka-Seltzer tablets, bicycle pumps, and rubber tubing. It's awesome.

The culprits of the poisoning soon become clear. A group of *full-on* zombies, their bodies decomposing, emerges from the trees and descends upon them, filled with jealousy and rage. As Alastair and Abigail take each other's hands before the battle begins, we realize their romantic union has kept them pure. This is a subtle nod, and a neat reversal, to *The*

Lovers of Dust and Shadow. And since Moldavia movies often coyly reference one another, we've just checked off another Moldavia trope.

Oren and Franklin keep urging me to just *play against logic*, since if you overthink any Moldavia movie the magic gets lost. So I just go for it and embrace the absurd while trying to stay faithful to the tone of the original film, winking at some of its more infamous moments. That's how great horror sequels are made.

While still very much undead, Alastair and Abigail are in love, and it's the magic of this emotion that has embalmed them in a way and enabled them to age slowly, and not decompose as quickly as the rest of their zombie brethren. Yes, this makes no sense—*but only if you overthink it.* Zombies make no sense anyway, as I noted in my journal. So Alastair and Abigail have built a sort of stable life together.

Alastair must contend with the betrayed castaways of the zombie army he built in *Zombie Children* and later abandoned for Abigail (because they were all somehow less human than him). This leads to some whizzing, Vietnam-inspired battle scenes through the trees—using slingshots, broken bottles, and torches. War is hell, man.

Once Alastair and Abigail defeat the zombie army, they don't slaughter them but build them up again, handing them back their dignity and making them a viable defense force—*a zombie fortress*, if you will—against more roving bands of zombie hunters. Alastair and Abigail become their leaders.

While the forest burns around them, sending sparks flying into the ink-black night, everyone has a feast of defrosted human meat at a banquet table ringed by garlands of calla lilies (boom!), and that night, feeling victorious and lustful, Alastair and Abigail have crazy zombie sex. They have to be careful to temper their passion, because when things get too heated they tear chunks of flesh from each other with their teeth, leaving slimy, gaping wounds and streaks of blackened blood.

The audience may think this horrifying sex scene is the Curdling, *and why does it come so early on?*, but I've tricked them twice, in fact. This is *not* the Curdling, but the Curdling comes next, so yes, it does come super-early for a Moldavia film after all!

Nine months later, Abigail is having Alastair's child, but let's just say, being undead and all, the state of her reproductive health is somewhat questionable. She's in agonizing labor for so long, Alastair is forced to tear open her uterus with his teeth and remove the baby—which looks like a gelatinous alien turd—with his bare hands.

The supervising sound editor tells me they'll be able to record some really gross Foley sound in post—partly by squishing and kneading a hunk of wet, raw meat.

Jasper makes an amazing fake wax stomach, something I can really sink my teeth into, partially decayed intestines and all. They slather it in goo, and a ton of fake zombie blood (all of it edible). I want this to be one of the most disgusting scenes ever filmed—but also extremely moving. Because, surprise! They have a healthy *human* baby! And Abigail is totally fine. Alastair just sews her stomach back up with some guitar string (torn from an old Gibson that just happened to be lying around their farmhouse).

As the baby grows older, in a series of flash-forwards, not only do Alastair and Abigail realize their baby is totally normal, but their son begins to age at three times the rate they do.

Ten years later, Alastair and Abigail have decayed only slightly (meticulous makeup work from Madge, and great continuity work from our script supervisor) while their little boy has aged into . . . Ferdinand (played by Gavin). Knowing the treacherous world they live in, Alastair and Abigail have to teach their child how to hunt and kill—to protect their family and their farm, but also so he can fend for himself and survive on his own—because that day will come.

This is something Ferdinand rebels against, wanting to keep his childhood innocence and his family intact. But the sad truth is, as they age, Alastair and Abigail are less in control of their primal zombie instincts. In two horrific instances, Alastair and then Abigail momentarily forget themselves and try to attack and eat Ferdinand. Thankfully, each time, the other zombie parent happens to be there to save their son. But as time goes on, it becomes apparent that neither of them can be a true parent to their son—they both pose a threat. They cannot be the parents Ferdinand needs.

They have to cast Ferdinand out—for his own good.

The weeks of filming go by in a blur. I thrive on the clap of the slate. Shouting *"Action!"* and having everything suddenly come to life. I love the mess of gaffer's tape, C-stands, booms, electrical cords; the glare of HMI lamps, the burst of walkie-talkies, the cluster of viewing monitors in the video village.

The electrical crew (the "juicers") adopted Jude before we began production. But he gets promoted to best boy, assisting the key grip—something that happened quickly because we're stretched tight in terms of crew, with the other production still filming (and now delayed with unforeseen technical hurdles).

When I'm not in front of the camera or actively discussing a scene with the other actors, I'm having pretty technical conversations with Jip, the set decorator, the property master, the costume, makeup, and special effects supervisors, the sound guys—about how to construct each scene.

Thankfully, our production sound mixer has composition skills; he used to assist my dad scoring his movies. He thinks he can write an original score for *Alastair & Abigail* that has Moldavia's signature unsettling synth sound, with a twist of his own. Then the music supervisor tells me it won't be too hard to get the rights to some indie dark metal music I suggested we use for underscoring, to create a foreboding atmosphere in certain scenes, and a more modern-sounding soundtrack.

Late at night, I have a series of conversations with marketing about updating the Moldavia logo and the website, as well as setting up Twitter and Instagram accounts, all featuring mysterious teaser info for the coming sequel. We decide to title the movie *Alastair & Abigail: A Zombie Love Story*. True Moldavia fans will recognize it as the sequel to *Zombie Children* and get excited. Non-Moldavia die-hards won't know it's the sequel to a pretty shitty movie.

Hayley and I know all our lines by now. But we still spend every night together in my room. Acting with her has been super-fun because we both decide to just let the past go. We propel ourselves through the story and relate to each other through our characters, as we would ourselves. This turns out to be the best decision; we don't get weighed down by the past or caught up in any residual negative emotions lingering from *Zombie Children*. We're making a different movie, after all.

As I expected, there's no PTSD stuff about playing Alastair again, because I've made him, and this project, my own. Hayley and I take loving care of the story, and the characters we're playing. And like she was as a kid, Hayley is a generous, luminous presence on-screen.

We've had to film way out of sequence because of continuing production issues on *No Chance in Hell* (the last Moldavia movie that will ever be credited to Lucien Heyward), and we keep losing key crew members to the other production for days at a time. And then to make matters worse, Gavin gets a bad cold. In the meantime, I film the scenes with all the other actors playing Ferdinand at different stages in his life. Alastair and Abigail aren't on-screen again till the very end—I restructure the film like this *very much on purpose* so I can concentrate on my directing duties. Doing both is hard.

Jude plays Ferdinand at age twenty. A strong and able hunter now, Jude-as-Ferdinand has only one scene in the film, where he scavenges ammo, slays a deer using only a pickaxe (we use the same fake cow rib cage), and then fist-fights another ravenous hunter to defend his venison meal. Jude wanted to box on-screen—he practically made it a contractual requirement. We have no stunt coordinator at Moldavia, so Jude carefully choreographs the whole fight with the burly electrician who's playing the hunter, and it actually turns out great. I guess now we have a stunt coordinator.

After the fight, I want to film Jude-as-Ferdinand walking all bloody through the forest away from the slain hunter as the midday light sifts through the trees. Jude turns back to me as we're rolling and says: "So this is like some real warrior-contending-with-nature, Terrence Malicky shit you're doing right here, huh?"

No one can make me laugh like Jude.

In the last scene of the film, Ferdinand, now a sickly old man (played by Lorenzo Mayberry, who doesn't fall asleep on me!), has spent his remaining years trying to make his way back to the farm where he grew up, so he can see his parents one last time before he dies. Sixty or so years later, Ferdinand has never experienced any kind of love as pure as that of his undead parents, and I guess that's the tragedy of the story. He's had a hard life—a loveless life, driven only by survival.

Ferdinand returns to the farm and finds his parents still there, only slightly more decayed, still *almost* as young as they were when they sent him away more than a half century ago. Recognizing him, even though he's an old man now, they all embrace. It's a beautiful reunion. Neither Abigail nor Alastair gets a chance to attack and eat Ferdinand. He dies in their arms a day later.

Alastair and Abigail bury their son in back of the farm, where he used to play as a little kid, and where all of them, at least for a short while, were the happiest, and I guess the most human. That night, Alastair and Abigail cuddle lovingly in bed one last time. Knowing they'll grieve forever, and that they'll never really die, they devour each other until there's nothing left of them but bits of bone and dust.

And that's how the movie ends. But it's not the last scene we shoot.

There's still one scene left, and I swear it's going to be the goddamn death of me. It's the scene where Alastair and Abigail banish Ferdinand from the farm so he'll survive. It's one of the most powerful moments in the film, and I can't pretend this scene about having to leave home doesn't have deep personal meaning for me.

I write five drafts of the scene, but none of them work. I realize it's not about the dialogue or the way the shots will be composed; it's about the raw emotion, especially on the part of Ferdinand. And that's where we run into trouble.

I didn't know what to expect from Gavin, but his general demeanor—which I can only describe as a sludge of slowly degrading hopefulness—gives a level of truth to Ferdinand I never thought we'd achieve. It's literally jaw-dropping to behold. It's luck.

But Gavin freezes during the filming of this one crucial scene. We spend nearly six hours shooting as I try to coax out his performance, pushing him to give me *more more more.* But it doesn't come. And that's the first time I get tense, remembering what it was like for me when I was a kid filming *Zombie Children.* Standing there for hours in the cold, not knowing what my dad wanted from me, and then him just berating me and hitting me until he finally declared: *Yeah, we got it.*

I feel the pressure to get this right—the pressure on me, the pressure on Gavin, like we're bound together during a deep-sea dive, our ears madly popping.

"I need you to be heartbroken, completely despondent," I tell him, acting totally cavalier, like this is all *whatever.*

"I am," says Gavin, not really understanding.

"Right now you're reading apathetic." I try to phrase this in a way he'll connect to. "Think about what's happening in the scene. Ferdinand is being forced to say good-bye to his parents forever. We need to nail this now." I point up. "We're losing the light."

But he chokes. And then it's too late, and we have to wrap for the day.

That night, I have a terrible dream.

My bathroom door swings open, and in the watery light I see my father drowning Aida in the bathtub—she's floating lifelessly, her eyes open. He's whispering in her ear like he's spooling the remaining life out of her body with his words. He looks up at me and grins in this sadistic way. "You know what to do."

"I won't," I tell him.

He shrugs and kicks the bathroom door closed.

The next day we start super-early in the morning but run into the same problem again. Gavin is stoic, when I need him to feel betrayed by his zombie parents, who are essentially telling him they can't love him anymore. But he can't get himself there. We film for four hours, probably over twenty takes, a few different setups, but then it starts to rain and we have to wrap early.

That's when I start imagining my dad lurking around the set wearing that same white tuxedo he was buried in, shaking his head at me in disappointment.

And that night I have another awful dream.

This time, my hands are around Gavin's throat. And I'm screaming at him:

"We all have to give something of ourselves to keep this place afloat! We all have to sacrifice something!" I start

throttling him until I see his tears flying into the air. I hear a clicking sound and realize it's his teeth.

The next day doesn't go any better. Gavin is actually getting *worse* as he loses what's left of his confidence, and starts unconsciously sabotaging himself.

He was always terrified to do this role, and now the cracks are starting to show.

I look over and see my dad sitting in the director's chair, lit cigar between his fingertips, laughing at me. Franklin catches me punching a wall as we head inside.

That's when an emergency production meeting is called.

CHAPTER NINETEEN

SCREAM ALL NIGHT

I SIT AT A TABLE IN THE EMPTY COMMISSARY, MY HEAD IN MY HANDS. I'm joined by Franklin, Oren, Hayley, Jip, the first A.D., and Craig, our focus puller.

I'm told we're now behind schedule.

"But this was going so well!" I cry into my hands.

"There's always one scene that becomes an albatross," says Franklin. "In every movie. Your father would talk about it all the time."

"Okay," I say, "so how would he solve it?"

"He would rethink the scene," says Franklin. "Which is what you need to do if you can't get what you need out of Gavin."

"That scene is the emotional core of the movie! If this scene doesn't work, the rest of the movie doesn't work. *This can't be done halfway.*"

"Perhaps Gavin's character just feels a muted sense of

shock," Franklin suggests.

I shake my head. I've seen the dailies. "What he's doing doesn't read like shock."

"Yeah," Jip concurs, explaining to Franklin that it reads like indifference.

"And it needs to be super-emotional!" I say.

"Then we switch the angle," says Craig. He means the camera stays on Hayley and me, and registers our horror instead of Ferdinand's. But I know that's not right. We have to see Ferdinand's pain because the rest of the movie is about Ferdinand, and him trying to overcome the tragedy of being ejected from his own family.

"I think you should take one more day on this," says Oren. "And then we wrap."

"If we spend any longer than that, we'll be hurting the studio," says Franklin.

"And *No Chance in Hell*?" I shout. "How much time have we spent dealing with their VFX crap now?"

"Too much time," Franklin admits. "The reshoots were unnecessary, and now unfortunately that time has eaten into *Alastair & Abigail*'s production schedule. I agree with Oren. I think you should take one more day with this scene. Then we rethink."

"Oh, fuck this shit," I snarl, leaving the table, banging my chair.

I have a very bad night—my worst yet. I feel like I'm failing. I've become obsessed with getting this one scene right.

I know it represents the soul of the movie, and it feels like everyone's fighting me.

I will myself not to have any more nightmares. But it doesn't work.

I'm drowning Gavin in that bathtub. He's kicking, thrashing, eyes wide, begging, but I keep pushing him under, while my dad stands over me, encouraging me. "But I'm going to kill him," I say, somehow unable to control my hands tightening around his throat.

My dad crouches beside me and puts his hand on my shoulder, with a firm, fatherly squeeze. "A little part of us has to die for every movie that gets made here."

I look at him, tears pouring out my eyes. *"Why?"*

He shrugs. "It's the curse of Moldavia."

"I can't destroy this kid just for the sake of the film."

"But it's so easy," he whispers into my ear. "This kid really believes his mom is coming back for him. All you have to do is tell him the truth."

He interlocks his hands with mine, applying more pressure, holding Gavin underwater. "But then who will I have become?" I ask.

Of course I know the answer to that.

"I know what you want," he says, patting me on the back. "You want your debut to be *special*—better than a typical Moldavia movie. It's what I always wanted."

Gavin's lungs are filling with water. "It has to be better if we're going to survive," I say. "But not this way."

My dad gives me a hard, questioning look—like I'm on

the precipice of finally making him proud, or failing him again.

"It's the only way," he says. "It's what I would do."

My tears fall into the bathwater, vanishing into tiny craters. "But I'm not you."

Gavin is completely submerged. His eyes glass over. A final curlicue of bubbles streams out of his mouth as his face turns blue.

"Who knows how long you have?" my dad says, his voice echoing, like he's God.

It rains all morning, so Jip suggests we film later in the day, when it's supposed to clear up, during the magic hour that scrapes the sunset. This will create more stress, since it's a slimmer window, but if we nail the scene it will be a beautiful thing. I agree, even though it's a risk. I can't pretend Moldavia isn't trying to stoke some of my father's ruthlessness everyone thinks is dormant inside me.

Later, on set, there's tension so thick you can taste it. Gavin looks shaky and pale, like he spent the whole night vomiting instead of sleeping. It works for his character, though. When we're ready to roll, I walk over to him, knowing I already broke my promise to him by pretending this would be smooth sailing. "Hey there."

"Hey," he says, in a choked voice.

"So Gavin, the thing is . . . we haven't really been getting what we need from you. And this is the last scene on the schedule. I need you to really go to that super-sad place."

"Okay." He nods quickly. "I'm sorry about everything."

I take a breath. "Do you know what I mean, though?"

"Yes," he says, still nodding rapidly, like he's been preparing, "I know."

The first take isn't terrible but nowhere near what I need. The second take sucks. During the third take a light blows, but it doesn't matter anyway, since Gavin is so nervous he messes up his lines. The fourth take is a major regression, the fifth take is even worse, and the sixth take is a wash because there's a problem with sound. Hayley and I are totally spent, since we're giving everything we have to the scene as well.

The seventh take is flat. "Blasted," someone whispers.

That's when my first A.D. tells me, looking at the sky, that we don't have much time left. I worry the darkening sky is darkening my heart. I walk over to Gavin. I start to hear the hornets buzzing. I'm heading into a tailspin.

"It's better, right?" he says, shifting from one foot to the other, eyes wide, hoping.

I open my mouth—not sure what's going to come out. The crew grows still. I feel their eyes on us. I have the studio to consider, people's livelihoods.

But honestly, fuck Moldavia, and this stupid movie.

Gavin is just a kid. He hasn't figured out yet how cruel life can be. How it can take everything from you, dig in its sharp teeth and not let go. He still has hope. I can't tarnish that. Moldavia isn't worth that. This movie isn't worth that.

I look into his eyes, and I see my whole life reflected back at me: covered in blood and losing consciousness next to a mangled bike at the bottom of that cliff, the hospital, the lawyers, the judge, the therapy sessions, beating the shit out of goons at Keenan, the nightmares, closing people off . . .

My father saunters over. He gives me a stony look and whispers in Gavin's ear: *Your childhood is over. Not only is it never coming back—it wasn't what you thought it was. It was a mirage.*

I lead Gavin to a more secluded spot.

My dad follows, whispering into Gavin's ear: *Your mom was an addict. She died of a drug overdose. She loved heroin more than you. She's never coming back for you.*

"Aren't you losing the light?" asks Gavin, nervously studying the sky.

"Don't worry about that," I say.

I sit on the ground. I motion for Gavin to sit beside me.

My dad whispers to Gavin: *And you'll never get that kind of love back ever again. You'll spend your whole life trying . . . looking for it . . . but you won't ever find it again.*

But then Hugo comes over, wearing one of his ratty flannels. And he whispers in my ear: *Remember what I told you, kiddo. You can either be defined by him or defined by everything you are that he could never be.*

"It's just a movie," I tell Gavin. "There shouldn't be all this pressure. I'm sorry."

"Yeah, but . . . ," says Gavin.

"My dad cast me in *Zombie Children* because I was a sad, unloved kid and Alastair was sad and unloved. You read my journal—I was just sort of forgotten about." I laugh, thinking again about what horror movies really are. "Isn't it funny," I tell him, "that in all these movies about monsters and vampires and things coming back from the dead, no one ever stops and says, *Wow, you know what, this is kind of cool. There is an afterlife, there is something more than all this disappointment and loneliness!*"

Gavin smiles. "Yeah. They're too busy running. Or screaming."

One of the camera ops starts wildly signaling to me that we're losing the light. I give him the finger.

"Did you want me to play Ferdinand because you think I'm sad and unloved?" Gavin asks me.

"Actually, I don't think you're all that sad. And I think a lot of people here love you. I think my dad loved you too. I think I just identified with you over the mom thing."

"I know my mom isn't coming back," he says.

That startles me. Did someone say something?

"I just . . . know she's not coming back for me," he says. "Or she would have by now. But I like to pretend she will. You know?"

"I know," I tell him, nudging him with my shoulder. "Because I know my mom isn't coming back either. I'm never getting her back the way she was."

"It just makes me feel better to think it," he says, "even though it's stupid."

"It's not stupid."

He's starting to tear up, which surprises me, because I had pretty much given up on that. "I guess that's what this scene is about, right?" he says, wiping his nose with the back of his hand. "Knowing you're kind of on your own forever. I was afraid to think about that."

Gavin is a lot sharper than I knew. I underestimated him. Everyone here underestimates everyone else. It's all about what use people have for the studio. No one stops to talk, or listen to anyone.

I feel awful that I treated Gavin this way; that I fell into the same trap—trying to see what his pain could do for me, instead of listening to him, respecting his feelings. He's had a rough road. And if anyone should understand that, and empathize, it's me.

Gavin laughs through his tears, and coughs a little. "I get it now, I get what the scene's about." He smiles to himself, sniffling, seeming to consider everything, this movie, and this moment. "I was just afraid. But I'm ready to do this. . . ."

I hesitate. "I don't want to film the scene if I'm just using your bad feelings . . . to make this movie better. I don't want to exploit that. It's not worth it to me."

Gavin's seriously crying now, covering his nose and his eyes. "No, I want to do it for my mom. I want to do it for her. That's the right choice. This'll be for her."

I lay my hand on his wrist. "You sure?"

Gavin, tears streaming out of his eyes, nods firmly.

I stand up. I reach for him, and pull him up. I signal to Jip to roll camera.

"ACTION!" I yell, running over to my mark.

I always remembered what Aida and Hugo told me. So,

over time, I let go of all that hurt and anger. They taught me that even in a never-ending sea of darkness, there's always a lighthouse somewhere, casting a beam of light. That's corny, but it's totally true. I've always looked for the light ever since. There's always someone who cares. And I know exactly what I have that my dad could never find in himself.

Compassion.

And, ironically, I have that because of him, because of everything I went through.

Now everything begins to make more sense to me: Why Aida told me never to come back. Why my mother told me to leave. Why my dad willed Moldavia to me.

Through his will, my dad was framing my future for me the same way he'd frame one of his shots—looking at me, and at everything I could be, through the small rectangle he'd make with his hands. His legacy would continue—*through me.* This was an attempted possession all along. My dad wasn't evil. He was just deeply flawed. I gave him too much power all these years thinking he was something greater.

We film the scene as written. Gavin gives me exactly what I need.

"Scream all night," I say, almost reverently, as I watch through the monitor.

CHAPTER TWENTY

RUSTY BLADES

I SKIP DINNER. LYING IN BED, I PUSH ASIDE ALL THE LOOSE PAGES OF screenplay, schedules, storyboard, sketches, and whatnot. I take out the Harvard brochure they sent me that I keep opening and closing and trying to forget about but can't throw away.

I've been keeping it under my bed like a dirty secret. I don't know.

The images of the campus are attractive—aggressively diverse groups of friends lounging together under blossoming trees in impossible sunlight. Students throwing Frisbees framed by Victorian Gothic architecture, poring over stacks of handsome old books speckled by light through stained glass. Students sitting in comfy-looking lecture rooms staring ahead, fascinated, pens between their fingers.

I try to picture myself there: going to classes, typing on a MacBook during lectures on Milton and Chaucer, living in a dorm. Going to parties on Friday nights holding red plastic cups filled with warm keg beer; pretending I like hip-hop.

I've had a hard time picturing myself at Harvard, probably because I can't picture myself anywhere. My whole life has seemed temporal, one fast-moving train connecting to the next. I've made do with whatever reality was presented to me until I could move on again. But, I don't know, I keep looking at the stupid brochure.

And I can't pretend it has nothing to do with Hayley; seeing those unfinished college applications like nicked dreams. I think it would hurt her if I didn't go, if she watched me get swallowed by Moldavia forever.

After all, her phone call is what really brought me back.

That's why I could never bring myself to call Harvard and tell them I was taking a gap year. It's July already; it's too late now to postpone matriculation. I guess I figured I was either going to go or not go at all—it was now or never.

I needed to have Harvard remain an option. Because I know at Moldavia, one year can easily turn into ten years.

But I also know I haven't fulfilled the terms of my dad's will yet.

Hayley knocks on the door and slips inside. She's got a sandwich for me on a plate. When she sees the Harvard brochure lying open on my chest, she smiles.

"How did you know I was hungry?" I say, reaching for the sandwich.

"Because you didn't eat anything all day."

I gobble the sandwich down, thinking we're like an old

couple already. Hayley lies down next to me. She takes the brochure and flips through it herself.

I brush the crumbs onto the empty plate, wipe my mouth, and put the plate on the floor. I lay my head on Hayley's chest, curling up to her, and we look through the brochure together. We laugh at some of the posed photographs inside.

"You never called Harvard, did you?" she says after a beat.

I don't say anything, but I figured she'd know. Hayley always knows what's up. I just lie there, listening to her heartbeat.

Hayley closes the brochure and rests it on the floor, next to my bed. "I had an awesome time," she says, running her fingers through my hair. "It was tough work, and I love that character. I don't think acting is my game, though. I'm very much a producer."

"You're many things. Whatever you want to be."

"I like being on the other end, watching everything come together." She tickles my knee. "But having a sensitive, artic-ulate director with a real vision felt like a gift."

"My mom wants me to go to Harvard."

I feel her breathing change. Her hand pauses in my hair.

"I saw her," I say. "I didn't tell you. She had a bad reaction to seeing me."

"Oh. I'm sorry," she says softly.

"I really enjoyed directing the movie. But I think I want to see what else I love doing. I want to experience as much as I can before the lights could go out on me."

"Then that's what you should do," says Hayley.

I want to ask her if she'd come with me if I go to college. But I know the answer already, and I don't want to hear it out loud.

After Hayley's mom died, I might have been the only one in the world who could have consoled her. And I wasn't here. She couldn't bring herself to undo my self-imposed excommunication just for her. She couldn't break me out of my new world—not until it was my own dad who was dying. I want to aspire to be as strong and selfless as she is. Hayley is my hero. "You know I'm in love with you, right?" I tell her.

"Yes," she says playfully, nibbling my ear. "And I you, Alastair."

Once we review the dailies of Gavin's big scene, everyone realizes we have what we need. Principal photography is finished. It took nineteen days. I approve the next Crepuscular Dusk, which, because of filming, had to be postponed. It'll be combined with a belated July Fourth celebration, so that should be fun for everyone.

We've all seen the raw footage of *Alastair & Abigail*, so we know we have something pretty awesome on our hands. I find myself starting to pull away from the crush of Moldavia. I task Oren with overseeing post-production, and tell him he can have Final Cut, which thrills him to no end.

Jude and Mistress Moonshadow seem to be working out. Jude never returns to our room, and they show up to the commissary for every meal holding hands. Despite their age difference and all, something about them is just sweet. It boils down to tiny moments: Mistress Moonshadow whispering something to Jude over dinner, and him laughing so hard (something only I used to be able to make him do), resting his head against her neck, closing his eyes as she presses her cheek against his. You can't argue with that.

I stay in bed for a while, catching up on sleep and reading about Colin Hanks. Hayley and I spend virtually every night together. We don't talk about the future, or the studio, or whether or not I'm going to college. We just hang out and watch movies and chat about bullshit. She makes me laugh.

I skip Crepuscular Dusk. I feign a cold. Hayley, Oren, Jude, and everyone else attends. But truthfully, I don't want to get sucked into this world any more in case I decide to leave it. Oren got fireworks. I watch them explode over the east lawn in red and gold, flooding my room with fiery light, flashing off all the pages of my printed-out research on Harvard.

Cassidy Blackwell, the founder and CEO of Rusty Blade Films, postpones on us twice. He's stuck in Vancouver. No one knows why. Then, about four weeks after we wrap production, Franklin sends me a message one morning: today is the day Cassidy will finally be visiting Moldavia, and I should probably make an appearance.

Sure enough, right after lunch, I watch through an upstairs window as Cassidy's canary-yellow Porsche rolls through the gates. He sort of *fox-trots out* like a cartoon tornado, shaking the hand of everyone in sight.

He's youngish—David Schwimmer with a sharper jawline—his thick black hair slicked back, wearing a dark chambray shirt, skinny jeans rolled up in cuffs, green-tinted sunglasses. He checks his watch three times before he even gets inside the castle. I roll my eyes and head downstairs.

I meet Cassidy Blackwell in the hunting room, where he's having coffee with Franklin. Franklin introduces me and adds, proudly, that I was accepted into Harvard. "Yale," says Cassidy, standing up to shake my hand. That's literally what he says: *Yale.* And then: "Call me Cass."

"Nice to meet you." He's such a *bro*, but I keep my tone polite.

"You too, dude. Wow, I'm such a big fan. I must have seen *Zombie Children of the Harvest Sun* eighteen thousand times!" He's sort of hopping about the room. His vibe is all childlike and bright, like Jude's was—like everyone's is, I guess, when they first see this place.

Franklin hands me a cup of coffee. I sit on the couch, facing Cass. I'm not wearing shoes—green-striped socks with small holes in them. Business casual.

"That movie inspired *Zombie Eclipse*, I'll totally admit it," he says. "Put Rusty Blade on the map. Put Lana Polari on the map. She's starring in the *Scorpion* movies now—billion-dollar franchise for Paramount. Chuck Baum directed the first one—did you see it?—great guy, we go surfing. Holt Van Wynn is great in them—good actor, good-looking guy, friend of mine, I bought his house in Malibu, now he's dating

Lana. She won't text me back anymore." He chuckles, slurps coffee. "Anyway. *Eclipse* spawned our first franchise. We started in limited release, then went wide after great word-of-mouth and a smart ad campaign. *Grossed eighty-two mill domestically.* Our production budget was four hundred K! One of the most profitable horrors in history."

Having a conversation with Cassidy is like having a conversation with someone that contains unrelenting oral hyperlinks. Everything he says subreferences something else: some achievement of his, some hit movie, a quick name drop of a celebrity he knows. It gives me a sharp ache in the center of my forehead. Also, his cologne, or whatever, is super-intense: like pine trees burning by a seaside cabin.

"The grounds are stunning," he says, taking a sip of coffee, craning his neck to look out the window. "When we were filming *Backpacker 7* in Puerto Rico—film was set in Turks and Caicos, but the tax breaks in *Rico*, man, we saved a bundle—film grossed two hundred mill worldwide—put Julie Heathen on the map; she's helming Sony's reboot of *Crosshairs* now—they paid her fifteen mill up front just for the first one. We dated briefly. Doesn't wear underwear. Anyway. We shot some of the movie in La Perla—Old San Juan? Kept running into Justin Timberlake, great guy, friend of mine, always sweaty for some reason, I bought his house in the Hamptons. But for the scenes set in the kingpin's house . . . we were filming at the villa of this, like, Spanish pop star—dude is like a billionaire and he's twelve years old, great guy, can never understand a word he says, even when he sings, *even in English*—it had grounds like this—just, like—endless green." He leans in. "Are you gonna go to Harvard?"

I smile politely, but there's no way I'm telling Cass about my future plans.

"Well," he says, contemplating his coffee mug. "It is such a thrill to be here." His tone is suddenly nostalgic. "Moldavia movies meant so much to me as a kid. Like everyone else, I always wondered what went on over here."

"I hope we can count on your discretion!" says Franklin with a friendly laugh, crossing his leg. "No photos inside the walls."

"No, no!" says Cassidy, waving his arms around. "I would never! *Never!* I have like seven iPhones and three iPads, none of them on me. I've scattered them across three continents. I always forget stuff in hotels. There might be one, my girlfriend's, in the car. Abbie Strauss. British actress. Starred in that *Chimney Sweeper* miniseries on PBS?"

I frown. "What's it called?"

"*Chimney Sweeper.* It's about a female chimney sweeper during the Blitz. Won an Emmy. Big hit. Know her? *Watch it?* Man, is she hot. Bit burned out, though . . . sudden fame, you know. She's resting. . . ." He cups his hands over his mouth and whispers: "*Rehab.*" He gets up and starts pacing the room.

"Can we get you more coffee?" Franklin asks.

"I'm good." He sticks his face real close to one of the mounted deer heads, laughs, then turns back to me with a grin. "This room, man."

I smile back. "I know."

He walks over to me and puts his hands behind his back, staring down at his expensive "work boots," swaying a little, like he's about to be chewed out by his headmaster for setting off cherry bombs in the commons. "So, I heard you've been working on something?"

I look at Franklin. He nods back. "Yes. I . . . directed a sequel to *Zombie Children*."

"Really?" says Cass, eyebrows a mile high.

"Really."

"Are you in it as well?"

"Hayley and I both reprise our roles."

"Now I'm *really* interested. I bet she's hot now, huh?"

I stop smiling at him.

He looks around the room. "*Zombie Children* has amassed quite the cult following. A sequel would be nothing to sneeze at. I was in talks with your dad, as you know—a true genius, by the way, and I'm *so so sorry*, by the way—about selling Moldavia to Rusty Blade. The facilities here could use a bit of an upgrade. But this estate, where all these Moldavia classics were filmed—I mean, it's truly one of a kind. The secrecy you've kept up all these years added value to that. The myth. You could rack up tens of millions a year just in fanboy tourism."

I turn to Franklin. "You think?"

"Rusty Blade's offer would be for the estate itself," says Cassidy. "The grounds and castle. As well as the Moldavia name, and the rights to the library."

My dad kept the negatives for all his films and the rights to his entire library. This would be giving up the studio and our family legacy—the very soul of Moldavia.

"This is all very preliminary, you understand," says Cass. "I have to talk to my board, have the estate appraised. My plan would be to keep the necessary brass in place, and use the Moldavia imprint to release slightly more upmarket horrors. Creature features—but more contemporary in style than what Lucien was making, with a more aggressive marketing strategy behind them—get them on the festival circuit, put new releases in theaters, expand the brand, develop original programming for streaming services. That's where everything's headed now. And we'd leave the castle behind, and move all production to L.A."

"I'm assuming there are no guarantees about keeping everyone's jobs here."

"The necessary brass, like I said," says Cass. "This is business. Hollywood."

"Right."

"Look: Our films do very well, but audiences tire of the same formula after a while. We're in preprod for *Backpacker 9* right now. But I'll tell you: *Backpacker 8* did not make as much money as *Backpacker 7*. And I know Moldavia has been struggling to find its own audience lately—young people on tablets. Streaming. Times change. The marketplace shifts." He snaps his fingers to accompany all the points he's making. "Video games now often have better storytelling than Hollywood movies."

"Well, definitely better than the *Backpacker* films," I say.

Cassidy laughs. "All I'm saying . . . we've all gotta work harder and harder these days. So this deal could be mutually beneficial."

I clear my throat. "How much are we talking?"

"I would very much like to see what you've been working on."

There's a pause.

Franklin sets down his coffee cup. "We can arrange for you to view some of the footage," he says. "If it's okay with Dario."

"It's fine with me," I say. "We have a rough cut, actually. Or so I'm told."

Cassidy leans in to me. "What's the title?"

"Alastair & Abigail: A Zombie Love Story."

"Man!" Cassidy claps his hands together. "I love it."

Franklin arranges a viewing of a rough cut of *Alastair & Abigail* for Cassidy in the screening room. Two hours later, Cassidy Blackwell, who is wearing quite the poker face, meets Franklin, Hayley, Oren, and me, in the library of the Lugosi Wing. Something about Cassidy's energy is a lot different now.

We sit at the oblong table. Cassidy introduces himself to Hayley and Oren. They both give him a curt hello. For reasons unknown, Oren is wearing a vintage World War II flight suit, which makes a lot of noise every time he moves. "Love the getup!" says Cassidy.

"Appreciated," says Oren stoically, the old leather squeaking.

We wait politely while Cassidy stares down at the table, preparing whatever he's going to say, lost in deep thought, whatever "deep thought" is for him (probably images of naked blonde chicks with fake boobs on surfboards). Then he looks at me. "Not gonna lie. You edit that thing right, you could really shake up the genre. That's a game changer."

I was confident, but his reaction still surprises me. "You think?"

"*Man, that scene* where Ferdinand is banished is powerful stuff. It elevates the movie, puts it on a different level. Just the kind of thing I've been looking for."

It's hard to hate him as much now when *that's* the scene that truly moved him.

"Auto-horrors," he says, gazing out the window, devising a marketing plan on the spot. "We all know what made *Zombie Children* such a cult phenomenon. It wasn't just your performance, it was what the movie *was*—this real-life father-son relationship unraveling on-screen. It was mesmerizing. And here you've gone and filmed a response—an autobiographical horror. That's something new." He grins at me. His teeth have definitely been whitened recently. "The writing, acting, directing, it needs some reeling in, sure, but the talent is there. The potential is something I can't ignore. You have a great visual sense. I'd argue for less poetry and more T&A, though. Gotta sell tickets, after all."

He means Tits and Ass. I look over at Hayley. She's stone-faced.

We all sit there, silently, waiting for what Cassidy Black-well will say next. "I didn't get along with my father either," he says quietly, staring at his hands.

"Yeah?" I try not to burst out laughing at his daddy-issues bullshit, even though I'm well aware of my own.

"You're talented," he tells me. "And I'm attracted to tal-ent, what can I say? And you have a potential hit on your hands here—maybe even a rebooted franchise if you rethink that ending."

No one says anything.

He runs his finger along the table as if he's writing an SOS message in blood. "Depending on how our negotiations go, and the appraisal of the estate, I'm imagining an offer in the forty-to-sixty-mill range."

When you first hear a figure like that, everything just stops and your vision gets wavy, and you realize that if you were animated there would be dollar signs in your eyes. It wipes out everything, all rationality. But then you think about all the debt, the creditors, the back salaries owed, and everything stops rumbling, postquake.

I take a breath and maintain my composure. "The terms of my dad's will directed us to sell the studio to Rusty Blade if we weren't solvent—"

Franklin whispers: "Or likely to be solvent—"

"—within six months," I add. "We have some time left.

Little more than half, actually . . . but I'm assuming you made some sort of offer to my dad before his death."

"I did," says Cassidy.

"One moment." I lean over to Franklin. He whispers in my ear that the offer is generous, meaning we'd be able to pay off debts, all the crew and staff who have been working for free, and it would help get Moldavia out of the red. But we'd still have an uncertain future.

I turn back to Cassidy. "You imagine an offer in the forty-to-sixty-million range—*which is a wide range*, by the way. That's in the neighborhood of what you offered my dad, I'm assuming: a senile old man writing his will, trying to distribute his assets, pay everyone off, not leave his family in any debt. And that's the offer you came prepared with today, I'm sure. But now that you've seen a rough cut of *Alastair & Abigail*, what would your offer be?"

"Well," says Cassidy, tapping the table. "Are we negotiating?"

"I don't know. Are we?"

"There's a lot to be considered still," he says.

I raise my eyebrows, expectantly.

Cassidy takes off his sunglasses. "Around a hundred mill."

I look at Franklin. He nods at me. We'd pay everyone off *and* be millionaires.

"But," says Cass, "that's for everything. Including distribution rights to *Alastair & Abigail* and all its potential sequels, as well as for you."

"Me?"

"If we acquire Moldavia, my stipulation would be that you come work for me—and operate Moldavia Films, which would be a banner of Rusty Blade. And I'd contract you to write and direct the first five features, including at least two more sequels of *Alastair & Abigail*. I'd allow you to choose your top brass. But we'd have final say on what gets made and what gets released."

Oren and Hayley draw in their breath.

That's a lot of money, *obviously*. But he wants to buy my future. He wants me to spit out more Alastairs—except they'd be his corrupted, sleazy version of the character that's pretty much defined my life; the character that I just reclaimed for myself. My cult following would inflame further, into something sordid that I'd never be able to shake. Our family legacy would be tainted. Plus I'm pretty sure I'd be miserable working for him. I didn't come back to Moldavia and nearly lose my mind dealing with this place (and filming *Alastair & Abigail*) just so Cassidy could own me, and own everyone here.

I sit back in my seat. "Thank you, Cassidy, but I don't think we're interested."

Everyone exhales.

"Before I got here, all I wanted to do was sell Moldavia," I tell him. "This place was meaningless to me. I ran away from here, and stayed away for much of my life. But now . . . I don't feel the same way."

Cassidy doesn't seem surprised. He just puts his sunglasses back on, cool as a cucumber. "I understand."

"Thing is"—I look around at everyone—"none of us are just a cog in the machine anymore. My dad's gone. We all created something, and we did it together. This isn't just a movie studio. It's a part of who we are. It's . . . a family. *It's our family.* I know that's kind of corny—"

"Totally get it," says Cassidy. He points at me: "You'll remain studio chief?"

I laugh and shake my head. "No way."

Cassidy drums his fingers on the table. "Interesting."

"I don't deserve that," I say. "I'm going to appoint two chiefs—Oren and Hayley. They'll run this place better than I ever could."

Cassidy stands, extending his hand. "Well. This was a pleasure. And I meant what I said: You're a real talent. I'll let you have it out with your cohorts. And we'll talk again, before those six months are up. But by then, of course, my offer may have changed."

"Of course," I say, standing up to shake his hand. "I understand."

"It was nice meeting you all," he says, patting down his pants, as Gavin leads him out of the room. A few moments later we hear the roar of a V8 twin-turbo engine zooming out of the gates. Franklin, Hayley, and Oren all turn to look at me.

"Just so you know," says Oren, coughing into his fist, "if we're not solvent in just a few months . . . and we're *forced* to sell to him . . . his offer will be forty to sixty million less than if we sell to him now and he gets the rights to *Alastair & Abigail.*"

"Right. He wants total control over the film. And he's hedging his bets that we don't know what we're doing from a marketing standpoint."

"What do you mean?" says Oren.

"He probably already has some idea what the castle and estate are worth. And now he knows we have a potential blockbuster on our hands. Otherwise he wouldn't have upped his offer after he saw the rough cut. He's assuming there are cobwebs in the marketing office, which a few weeks ago *there were*. But now we have a half million followers on Twitter. Did you know that? We have fans out there."

"We have *no time*," says Oren.

"We have some time," says Hayley.

"What do you suggest?" asks Oren.

"The movie is in the can. Cut it fast. And then reach out to Dad's old Hollywood contacts and find a U.S. distributor. Get a deal in place. Put the film on the festival circuit. There's time to make at least some of those deadlines. Then hop on a plane and sell distribution rights in all the foreign markets. It's a risk. But it's not a fantasy."

"No, it's not a fantasy," Franklin concurs.

"Otherwise, look, we can just sell the studio to him now. Everyone gets paid. We leave the castle, retire to Florida or wherever, and live comfortably. People find new jobs, begin fresh lives, and Cassidy gets to use the Moldavia name to make his *upmarket contemporary creature horrors* with more tits and ass."

"So basically, sell our souls," says Oren.

"Welcome to Hollywood," I tell him.

Oren looks at the ceiling and closes his eyes. "Say good-bye to Moldavia forever. . . . *Wow*," he says, shaking his head, and then he looks at me with a frown. "Where's Florida?"

"Cassidy knows this business," I tell them. "You saw his reaction to *Alastair & Abigail*. Things turned out well with this sequel. We got lucky."

"It is a big risk," says Oren. "But I can't imagine selling Moldavia to someone like Cassidy Blackwell if there's even a chance we can make it on our own."

"There's a real chance," says Franklin. "I saw the rough cut too. If we market this right, we could have a real hit on our hands. We could come out of this on top."

"Dario," says Hayley, scooting her chair out from the table, "you don't want to be studio chief?"

"No, it should be you guys."

"It should be Hayley," says Oren, looking at her. "I'm comfortable just producing, writing, lending a hand wherever one is needed. I think that's best."

I make a knighting gesture at Hayley. "Then it's you."

The disbelieving, overwhelmed, rapturous look on Hayley's face tells me that this is what she always wanted. "Oh boy," she says, waving a hand in front of her face, fighting back tears, "I did not expect this. I'm honored. Thank you."

"Dario," says Franklin, "are you going to college?"

"Have we met the conditions of my father's will?"

Franklin clears his throat. "Solvency means our assets are greater than our liability. However, the wording of your father's will was very particular: You are free to leave the estate within the six-month period if the *likelihood* of solvency is achieved. And I believe, with *Alastair & Abigail*, we have achieved that."

"I'd like to actually study film. And English. And history. And economics, I think. Psychology too. I don't know who I am yet. I want the opportunity to find out."

Franklin nods at me, all proud. Oren gives me a hearty thumbs-up. Hayley is glowing. In a way, it was Moldavia that made me realize how much more I want to experience, how much more I want to learn.

"We should have a board of directors," says Hayley, "like any normal studio has."

Everyone agrees. So we discuss a new structure for Moldavia. Oren, Franklin, Hayley, and I could be on the board to make decisions and green-light projects. My dad is gone now, so there doesn't have to be one lone visionary leading the studio into a cloud of nihilistic madness. This way, I'd always be connected to Moldavia, but not *bound* to it.

"We should hire outside directors," I suggest.

This gets an enthusiastic response. We talk about hiring all the hotshot indie guys from all the hot festivals. The Moldavia name still carries weight, and young genre filmmakers know that. Maybe once the cash-flow situation is resolved, Moldavia could retain the castle and grounds as home base but find ways to shoot on location, in more far-off, exotic locales.

Meanwhile, Cassidy's ideas about "fanboy tourism"

weren't so far out. If shooting schedules were planned way ahead of time to accommodate it, tour groups could come in to view the grounds while production teams shoot around them. We'd be shedding our much-guarded secrecy, but tours could be a great revenue stream for the studio. Things start to come together in a new way—because we're rethinking what Moldavia really is, what it could be, and what it means to us and to horror fans.

We decide to officially announce all the changes to everyone at Moldavia during the next Crepuscular Dusk.

After our meeting, I walk across the eastern lawn to clear my head, and find myself on this hill. There was a moment here I remember very well. We had finished an all-night shoot of *Zombie Children*, and it had gone well. The crew cleared out quick, and my dad didn't immediately run off somewhere, so we were the only two left. That was rare.

The sun was coming up. We stopped for a moment. He put his hand on my shoulder. And we just watched the sunrise, side by side like that, without ever saying a word. Then it was over. The grounds were alight with sweeps of neon pink, shining brilliantly off the windows of the Lugosi Wing, and my dad turned and walked swiftly back toward the castle, while I hurried to catch up.

And they say you never remember the good stuff.

CHAPTER TWENTY-ONE

BEAUTIFUL NIGHTMARES

ON THE WAY TO MY ROOM, I SEE OREN'S DOOR IS OPEN. HE'S LYING ON his futon, watching a movie. He's still wearing his leather flight suit, and he's eating popcorn from a bucket on his chest. I expect to see some Italian horror flickering on his old TV, but I'm surprised to see he's watching *Zombie Children of the Harvest Sun.*

I plop down next to him, put my arms behind my head, and watch the movie with him. He's at the scene where Alastair, standing in a dead cornfield, lit up red from the setting harvest sun, first amasses his child army of the undead. It's funny, watching it now; it's slow in places, but I find myself enjoying it—so much so, *I forget I'm in it.*

I don't see the blood, sweat, and tears that went into making it. But then again, you never see what went into making any movie. There's just the result of it all.

Zombie Children is just a horror movie—an inconsequential piece of fluff. It's scary in some places, silly in others, but overall it's just fun.

People made more out of it than what it is. I don't think it deserved to be panned so harshly, and I don't think it deserved to be obsessed over either. But people see what they want to see; feel what they want to feel. And there's nothing you can do about that. "It's better than I remember," says Oren, crunching popcorn.

"Yeah. This movie is *pretty good.*"

"For a Moldavia movie, anyway."

"Well, yeah." I laugh. I'm so into this moment. I'm smiling. And then I remember what Aida once told me.

One day you'll look back on your time here, and all of us, and you won't feel the pain you do now. When that moment comes, you'll know you've made it through all the darkness God drew for you, and come out into the light.

Oren and I don't say anything else, even after the credits roll. I never even ask him what made him want to watch this again in the first place—although I kind of get it.

That night, I must be more tired than I realized, because I fall asleep super-early, before Hayley gets a chance to join me.

The nightmares haven't totally ceased.

I have a tense dream about carrying Hayley through the Moldavia gates. But every time I do, she turns to dust—over and over again.

Oren wakes me in the middle of the night, his hand pressed down on my chest, over my heart—in this firm, stabilizing way. "Huh," I say, trying to brush him away.

"The hospital called," he says.

I sit up, not fully awake, rubbing at my eyes. "What?"

"Kingside Park called. Mom's gone."

I try to get myself fully awake. "Escaped?"

He almost laughs a little. "No, Dario."

My heart starts beating real fast. "What happened?"

"She died in her sleep. Her heart stopped."

I slap my hands over my eyes. "Oh no."

Oren sits heavily on the edge of my bed. "She was on a lot of medication for a long time. It took a toll on her body. It's a terrible surprise. But not a total shock."

I look around. "Where's Hayley?" I forgot we didn't spend the night together.

"In her room. She was just told."

I hug myself. "Mom was waiting to see me one last time . . . and then she . . ."

"Dario," says Oren, "you gave her such a gift . . . seeing her again like that. Maybe it's time to stop beating yourself up for every little thing."

That sounds so weird, coming from Oren.

He tells me, bittersweetly, that all the money going toward her care at the hospital will now redirect back into Moldavia.

Oren pulls me in, and we hug. Something we've never really done before. Soon enough, we're both crying and saying *sorry* to each other.

Look, maybe I was wrong: Saying sorry can mean something after all. I guess it's all about context, because right now it feels like an all-encompassing forgiveness through time and space for everything we've torn at each other over, everything that's kept us at odds all these years.

Moldavia is, in so many ways, an extraordinary place. Jude put it best: *a beautiful nightmare.* But it has this uncanny ability to beat me up in new and different ways. And it's not just Moldavia proper, but the world that surrounds it, all its islands, like the one my mom was on, all of Moldavia's tentacles. I guess I always knew that I could return to Moldavia, but I could never stay. Hayley knew. My mother knew. Deep down, I obviously knew. There are just too many ghosts here. And I have a different path to take.

When someone dies, at first there's shock. Shock makes you really tired without the ability to sleep. I stay in bed for the rest of the next day.

Gavin brings me some food.

"You're a big part of why *Alastair & Abigail* succeeded," I tell him, "and why the studio will survive, so thank you."

Gavin seems overcome. "I know things could have gone a certain way during filming. And I know you made sure it wouldn't get bad."

I open my mouth to say something, but he starts speaking really fast:

"My dad was some dude my mom met in Vegas. She called him the Dirty Cowboy. That's all she said about him. I don't know what he meant by that or who he is or was.

We're not really brothers, Dario."

I laugh, all muted and hoarse. Gavin always knew what I was wondering. I lay my hand on his wrist. "Yeah we are, man," I tell him. "We're totally brothers."

I think that's what Gavin needed to hear.

Jude comes in a little later. I pull him into a bear hug. I grab his fists and hold on to them in my hands, like I'm keeping them from swinging. They're the hardest part of Jude. "How are you?" I ask, pressing my forehead into his.

He nods, trying not to cry. He grips my shoulders, as if he's using me to keep his balance. "You're going to be the best stunt coordinator Moldavia never had," I say.

Jude burbles out a happy laugh through his tears.

"We've made deals with each other in the past, yeah?" I tell him. "Well, I'm gonna go to Harvard, okay?" Jude buries his face in my neck. I slap him on the back. "But listen, *listen*, you take care of everyone here, okay? And yourself."

"Yeah," he says.

"*Look at me.* You never go looking for your stepdad. You don't go down that path. Ever. Hear me?"

Jude nods, playfully punching me in the shoulder. "I won't."

I know he means it.

Jude hangs around a little longer, wanting to reminisce, I guess, about being roomies. But it doesn't feel the same. And then he leaves, to go back to Elena.

†††

Hayley comes in last.

"You look like a total mess," I say, a little playfully. Her eyes are all red. She gives me a hapless *what the hell do you expect?* look.

We kiss a little.

"I want to give you something," I say. I root around in my armoire, find the little trimmed photo of myself, and hand it to her. "My mom gave this back to me. . . ."

Hayley looks at the photo and smiles, wiping her eyes with the heel of her hand. "Oh, look at that. You're so cute." She clicks open the face of the locket and sticks the photo inside. Then she presses the locket tightly to her breast.

"Are you happy?" I ask her. "I mean, about everything . . . is this what you want?"

"It is." She nods, her mouth a quivering line. "Thank you, Dario."

"I don't know what to do now," I say, looking around the room.

"Yes, you do," she says, kissing me on the forehead. She leaves her hand on my cheek for a second. "You always know what to do."

For a while we don't say anything. We just stand there.

"One day, maybe," she says, almost to herself, looking around the room.

I don't ask her what she means. I kind of already know. We just have different paths right now. One day, maybe we won't.

"I should take a nap," she says, running a hand through her hair, moving toward the door. She holds on to the doorknob for a moment, turning it, polishing it with her thumb. "I didn't get much sleep. . . ."

And then she's gone, all at once, closing the door behind her.

And of course I know if I'm going to leave this place, I better do it.

Quietly, I drag the steamer trunk out of the closet.

I spend one final night at Moldavia.

I have one dream I can recall: my dad walking off toward the lake. Then my mother, young, beautiful, and healthy again, appears from the low-hanging fog and takes his hand. She blows me a kiss as they walk toward the lake.

My dad stops, looks over his shoulder, and smiles at me.

"Ignosce mihi," he murmurs.

Then they walk into the lake and disappear into the water, still holding hands.

I feel so grateful that I got to return to Moldavia. And that's freakin' hilarious.

Man, after Oren's guilt-inducing phone call at Keenan all those months back, it felt like this place was a bear trap on my future. I was so pissed.

But now, because of Moldavia, I feel like I'm actually free to claim that future. I have a greater sense of its value and what it should be. I made shit right. I healed so many wounds I didn't even realize were still gaping. I helped people. That's the best part. Weirdly, I have my dad to thank for all that.

The spiders will always hatch out of the flowers. But now I like to think about the moments before, when they're just flowers, blooming, and they can be pinched closed, so all that prettiness lasts a little longer before the inevitable horror comes.

That's how I'll always think about this place now.

The next day, before dawn, I go to Hayley's room. I lay my palm flat on her door. It's silent inside, but I get the feeling that Hayley is doing the exact same thing on the other side. Or maybe I'm just imagining that, I don't know. I kiss her door.

I strap the steamer to the luggage rack on top of the car. I get behind the wheel and roll down the driveway. The gates open, and I'm out. Just like that.

I get on the highway.

I see that green sign on the opposite side now: Moldavia Studios, 14 miles.

As I drive, scenery goes flying past that doesn't look totally real. It looks like the stuff you decorate a train set with, all the little trees and houses, hobby store crap, rainy Saturday afternoons with dads wearing stained sweatshirts.

I had a train set once. I loved it while I was able to play with it for those few weeks. I was so happy my dad gave me that, that he gave me something. But the sad truth is, a lot more people enjoyed watching it burn—it made for a very cinematic moment in an otherwise forgettable movie.

It's early morning and there aren't many cars on the roads, and those that are seem curious to me. I wonder who's in them, where they're going, and what they're escaping from. Because, I think, we're all escaping from something.

I'll call Harvard and see if they'll let me sleep in an empty dorm. If not, I'll find a motel to crash somewhere in Cambridge. School starts fairly soon anyway.

I drive for a long time, going eighty, into the brightening sky. And then the weirdest thing happens: *I get second thoughts.* I'm not sure this is the right decision at all, ghosting it like this. Maybe I should have stayed. Maybe this is madness. . . .

All I want to do is talk to Hayley.

And then I remember something.

I pull over into the emergency lane. I get out, take the steamer trunk down, and open it. I pull out everything in a frenzy: books and clothes and papers, all of it scattered on the side of the highway now, some of it blowing away.

I find my journal and snatch it, holding it to my chest with both hands like it might blow away too. I walk away from the car and sit in a clump of weeds on the edge of the highway. I page through the journal until I find what Hayley wrote, near the end of the journal. I remember us sitting in that closet, all those years ago, when she wrote it.

I remember it like it was yesterday.

I want to tell you to do something.

So tell me.

But I don't really want you to do it. It would hurt.

Then I wouldn't do it!

I mean, hurt me. . . .

I handed her the journal and the pen. *Sometimes writing stuff down is easier. Tell me only the last word. And write the rest . . .*

Away, she whispered to me.

I still remember how her lips felt, brushing against my ear.

And she wrote the rest down.

I didn't write it on the very last page. It's toward the back. So you'll have to search to find it.

So it'll always be there if I need it. . . .

I laugh a little through my tears. And after all these years, I finally look.

Hayley only wrote me one goddamn word.

Run.

ACKNOWLEDGMENTS

I'D BE WANDERING ALONE IN A DARK MEADOW WITHOUT THE SHINING light of my agent, Victoria Marini, who never lets a neurotic text go unanswered, never lets me pay for a drink, and shepherded me through the turmoil and ecstasy of writing and publishing my first novel. She is a great protector, an intrepid agent, a smart, sharp editor, and a fantastic friend, who can always make me laugh out loud. Thank you for believing in my writing, my characters, and the dark screwball world of Moldavia, and everything it could be.

And thank you: Penelope Burns, Lia Chan, and everyone at ICM and the Irene Goodman Agency.

Thank you, from the bottom of my heart, to Donna Bray and the team at B+B and Harper, particularly my visionary editors, Viana Siniscalchi and Kelsey Murphy. I was constantly amazed by your ceaseless passion and your uncanny insights. You worked so hard, nurturing my vision with such wisdom and sensitivity.

Many thanks, also, to Alessandra Balzer, Kristin Daly

Rens, Jordan Brown, Claire Caterer, Renée Cafiero, Gina Rizzo, Bess Braswell, Michael D'Angelo, Mark Rifkin, Josh Weiss, Kim Stella, Vanessa Nuttry, and Tiara Kittell.

Thank you, Tom Whalen, Jessie Gang, and Alison Donalty for that stunning, knee-quaking cover.

I am so lucky to have a certifiable force field of brilliant, generous friends and relatives in my collective orbit. People who read draft after draft of my early manuscripts, including various iterations of *Scream*, offering incisive, supportive criticism at every stage:

- Brian Murray Williams, who carries a torch all his own, and is always *always* there for me.
- My brother, Jordan Milman, for his undying support, for which I'm forever grateful.
- My sister-in-law, Lorin Milman, who is my most passionate fan and most important beta reader.
- My wonderful parents, Evelyn and Harvey, for all their years of love, support, and encouragement— and for inspiring me to write.

Also: Max Van Bel, Simon Pearl, Devin Vermeulen, Ben Rosenbaum, Alexis Percival, Josh Taylor, Howard Abrams, Michele Jaslow, Beth Kingry Northington, Soman Chainani, Michael Barakiva, Ben Haber, Patrick Carman, Jeff Garvin, and Goldy Moldavsky.

A heartfelt thanks to my fellow Electric Eighteens, for your guidance during the editing process, especially my dear friend Lindsay Champion, and to Pete Knapp and Jocelyn Davies for your early support.

I am forever grateful to Marisa Yeres Gill, who unblinkingly delivered an early manuscript of mine right to publishers, starting me down this mad roller coaster ride.

A shout-out to some teachers of mine, from grade school to college, who encouraged and fostered my nascent creative impulses: Alice Yugovich, Kathy Connon, Jeanne Cooper, Paul Sheehey, Sharon Achinstein, and Albert Cirillo.

I am beholden to my dear friend, clinical psychologist and professor Lauren Weinstock, PhD, for giving me a deeper understanding of mental illness and helping me depict Isabella Moldavia's schizophrenia with as much sensitivity and accuracy as humanly possible. Any failure to do so is strictly my own.

On this front, I must also extend my deepest gratitude to Andrea, as well as to Elizabeth Roderick, for their crucial feedback.

Thank you to Marlyn E. McGrath and William R. Fitzsimmons at Harvard Admissions, for answering my questions about the current application process.

In my research into mental illness, moviemaking, horror films, and creaky old movie studios, I found these various sources, films, and works of literature particularly insightful: the American Psychiatric Association's *Diagnostic and Statistical Manual of Mental Disorders (DSM-5); I Never Promised You a Rose Garden* by Hannah Green; *The Quiet Room* by Lori Schiller & Amanda Bennett; *No One Cares about Crazy People* by Ron Powers; *Lowboy* by John Wray; *Tarnation* (documentary, written and directed by Jonathan Caouette); *The Filmmaker's Book of the Dead* by Danny Draven; *The Slasher Movie Book* by J. A. Kerswell; *Horror! 333 Films to Scare You to Death* by James Marriott & Kim Newman; *All I Need to Know about FILMMAKING I Learned from THE TOXIC AVENGER* by Lloyd Kaufman & James Gunn; *The Hammer Story* by Marcus Hearn & Alan Barnes; *The Art of Hammer* by Marcus Hearn; *Making Movies* by Sidney Lumet; *Electric Boogaloo: The Wild, Untold Story of Cannon Films* (documentary written and directed by Mark Hartley).